THE BORROWED

THE BORROWED

CHAN HO-KEI

TRANSLATED FROM THE CHINESE
BY JEREMY TIANG

BLACK CAT
NEW YORK

Printed in the United States of America

First published by Crown Publishing Company, Taiwan, in 2014

First published in the English language in
Great Britain in 2016 by Head of Zeus

First Grove Atlantic edition: January 2017

Library of Congress Cataloguing-in-Publication data available for this title.

ISBN 978-0-8021-2588-0
eISBN 978-0-8021-8982-0

Black Cat
an imprint of Grove Atlantic
154 West 14th Street
New York, NY 10011

Distributed by Publishers Group West

groveatlantic.com

17 18 19 20   10 9 8 7 6 5 4 3 2 1

CONTENTS

I will well and faithfully serve Her Majesty and Her Heirs and Successors according to law as a police officer, I will obey, uphold and maintain the laws of the Colony of Hong Kong, I will execute the powers and duties of my office honestly, faithfully and diligently without fear of or favour to any person and with malice or ill will towards none, and I will obey without question all lawful orders of those set in authority over me.

— HONG KONG POLICE OATH,
version used until 1980

I

THE TRUTH BETWEEN
BLACK AND WHITE:

2013

1

Inspector Lok had always hated the stench of hospitals.

That antiseptic tang was wafting through the air now, assaulting his nose. It wasn't that he had bad memories of these places, but the reek reminded him too much of a morgue. He'd been on the police force twenty-seven years and seen countless corpses, yet still couldn't get used to this smell – but then who, necrophiliacs aside, gets a thrill out of dead bodies?

Lok sighed, his heart even heavier than when he had to oversee an autopsy.

Standing by in his neat blue suit, he gazed disconsolately at the occupant of the lone bed, a white-haired man whose eyes were shut, his wrinkled face ghastly pale beneath a respirator mask. Fine tubes pierced his liver-spotted hands, connecting them to several monitoring devices. A seventeen-inch screen above the bed showed the patient's vital signs, lines wavering slowly from left to right the only thing showing he was still alive, not a well-preserved corpse.

This was Inspector Lok's mentor of many years, the man who'd taught him everything he knew about crime solving.

'Sonny, let me tell you – you don't solve cases by meekly following the rules. Sure, among the uniforms, obeying orders is an iron-clad principle, but as officers our first duty is to protect civilians.

If the rules cause an innocent citizen to get hurt or impede the course of justice, that's ample reason to disregard them.'

Lok smiled grimly as he recalled these words, variations of which were never far from the older man's lips. Since his promotion fourteen years ago, everyone had called him Inspector Lok, but his mentor continued to use that ridiculous little-boy name, Sonny. After all, as far as he was concerned, Lok really was no more than a child.

Before his retirement, Superintendent Kwan Chun-dok had been Commander of the Central Intelligence Bureau's Division B. The CIB was the agency in charge of researching, gathering, and analysing crime reports from the various regional bureaus. If the CIB were the brain of the police force, then Division B would be its prefrontal lobe, the part responsible for deduction, sifting and sorting information, pulling together clues to reveal what even eyewitnesses might not have noticed. Kwan had begun leading this core group in 1989 and had quickly become the guiding spirit of Intelligence. In 1997, Constable Sonny Lok had been transferred to Division B, becoming Kwan's 'disciple'. Although Kwan was only Lok's commanding officer for half a year, he continued working as a police consultant after retirement, which gave him more opportunities to guide Sonny, twenty-two years his junior. For the childless Kwan, it felt like having a son.

'Sonny, waging psychological war against a suspect is like playing poker – you have to mislead them about your hand. Say you're holding a pair of aces, you have to make them think you have low cards of different suits; but the worse things get, the harder you bluff, making them think victory is within your grasp. That's how you get them to give themselves away.' Like a father instructing his child, Kwan passed on every one of his tricks.

After many years together, Lok treated Kwan like his father, and knew his personality inside out. While others referred to Kwan as 'Sir', Lok called him 'Sifu', which meant 'mentor' in Cantonese. His colleagues in the force gave Kwan all kinds of nicknames: 'Crime-Solving Machine', 'Eye of Heaven' or 'Genius

Detective'. Lok thought the most suitable was something Kwan's late wife once said: 'He's basically the sort to count every strand of dead grass. You might as well call him Uncle Dok.'

In Cantonese, 'Uncle Dok' is a common name for the tightest of tightwads. It also happened to share the last syllable of Kwan's own name. Thinking of this pun from so many years back, Lok couldn't help smiling.

Scarily capable, fiercely independent, obsessively attentive to every detail – this was the oddball character who'd lived through the leftist unrest of the sixties, the police mutiny of the seventies, the violent crime of the eighties, the transfer of sovereignty in the nineties, the social changes in this new millennium. Across all these decades, he'd quietly solved hundreds of cases, silently filling a glorious page of the history of Hong Kong policing.

And now this legendary figure had one foot in the grave. The gleaming image of the police force he'd built up had started to fade, and by now, in 2013, the profession was looking distinctly tarnished.

After ridding themselves of corruption in the seventies, the Hong Kong Police had earned the reputation of a selfless, reliable organization. There might have been the occasional black sheep, but the vast majority of the populace were able to see these as exceptions What changed this view was politics. In 1997, after the territory was handed over from Britain to China, a society that had once been able to contain different value systems began to be torn apart into political factions. Rallies and protests became more heated, and the use of hardline tactics against protesters provoked murmurs about where the police really stood. The police were supposed to be neutral, but when the clashes impinged upon government institutions they seemed to hold back rather than performing with their usual superb efficiency. People started insinuating that in Hong Kong, power was now able to crush justice, and that the police were just the stooges of those in authority, closing one eye when it came to groups supported by the government, serving no one but the politicians.

In the past, Inspector Lok had refuted such criticisms. Now, though, he was starting to suspect they might hold some truth. More and more of his colleagues seemed to regard their position as just a job, rather than a sacred calling, and did nothing but follow orders, the same as any other salaried worker.

Now and then, he'd hear the refrain, 'The more you do, the more mistakes you make, so better do less.' When he joined the force, back in 1985, he had been motivated by a longing for the *status* of a police officer – the duty to keep the peace and uphold justice. These new officers seemed to regard ideas like justice purely theoretically. Their goals were to maintain a good discipline record, rise through the ranks as quickly as possible, safely reach retirement and start drawing on their generous pensions. And as the public began to notice the growing prevalence of this mindset, they thought less and less of the police.

'Sonny, even... even if the public hates us, our superiors force us to act against our consciences and we find ourselves attacked on all sides... don't forget the basic duty and mission of the police... make the right decision...' the superintendent had gasped shortly before losing consciousness, fighting for breath and clutching Lok's hand.

Lok understood very well what the 'duty and mission' were. As the head of the Kowloon East Crime Unit, he knew he only had one task: to protect the people by catching criminals. When the truth was obscured, he had to turn chaos into order, justice's final line of defence.

Today, he would ask his mentor to spend what might be left of his life to help solve a case.

The afternoon sunlight sparkled on the azure bay outside, dazzling as it came through the floor-to-ceiling windows. Apart from the machine noises indicating the patient was still alive, there was also the tapping of a keyboard, coming from a young woman in a corner.

'Apple, have you finished? They'll be here soon.' Inspector Lok turned to her.

'Almost done. If you'd told me sooner you wanted changes to the program, it wouldn't be in such a mess. It's not hard to change the interface, but coding takes time.'

'I'm relying on you.' Inspector Lok knew little of computers but completely trusted Apple's skills.

Apple didn't even look up to speak to him, focusing on her keyboard. She wore an old black baseball cap, under which were loose brown curls and a face completely free of make-up, thick black-framed glasses perched on her nose, a black T-shirt and some ancient overalls, plus flip-flops that revealed toenails painted black.

Someone knocked at the door.

'Coming,' he called. In that instant, his expression returned to its customary alertness, like a hawk sighting prey – the eyes of a criminal investigator.

2

'SIR, THEY'VE ARRIVED,' said the inspector's subordinate, Ah Sing, opening the door. Behind him, a stream of people came single file into the hospital room, their faces betraying doubt.

'Mr Yue, I'm grateful you could find the time to come.' The inspector left Kwan's bedside and crossed the room. 'It's good that all five of you are here. If anyone had been busy, the investigation might have been delayed another few days. Thank you all.'

His courteous words were, the assembled company knew, just a veneer of politeness. After all, what lay before them was a murder case.

'I'm sorry, Inspector Lok, but I don't understand why we need to be here.' The first to speak was Yue Wing-yee. Normally, the police interviewed eyewitnesses or suspects at the station, or else at the scene of the crime, not in a single room on the fifth floor of Wo Yan Hospital in Tseung Kwan O. This private hospital happened to be part of the Yue family's holdings, but that had absolutely nothing to do with the case, as far as Wing-yee knew, and he could not imagine why they were here.

'Please pay no attention to the family connection, it's just a coincidence. Wo Yan happens to have the best facilities in Hong Kong – so it's no coincidence that our Police Consultant was transferred here a short while ago.' Inspector Lok explained smoothly.

'Oh, I see.' Yue Wing-yee still seemed uncertain, but asked no further questions. Dressed in a grey suit and rimless glasses, the thirty-two-year-old still had a boyish look about him, despite now being the head of his family's firm, the Fung Hoi Consortium. Wing-yee had always thought he might take over the business someday, though he hadn't expected the burden to fall on his shoulders so suddenly. After his mother's death and his father's recent murder, he'd had no choice but to assume this role and to take the lead in dealing with the police.

Since finding his father's bloodstained corpse the previous week, he had been thinking of his older brother's accidental death more than twenty years ago. He couldn't stop seeing his brother's face, and each time a spasm of bitterness surged up his throat. It had taken him years to escape the pall that early death had cast over his own youth, and to get used to the nausea each time he recalled it.

The recurrence of this ache brought home to Wing-yee that he could never completely forget Wing-lai's death. All he could do was mutely accept his responsibilities. *If Wing-lai were still alive, he'd definitely be able to handle this situation more calmly than me*, thought Wing-yee.

Even though he felt nervous every time he had to speak to Inspector Lok, Wing-yee was much more at ease in the familiar surroundings of Wo Yan than the stark police station. He wasn't a doctor, but nonetheless knew the hospital intimately – not because of his senior position within the consortium, but because during his mother's last illness, he'd visited her here every couple of days.

Before that, he'd inspected the place once a year at most. Fung Hoi had many other property and shipping enterprises to look after; in fact, these were the backbone of the business. Wo Yan was not a particularly lucrative investment, but it brought prestige to the consortium, leading the field in importing innovative

techniques from abroad – minimally invasive surgery, DNA testing for hereditary diseases, radiation treatments for cancer.

But then, as if in a third-rate melodrama, he found that own-
ing this hospital with its advanced equipment and impeccable
staff was no help to Mrs Yue as she lay dying of cancer aged
fifty-nine.

'Inspector Lok, you and your colleagues have been bothering us for quite a few days now. I'm guessing it's when you can't
solve a case that you need to make this kind of fuss, to show
your superiors you're trying?' This came from the young man
standing behind Wing-yee – Yue Wing-lim, eight years his junior.
Unlike his sophisticated brother, Wing-lim came across as rather
frivolous, decked out in fashionable, expensive clothes, his hair
dyed bright red. Even when speaking to a police officer, he
appeared to have no fear – it seemed there was nothing that could
frighten him.

Wing-yee turned to glare at his younger brother, though to
be honest he'd been thinking the same thing, as had the other
three people present – Wing-yee's wife, Choi Ting, the Yue family retainer Nanny Wu, and their private secretary, Wong Kwan-
tong, known to everyone as Old Tong. They'd all been summoned
to the station the previous week to make detailed statements,
and no one had any idea how answering further questions could
aid this investigation.

'The Yue family is so well known, and Fung Hoi so important to Hong Kong's economy, the media is scrutinizing every
detail of this crime,' said Inspector Lok slowly, not seeming to
take offence at Wing-lim's words. 'This case is being taken very
seriously at the highest levels, and we hope to solve it as quickly
as possible, so as not to cause a scandal in the business world.
That's why I've had to seek help from my mentor, and why I'm
asking you all to spend a little more time going over the case.'

'What superpowers does your mentor have?' Wing-lim's
barbed tone suggested he had no high regard for this officer.

'He's ex-Superintendent Kwan Chun-dok, former Director of

the Hong Kong Island Crime Unit. Now he's a special consultant. No crime is unsolvable where he's concerned. In more than thirty years on the force he has a hundred per cent success rate.'

'A hundred per cent?' exclaimed Wing-yee, astonished.

'One hundred per cent.'

'You... you must be exaggerating. How could anyone have a perfect record?' Wing-lim no longer sounded as certain of himself.

'Could I enquire where this Superintendent Kwan is?' asked Old Tong, the white-haired secretary. He glanced at Apple, tapping away at her keyboard in a corner of the room, but it seemed unlikely this girl in her early twenties had headed a Crime Unit.

Inspector Lok turned to look at the bed. It took everyone a second to realize this was his answer.

'That old man is Superintendent Kwan?' gasped Yue Wing-yee.

'Yes.'

'What's... what's wrong with him?' Wing-yee regretted the words as soon as they left his mouth. Illness ought to be a private matter, and asking so directly could annoy this officer he'd hoped to get on his side.

'Liver cancer. Terminal.'

'So this... old geezer is going to solve my daddy's case?' Wing-lim continued to sound irreverent, but in fact had made an effort by swallowing the words 'decrepit wreck'.

'Wing-lim, be more serious.' This came not from his older brother, but from Old Tong. Wing-yee pursed his lips in displeasure, but said nothing.

'Inspector Lok, did you bring us here to repeat our statements for this... this Superintendent Kwan?' asked Choi Ting. She seemed unused to being lady of the household, and spoke with a desperate fear of saying the wrong thing.

'Precisely.' Inspector Lok nodded. 'My mentor is unable to travel to the Yue mansion or the station, so I had to trouble you all to come here.'

'But... can he speak?' Choi Ting stared at the old man. She'd been a doctor before marrying into the Yue family, and seeing the tubes in the patient's mouth and nose, not to mention his respirator, she knew this wasn't possible.

'No, nor move. He's in a coma,' said Inspector Lok dispassionately.

'So we're too late!' exclaimed Wing-yee.

'What stage?' asked Choi Ting.

'Stage three.' This meant no eye movement, speech or physical activity.

'If Superintendent Kwan can neither speak nor move, how will he help you?' asked Old Tong. 'Inspector Lok, is this a joke?'

'He can still hear,' said Lok sombrely.

'So what if he can hear?' said Choi Ting. 'How will he tell us what he's thinking? The man's in a full-blown coma.'

'As long as he can hear us,' Inspector Lok pointed at the geek girl sitting behind him, 'she can do the rest.'

The young woman said nothing, pounding at the keyboard and ignoring the odd looks all five visitors were giving her.

'She's called Apple, she's a computer expert.'

'Oh, really?' Wing-yee clearly felt this explanation was superfluous, given that Apple had in front of her three screens of different sizes, a tangle of multicoloured cables and a laptop covered in cartoon stickers.

'What can a computer expert do? Pluck out the guy's brain and hook it up to her CPU?' jeered Wing-lim.

'Well, more or less.'

No one had expected this from Inspector Lok, let alone with a straight face.

'It's a bit complicated to explain – best to try it for yourself. We've modified the program to let you experience it.' The inspector turned to Apple. 'Is it ready?'

'Yes, just about,' said Apple, handing over a black rubber headband, about two centimetres wide, a grey wire connecting one end to her blue laptop.

'This is how we'll pluck out Superintendent Kwan's brain,' explained the inspector. 'Mr Wong, could I borrow you for my demonstration?'

Old Tong stepped forward uncertainly.

Inspector Lok seated him on the sofa, then placed the band around his forehead, where it looked like the Monkey King's golden circlet. The two ends clamped onto his temples, and Old Tong could feel countless little protrusions sinking into his skin. The inspector gently adjusted the band.

'Right, that should do,' said Apple, still staring at her screen.

'Do you all know what EEG is?' he asked.

'Electroencephalography,' answered Choi Ting.

'Yes, that's right. Our brains are made up of nerve clusters, and when we think, tiny electric impulses move between these clusters – which we can measure, through EEG. Scientists call these brain waves.'

'And this thing can turn brain waves into speech?' Wing-yee was astonished.

'No, current technology doesn't go so far yet, but for several years now we've been able to track the condition of the brain, and with recent breakthroughs, very simple equipment is all that's needed.'

'The main difficulty has been in working out which readings are brain waves and which aren't,' Apple cut in. 'Take this room – the medical equipment alone creates huge amounts of interference. You used to need a special environment to do an EEG, but now you can cut out all this "noise" on the computer. I wrote this program myself, using a formula from a Berkeley research team's library. As for the interface, it—'

'To put it simply, this device is able to detect a person's thought as soon as he has it,' the inspector interrupted, pointing at one of the screens. Apple turned the screen round and everyone saw a rectangle divided in two, the top half white, marked YES in black letters, the bottom half black with NO in white letters. On the line between the two was a tiny blue cross.

'Mr Wong, please concentrate, and imagine the blue cross moving,' said Inspector Lok. Old Tong had no idea what was going on, but did as he was told.

'It's moving,' Wing-lim cried out. And sure enough, the cross was inching upward, hitting the letters YES with a ping.

'There's a significant difference between when the brain is concentrating and when it is relaxed,' said the inspector, gesturing at the screen. 'When Mr Wong focuses his attention, his mind produces... produces...'

'Beta waves – that is, between twelve and thirty Hertz.' Apple stuck her head out from behind the screen. 'When the brain is at rest, it produces alpha waves of eight to twelve Hertz.'

'Right, beta waves.' Inspector Lok chuckled, thinking what a terrible scientist he'd make. 'Mr Wong, please let your mind grow still – maybe look out at the ocean? – and the pointer will settle down. You can control its movement by switching between concentration and relaxation.'

The assembled company stared dubiously at the screen as the pointer slowly bobbed up and down. But Old Tong's expression told them all this was no fakery.

'It's true! When I try to make it move upwards, it really does rise! And when I stop thinking, it falls,' he exclaimed, full of wonder.

'You may all try it, if you like,' said Inspector Lok, removing the band.

Wing-yee was always curious about new discoveries and would normally have been the first to volunteer, but didn't want to draw attention to himself.

'Hang on,' Old Tong asked, 'this young lady says she wrote the program, but what about the hardware? This rubber thing looks like it was specially manufactured.'

'I bought it,' replied Apple.

'Where would you buy such a thing?'

'Toys "R" Us.' Apple produced a cardboard box. 'Toys controlled by brainwaves have been in shops for a few years now

– this is nothing new. All I did was modify an off-the-shelf product. I've also been able to turn toy 3D cameras into virtual reality inductors...'

'Are you actually suggesting we place this device on Superintendent Kwan, so he can tell us the results of his deductions?'

'That's right.'

'But this only allows him to say "Yes" or "No" – how will that solve the case?'

Inspector Lok swept his sharp gaze across the group. 'Even "Yes" and "No" can have a big impact. Besides, he's much better at controlling this machine than the rest of us.'

He stepped gingerly across the cables to place the band gently around the old man's forehead, adjusting it until Apple said, 'Okay.'

'Sir, can you hear me?' Inspector Lok sat on a chair by the head of the bed.

The computer pinged crisply, and the blue pointer leaped onto YES.

'Why did it jerk like that? Is it broken?' asked Yue Wing-lim.

A dull beep – *dub-dub* – and the pointer swooped onto NO.

'As I said, he's become adept at using this apparatus,' said the inspector. 'This is how he's communicated every time he's been in a coma state – about a month of practice. The system's gathered so much data about his brain, the likelihood of error is virtually zero.'

'Could anyone really improve their powers of concentration so quickly?' said Choi Ting, her eyes flicking in astonishment between the old man and the screen.

Ping. The pointer said YES.

'Blind people can judge distances through sounds, and deaf people learn to read lips – people discover their potential in extreme circumstances.' Inspector Lok's hands were clasped, resting in his lap. 'Besides, this is his only means of communicating with the outside world now – he had no choice but to learn how to use it.'

The pointer drifted slowly back to the centre, as if insisting it was now part of Kwan's body, and he wouldn't have anyone impugning its accuracy.

'In order to speed up the investigation, I've asked all five of you here today, so Superintendent Kwan can fully understand the situation. We were going to carry out the questioning after he regained consciousness, but with my superiors so eager for an outcome, I've had to resort to extraordinary measures. Naturally I'll do the bulk of the questioning, and the superintendent will come in with responses and suggestions where necessary.'

Ping. YES.

'Why are you interrogating us? Wasn't he murdered by a burglar? I thought that was clear,' snapped Wing-lim impatiently.

'I'll go through all of that, and explain the details of the case to Superintendent Kwan,' said the inspector, ducking the question. 'Would you please take a seat?'

Old Tong was already sitting down. Wing-yee, Wing-lim and Choi Ting joined him on the sofa, leaving Nanny Wu, who hadn't yet said a word, to hesitate a moment before taking the wooden chair by the door. From the middle of the sofa, Wing-yee's vision was partly blocked by the table across the bed – he could only see half the old man's face. Still, everyone was paying more attention to Apple, or rather the seventeen-inch black-and-white screen next to her that had now replaced Superintendent Kwan's mouth.

3

'AH SING, PLEASE record this,' ordered the inspector. His assistant, perched on a stool behind Apple, switched on a compact little digital camera, making sure he could see everyone on his viewfinder before nodding at his superior.

'Sir, I'll start with an overview of the case.' The inspector pulled a notebook from his pocket and flipped it open. 'On the night of 7th to 8th September 2013, that is the early hours between Saturday and Sunday, there was a murder at Fung Ying Villa, number 163 Chuk Yeung Road in Sai Kung. This was the residence of Fung Hoi Consortium's director, Yuen Man-bun, and his family; the deceased is the property owner, Yuen Man-bun himself.'

Hearing his father's name, Wing-yee's heart pounded.

'The victim was sixty-seven years old. In 1971 he married Yue Chin-yau; as she was the only child of the Yue family, he agreed to have their children take her surname. In 1986 he assumed the directorship of the family business, and when his father-in-law Yue Fung passed away the following year, he became the head of the household.' Inspector Lok turned a page. 'He had three children. The oldest son, Wing-lai, died in a car accident in 1990. Second son Wing-yee and third son Wing-lim still live at the above address. Wing-yee was married last year, and his wife, Choi Ting, moved in with him and his parents. The victim's

wife, Yue Chin-yau, passed away this May. Apart from the four
people mentioned, Fung Ying Villa is also home to a private secretary, Mr Wong Kwan-tong, and a maid, Ms Wu Kam Mui.
These six people were the only ones present the night of the incident. Do you need me to repeat any of that, sir?'

Dub-dub. NO.

'Next, the setting and events of the crime.' Inspector Lok
cleared his throat, and continued unhurriedly, 'Fung Ying Villa
is a three-storey building that, together with its grounds, occu-
pies half an acre of land on Chuk Yeung Road near Ma On Shan
Country Park. This mansion has been the Yue family residence
since the early 1960s, housing three generations of the family.'

The inspector glanced at the group, noting Nanny Wu's gentle
nodding, as if she was thinking back to the glory days of the old
master building up the consortium in the sixties and seventies.

'At half past seven on the morning of the 8th, Yue Wing-yee
noticed his father wasn't in the living room reading the newspaper, as was his habit, and subsequently found him dead in the
study on the first floor. In the police investigation that followed,
it was initially thought that the deceased had surprised a burglar
and been attacked.'

A shiver went through Wing-yee.

'The study window had been broken, and the room showed
signs of being ransacked.' Inspector Lok put down the notebook, glancing at the face of the old detective in the bed. Having gone over it so many times in his mind, he could describe the
scene from memory alone. 'The flame trees in the garden were
close enough to the study window that a criminal could easily have gained access that way. There were strips of sticky tape
fixed to the outside of the window to prevent the glass making a sound when broken – suggesting an experienced burglar.
We found a roll of waterproof tape on the ground beneath, and
the lab has confirmed it matches what's on the window.'

The blue cross on the screen remained motionless, like an
attentive listener.

'Yuen Man-bun's study was four hundred square feet in size. Apart from the usual office furniture, there was a rather unusual item: a steel cabinet a couple of metres high and a metre wide. This contained a number of spearguns – Mr Yuen used these to hunt fish while deep-sea diving, and had a licence to do so. Next to it was a styrofoam box, a metre square, full of old newspapers and magazines. According to the family of the deceased, he used this for target practice in his spare time.'

'No, Inspector Lok, it wasn't practice,' blurted Wing-yee.

'Not practice? But Mr Wong said—'

'The boss used it as a target,' Old Tong explained. 'But it wasn't practice. He'd had arthritis for several years, and his left leg grew too weak for him to dive, meaning he could no longer go fishing. So he had me build him this set-up to play with his spearguns in the study, reliving the old days. In fact, you shouldn't use a speargun on land, it's very dangerous.'

'Ah, so I had it wrong. Anyway, this was the situation, sir.'

Ping. Kwan seemed to be urging him on through the computer.

'Both the safe and the speargun cabinet showed signs of being attacked with a chisel, and while the safe remained intact, the intruder had managed to force the cabinet open. Books and documents had been swept off the shelves and flung all over the floor, the desktop computer screen had been smashed and the contents of the drawers tipped out. All in all, about two hundred thousand Hong Kong dollars in cash was taken from the room, but the deceased's ring and the jewelled letter-opener on the desk were left behind, as was an antique gold pocket watch worth three hundred thousand Hong Kong dollars.'

Listening to his superior's account, Ah Sing remembered the first day of the investigation. When he'd learned that the missing two hundred thousand (about twenty-five thousand US dollars) was kept in the study as 'petty cash', he'd realized just how distant his own life was from the Hong Kong elite.

'The investigators found no footprints or fingerprints in the

room, and believe the intruder must have worn gloves.' Once
again, the inspector opened his notebook. 'So much for the scene
of the crime. Next, the incident itself.'

Ping.

'Forensics put the time of death between half past two and
four a.m. The deceased was found lying next to the bookcase.
There were two contusions to the back of his head, but the fatal
wound was in his belly – he was shot by a harpoon from the
speargun, and bled to death.'

The glint of that thin metal shaft protruding from his father's
belly seemed to flicker before Wing-yee's eyes.

'I'll describe the murder weapon in more detail.' Inspector Lok
turned over a few more pages. 'The harpoon was 115 centimetres
long, with barbed hooks along the top three centimetres. It was
these that pierced multiple organs and caused massive loss of
blood. On the floor in the middle of the room, we found a carbon-
fibre speargun manufactured by the South African company
Rob Allen, model number RGSH115, barrel length 115 centimetres long, the shuttered tip fitted with a thirty-centimetre rubber
tube. The only fingerprints on the gun belonged to the deceased.'

When Inspector Lok first took on this case, all the terminology
had muddled him, so he'd spent some time mastering it. The speargun used the elasticity of the rubber tube to fire the harpoon,
just like a slingshot. With the harpoon gripped by the trigger
mechanism, the diver would pull the tube back, hooking it to the
ammunition. Pulling the trigger released the rubber tube, propel-
ling the harpoon forward.

'We've inspected the cabinet, and ascertained that this speargun is from the deceased's collection, because there was a com-
partment for three weapons that only held two of different
lengths, an RGSH075 and an RGSH130, leaving the middle
rack empty. There was also an extra-long RGZL160 – Rob Allen
Zulu model – and a seventy-five-centimetre RABITECH RB075
aluminium alloy gun, but these were broken down and stored
in carry cases. The cabinet also contained harpoons of varying

lengths, from 115 to 160 centimetres, which our investigators confirmed were of the same make as the one in the victim's body.'

'Father never used the Zulu,' said Wing-yee, visibly stirred. 'He said he bought it to go shark-hunting, but before he could take it out even once, his arthritis had left him unable to dive.'

Inspector Lok made no response to this, but went on, 'Also in the cabinet was other equipment for diving and fishing, including scuba masks, wetsuit hoods, oxygen regulators, gloves, harpoon lines, a screwdriver, Swiss army knives, and a twenty-five-centimetre diving knife. Our initial investigation suggests that the murderer forced open the cabinet and killed the victim with his own speargun.'

Ah Sing swallowed. Although he'd seen plenty of corpses in his two years as Inspector Lok's assistant, when he thought of that long, barbed metal spear slicing into a soft belly and making mincemeat of someone's innards, his hair stood on end.

'Apart from the fatal injury, the two head wounds were odd,' continued the inspector. 'According to forensics, the second blow was received some time after the first. The bloodstains on the victim's collar and the injuries themselves suggest a half-hour gap between the two. The exact circumstances are still unclear, but we've identified the weapon – a metal vase that normally stood on the desk. There were no fingerprints whatso-ever, suggesting the murderer wiped it thoroughly after assault-ing the victim.'

Inspector Lok looked up from his notebook, sweeping his gaze across the assembled people, coming to rest on the patient.

'As for the position of the body, that's what makes me most suspicious.' The inspector's brow furrowed. 'He was lying by the bookcase, with a family album beside him, from which investi-gators lifted some bloody fingerprints. The bloodstains on the floor show that after sustaining the fatal injury, he crawled five metres or so from the desk to the bookshelf, where he looked through the album. Forensics estimate he died more than twenty minutes after the harpoon struck him. At first I assumed he was trying to leave us a message, but there's no pattern at all to the marks in the book. He simply wanted to look at the old photographs. Even stranger, there were marks showing duct tape had been wrapped around his wrists and calves, as well as covering his mouth, but all this tape had been ripped off by the time he was found, and wasn't anywhere in the room.'

When these test results had come in a few days ago, Ah Sing had suggested this might not have been the work of the murderer – what if the deceased was into S & M, and the tape marks came from a bondage session? This earned him some filthy looks from his female colleagues, as if *he* were the pervert. Inspector Lok brushed off his theory, chuckling, 'I suppose you're the sort who thinks rich folk are all completely depraved, with secret fetishes?'

'Leaving aside the anomalies,' Lok continued, 'the scene suggested a burglar smashing the window to gain entry to the study, and upon being surprised by the deceased, knocking him unconscious with the vase, binding him and continuing to rummage. He'd have found the safe but been unable to open it, and so threatened the victim with the speargun, demanding the combination, and when he refused, shooting him dead. The criminal snatched the two hundred thousand in cash and fled...'

Dub-dub. The negative tone again, as the pointer moved to NO. The witnesses looked at each other, shocked.

'Sir, are you saying the murderer wasn't an outsider?'

Ping. The pointer slid breezily onto YES.

Inspector Lok looked startled. 'You're right. Further investigation made it seem less likely the criminal was an intruder. We found no evidence of climbing outside the window, nor footprints in the flowerbed below. I wondered if he might have entered some other way, for example rappelling from above, but there were no marks on the roof either. There's still the possibility of a helicopter...'

Dub-dub. The old detective seemed to be mocking his disciple for missing an obvious truth.

'Sir, do you already know from what I've said that this was an inside job?'

Ping. Another swift YES.

'Was it how the window was broken? Evidence that the victim was killed with a speargun? Signs that the room had been ransacked?'

The pointer remained still in the centre of the screen.

'Was it the desk? The bookcase? The vase? The floorboards?'

Ping.

The inspector repeated, 'Floorboards,' and the pointer responded.

'Floorboards? But there was nothing on them – neither fingerprints nor footprints. They were completely clear,' Ah Sing interrupted.

Inspector Lok turned suddenly to look at Ah Sing, then back at his mentor, enlightenment spreading across his face. 'That's right!' He smacked his forehead.

'What?' Ah Sing looked uncertain, as did the Yue household.

'Ah Sing, when have we seen such a spotless crime scene before? No fingerprints, fine, that's easy enough, most burglars know to wear gloves. But footprints don't prove much one way or the other, and home intruders seldom avoid them. Much simpler to buy a new pair of shoes and burn them after the burglary.'

'But it's possible a murderer would take special care to wipe the floorboards to cover his tracks,' argued Ah Sing.

'If that were the case, how would you explain the documents and other objects scattered across the floor? If we assume the murderer walked across the flowerbed, broke into an empty room, and killed Mr Yuen when he came in unexpectedly, wouldn't he have cleared everything off the floor before wiping his footprints away? Why get rid of the evidence of murder and leave behind the appearance of a ransacked room, instead of just running away in the first instance? That makes no sense.'

Listening to their dialogue, Wing-yee realized why

Inspector Lok had wanted the superintendent's help. Merely hearing a description of the scene, this immobile man had reached a conclusion it had taken the police vast amounts of manpower to arrive at. Wing-yee shivered, afraid this old detective, unable to move a finger, would nonetheless see right through him.

He was terrified he wouldn't escape this penetrating insight, because he was a killer.

4

'IF IT WASN'T an outsider...' Choi Ting said suddenly, dragging Wing-yee back from his reverie.

'Then the murderer must be one of the five other people in the house at the time,' said Inspector Lok coldly.

In an instant, the five witnesses – now suspects – understood what lay behind Lok's investigations over the last three days. He'd met each of them in turn, asking about the relationships within the family, the deceased's past, and so forth. And that strange question, 'If the murderer weren't an intruder, who would you think it was?'

'You bastar— So all of this was a trap?' spat Wing-lim. This time, Old Tong didn't try to silence him.

'Mr Yue Wing-lim, let's be clear.' Inspector Lok turned his hawklike gaze to the younger man, speaking very distinctly. 'My job is to find the truth and uphold justice for the deceased. I don't need any of you to like me. The police stand on the side of the victim, speaking for those who have no voice.'

Ah Sing noticed the emphasis on the words 'any of you'.

The temperature of the room seemed to plunge several degrees. Reverting to his previous tone, Inspector Lok went on, 'Now, if you have no objection, I'll go through the information we've gathered this week concerning various individuals.'

Ping. No one else spoke, but the old detective was letting them know he approved.

'First, the deceased.' Inspector Lok flipped to the relevant page. 'Yuen Man-bun, sixty-seven years old, male, director of Fung Hoi Consortium. According to various statements, the deceased was known to be a ruthless businessman, buying up small companies, using, shall we say, extreme tactics against his opponents, so much so that he was nicknamed the Fung Hoi Shark. This was a completely different ethos from that of the founder of the consortium, Yue Fung. Yet through the Asian financial crisis of 1997 and the global economic slump of 2008, Fung Hoi's profits continued to rise unabated, which would seem to show Mr Yuen's strategy may well have been the right one. Leaving this aside, most of his employees thought he was a friendly boss, even if his demands were somewhat stricter than average.'

Ah Sing always felt such praise from employees must be flattery. Even with the boss dead, the successor would be his son, and if any criticisms were to make their way back to the future boss's ears, there'd be consequences. Describing a 'shark' as 'friendly', well, that was the best joke he'd ever heard.

'Yuen Man-bun was originally Yue Fung's subordinate. Fung Hoi started out as a small-scale plastic goods factory, but in the late sixties it branched out into property investment, and Yue Fung took the opportunity to float the company's stock on as many of Hong Kong's exchanges as possible. At the time, Yue Fung preferred to hire young men, and twenty-three-year-old Yuen Man-bun's sharp mind left a strong impression on him. This clerk quickly rose to be Yue Fung's personal assistant. Another person received a promotion at that time: the twenty-year-old Wong Kwan-tong, now aged sixty-four and one of our suspects.'

Hearing the inspector mention his name, Old Tong unconsciously straightened.

'According to some retired workers who knew the family, there was a persistent rumour that Yue Fung hadn't just hired a personal assistant, but also an "imperial son-in-law". He was sixty, and had no descendants but a teenage daughter. Being an only child himself, he feared the Yue family would die out. His solution was to find a young, capable man to marry into the family, and run the consortium when the time came. Some people pointed out that when they were younger, Yue Chin-yau got on far better with Wong Kwan-tong, who was more her own age, but in the end it was Yuen Man-bun that she married.'

'Inspector Lok, you can't possibly be claiming this as my motive for murder?' Old Tong broke in. 'It wasn't Old-boss who chose her husband, it was the lady herself, and while I was close to Yue Chin-yau, we were never in love. Anyway, this was forty years ago. Who'd kill a love rival over ancient history? I've been working under him all this time.'

'I'm just narrating, there's no further meaning. My mentor will make his own analysis.'

'That's right.' Nanny Wu spoke for the first time. 'Tong can't be the killer. He was good friends with Boss-man and young Missy. Those two got hitched in April 1971, just as the Kam Ngan Stock Exchange was getting started. They listed the company there, and in order for Boss-man and Missy to go off on their honeymoon, Tong took over that whole job without a word of complaint, while letting the old man believe his son had found time to do it in the midst of all his wedding preparations. Those two were close as brothers. Tong wouldn't do anything so cruel.'

By 'Boss-man', of course, Nanny Wu meant Yuen Man-bun. And for all that Yue Chin-yau had afterwards become her 'Boss-lady', the old woman had never called her anything but 'Missy'.

The inspector glanced at Nanny Wu, then went back to his notebook. 'That's right; everything Ms Wu Kam-mui just said is accurate. Let's see what we know about Ms Wu.'

Not having expected the arrow to point in her direction, Nanny Wu grew panicky.

'Ms Wu Kam-mui, sixty-five years old, crossed illegally from the mainland in 1965. She met Yue Fung and his wife and started working for them. At the time, indentured servants were illegal in Hong Kong, but many households nonetheless had an *amah* or *mui tsai*. At the age of just seventeen, Ms Wu became Yue Chin-yau's nanny. In 1965 – that means Miss Yue would have been just twelve... no, thirteen...'

'Eleven,' Nanny Wu said cautiously, a handkerchief twisting in her hands.

'Right, eleven.' The inspector nodded gently. 'And from that point, Ms Wu became Miss Yue's permanent maid, accompanying the household for more than forty years, up to the present day. According to the other witnesses, Ms Wu's relationship with the deceased couple was always very good.'

From what the others had said, Nanny Wu might have been an employee, but as far as Chin-yau was concerned, she'd been more like an older sister, taking care of her, sharing the secrets of her heart. When Yue Chin-yau had died four months ago, Nanny Wu had wept every bit as much as the rest of the family, and had more sleepless nights afterwards than anyone else.

'Yuen Man-bun and Yue Chin-yau were married in 1971 and had their eldest son, Wing-lai, that year. He died in a car accident, but we've already mentioned that—'

Dub-dub.

Everyone jumped at the computer's NO sound.

'No? Sir, do you want me to say something further about Yue Wing-lai?'

Ping. YES this time.

Inspector Lok scratched his head, a little helplessly.

'In 1990, the car Yue Wing-lai was driving veered off Clear Water Bay Road and plunged downhill, leaving him in a coma. He died in hospital two days later without regaining consciousness... That's all I have here. Ah Sing, you were in charge of investigating the Yue family connections; do you have anything to add?'

Looking unprepared, Ah Sing scrambled to pull out a brown notebook from his pocket and anxiously flipped to the right page. 'Ah, Yue, Yue, Yue Wing-lai, only eighteen at time of death. Studied in Australia from ages of thirteen to seventeen, but his results were so poor his father forced him to return to Hong Kong, where he enrolled in the foundation course at St George's School. Because he'd already gained his driving licence abroad, he got a Hong Kong licence as soon as he turned eighteen, without having to take the test. Family friends say that unlike his business-minded father, Yue Wing-lai lived for pleasure. He frequently got into trouble, growing estranged from his parents. Oh, this is interesting, he was born on the Mid-Autumn Festival, and died on April Fool's Day...'

'Ahem.' Inspector Lok coughed a couple of times. Ah Sing looked up to see all five suspects staring at him, upset.

'My subordinate is inexperienced and unguarded with his words,' said the inspector. 'If he's been disrespectful to the deceased, please forgive him.' Ah Sing quickly nodded in apology.

Seeing no further reactions, Inspector Lok continued. 'Next, I'd like to discuss Yue Wing-yee. May I proceed, sir?'

Ping. YES.

'Yue Wing-yee, aged thirty-two, is the second child of Yuen Man-bun and Yue Chin-yau. Like his elder brother, Wing-yee studied at St George's School, then went to America for a degree in Business Administration, following which he returned to take on the deputy directorship for the Fung Hoi Consortium, that is, second in command to his father. Various people have testified that Wing-yee's character is very different from Wing-lai's, serious about his work, every bit as capable as his father and even his grandfather. His father respected him a great deal – they had an excellent relationship.'

Despite the compliment, Wing-yee's expression remained tense. Inspector Lok must think he was unhappy at Ah Sing's negative remarks about his older brother, but in fact he was still feeling intense guilt. He started to think that if this comatose detective did find the truth, even if that meant him going to jail, he'd feel relieved.

'Yue Wing-yee married Choi Ting last year. Choi Ting, aged thirty-four, is the youngest daughter of Choi Yuan-sam, founder of Choi Electronics. Before leaving her job on her marriage, she was a general practitioner at Cedar Medical Centre.' Inspector Lok fixed his gaze on the Yue daughter-in-law as he went on. 'There are rumours that Choi Ting's union with Yue Wing-yee was necessitated by Choi Electronics having fallen into debt in recent years, requiring a capital injection from the consortium—'

'Don't you dare sling mud at me, Inspector Lok.' Choi Ting's face had grown red and twisted with fury. 'You're implying I married Wing-yee for money—'

'I'm just reading the report, and I stress that these are only rumours,' the inspector said calmly. 'But after all, of the five people here, you have the strongest motive for murder. Wing-yee and Wing-lai stood to inherit from their father's death, but they weren't in urgent need of money. It's your family that's in need of cash. There've been reports that Choi Electronics has already lost one hundred and eighty million Hong Kong dollars this year – that's more than twenty-three million US dollars – and if Wing-yee were to become the director of Fung Hoi, transferring funds to your father would become much—'

'You... you bastard! This is all lies! I, I...' Choi Ting's poise was shattered by her apoplectic outburst, until it seemed she might scream. She stood up, glaring wildly at the inspector.

'Inspector Lok, you've guessed wrong.' Old Tong patted Choi Ting's arm, motioning her to take her seat again. 'Choi Electronics is undeniably in financial difficulties – that's a fact. But Boss-man was clearly aware of the company's potential, and even before Master Wing-yee's wife entered the household, he was already collaborating with them and providing monetary assistance from time to time. It was through these transactions that Master Wing-yee first met Miss Choi. Inspector, you said earlier that Old-boss was known as the "Fung Hoi Shark" – he never made a bad deal. I have many documents proving that he was already planning to invest in Choi Electronics before his death.

If Second Mistress was indeed the murderer, wouldn't she be damaging her own interests?'

Inspector Lok said nothing, only looked away from Choi Ting and returned to his book. Choi Ting felt this wasn't necessarily a sign of weakness – his silence didn't indicate agreement with Old Tong's words. Like a veteran gambler, he'd keep his cards close to his chest, leaving his opponents guessing.

'Finally, the third son of the deceased, Yue Wing-lim. Twenty-four years old and an engineering student at the Chinese University of Hong Kong, though he's currently taking some time off. We heard he wasn't close to the deceased, but had always been particularly filial to his mother, visiting her almost every day when she was hospitalized. The victim asked of Wing-lim that he finish his studies and start working at the consortium, but he wanted to become a professional photographer instead, so there was some friction between the two.'

This had come to light the day before, when the inspector asked Old Tong to guess who, other than a burglar, might have been the murderer – though the older man had insisted at the time that Wing-lim couldn't possibly be the killer.

'Huh.' That was Wing-lim's only comment – he wasn't going to kick up a fuss like his sister-in-law.

'That's all the background information we have about the Yue household. Now I'll move on to their whereabouts before and after the—'

Dub-dub. NO.

'What?' A pause, as if he'd forgotten the other person couldn't speak. 'Sir, do you want me to ask further questions? About this information?'

Dub-dub.

'Oh? But... you want to ask about a particular person?'

Ping.

'Is it a man?'

Dub-dub.

'Is it Choi Ting?'

Dub-dub. Nanny Wu looked stunned.

'Is it Wu Kam Mui?'

Dub-dub.

Baffled that the only two women present had received a NO, Choi Ting was about to speak when she heard Inspector Lok say, 'Then... you want to know more about Yue Chin-yau?'

Ping. The five suspects let out a sigh of relief, though this was even more confusing – why was the old detective so interested in dead people? First Wing-lai, now this.

'Sir, Yue Chin-yau's background is quite straightforward, there's not much more to say.' Still, Inspector Lok flipped through his notebook for the right page. 'Only daughter of Yue Fung, wife of Yuen Man-bun, three children – we've covered all that. Died of pancreatic cancer this May, aged fifty-nine. Apart from a bout of post-partum depression a year after the wedding, there's been nothing of significance. Sir, do you think she has anything to do with the case?'

The pointer refused to pick YES or NO, but moved rhythmically between the two.

'Do you mean "perhaps"?'

Ping.

'Then let me ask – do you have anything to add?' Inspector Lok turned back to the other five. They looked at each other, but no one wanted to speak first.

'No?'

'There's just—' Nanny Wu began timidly. 'It may be nothing, but the night of the crime, it was the hundredth day after Missy's death, and I'd prepared some hell money and offerings to burn for her.'

'Ah, that's right, Mr Wong mentioned that too,' said the inspector. 'And he said you'd had a paper mansion just like Fung Ying Villa made specially for her.'

'Missy lived here all her life, I was afraid she'd find it hard getting used to a different house...' Nanny Wu's eyes grew red.

Ah Sing recalled the sweet scent of burning joss paper that

permeated the house during their investigations. He'd thought at the time they must be devout Buddhists or Taoists, praying to their ancestors every weekend.

'This old dude isn't saying Mom came back from the grave to kill my dad, is he?' blurted out Wing-lim. Before Old Tong could scold the boy for making a joke in such poor taste, everyone's attention was drawn to the screen, where the pointer was once more hovering to mean 'maybe'.

'What nonsense is this?' chuckled Wing-lim, though they could all tell his smile was forced.

'Sir, are you saying the murderer... is Yue Chin-yau?'

The pointer remained still in the middle of the screen, neither YES nor NO.

'Then... Sir, your intuition hasn't told you the answer as it did before, and you need to hear more evidence?'

Ping. A definite YES.

'In that case, I'll go on with my report, and you can give us more instructions later?'

Ping.

Wing-yee tried frantically to conceal his uneasiness at this exchange. Each time the computer let out one of those tones, he felt it pierce through him, as if the old detective's spirit were burrowing into his skull, digging for the buried secret.

He felt close to collapse.

5

'LET'S MOVE ON to the day of the crime.' The inspector's voice remained steady. 'According to various testimonies, nothing out of the ordinary happened on Saturday night – it was just like any other weekend. All six members of the household ate dinner together. The only difference was they were preparing to burn offerings to Yue Chin-yau afterwards, which made the food turn to ashes in their mouths, so to speak.'

This was a direct quote from Old Tong.

'After dinner and the offerings, everyone returned to their own room, around eleven. Wong Kwan-tong and Wu Kam Mui have rooms on the ground floor. The deceased's study and bedroom are on the floor above, while Wing-lim's room and that of Wing-yee and his wife are on the top floor. Frustratingly, no one can prove where they were – everyone claims to have been in his or her room, alone – except for Yue Wing-yee and Choi Ting, who were together, but each has testified they wouldn't necessarily have noticed the other slipping out, because both were in the habit of going to the bathroom during the night.'

Inspector Lok paused. 'In other words, none of our suspects has an alibi.'

Even a rookie like Ah Sing could tell how upset the household was at these words.

'The deceased's bed was undisturbed, suggesting he hadn't slept at all, but remained in the study until his death. Of course, we can't rule out the possibility that he was in the bedroom or bathroom, and happened to walk into the study just as a burglary was taking place.' The inspector stroked his chin. 'As to whether the murderer or victim entered the room first, and what happened between them, we haven't been able to work out a logical hypothesis, because the ransacking prevents us reconstructing a sequence of events. But we can confirm that nothing is missing from the safe, which held diamond jewellery and antiques worth eight million US dollars, bearer bonds to the value of twelve million US dollars, stock certificates for four enterprises, an original copy of the deceased's will, and an old Fung Hoi Consortium accounts book, dating back forty years and signed by the deceased. Mr Wong Kwan-tong suggested the latter might have been kept as a memento, as it was the first set of accounts dealt with by Mr Yuen upon becoming Mr Yue Fung's personal assistant.'

From their expressions, it was clear the others were already familiar with the contents of the safe. When the police locksmith had got it open, Ah Sing and the inspector had been thoroughly startled by the bonds and diamonds. Why would this tycoon keep such valuable items in his own home, far less secure than a bank vault or the Fung Hoi Building?

'Speaking purely hypothetically,' continued the inspector, 'the murderer's target might have been the will. Perhaps he crept into the study and was trying to get the safe open when Mr Yuen entered. After a struggle, the murderer knocked the victim out with the vase, tied him up, then threatened him with the spear-gun to force him to reveal the combination, hitting him on the head a second time. When Mr Yuen resisted, the killer shot him dead – or perhaps that was an accident. To create the impression of a burglary, he smashed the window and ransacked the place. He'd have worn gloves and shoes that wouldn't leave prints, to prevent the police suspecting it was an inside job. Perhaps he had hoped to slip in and out quietly, but instead encountered the victim, with tragic consequences.'

This nonchalant mention of the will seemed to hint that the Yue brothers and Choi Ting were the likely suspects, but none of the three was stupid enough to speak now. They knew the inspector would be watching for a reaction.

Dub-dub. NO.

'What is it? Did I say something wrong?'

Ping, ping, ping. The pointer repeatedly jabbed at YES, as if the old detective were frowningly rebuking his junior for getting things so wrong.

Inspector Lok looked quizzical, trying to find the right question.

'Is something about the room leading our investigation in the wrong direction?'

Ping.

'What should we pay more attention to? The victim? The suspects' whereabouts? The method? The murder weapon—'

Ping.

'The weapon? The speargun?'

Ping.

Inspector Lok hesitated. 'The speargun... That's right, I forgot. Of our five suspects, only Wong Kwan-tong and Yue Wing-yee have any experience of diving and spear-fishing – they'd been out to sea with the deceased.'

'Hang on! This is a child's game, and you're going to use it as evidence to say one of us two is the killer?' protested Old Tong. Wing-yee was silent, his eyes uncertain as he watched the exchange.

'But this is a key point,' said the inspector, his face glowing with realization. 'The killer murdered Mr Yuen with the speargun, which means he knew how to operate it. Otherwise, wouldn't it have been simpler to use the diving knife from the same cabinet?'

'But... But...' Old Tong was growing agitated.

Dub-dub.

'Sir, do you have something to add?'

Ping.

'Are you going to say who did it?'

Dub-dub.

The suspects were intrigued – surely with this development, the old detective could name the murderer?

The inspector looked pained. Old Tong guessed that he must be finding this hard, knowing his mentor wanted to say something but having to guess what.

'Sir, is this about my earlier hypothesis?'

Dub-dub.

'About the deceased?'

Dub-dub.

'About the five suspects?'

Dub-dub.

'Then... about the Yue family?'

Ping.

'About the scene of the crime?'

Dub-dub.

'About Fung Hoi Consortium?'

Dub-dub.

A question mark seemed to form above the group. What else could there be?

Ah Sing broke in. 'Is it about Yue Chin-yau?'

Ping, ping.

The suspects looked at each other. Why bring up the late wife again?

'You answered YES twice,' said Inspector Lok. 'Apart from Yue Chin-yau, do you also want to talk about Yue Wing-lai?'

Ping. The swift YES was like a leap of joy at the inspector having hit on the answer.

'You old fool! Why keep yammering on about dead people?' yelled Yue Wing-lim.

Inspector Lok looked up to see the befuddlement in their faces. A while ago, when Ah Sing had mentioned Yue Wing-lai, they'd

been unhappy, as if he'd offended them. Now anyone could see
what lay behind that – they didn't want Wing-lai mentioned, the
same way they wouldn't want to touch something dirty.

One expression in particular grabbed Inspector Lok's attention. Nanny Wu's eyes were wet, her face full of torment.

'Ms Wu, if you have anything to share with us, please do.
I can guarantee it won't go any further than this room,' Inspector Lok reassured her, guessing this was a family secret.

Nanny Wu glanced at the other four, and as no one seemed
to object, took a deep breath and said slowly, 'Inspector, I'm
sure Superintendent Kwan has already guessed this, but I'll say
it anyway... Master Wing-lai wasn't Boss-man's biological son.'

'What?'

'Only the family knows the ugly truth.' She clenched her teeth.
'When she was very young, Missy had an unfortunate encounter,
and someone put her in the family way.'

'Why don't you just say it – she was raped!' Old Tong's face
was full of anger.

Nanny Wu's brow furrowed and she looked in anguish at Old
Tong before going on. 'This was in the winter of 1970... No, January 1971, close to Chinese New Year. Missy was just seventeen,
doing well at school, but she fell into bad company. The old master asked me to keep a tight watch on her, but one evening she
slipped out. The whole family was out looking everywhere, and
the old master even went to the police station to ask his friends
for help. The next morning, I got a phone call from Missy, crying her eyes out. She was at a phone booth on Kowloon Peak,
wanted me to come alone to get her, not tell the old master.
I couldn't get there on my own, I had to ask Man-bun, I mean
Boss-man, to drive me. He'd just come back from hunting for
Missy all night, not a wink of sleep. Ah, we were all exhausted
that day. Tong hadn't slept either – he must have gone over the
whole of Kowloon.'

Even before she was done, the inspector and Ah Sing, and
even Apple, could guess how this would end.

'When we found Missy, she was squatting by the roadside with her arms around her knees, her dress all ripped – it broke my heart. She hugged me and cried some more, and all we could do was help her into the car to rest. She said her so-called friends had taken her out for a spin, and there they were listening to music and boozing, when someone produced a rolled-up cigarette and got her to try some, but after a few drags she felt light-headed, and someone was tugging at her clothes. When she woke up, she was alone at a shelter near the Kowloon Peak car park, her dress all open – oh, it was awful...' Nanny Wu was weeping now. 'And that's how Missy got raped by a stranger. She begged me not to tell the old master, and at that moment my heart was so weak for her, I agreed. Even went back home to get her clothes to change into. The old master thought she'd just stayed out all night partying, gave her a good scolding, and that should have been it, only two months later trouble showed itself... Missy told me her time hadn't come, and I realized how serious the situation was.'

Sex education in schools had been much more limited back then; Ah Sing thought how much damage this policy had caused.

'There was no keeping this from the old master. Surprisingly, he didn't lose his temper, he and the old mistress just hugged Missy and cried. He got a doctor he knew to examine her, and she was going to get rid of it, but the doctor said if she did that she might never be able to get pregnant again. She was the old master's only child, and if she couldn't have kids, that'd be the end of the Yue family. All along, the old master had felt uneasy about only producing a single girl, thinking he'd let down all his ancestors, but at least any child she had would still have Yue blood in its veins, and he'd just need to make sure it got the name as well. Now it seemed the heavens were taking even that away—'

'So Yue Fung made Chin-yau have the baby?' asked Inspector Lok.

'He didn't insist, but she wanted that too, if only to protect the family name.' Nanny Wu slowly dabbed away her tears. 'If a scandal like this got out, it would hurt the old master's reputation. Things weren't as liberal back then. People would have said he couldn't even control his own daughter, how could he run a company? The only choice was to get Missy married off as quickly as possible.'

'So Mr Wong and the deceased really were brought in as potential sons-in-law?'

'No,' said Old Tong. 'Old-boss had only been looking for young assistants when he hired us, but because we were around her so much, we'd grown close to the mistre— to Chin-yau, and so he ordered one of us to marry her.'

'Which means you had the chance to become head of the Yue family?' Inspector Lok asked, his eyes bright as lightning.

'You could put it that way,' Old Tong smiled bitterly. 'But I gave it up. All right, I'll admit I was fond of Chin-yau, but I couldn't bring up a child that wasn't my own. But Brother Man-bun – Boss-man – he was more open, willing to step forward right away and say the little life in her belly was innocent. Maybe he was attracted to the status of being the Yue successor. But back then, it wouldn't have been easy to accept another man's kid and a wife who'd been ruined. So you see, he must truly have loved Chin-yau. That's something I could never have done.'

'The boss-man was very good to the child,' said Nanny Wu. 'Even if he wasn't his, he always loved him.'

'Because of what happened, Old-boss felt local medicine was inadequate, and many years later he set up Wo Yan Hospital,' said Old Tong. 'If there'd been safer abortion techniques available at the time, ones that didn't endanger future pregnancies, Chin-yau wouldn't have suffered so much, especially getting depression after Master Wing-lai's birth.'

'Does that mean Wing-lai's rotten character came from the rape?' Ah Sing's nonsensical exclamation seemed to pour salt in the wound, but no one tried to deny it. Only Old Tong smiled bitterly.

'That's right. Wing-lai's rotten character... might actually have come from his father.' He shook his head as he spoke.

'Tong, never mind if Master Wing-lai was stubborn and badly behaved, he's dead now. Don't say bad things about him,' said Nanny Wu, but without much resolve.

'How did Superintendent Kwan know all this?' asked Choi Ting suddenly. 'Did he work out what went on with Uncle and Granny, just from what we said?'

Ping. The pointer moved to YES, then hovered around the middle of the screen.

'What does that mean?'

'Probably that he saw most of it, but needed to guess the details.' Inspector Lok seemed preoccupied, falling silent for a moment. 'That's right, didn't Ah Sing mention that Yue Wing-lai was born at Mid-Autumn? Yuen Man-bun and Yue Chin-yau were married in April 1971, and had their oldest son that same year. Mid-Autumn is September or October, less than seven months after the wedding. Even if the baby were premature, that'd still be implausible, unless it was a shotgun wedding... If the father had been one of these "imperial sons-in-law", then Wong Kwan-tong would have been the more likely candidate, because we've heard that Chin-yau got on better with him. Even if it was Yuen Man-bun who'd raped Yue Chin-yau to get her pregnant so Yue Fung would force them into marriage, that wouldn't necessarily have meant he'd gain control of the consortium – Yue Fung might have instead instructed Wong Kwan-tong to groom the young Wing-lai as his successor. So we have to consider that the father of the child was someone else altogether.'

Ping. Like praise from the old man.

'Then Yue Wing-lai...'

Before the inspector could finish his sentence, Wing-yee abruptly stood up. Only now did everyone notice how pale he had grown, his face clenched tight, his brow covered in sweat. His nerves were a rubber band about to snap.

'Wing-yee, what's wrong? Are you sick?' Choi Ting urgently asked her husband.

'I... I want to turn myself in. I'm the killer.'

The company was taken aback by the unexpected confession.

Yue Wing-yee's hands were trembling. He plucked off his glasses and kept turning his head to glance behind him, as if someone he couldn't see was staring at him.

'Mr Yue, what are you saying?' Inspector Lok glared at him.

'I said, I'm the killer. Please, please don't let Superintendent Kwan say anything further, I'll admit everything.' Wing-yee hid his face.

'Why would you kill your own father?' Nanny Wu's tears started flowing again. 'You always got on so well with him! Were there problems at work? Was it because of debt? Or—'

'No, no, I didn't kill Father. I meant my brother.'

6

'YUE WING-LAI? BUT didn't he die in a car accident? And at the time you'd have been... just nine years old!' The sudden revelation made even Inspector Lok lose his imperturbability.

'Yes, I killed my older brother when I was nine, and kept the secret for more than two decades.' Wing-yee sat down again and covered his face with his hands.

'How did you kill Wing-lai at the age of nine?'

'That day was April Fool's.'

'So?'

'I wanted to pull a prank, so I asked Old Tong to help me find... scary toys.' Wing-yee's voice trembled. 'They were fake soda cans, and when someone pulled the tab, the bottom of the can would open and dump rubber insects all over you.'

'Argh! Those things!' Nanny Wu's exclamation suggested she'd been one of his victims.

'I thought it would be fun to plant one of them in my brother's car...' Wing-yee clenched his jaw, his fingers digging into his scalp. 'After the accident, I heard people saying they didn't understand how he could have gone off the bridge – the road was wide there, not dangerous at all, it was as if he'd been startled by something and turned the steering wheel...'

Inspector Lok winced, not having expected this old matter to suddenly rear its head.

'Ah... Mr Yue, we're currently investigating your father's death. Wing-lai's accident isn't within the scope of this case, and we won't look into it right now. I'm not a judge, and can't pronounce you not guilty, but in my experience, something like this would almost certainly be called an accident, and I don't think anyone's going to press charges. After we've dealt with your father's killer, let's look into how to resolve this other matter – okay?'

Wing-yee raised his head, looking like a little child caught being naughty, and nodded.

'Sir, did you know about this as well?'

Ping. An unhesitating YES.

'And does this have anything to do with Yuen Man-bun's murder?'

Unexpectedly, there was no response, and the pointer remained neutral.

'Sir? Yue Chin-yau's rape, Wing-lai's birth and accidental death – do these have any bearing on the Yuen Man-bun case?'

The pointer wobbled on the centre line, which they all understood to mean MAYBE.

'Perhaps, sir... you saw the inconsistencies and contradictions in the details, realized there was a puzzle there, and brought up the matter to prove your suspicions right?'

Ping. An enthusiastic YES.

'Dammit! This old bastard enjoys picking at other people's scabs!' Wing-lim stood up, agitated. 'So to satisfy your curiosity, you have to publicly humiliate my mom. All you pervs staring at her with your filthy eyes, pointing and laughing.'

'Mr Yue, please try to stay calm,' said Inspector Lok, conciliatorily. 'I apologize on behalf of my mentor, and ask for everyone's forgiveness. Superintendent Kwan would never let a suspicious point go, which is why he wanted to verify those events we've just talked about. After all, he's already ascertained the killer must be a member of the household, so your family past might be relevant. I imagine now that he understands the ins and outs of this case, he probably knows who the killer...'

Ping. Confirmation, even before the inspector could finish his sentence.

'You know who the killer is?' This was Ah Sing.

Ping.

'Then ask him to say the name!' called out Nanny Wu.

'No, before that, let's make sure of the evidence,' said Inspector Lok. 'Without sufficient evidence, pointing out the murderer won't do any good. They'd just deny it, and we'd be left with nothing but speculation.'

Ping.

This line of reasoning in fact came from the superintendent himself. Inspector Lok remembered being lectured by his mentor more than once as a young man: 'What's so hard about knowing who's guilty? The difficulty is in giving the suspect no wiggle room, so they have no choice but to admit it.'

'Sir, in everything that's been said up to now, has the killer slipped up and left us an opening?'

Ping.

'Really?' Ah Sing butted in. 'I see a pile of possibilities, but no actual clues. It's not like the victim left us a message—'

Ping. This one seemed especially emphatic.

'A message before he died?' Inspector Lok queried. He flipped open his notebook. 'Was it the photo album? But we didn't find anything—'

Dub-dub.

'Was the message in the album?'

Dub-dub.

'On the victim's body?'

Dub-dub.

'The bloodstains?' asked Ah Sing.

Dub-dub.

'Ah Sing, we haven't even mentioned the bloodstains.'

'Right, yes. Um... was it something in the room?'

Dub-dub.

'Nothing in the room?' Ah Sing was startled. 'Then, something outside the room?'

'That's a dumb question – if it wasn't in the room, then it must be out—'

Dub-dub. The NO interrupted Inspector Lok.

'Huh?' Everyone now looked thoroughly confused.

'What does that mean?' said Wing-lim. 'Inside and outside are the only possibilities!'

'Was it on the door?' said Old Tong.

Dub-dub. This one sounded like 'Nice try, but no.'

'Nothing could be neither inside nor outside the room,' yelled Wing-lim.

Ping. Finally, the screen agreed with someone.

'No?' The inspector was deep in thought for a moment. 'Sir, are you saying the deceased left no message?'

Ping.

'The old fool must be brain-damaged! First there was a message, now there isn't,' sneered Wing-lim.

'No, I understand what he's saying,' smiled Inspector Lok. 'What he means is, the clearest message the victim could leave was no message at all.'

The others blinked uncomprehendingly at him.

'Initially, we thought the killer was a burglar – in which case, the victim wouldn't have known their name. But after investigating, we've realized the murderer must be a member of the household, so the deceased should have been able to leave behind a clue to their identity.'

Inspector Lok glanced at the superintendent before continuing, 'Let's look at it objectively. First of all, did the victim have the ability to leave any words behind? He had a harpoon through his belly and was bleeding freely, but even if he couldn't find a pen, a finger dipped in blood would have done to write the killer's name. There were signs he'd been tied up, but when he was found, his limbs were unrestricted. Next, was there enough time? It would seem so, because he was looking through the photo album before he died. So the fact he left no clue at all seems abnormal.'

'So what's the meaning behind this no-message message?' asked Old Tong.

'He could have left a message or called out for help, but didn't, which means... he'd rather die than let anyone know who the killer was.'

Inspector Lok's deduction left the group stunned.

'You mean he was trying to protect the murderer?'

Ping.

Having stayed silent for some time, the computer came back into the conversation in answer to Old Tong's words.

'Maybe... maybe there *was* a message, but the killer wiped it away?' said Choi Ting.

'Mm, no,' said the inspector. 'After Mr Yuen sustained the fatal injury, he didn't crawl towards the door, but to the bookcase for the photo album, as if he'd given up hope of being rescued. He might have realized he was close to death, and so decided to curl up in a corner and pretend he'd been killed by an intruder, in order to protect the real criminal.'

Inspector Lok smiled suddenly, as if something had just become clear through the fog.

'I think I understand what happened just beforehand. The killer and victim were speaking together in the study. The murderer became angry about something or other, picked up the vase and knocked out Mr Yuen. Perhaps thinking they'd killed him, they quickly made the room look like it had been ransacked, prised open the gun cabinet, chiselled some marks on the safe, then swept the contents of the bookcase onto the floor. While this was going on, the victim came to. Panicking, the killer knocked him out again with the vase, then decided murder was the only option, so grabbed the waterproof tape – that must have come from the cabinet with the diving equipment – and bound Mr Yuen's arms and legs, then pushed open the window and stuck tape to the outside to make it look like a break-in, and finally finished him off with the speargun.'

Inspector Lok paused. 'After the harpooning, thinking the victim was dead, the murderer pulled the tape off his limbs and fled. But in fact, Mr Yuen still had enough strength left to get to the bookshelf...'

'Hang on, why would the murderer pull the tape off?' asked Choi Ting.

'That's...' Inspector Lok stuttered to a stop.

Ping.

'Sir, do you have something to say?'

Ping. To Lok, this sounded like Kwan was saying, 'Of course.'

'About Ms Choi's question?'

Ping.

'The killer pulled the tape off on purpose?'

Ping.

'Was this... to distract attention?'

Dub-dub.

'To harm the victim?'

Dub-dub.

'Then... the murderer slipped up, and had no choice but to untie him?'

Ping.

Inspector Lok rubbed his chin with his left hand, sunk in thought. Apart from Yue Wing-yee, whose head was lowered in despair, the other four were looking fixedly at him, hoping he'd be able to explain the old detective's words. After some time, the inspector's head snapped up and he asked the old man, 'Sir, was my hypothesis earlier completely correct, including the *sequence* of events.'

Ping.

A smile reappeared on Inspector Lok's face. He said to Choi Ting, 'The murderer made a basic error, so he had no choice.'

'What mistake?'

'He got the order wrong.'

'What order?'

'Sticking the tape to the window, and binding the victim,' he said with satisfaction.

The suspects looked confused, and it was Ah Sing who said, 'That's right, an intruder would have to break the window before entering and then tape up the victim. So the unused tape left on the roll should have a matching edge with the tape on the victim's limbs. If it joined up with what was on the window instead, investigators would realize there was a problem.'

'When the murderer realized their mistake,' Lok said, 'they'd have had to remove the tape either from the window or the victim's limbs. The latter would make more sense, as the other option would involve also dealing with broken glass.'

'What's the big deal? It's just a few bits of glass,' protested Wing-lim.

'Tape can be burnt, but not glass.'

'Burnt?' asked Nanny Wu.

The inspector pointed a finger at Nanny Wu. 'You did the killer a big favour.'

'What? Don't you dare accuse—'

'I'm not accusing you of anything, just saying something you did inadvertently helped the killer. You were burning hell money for Yue Chin-yau the night before, filling the house and garden with the smell of smoke.'

'But that doesn't— Oh!' Choi Ting didn't finish her sentence.

'The criminal will have burned the tape, then flushed away the ashes and other remains. By the way, I imagine that's also what happened to that two hundred thousand Hong Kong dollars.'

'What?'

'Which is why only the money was taken, not the rings or antique watches and so forth. Those would be too troublesome to deal with, and too easily found by the police if they were concealed on someone's person or in their room. Besides, the murderer certainly wasn't motivated by money.'

'So who did it?' urged Choi Ting.

'If the deceased would rather die than name his killer, it was probably one of his sons,' said Ah Sing.

Yue Wing-lim leaped to his feet again, while Wing-yee continued to clutch his head, apparently still not recovered from his confession.

'At the very least, I presume the deceased wouldn't have protected his old retainer or secretary in this way,' said Inspector Lok. Seeing Choi Ting about to object, he added, 'And I'm sure Dr Choi would be able to tell unconsciousness from death, and would have noticed if the victim was still alive after she'd fired a speargun at him. Yuen Man-bun's death was at least partly due to his not seeking help – the killer left before finishing the job. Choi Ting would have made sure he was dead, rather than leaving him still able to crawl over to the photo album.'

'Which leaves Wing-yee or Wing-lim.' The thought popped into everyone's head.

'So that means Wing-yee was the killer,' proclaimed Ah Sing. 'Out of the two brothers, he was the only one who knew how to use a speargun.'

'It's not that difficult to pull a trigger,' said Inspector Lok.

'But sir, as you know, an inexperienced person wouldn't find it easy to get the rubber tube in place – the slightest mistake and they'd hurt themselves.' Ah Sing tried to sound like an expert despite having, like Inspector Lok, learned about spearguns just that week.

Ping. The old detective broke his silence.

'The speargun? Sir, would you like to talk about that?'

Ping.

Now everyone remembered that the old detective had been asking about the gun before they got distracted by the revelations about Yue Chin-yau and Wing-lai.

'Have we missed an obvious piece of evidence?'

Ping. This YES somehow sounded reproachful to Lok.

Inspector Lok opened his notebook again. 'What about the speargun? The deceased was hit in the belly by a 115-centimetre steel harpoon, and died of blood loss. On the floor was a RGSH115 carbon-fibre speargun: 115-centimetre barrel, shuttered opening, thirty-centimetre rubber tube...'

'Wait – what?' Unexpectedly, this came from Wing-yee. He still appeared utterly dejected, but was now looking at Inspector Lok in confusion.

'What's wrong, Mr Yue?'

'Could you repeat that?'

'What I just said? The victim was killed by a 115-centimetre steel harpoon; there was a RGSH115 carbon-fibre speargun on the floor with a shuttered opening...'

'The RGSH115 couldn't possibly fire that harpoon,' said Wing-yee with certainty.

'Why not?'

'Wrong length.'

'Both the barrel and the harpoon were 115 centimetres long, isn't that right?' said Ah Sing.

'The speargun ought to be shorter than the harpoon! You'd use a seventy-five-centimetre speargun for a 115 centimetre harpoon!'

'That's right! I thought something sounded wrong,' said Old Tong.

Ping. Confirmation from the computer.

'But is it really not possible to fire a 115-centimetre harpoon from a speargun of the same length?' Ah Sing seemed determined not to let this point go.

'You might manage with another model, but not the RGSH115.' For an instant, Wing-yee seemed to have switched from suspect to detective. 'Because of the shuttered opening.'

'What does that have to do with it?'

'The harpoon has barbed hooks at one end. You might be able to force it through an easy-release gun, but the shuttered opening is just a round hole, and if the harpoon is shorter than the barrel, the barbs will catch on the aperture. Did you see any damage to the harpoon or barrel?'

Inspector Lok shook his head. 'So the harpoon was fired from another gun?'

'Probably the RGSH075 or RB075.'

Ping.

Wing-yee had an eerie sense that the old detective was absolving him of his brother's death.

'Which means the murderer didn't know anything about spear-fishing, and mixed up the 115 and 075 guns... Wing-lim?' Choi Ting stared in trepidation at her brother-in-law, sitting beside her.

'Nonsense,' Wing-lim said nonchalantly. 'Seeing as I don't know about spearguns, how could I have loaded one? Or if you think I secretly did know, then anyone might have mixed up the two guns. From this angle, I'm the least likely suspect.'

Inspector Lok said nothing. His left hand went back to his chin as he stared thoughtfully at Wing-lim, as if searching for a flaw in his statement.

Dub-dub.

'Sir, was that a no?' said the inspector. 'Are you disagreeing with Yue Wing-lim?'

Ping.

The old detective might as well have jumped from his bed and pointed at Wing-lim, declaring in his bass voice, 'Don't deny it – you're the murderer.'

Wing-lim was clearly rattled by this, but in a matter of seconds had returned to his previous insouciance. 'Fine, let's see what evidence this old coot has.'

'Sir, do you have proof?'

Ping. Again, Lok imagined the old detective tossing that out lightly, facing off with the suspect.

'But wasn't Yue Wing-lim right to say he doesn't know how to use a speargun, so couldn't have loaded it and used it to kill someone?'

Dub-dub, ping. NO, then YES.

'He didn't load it, but did kill someone with it?'

Ping.

'But if he didn't load it, how... Aha!' yelled Inspector Lok. 'Yuen Man-bun loaded it himself! Wong Kwan-tong mentioned that Yuen Man-bun often practised harpooning in his study. That's what he must have been doing that night!'

Ping.

'Then the damage to the gun cabinet must have been faked! It wasn't locked to start with, so Yue Wing-lim did that to create a false impression. He grabbed the waterproof tape, gloves and so forth right away, as well as the tools for prising the door open. He didn't use a knife because he was afraid of getting the victim's blood on himself, and besides, he didn't know how to operate a speargun, so that would deflect suspicion from him.'

Ping.

'The victim was playing with the speargun in his room when Yue Wing-lim entered. They started arguing, and then the attack with the vase, the fake burglary, the speargun murder... Hang on, why would the culprit swap the guns? He'd already be wearing gloves when he fired...'

Ping, ping, ping, ping... A series of YESes, the pointer jumping about like something in an arcade game. They were at the point of cracking the case.

Inspector Lok looked up abruptly, one finger pointed at Wing-lim, his gaze hawklike. 'You had to change the spearguns because you'd left some damning evidence on the real murder weapon.'

Wing-lim had grown pale, but continued to hold himself upright, facing the accusation head on.

'You fired the speargun at the victim, but because you weren't familiar with it, only managed to hit him in the belly. You tried to fire again – but didn't know how to load it! The mechanism is quite fiddly, you have to keep the grip pressed against your chest while pulling the rubber tube with both hands. Anyone unfamiliar with the device would easily get hurt by the moving parts. Thinking the victim was dead anyway, you gave up on shooting him again and tried to get rid of the immediate danger.

You wanted to replace the RGSH075 with a gun of equivalent length, but the RB075 was disassembled, and you didn't know how to put it together. So you could only use the RGSH115, not thinking how the harpoon would work with the shuttered opening. Now we know what the real murder weapon is, we can—'

Just at that moment, Wing-lim showed his guilt: he tried to run. In one step, he leaped over his brother and sister-in-law to the door, only to find it wouldn't open, and in a second he felt a pair of hands grabbing him. Ah Sing had reacted almost as soon as Wing-lim jumped up, and quickly pushed him to the floor, easily pinning him down.

'Do you think I'm a total rookie? I told Ah Sing to lock the door when he closed it,' said the inspector. Everyone looked at the door, now noticing the catch had indeed been flipped.

Ah Sing now had Wing-lim in handcuffs. Wing-yee, Choi Ting and Old Tong stood, leaving him alone on the sofa. Nanny Wu longed to ask why on earth he'd kill his own father, but the thought of her Missy having produced such an unworthy child left her sobbing and unable to speak.

'Yue Wing-lim, why did you murder your father?' asked Inspector Lok.

He grunted, but didn't reply.

'By trying to flee, you've already admitted your guilt. I'm sure the investigators will find your DNA on the murder weapon. You have the right to remain silent, but anything you say may be used against you... But I have to add that if you don't make things clear, your family will have no idea why you'd do what you did.'

'I... I wanted to be a photographer,' spat out Yue Wing-lim.

'And?'

'The old man wouldn't let me. We quarrelled, I hit him, and then what you said.'

'Just for that?' Nanny Wu couldn't stop herself asking.

'Just that. And because once he was dead, Second Brother would take over the directorship and stop pestering me to join the firm, and I'd be able to use my inheritance to focus on photography. Two birds with one stone.'

Nanny Wu slapped him across the face. 'These devilish reasons – if Missy could hear you from the afterlife, her heart would break.'

Wing-lim made a guttural sound and looked down, avoiding Nanny Wu's eyes.

'So the case is solved. Thank you all for taking part in the investigation, and to my mentor too.' Inspector Lok remained by the bedside. 'Ah Sing, turn off the camera. Apple, you can put away the computers too.'

Dub-dub.

Everyone turned towards the screen and its NO.

'Sir, what is it?'

Dub-dub.

'Sir, are you saying... this case isn't over yet?'

Ping.

Their eyes were fixed on the screen. Wing-yee was paralysed, convinced the old policeman was going to go after him for his elder brother's death now.

Inspector Lok's brow crinkled. 'Not finished? What did we miss?'

The pointer remained stationary.

'Sir?'

Whoosh. Out of nowhere, a dialogue box popped up on the screen: 'ERROR :: Interface Linkage Exception / Address: 0x004D78F9' and a bright red exclamation mark.

'Apple, what's up?' asked the inspector.

'A bug.' Apple's head was bent over another screen. 'I'll see what I can do.'

'How long will it take?'

'Anything from half an hour to half a day. Might be hardware. I'll have to go home and get a spare.'

Inspector Lok glanced awkwardly at the family, then the figure in the bed. 'Then we'll stop for today. Apple, see if you can fix the bug tonight and come back here with me tomorrow morning, to ask the superintendent what else he has to say. He might even have woken by then, and be able to speak to us in person.' Inspector Lok turned to the other four. 'I'll be in touch if anything needs clarifying.'

The setting sun had dyed the ocean red. Ah Sing put away the video camera and held on to Yue Wing-lim as they waited. Apple only put away one computer, leaving the two other machines and a floor covered in cables. Yue Wing-yee, Choi Ting, Old Tong and Nanny Wu had already left the room. Inspector Lok stood beside the bed, looking down with respect and admiration at Kwan Chun-dok, taking his hand as he said, 'Sir, I'm going. I'll keep working as you would have, and get to the bottom of this case.'

A corner of the superintendent's lip seemed to curl upwards a little, but Inspector Lok knew this was just an illusion caused by the setting sun.

7

AT NINE THE next morning, Inspector Lok and Ah Sing arrived at Fung Ying Villa. There were already several reporters lurking outside who'd received news of Wing-lim's arrest and hoped to snatch an exclusive from the family. Seeing the police car, they rushed towards the main gate, but were blocked by the security guards hired in haste the night before. They could only watch the inspector walk up to the house.

'Good morning, Inspector.' Nanny Wu answered the door. Her eyes were bloodshot, and she clearly hadn't slept well.

'Good morning, Ms Wu.' Inspector Lok seemed worn out too. 'Are the others home?'

'They're all here.' As she spoke, Wing-yee and Old Tong appeared in the vestibule. It was Sunday, and they weren't needed at the office. 'Tong was running around all night trying to find a lawyer for that brat, while Master Wing-yee phoned everyone he knew. None of us slept well.'

'My wife is in our room. Inspector Lok, did you come here because of me?' Wing-yee asked. He was relieved to have given up the secret that had plagued him for twenty years, even if it caused a schism in the family.

'No, we'll talk about that later.' The inspector turned to Old Tong and said sternly, 'Mr Wong Kwan-tong, you are under arrest on suspicion of murder. Please accompany us to the police station to help with our inquiries. You have the right to remain silent, but anything you say will be recorded and may be used against you.'

The formal police caution statement stunned all three of them. Wing-yee and Nanny Wu swung around to look at Old Tong.

'So the mur... murderer wasn't Wing... Wing-lim, but Old Tong?' Wing-yee struggled to get the words out. The inspector ignored him.

Old Tong's expression went from shock to sadness, and he only furrowed his brow a little as he asked, 'May... may I put on my jacket?'

Inspector Lok nodded. He waited till Old Tong had the garment on before handcuffing him.

'Wing-lim must be spouting all kinds of nonsense at the station, trying to drag the rest of us down with him. Don't worry,' said Old Tong to Nanny Wu and Wing-yee as he left.

The three of them got in the car and departed, cameras flashing non-stop as they passed through the gate, all the reporters trying to get a shot of the inspector and Old Tong in the back seat. They drove along the highway towards Kowloon East Regional Headquarters in Tseung Kwan O.

In the car, the three men were silent. Ah Sing glanced at the other two in the rear-view mirror from time to time, but both kept up a poker face. Old Tong seemed self-possessed, not anxious at all, as if his confusion at being arrested earlier was all for show.

Inspector Lok broke the silence first. 'It was you who incited Yue Wing-lim to murder Yuen Man-bun, wasn't it?'

'Is that what Wing-lim said?' Old Tong didn't turn, but looked directly ahead.

'No. He hasn't said a word, not even to that lawyer you found for him.' The inspector was certain the old man already knew this; there was no way the lawyer wouldn't have reported back to him.

'Then why do you think I incited him to do it?' said Old Tong calmly.

'The motives he admits to don't stand up at all. Killing his father because he wanted to be a photographer? That's laughable. As an impulsive act, sure, that might explain the attack with the vase. But shooting with a harpoon? That's not something that happens on the spur of the moment.'

'You think Wing-lim wasn't the murderer?'

'No, he did it. The DNA evidence shows it – because he wasn't familiar with the loading mechanism, a hook on the rubber tubing grazed his left wrist. He probably tried to clean up the blood, but what the naked eye can't see, police technology can still pick up.'

'So it was him.'

'But even if he'd attacked his father over his choice of profession, there'd be no reason to turn it into murder. Say he impulsively knocked his father out, and thought he'd killed him, so tried to make it look like a burglary – fine. But when his father came to, he knocked him out again, and even shot him with a speargun – that's completely over the top. This wasn't a premeditated crime; the scenario he created is full of holes. Yet it was an unspeakably vicious assault, as if he felt he had no choice but to kill his father. So I think he must have had a real hatred for the deceased that had lain dormant for a long time, but flared up because of some argument.'

'I can't speak for Wing-lim's own issues.'

'That's the one thing I can't understand. What kind of deep vendetta could a twenty-four-year-old have against his own father? Most murders of parents take place when the killer has a long-term resentment against their victim, and more importantly, has never felt any familial warmth since childhood. Yue Wing-lim doesn't fit the profile – it's clear from his words and behaviour that he got on very well with his mother. Money plays a big part in most patricides, but I don't think Wing-lim was in financial difficulties, and besides, Yuen Man-bun paid for all his children to go to university. There surely couldn't be enough accumulated anger to provoke this kind of act.'

'Yuen Man-bun paid for his kids' education because that was

his duty. He wasn't a good father – he only cared about money, power, reputation and status. He liked Wing-yee, but only because he had the potential to do well in the business world.'

Inspector Lok noticed Old Tong had stopped calling Mr Yuen 'Boss-man', and was just using his name – his pretence of respect for the deceased completely dropped.

'Even if Yuen Man-bun wasn't as warm towards his sons as he could have been, I don't believe that would cause Wing-lim to commit murder. There'd need to be some kind of deeper reason to provoke such an extreme act.'

'Did the unconscious Superintendent Kwan deduce that?'

'No, that was me.' Inspector Lok smiled, although his tired eyes told a different story.

'And you think I was this "deeper reason"?'

'Yes.'

'Inspector Lok, you think too highly of me.' Old Tong's grin looked forced, like a mask. 'I'm just a humble secretary...'

'But you've been with the Yue household a long time.'

'So?'

'So I believe you're at the core of this case. Do you remember, at the police station last week, I asked you, "If the murderer weren't an intruder, who would you think it was?"'

'I remember.'

'And you answered that of all the family, Yue Wing-lim had the worst relationship with the deceased, though he'd never kill his own father.'

'I guess I was wrong.' Old Tong shrugged.

'Do you know what answers the others gave?'

'What?'

'Wing-lim said he didn't know, and the other three gave three different names, all people connected to companies that were subject to hostile takeover by Fung Hoi.'

'Oh?' Old Tong hesitated.

'My question was really, "Who do you think harboured ill intentions against Yuen Man-bun?" The others thought of his business enemies – which the "Fung Hoi Shark" would surely have plenty of.' Inspector Lok's voice was calm. 'But you, as his secretary, didn't reach for these names. Instead, you assured me Wing-lim wasn't the killer. I don't believe this was a slip of the tongue, or that your mind momentarily went blank. You supposed in that moment that I was asking only about the Yue household. Which means that even if you weren't the murderer or chief plotter, you still knew more than you should.'

'A fascinating supposition,' said Old Tong placidly. 'But that's just your little fantasy.'

'That's right, I've got no evidence at all,' smiled the inspector. 'Only my instincts. For that matter, I have an even bolder hypothesis.'

'What might that be?'

'Yue Wing-lim isn't Yuen Man-bun's son. He's yours.'

'Ha!' Old Tong burst into laughter. 'That's original. Let's hear more.'

'If Yue Wing-lim were the result of you and Yue Chin-yau having an affair, that would explain some of the strange things I've noticed. Why did Wing-lim get on so badly with Yuen Man-bun? Why such hatred for Mr Yuen? Why so insistent he committed the murder because he wanted to be a photographer? It would be far more convincing if his biological parents were both under Yuen Man-bun's thumb, and his mother died in great sadness, creating a grudge against his so-called father.'

'That's rather overblown, don't you think? Like some crappy eight o'clock soap.'

'Isn't real life just as ridiculous? I actually have a fair bit of evidence to back me up. Firstly, your attitude towards the two Yue sons – you're respectful to the elder one, calling him "Master Wing-yee", but with Wing-lim you just use his name. You don't even hold back from scolding him in front of outsiders, and Wing-lim, who talks back to his older brother, sits there quietly and takes it from you. Isn't that odd? You're just his father's personal secretary, why would he give you so much respect? You might be a long-serving member of the household, but I don't think that'd mean much to this young punk.'

'Logical, but still a bit thin,' sneered Old Tong. 'Just think about it – if I'd had a secret affair with Chin-yau, and deceived Yuen Man-bun into raising my son as his own, wouldn't that already be my revenge? Killing him would seem excessive.'

Lok was silent, apparently thinking about this.

'Inspector Lok, your fantasies are comical.' Old Tong suddenly stopped smiling. 'But if you're going to make wild guesses, so can I – even crazier ones. Of course, this is completely fabricated, with no proof at all. Even if you write it down, my lawyer will call it "pure supposition" and get it thrown out of court. Want to hear it?'

'Please.'

'First of all, if I were behind all this, I wouldn't be stupid enough to directly incite Wing-lim to commit murder. If you want to use a person like that, you create the right conditions – plant seeds of hatred, allow the desire for revenge to fester slowly. At a certain point, this tips over into murder. Anyone could become a killer, given the right circumstances. This is all hypothetical, of course.'

'Fine, noted. Please continue.'

'The nature of that hatred isn't even particularly important. If I were nurturing Yue Wing-lim's loathing, I'd certainly make use of a more plausible reason to indoctrinate, heh, my own son – you insist he's my child, so let's go with that, but it's not a sufficient reason to commit murder. What could make Wing-lim so full of fury that he'd actually take a life?'

Old Tong's eyes were fixed on a horizon only he could see.

'For example, if someone he loved got badly hurt. You know what I mean, Inspector? Hatred and love are two sides of the same coin. Want to make Peter truly loathe Paul? Tell Peter that Paul hurt someone Peter loved deeply.'

'Loved deeply?'

'Such as his mother.'

'Hurt in what way?'

'Such as... Yue Wing-lai being Yuen Man-bun's biological son.'

'Biological? But...'

'What if Yue Chin-yau's rapist was none other than Yuen Man-bun?'

The air in the car seemed to solidify.

'Supposing, just supposing...' Old Tong's manacled hands plucked at his sparse white hair. 'If Yuen Man-bun had been jealous of his young colleague growing closer to Old-boss's daughter, realizing his chance of becoming the chosen son-in-law was slipping away, he might hatch a diabolical plot – making use of company funds to bribe some ruffians to spend time with Chin-yau, and then, at one of their parties, knock her out with drugs and alcohol, leaving Yuen Man-bun free to have his way with her. He'd have known the timid Chin-yau wouldn't dare tell her parents, and as long as innocent Nanny Wu played her part, the whole thing would be hushed up. The best-case scenario would be Chin-yau getting pregnant, leaving Yue Fung the unpalatable choice of marrying off his daughter or facing unspeakable scandal. Or she might have an abortion, but even then this inglorious episode would leave her vulnerable to Man-bun stealing her from me under the guise of compassion. Or at worst, if she didn't get pregnant and went on to marry me or someone else, he wouldn't have lost anything, and would at least have got to satisfy his animal lust.'

Inspector Lok let out an icy breath. 'This... this is all plausible, but it contains things you couldn't possibly know.'

'On the contrary. Let's say because of work, I had occasion to speak with Triad members, and learned about underground gossip from a decade before.' Old Tong smiled mirthlessly. 'The "Fung Hoi Shark" used all kinds of tactics, sometimes turning one faction of the underground against another. As his secretary, I'd naturally meet these people, and who'd have thought this world was so small – some little nobody helps Yuen Man-bun rape Yue Chin-yau, and ten years later there he is, a Triad big shot. Drinking with me one day, thinking I was friends with Man-bun, he let slip some things he shouldn't have.'

'So you incited your son to kill Yuen Man-bun in revenge for having stolen your authority and position?'

'Inspector Lok – again, speaking hypothetically – it hardly matters whether I wanted revenge because I'd lost my position, or because Yuen Man-bun's underhanded tactics hurt someone I cared about. Maybe it was just anger at being betrayed by someone I treated like a brother. Maybe I played a long game, and eventually gave as good as I got?'

It was just for an instant, but the inspector noticed something flash across Old Tong's eyes. Something like hatred, but mixed with anguish.

'But this revenge came so late, forty years after the event...' Lok said.

'Ah, in this scenario, vengeance began a long time ago. Why kill, when it's so much more fun to make your victim suffer a living hell?'

Inspector Lok stared at Old Tong. He knew very well this 'supposition' was really a confession, but the fact Old Tong was willing to say all this meant only one thing: he was certain the inspector would be unable to find hard evidence.

'For instance?'

'For instance, letting the bastard die.'

'Wasn't that a car accident?'

'Car accidents can be man-made. A little damage to the steering column, or pedals, or brakes. For a young speed demon, that'd inevitably be fatal. Of course, the remains of the car were destroyed long ago, so you'll have to treat it as an accident – this is just "supposition".'

'Weren't you afraid of hurting Yue Chin-yau?'

'That wouldn't happen. She might believe Yuen Man-bun to be a good husband who'd never treat her badly, but Wing-lai was the product of rape. She'd be sad if Man-bun were to die, but as for Wing-lai, only Man-bun knew the truth about his parentage and would feel sorrow. And because he couldn't tell anyone the truth, he would have to hide his grief in front of the household – no more than he deserved.'

'Why wait till Yue Wing-lai was almost twenty before you struck? I thought you'd learned the truth from the Triad guy a decade after the event.'

'I'm not the sort of idiot who trusts whatever some two-bit gangster tells me. I only believe my own eyes. Heaven was good to me, and in 1990, I received a gift.'

'What gift would that be?'

'The DNA Testing Centre at Wo Yan Hospital.'

Lok remembered that Wo Yan was indeed the first medical centre in Hong Kong to have brought in DNA-testing RFLP technology. As well as uncovering hereditary conditions, it could also be used to confirm blood relationships.

'As the private secretary of the consortium's director, it was child's play to arrange for the entire family to undergo a complete physical examination. Just a drop of blood would do – it wasn't hard to use the boss-man's name to secretly run a couple of tests.'

The inspector grew certain that he was facing a formidable opponent – one who must have been every inch a match for Yuen Man-bun.

'Why didn't you seek revenge against the second son, Wing-yee?'

'Who says I didn't?'

Inspector Lok stared in surprise at the other man.

'Who do you think gave him the idea that he'd killed his older brother?' said Old Tong. His tone was deadpan, but Inspector Lok could tell he was suppressing a smile.

The inspector could see the whole thing now. Wing-yee had said it was Old Tong who gave him the joke can. Probably he also encouraged the boy to place it in his brother's car, and after the accident, would have murmured, 'Young master, don't worry, I won't tell anyone what you did,' affecting the child's judgement. For someone as cunning as this, it would be simplicity itself to manipulate a nine-year-old kid.

'So Yue Wing-lim...'

'I've never told him I'm his biological father, just quietly taken care of him. Even without knowing the truth, under my influence, he came to share my thoughts, my hatred for Yuen Man-bun. After Chin-yau died, he happened to come across a couple of DNA reports – now, who could have left those lying around for him to see? – and I "had no choice" but to tell him how Yuen Man-bun had assaulted and deceived his mother back in the day.'

DNA reports, Inspector Lok guessed, showing that Yuen Man-bun was related to Yue Wing-Lai, and that Old Tong himself was Wing-Lim's father.

Inspector Lok mumbled to himself. 'Already on edge from the hundredth day anniversary of his mother's death, Wing-Lim confronted Yuen Man-Bun, asking if he'd raped his mother, and in his agitation attacked him with the vase, then wrestled over whether to get rid of this hated man. With the second blow, he made up his mind to commit murder. Then the sequence of events we imagined yesterday. To get vengeance for his mother, he'd kill someone like this. Did Yue Wing-Lim never talk about his own identity? Right, he wouldn't want to mention his mother's affair, because he respected her too much to trash her reputation even when confronting his enemy. And so Yuen Man-bun would rather die than reveal what had happened. He thought his son was just taking revenge for his mother. Before dying he even looked at the photo album – he must have regretted what he'd done to Chin-yau...'

'Wrong!' yelled Old Tong. 'That man regretted nothing! He only missed the bastard who toppled off the cliff, and in his last moments wanted to relive his glory days. That scum still had the fake accounts he used forty years ago to steal company money to bribe those gangsters with. I'm sure it wasn't to cover his tracks, but as a trophy! The first souvenir of his road to success!'

'Anyway, Yue Wing-lim carried out this murder solo, without

any urging from you.'

'Hypothetically, yes.'

'You're sending your own son to prison. Can you live with that?'

'What son do I have?'

'But isn't Wing-lim...'

'I said "supposing"! I don't have a son!' Old Tong smiled craftily. 'The police are free to test my and Wing-lim's DNA – you won't find any blood tie between us. Just think. Wouldn't the most perfect revenge be to have your enemy killed by his own son?'

Inspector Lok was tongue-tied.

Old Tong continued calmly, 'The first step would be to kill the eldest son just as the youngest was born. Their father would believe rumours that the child was unlucky and would bring harm to the family, so they would become estranged. That's when the plotter would make sure to grow closer to the youngest child, allowing him to feel a father's love from another source. Add in a fake DNA report, and twenty years later this scenario would spell success. As the plotter wouldn't actually be related to the youngest son, even if the boy were to say something, he'd be unable to prove it. But I think this child will keep his promise, and not say a word against his "natural father". He'd rather make some excuse like his father forcing him into business, to take the guilt upon himself.'

So that's why Old Tong was so forthcoming – Inspector Lok now saw where this confidence had come from. He was right; the string of suppositions wasn't sufficient to prove his guilt. The physical evidence had vanished, and all that was left was testimony, which alone would never convict him. As long as Old Tong refused to admit his guilt, Yue Wing-lim's words would be taken at face value.

Old Tong's speech was the final scene in his drama of revenge – and Inspector Lok was the audience.

Inspector Lok felt a chill through his heart. If he wasn't able to stop this brilliant, evil man today, how many more people would be hurt? Perhaps Yuen Man-bun had got what was coming to him, but his three children were innocent. And even if Lok could persuade prosecutors to drop the murder charge, Wing-lim was very likely to be found guilty of manslaughter. Then there was the unjustified guilt Wing-yee had shouldered for twenty years, let alone Wing-lai's accidental death – all their lives had been snatched away by this monster.

The car turned to enter the main gates of Police Headquarters.

'Inspector Lok, I've enjoyed our little chat, but I believe you're only allowed to detain me for forty-eight hours, and you certainly won't find any evidence within that time. Yuen Man-bun's death has nothing to do with me.'

'I don't need forty-eight hours. I imagine you'll be arraigned and formally charged by tomorrow.'

'Oh, and how would that happen? Everything I said was a supposition, just a joke. You won't be able to find anything connecting me to the Yuen Man-bun case.'

'Who said anything about Yuen Man-bun? I'm arresting you under suspicion of the murder of retired Superintendent Kwan Chun-dok last night.'

Old Tong gaped at him.

'How... you... you have no proof.' His response wasn't 'Superintendent Kwan is dead?' nor a rebuttal of the charge, but this stiff little statement of self-defence.

'I do.' Inspector Lok pulled out his smartphone and tapped on the screen. Old Tong took one look and almost fainted – it was the hospital room, and a man sneaking in to switch the IV bag.

The man in the video was Old Tong.

'That's not possible... yesterday... you'd put away the camera... I didn't notice...' He was panicking.

Inspector Lok didn't even look at him. 'I don't care about Yuen Man-bun's case. I have hard evidence now that you tried to kill Kwan Chun-dok. We found a large dose of morphine in the IV bag, as well as the gloves and phials you discarded. Today the pathologist will carry out an autopsy, which, together with this video clip, should be enough to put you away.'

'No, that's not possible... This was a patient in the late stages of liver cancer, no doctor could be sure of the cause of death... Ah!' Suddenly he started screaming, 'It was you! You laid a trap for me! This was all a plot.'

Ah Sing opened the car door and several officers caught hold of Old Tong. He didn't stop roaring as Lok ordered, 'Put him in a holding cell for now, I'll deal with him later.'

The inspector stayed in the back seat of the car, watching as Ah Sing led the struggling man away. He didn't move for a long time.

'Sifu, did I do well?' he murmured.

A week earlier, while examining the speargun, he'd already noticed the discrepancy – a 115 cm gun couldn't possibly shoot a 115 cm harpoon. The investigators quickly found the real weapon, which yielded the killer's DNA. Normal procedure would have been simply to request a DNA sample from everyone in the Yue household in order to determine who was guilty, but he'd felt something was wrong.

The scene of the crime was just too bizarre. The two injuries to the back of the head, the incompetent murder method, the victim choosing to look at a photo album instead of seeking help... it didn't add up.

And so, he did what his mentor would have done, and adopted an unorthodox method.

First, he summoned the suspects to the station for questioning, but also so he could surreptitiously harvest their DNA by offering them drinks, then sending their cups to the lab.

DNA evidence showed the murderer was Yue Wing-lim.

Knowing the killer's identity deepened the mystery. No combination of means, method and motive made any sense, and the inspector grew certain there must have been some kind of plot behind this, or that someone had incited Wing-lim to kill.

When Old Tong stated so emphatically, 'Yue Wing-lim would never kill his own father,' that only strengthened his belief in his instincts. This old fellow was a first-rate chancer.

After accompanying Superintendent Kwan for so many years, Inspector Lok had encountered quite a few worthy opponents, and learned to detect that whiff of the extraordinary from their every move and gesture. Old Tong gave him that sensation, and even without evidence, the inspector knew this old man was at the centre of the case.

The problem was, given the bureaucratic system they worked under, his superiors weren't going to accept his instincts as proof. Yuen Man-bun was an important figure in the business world, and the case would devolve into a tangle of government, police, financial and societal interests.

'I'm guessing it's when you can't solve the case that you need to make this kind of fuss, to show your superiors you're trying?' Yue Wing-lim's sarcastic words had touched on the truth. Inspector Lok had indeed received orders from his boss to crack the case as quickly as possible, to shut the public up and remove the impression that the police were incompetent.

Lok's worry had been that the younger man would take on all the guilt, and his superiors would close the case without seeing any need to investigate further. 'Don't cause trouble for yourself' was the ethos of today's civil servants and police higher-ups, only interested in generating reports and keeping their positions. The truth didn't interest them. Yet to Inspector Lok, bringing the real killer to justice was the only mission of the police. He couldn't accept anyone committing a crime and walking free – his true loyalty was to the people of Hong Kong.

In this difficult position, he thought of his mentor.

'Sonny... just let me die...' This had been Kwan Chun-dok's plea the umpteenth time he regained consciousness, several days before the Yuen Man-bun case.

'Sifu, don't talk nonsense... The best detective of his generation shouldn't just give in to death like that,' said Sonny Lok, clutching the superintendent's hand.

'This... this isn't giving in...' Kwan Chun-dok fought for breath, spitting each word out. 'I just don't want to linger on... What's the point of prolonging my existence with machines and medicine... My brain is all confused... I hurt all over... I think... I've finished my life's work... it's time to go...'

'Sifu...'

'But... but Sonny... life is precious... don't waste it... Sonny... I give you my life... make good use of it...'

'Sifu, what on earth do you mean?'

'I'm giving you the rest of my life... do what I would do... look beyond the rules... don't let me die in vain...'

With a chill, Sonny Lok understood what his mentor meant. He wasn't one of those cops who followed every rule and regulation, but still the superintendent's parting instructions left him with no alternative.

'Sonny...'

'I understand,' said Lok, after a long time. He squeezed out a smile. 'Still "Uncle Dok", after all.'

'Ha... I'll see my wife again soon... she must be waiting impatiently... Sonny... take care of yourself... don't forget what the police are here for...'

And for just a second, Sonny Lok glimpsed past glories in his mentor's failing eyes.

The following day, Kwan's blood ammonia levels spiked, leaving him in a coma. Doctors told Lok that his organs had deteriorated so much, he might never wake again. The cancer cells had spread too far.

Just as the inspector was wondering how to put his mentor's parting words into action, the Yue case came up. The more he looked into it, the clearer it became that conventional methods wouldn't reveal the truth. He was at the poker table with no chips and a weak hand.

It seemed like fate – Kwan Chun-dok would be his trump card.

Caught on the back foot, Inspector Lok went on the offensive and set a trap – with his mentor as bait. Kwan would have wanted it this way.

And sure enough, the old detective's life wasn't wasted.

The apparatus to measure brain waves actually did work, as Old Tong demonstrated, so the suspects were convinced it was the unconscious detective solving this case. But as Choi Ting said, no one would be able to control their thoughts with such accuracy. Kwan Chun-dok's supposed responses were, in fact, all engineered by the inspector. Apple owed the superintendent a favour, so Lok asked her to build the machine and connect it to two pedals. If Lok pushed down with his left foot, the pointer would move to YES, while his right foot produced a NO. With the hospital bed in the way, only Apple and Ah Sing could see the movement of his legs.

At the last moment, the inspector asked Apple to add a pop-up error message, meaning she had to change the program on the spot – fortunately, she managed this in time, and everything went as planned. She hadn't expected Lok to be such a good actor, answering his own questions convincingly, completely fooling the suspects into believing Superintendent Kwan truly was a genius who could solve crimes while unconscious. As the inspector suspected Old Tong was most likely to be manipulating Yue Wing-lim behind the scenes, he made sure the old man was the one who tried on the band, so he'd be firmly convinced the superintendent was calling the shots.

Inspector Lok had already gathered enough evidence from the scene of the crime to have more or less deduced the sequence of events. He had to pretend ignorance, making use of his mentor to point out inconsistencies, so the true murderer would believe the patient in the hospital bed had a complete grasp of the situation. Superintendent Kwan had taught him that misleading your opponent is an effective tactic, the way mediums make use of psychology to cheat people, creating the impression that they can commune with spirits through the use of ambiguous words.

Lok knew next to nothing about Yue Chin-yau and Yue Wing-lai's past, but had sensed a reserve towards the late eldest son while carrying out his investigations, and also noticed Wing-lai's date of birth was a little too close to his parents' marriage. Added to the recent death of Chin-yau, who seemed to have been the nucleus of this family, it seemed likely there were some secrets here. And so he teased his audience by drawing back each time he seemed about to reveal the murderer, dazzling them, leading the conversation back to those two earlier deaths, inducing them to reveal facts no outsider knew, falsely claiming his mentor deduced the truth from their words alone. The inspector also knew very well that the identification of Wing-lai's real father could be no more than conjecture, but in this charged atmosphere, no one would be able to look at the matter objectively and ask questions.

Because of 'Kwan Chun-dok's' preternatural performance, Old Tong began to worry there might be a flaw in the plan he'd been working on for so many years. That error message was the final bit of bait: what had the genius detective been about to say? Was he about to point out a flaw in the story that he, Tong, hadn't noticed?

These worries niggled away at Old Tong, growing larger in his mind. Inspector Lok was sure to let everyone know he and Apple planned to visit the ward again the following morning. Under such pressure, even the most cunning criminal might make the wrong choice.

And sure enough, Old Tong tried to cover his tracks, but instead ended up tying the noose around his own neck.

When Yue Chin-yau was dying of pancreatic cancer, the man who'd secretly loved her all along, Old Tong, visited her daily together with her youngest son. As a result, he knew the workings of the hospital very well, including where medicines were kept, when visiting hours ended, how to inject someone with morphine... He also learned the effects of morphine on the human body, and so thought of this method to kill Kwan Chun-dok.

An overdose of morphine constricts the respiratory system, causing the victim to suffocate – also the way many cancer patients die, meaning the hospital wouldn't find his passing suspicious. Essentially, this murder would have been foolproof – if someone hadn't been lying in wait.

Old Tong hadn't missed anything; the cameras had indeed been cleared away. What he didn't know was that the two computers left behind by Apple had been fitted with night-vision video lenses, so everything that happened would be captured and sent over the internet to her and Inspector Lok. They'd spent the night staking out the hospital from a nearby parking lot, keeping an eye on the room. The moment Old Tong struck, Inspector Lok felt a great jolt of sorrow, but also relief that his mentor wouldn't have to suffer any longer.

The brain-wave apparatus had worked as advertised, and the Yue family would testify that the unconscious superintendent had 'assisted in solving the case'. All Inspector Lok needed to do was stand up in court and insist Apple had merely forgotten to turn off the recording function on her computers, and Old Tong would be left with nothing to say. They'd have both physical evidence and damning testimonies. As for whether or not Old Tong admitted his part in Yuen Man-bun's death, the inspector no longer cared. 'We'll leave the prosecution to deal with those details.'

A couple of taps on his car window. The inspector looked up to see Ah Sing.

'Sir, my condolences,' he said, opening the car door and sticking his head in.

'Ah Sing, if someday I get ill and fall into a coma...'

Ah Sing looked Inspector Lok directly in the eye and nodded firmly.

The inspector smiled bitterly. He knew these methods lay in a grey area, and even though he wouldn't be caught, they weren't that different from Old Tong's 'foolproof' crimes. Without question, they went against many principles, but Inspector

Lok remembered well something his mentor had once said: 'You have to remember, the real duty of the police is to protect the residents of this city. If the rules cause an innocent citizen to get hurt, or stand in the way of justice, then we have more than sufficient reason to push aside these inflexible statutes.'

When an officer joins the force, they go through an oath-taking ceremony. The words had altered because of the change in the country's sovereignty and restructuring of the force, but concluded in more or less the same way: 'I will obey without question all lawful orders of those set in authority over me.' Kwan Chun-dok's aims clearly challenged this sacred vow, but Inspector Lok understood the difficulty his mentor was in.

In order to allow other people the luxury of certainty, Kwan Chun-dok had spent his life on the border between black and white. Inspector Lok knew that even if the police force were to descend into corruption or bureaucracy, in thrall to the rich and powerful, placing politics over people, his mentor would continue to keep the faith, to do everything in his power to bring about justice as he knew it. The job of the police is to reveal the truth, to arrest the guilty, to protect the innocent – but when the rules are unable to bring criminals to heel, when truth is obscured, when the innocent have nowhere to turn, Superintendent Kwan was willing to leap into that swamp of grey, using the methods of the unlawful against them.

Allowing justice to shine in the space between black and white – this was the mission Sonny Lok inherited from Kwan Chun-dok.

II

THE PRISONER'S DILEMMA:

2003

1

'Sifu, I don't think I can do this any more...'

'Don't worry, Sonny. The Crime Unit was only playing a supporting role in this op, you won't have to be the fall guy.'

'This was my first time in charge. You know how awful my record is – it wasn't easy to get a chance at squad leader, and I've fallen flat on my face.'

'This really is nothing. If you couldn't deal with a little setback like this you'd really be unfit to take command.'

'But...'

On the bleachers of Macpherson Playground, Sonny Lok guzzled his beer, unburdening himself to his mentor Kwan Chun-dok. It was after ten at night, and Macpherson was one of the few quiet spots in the crowded district of Mong Kok. Floodlights shone down on the empty field, while three or four stray cats prowled across the seats. In such cold weather, most people would rather stay indoors than subject themselves to the biting winds. If it were summer, this place would be full of small groups of noisy youngsters, courting couples, and homeless people snoozing on the long benches.

Kwan Chun-dok and Sonny Lok often enjoyed an icy beer in the cold winter months, meeting in the vastness of the soccer stands. Here, they could speak freely about sensitive work matters without fear of being overheard, and as Kwan was fond of pointing out, bars were a rip-off. 'For the price of a pub beer, you could get three cans at the supermarket, so why throw money away? If you want bar snacks, a packet of nuts doesn't cost that much.' This was his standard response, each time Lok suggested going out for a drink.

That night, Lok had sought out his mentor to bend his ear about some bad luck he'd had. 2002 had actually been a good year for him, both in terms of career and family, with his wife becoming pregnant after two years of marriage – he'd be a father soon. Around the same time, he was promoted from probationary to full inspector, and put in charge of the Yau-Tsim District (Yau Ma Tei and Tsim Sha Tsui) Crime Unit Team 2 in West Kowloon.

Sonny Lok had graduated from the Police Academy aged seventeen, and was now twice that age. He was fairly bright and enthusiastic, but his luck wasn't good – and his misfortunes, coupled with his introverted personality, meant his personal file was filled with criticism. In the Hong Kong Police Force, promotion is earned not just by passing a test but, more importantly, by having a clean record. Hence Lok was overjoyed to receive his probationary inspectorship in 1999, never expecting that a mere three years later he'd be the head of a team within a Crime Unit.

But he also didn't predict that his first outing on the frontline would end in such a sound defeat – a disastrous beginning to 2003.

In the early hours of Sunday 5 January, the police launched Operation Viper, a large-scale drug bust that simultaneously raided a dozen karaoke joints, nightclubs and bars in the Yau Ma Tei and Tsim Sha Tsui districts. Kowloon West Region Crime Wing led the op, which involved more than two hundred officers from the Regional Anti-Triad Unit, the Regional Special Duties Squad and Crime Units from the various districts – including Lok's. Such wide-ranging operations usually produced results, curbing Triad and drug-dealer activity for a few months. Operation Viper, however, was a resounding failure.

The entire operation netted less than a hundred grams of ket-amine, a few dozen grams of amphetamines and a tiny amount of cannabis. Fifteen people were arrested, though only nine were charged in the end. In the language of the marketplace, the ret-urn on the investment was abysmally low.

As with any other failed venture, people lined up afterwards to assign blame. Because they hadn't returned empty-handed, the press didn't give the police too hard a time, but the frosty atmo-sphere during the internal inquiry left Lok thoroughly on edge.

'I believe the reason we only seized a small quantity of drugs was mistaken information from the Intelligence Unit.' Inspector Au-yeung, Commander of the Regional Special Duties Squad, fired the first shot.

'I'm pretty sure there was nothing wrong with the intelligence. For all we know, it may have been a leak from within the RSDS that tipped off the dealers,' drawled Inspector Ma, head of the Kowloon West Intelligence Unit.

'Are you implying there's a snitch on my team?' Au-yeung glared furiously.

'Au-yeung, Ah Ma, let's not lose our tempers,' said Benedict Lau, Commander of the Kowloon West HQ and chair of the inquiry. 'Blaming one another won't help matters. First, let's see if there were any issues with deployment.'

Superintendent Lau ran the Kowloon West Crime Wing, and was the highest-ranking officer present. Sonny Lok breathed a sigh of relief at the thawing atmosphere, not realizing what was to come next.

'Let's start with the Lion Pub on Prat Avenue, Tsim Sha Tsui East,' continued Superintendent Lau. 'According to Intelligence, the Hung-yi Union pusher "Fat Dragon" works that patch. Our sentry saw him enter the building, but when we moved in he was nowhere to be found. Yau-Tsim Crime Unit Team 2 was in charge of that pub. Inspector Lok, you were the commanding officer. Would you care to explain?'

All eyes in the room swivelled to stare directly at Sonny Lok.

Stammering, he reported on his placement of officers, said he believed Fat Dragon might have fled from the roof, and described the layout of the place. He wanted very much to explain that although he'd posted officers at every exit to the bar, if the dealer had been given a tip-off before the operation commenced, that was out of their control – but this would point the finger at Intelligence, and Inspector Ma outranked him.

Of course, if he didn't point the finger at anyone, their fingers would all point at him: 'Why wasn't anyone posted on the roof?' 'If the suspect escaped over the rooftops, wouldn't posting sentries at the exits of neighbouring buildings have prevented that?' 'Could it be that Fat Dragon simply walked out the front door, and your officers somehow missed him?'

What they were looking for, thought Sonny Lok, was a scapegoat.

'Sifu, my deployment was impeccable. I'm certain I didn't miss anything. Fat Dragon didn't linger in the bar like normal – that's not something I could control, is it?' On the bleachers, Lok took a swig of beer and allowed the alcohol to prod him into grumbling.

'It doesn't matter. It's not like Fat Dragon was the only one who escaped that day; the whole operation only netted a few small fry. Benny isn't going to blame you especially.' Kwan Chun-dok gulped some beer. Lau was younger than Kwan, and had been his subordinate in the past. The two had worked together at Criminal Intelligence Bureau in Headquarters, Lau in charge of Division A – suspect surveillance and handling informants – and Kwan running Division B, which analysed intelligence reports.

'But...'

'No buts.' Kwan stroked his stubbly grey chin, smiling. 'Fat Dragon wasn't even the main target – the man they really want is that "Giant Deep Sea Grouper".'

Lok knew who his mentor was referring to. Fat Dragon was a middle-ranking member of the Hong Kong Triad Hung-yi Union, while the big fish above him was the brains of Hung-yi's activities in Yau Ma Tei and Tsim Sha Tsui – Chor Hon-keung, aged forty-nine. The police suspected him of being involved in many illegal activities, but had so far been unable to nab him.

Unlike other underground figures who stayed out of the lime-light, Boss Chor was a well-connected entrepreneur. In the early 1980s, he had taken advantage of the booming Hong Kong economy to buy up bars and nightclubs, finding these legiti-mate businesses excellent for money-laundering. Each nightspot he opened was classier than the last, attracting a clientele of pop stars and record producers. Gradually, he realized that the entertainment world was a short cut to the social status he craved. Around 1991, he founded the Starry Night Entertain-ment Company and set himself up as an agent, with dozens of singers and models on his books. In recent years, he'd dipped his fingers into the movies, collaborating with film studios on the mainland.

'We're not going to get Boss Chor as easily as that,' sighed Lok. 'His underlings are so loyal I don't think they'd give us any-thing on him, not even if we tortured them.'

Chor ruled his inner circle with a combination of favours and threats that ensured utter compliance. His subordinates knew that if they betrayed their boss, they could run to the ends of the earth and he'd still hunt them down and kill them. But if they obligingly took the rap for him, they'd be set for life. Even while they were inside, their families would be well taken care of. For this reason, the Anti-Triad and Special Duties Squads had long regarded prosecuting Boss Chor as an impossible task, and focused instead on attacking his underground businesses as much as possible.

In Yau-Tsim, Hung-yi was the biggest Triad presence, with Chor's clubs and bars comprising eighty per cent of the drug market. The remainder was in the grasp of another Triad, Hing-chung-wo, a Hung-yi splinter group. Five years previously, Hung-yi had controlled Kowloon, but when the boss of the Yau-Tsim area died in an accident, the top cadres ran into intractable disputes trying to carve up the territory amongst themselves. The successor ought to have been the deceased's right-hand man, Yam Tak-ngok, known as Uncle Ngok. Unexpectedly, Chor Hon-keung staged a coup, secretly gathering support from the heads of various districts until he'd snatched the job for himself. Uncle Ngok still cherished the older generation's idea of honour amongst thieves, and if Chor had openly challenged him for the leadership, he'd have relinquished power and remained in the Triad as his number two. Instead, Chor's low-down tactics led him to leave. He decided to set up a new organization, taking dissenters with him, with the reasoning that this would prevent a bloody internal battle.

Unfortunately, showing kindness to jackals and wolves inevitably means inviting cruelty upon yourself. To begin with, Boss Chor appeared to treat this new rival with respect, proclaiming grandiosely to his gangland friends, 'Hing-chung-wo sprang from Hung-yi, so we are part of the same family, and if we allow Uncle Ngok some of this territory, the benefits to both of us are clear.' Yet he soon began using schemes and tricks to swallow up Hing-chung-wo's strongholds one by one, and five years on had turned a fifty–fifty split into eighty–twenty.

The Anti-Triad Squad believed that Hing-chung-wo's continuing decline must eventually goad Uncle Ngok into action. They knew an old-school gent like him wouldn't use the police against his enemies, but they expected him to leverage his underworld connections. He might not be as powerful as Boss Chor, who had the funds to hire more thugs, but his long history in organized crime had given him a certain amount of influence, and if he were to ask the other gangland bosses for help, Chor Hon-keung would have something to worry about.

But the police were wrong – they'd forgotten what the years can do to a person.

Yam Tak-ngok had steadily grown weary of the underworld. He was an old man now, and his fighting spirit had waned. Hing-chung-wo was haemorrhaging members, who were either switching their allegiance to Hung-yi or washing their hands of the business altogether, and Uncle Ngok silently condoned their departure. At this point, his support base consisted of a few loyal subordinates who'd stood by him all these years, as well as some who were unable to stomach Boss Chor's arrogant ways.

While Yau-Tsim was still run by the previous Hung-yi boss, the police had been able to maintain some degree of control over the territory, but once Boss Chor arrived on the scene, they had a big headache. Chor would appear at film premieres, soirées, charity banquets and the like, always with a big smile on his face, the model of respectability. There was gossip in artistic circles, for instance when an up-and-coming director got beaten up in a nightclub by unknown assailants after he had made fun of a fashion model represented by Chor. Eventually, he had to settle the matter by ceremonially offering Chor tea as an apology. As for the attackers, when they were arrested they insisted they had no idea who Chor Hon-keung was, and took all the blame themselves. Other rumours told of actresses being kidnapped, radio broadcasters being threatened – and not one of these cases could be directly linked to Chor. When a magazine suggested Chor was behind these unhappy events, he sued them for defamation, and the magazine's publishers finally had to print an apology and pay him a huge sum in compensation.

What's more, all of this was just the tip of an iceberg. The Chor known to the police and Triads was ten times more vicious than the general public was aware. When he first took over, the police began to notice that informants were dying in car accidents, or simply vanishing. Quite a few of these people were addicts who'd turned to the police to fund their ketamine, cocaine, heroin or crystal meth habits; now, many of them abruptly succumbed to 'overdoses'. The Intelligence Unit knew this was fishy, but without hard evidence, there was no way to even begin an investigation.

In other words, Boss Chor was a thorn in the side of the police, and they could only treat the symptoms but not the cause.

What Sonny Lok hadn't expected was that in Operation Viper,

even these symptoms would go untreated.

'Sifu, surely a scumbag like Boss Chor, pretending to be a proper businessman, will slip up one day and be brought to trial, won't he?' Lok drained his beer.

'From what I've seen, a shrewd operator like him will be hard to catch hold of,' said Kwan calmly. 'He's not going to leave traces of his guilt, and even if he did, no one's going to take the risk of giving evidence against the notorious Boss Chor.'

'But why can't we just bring him in for questioning? Even if we don't get anything on him, we might give him a fright.'

'If you already know you won't get anywhere, what's the point? Annoying a chap like that without proof, you'll just end up being scrutinized by the Independent Police Complaints Council, and there'll be more ugly marks on your record. Why gamble when you know there's no winning card?'

'If even you talk like this, then I guess we really have no way of dealing with him. Operation Viper showed our hand; Boss Chor may have known we had our eye on him, but now he's seen all our cards. I don't know where we go from here.'

Lok hadn't realized what a hot potato this Yau-Tsim post was. The Special Duties Squad couldn't find any evidence of Boss Chor selling drugs, the Anti-Triad intelligence reports failed to implicate him, leaving the Crime Unit nothing to do but investigate those 'accidental deaths' due to drug overdoses and the performers getting attacked by unknown persons. Unless one of Chor's inner circle or a subordinate with an inside knowledge of Hung-yi was willing to testify, Boss Chor would continue to dominate the scene, becoming the emperor of the Yau-Tsim underworld.

'Don't worry. You've only just become a team commander, you'll have to adapt slowly. Don't let your subordinates sense your doubt.' Kwan patted his disciple on the shoulder. 'You have to be patient when you're angling for a big fish. If you can't get him on the hook right away, just still your heart and wait, and keep an eye on the surface of the water. You may only have an instant, when the opportunity arrives...'

'Any opportunity would be welcome.' Lok smiled grimly. 'But sir, enough about me. How's work been treating you?'

'Not too bad. I'm just helping out at Headquarters: Organized Crime and Drugs.'

'Does HQ Narcotics include you in their investigations, Sifu? Do you have anything you can tell me?' Lok had West Kowloon and Yau-Tsim between him and Headquarters, and without his mentor giving him the inside scoop, he had no way of knowing what those at the top were up to. Even during his three years in Intelligence he had felt like he was just following orders, not seeing the larger picture at all.

'Sonny, you know the rules – unless I decide something will help your investigation, I won't tell you anything concerning other departments.' Kwan pulled off his black baseball cap – its edges worn, a little grey insignia sewn onto the right side of the brim – and ruffled his hair. 'You wouldn't want me to tell Benny Lau about your little rant, would you?'

Lok smiled bashfully. Lau was his boss's boss, and if he were to hear of anything untoward, there'd be consequences.

'We should get going.' Kwan Chun-dok stood, his left hand giving his lower back a couple of quick rubs. 'If I get home too late, my wife will give me a hard time – though she'll nag anyway when she sees I've been drinking. I'm not supposed to – bad for my joints. Sonny, don't think too much about it, your time will come.'

'Sure.' Lok nodded helplessly. A year ago, he'd started to notice his mentor was ageing. Greying hair aside, he'd never heard Kwan complaining about any physical ailments. Lok knew police officers retired earlier than regular folk, partly because of the stress of the job. Constantly facing life-and-death situations became torture for someone in their forties or fifties.

Kwan Chun-dok lived at Prince Edward Road West, a little over ten minutes' walk from the Macpherson Playground. Sonny was on Hong Kong Island; not having driven, he would have to take a minibus home.

'See you later.' Kwan pulled on his cap, grasped his stick and walked slowly in the direction of Argyle Street.

After parting from his mentor, Sonny Lok walked along Nathan Road, boarding the Shau Kei Wan bus near Shan Tung Street. There were only three other passengers. The driver was idly flipping through a magazine, waiting for all sixteen seats to be full before he set off. The speakers blared a local radio station, music interspersed with DJs chatting and joking.

Sonny Lok stared out the window.

Mong Kok was dazzling as always. The multicoloured neon lights, glittering shop windows, throngs of pedestrians – as if the city knew no night. This bustling scene was a microcosm of Hong Kong, a city that relied on finance and consumption for survival, though these pillars were not as sturdy as people supposed. In recent years, unemployment was up and growth was slowing, and the government's performance was slipping – almost ripping through the veneer of a flourishing economy. Mong Kok was like an engine that couldn't stop running, fuelled by cash day and night, and when the legal sources of this fuel ran dry, dirty money came in to fill the tank.

Once Boss Chor had complete control over Yau-Tsim, Lok reckoned he'd set his sights on Mong Kok. This district had grown turbulent in recent years, and Chor would probably have to use even stronger tactics to defeat all his rivals and seize the drug trade entirely for himself.

'Let's have a new tune! This is "Baby Baby Baby", the latest from Candy Ton. Her album is being released on the 30th.'

Sonny Lok felt a wave of disgust rising in him. Even though the song now coming through the speakers had a catchy beat and the singer's voice was sweet, it made him sick.

This girl, Candy Ton, belonged to Starry Night Entertainment. And her music was like a layer of sparkling white sugar concealing rotting flesh below, black and full of maggots.

2

THE WEEK AFTER Operation Viper, Sonny Lok handed his report to Superintendent Lau. Just as Kwan had predicted, there were no internal sanctions after the inquiry, and even though Lok couldn't furnish a satisfactory reason for his failure, his team didn't receive any blame. During this time, he was careful not to show even a trace of despair in front of his subordinates, frequently repeating, 'We just ran into a bit of bad luck, we'll do better next time.' As a result, his team began to place a little more trust in their young new commander.

The Crime Unit mainly investigated cases of murder, grievous bodily harm, kidnapping, sexual offences and armed robbery. Underworld activity was the remit of the Anti-Triad Unit, and narcotics of the Special Duty Squad. For the moment, Sonny Lok set aside the affair of Boss Chor and the Hung-yi Union, and buried himself in his other work. The Crime Unit had a whole heap of open cases, not to mention all the administrative work that would take lots of overtime to complete. Even though they could kick simple cases down to the Investigation Team, in this crowded city the Crime Unit's work was never done.

'Commander, have you heard the rumour?' said Lok's subordinate Ah Gut, putting down his newspaper. It was eight in the morning of 16 January, and Lok had just walked into the office.

'What rumour?' Lok set down his briefcase.

'Eric Yeung Man-hoi was attacked last night, in a nightclub on Granville Road.'

'Eric Yeung Man-hoi? Who's that?' Lok couldn't connect this name to a case.

'You know, that new movie star.'

Lok stared at Ah Gut, his expression protesting, 'I'm not a tabloid reporter, how would I know this stuff?'

'Commander, even if you don't know who he is, we might have to take this case.'

'Sure. Granville Road is within our beat, and the victim's a public figure, we ought to... Will those entertainment journalists start bothering us? Those idiots don't even know what to ask...'

'No, Commander, Eric Yeung hasn't filed a police report, and this is just a rumour. I don't even know if it actually happened.'

'Just a rumour? Actors get drunk and make trouble all the time. If no one called the police, our unit has no reason to get involved.'

'This wasn't a bar brawl. He walked into an ambush. That's a Triad tactic.'

Lok now understood what Ah Gut was getting at. 'Boss Chor?'

'Probably.' Ah Gut grimaced. 'A fortnight ago, at a New Year's Eve party at Jay's Disco on Canton Road, Eric Yeung met Candy Ton – the singer, seventeen years old, one of Boss Chor—'

'One of Boss Chor's Starry Night entertainers, I know.'

'Right, so Yeung probably had too much to drink, lunged at the girl, groped her and what not, and when she pushed him away, he started calling her a stinking whore, Boss Chor's plaything... Candy Ton left in a hurry after that. Then last week, *Eight-Day Week* ran an exclusive report with pictures, though with so many embellishments, who knows what really happened.' *Eight-Day Week* was a gossip rag that had skewed reporting down to a fine art.

'So you think Candy Ton complained during their pillow talk, and Chor Hon-keung sent some thugs to teach the young pup a lesson?' The word was that Boss Chor had had a fling with every actress and female model on his roster. If you wanted the boss to boost your career, you first had to offer him your body.

'That's my guess.'

'Why would Boss Chor wait two weeks to retaliate?'

'Yeung was in Shanghai shooting a movie. Only got back two days ago.'

'Oh, I see.' Lok sat down, his hands intertwined. 'How bad are his injuries?'

'I heard not too bad, just some bruises on his pretty face, a few punches to his torso.'

'He didn't go to the hospital?'

'No.'

'And he didn't call the police, so he probably knows who was behind it.'

'Seems likely.'

'Then there's nothing we can do.' Lok waved dismissively. 'He wasn't beaten to death, so we can't get involved. Even if public opinion forces us to do something, going by what's happened before, we'll just arrest some two-bit gangsters who'll say they came up with the whole idea, and Boss Chor keeps that innocent look plastered on his face, maybe even scares Eric Yeung into having a meal with him, so the papers have a picture of them being all buddy-buddy. Case closed.'

'This time it's different. There might be trouble ahead.' Ah Gut crinkled his brow.

'How's that?'

'There's no proof, and this only came out after the attack, but if it's true, this won't blow over as easily as before...' Ah Gut paused. 'Eric Yeung's biological father is named Yam.'

Sonny Lok stared at Ah Gut, stunned. 'As in Yam Tak-ngok? Uncle Ngok?'

Ah Gut nodded.

Lok leaned back in his chair, tapping his forehead. This did put a wrinkle in it. Given the existing Chor–Yam rivalry, now that one had attacked the other's son, there might well be some payback.

'Any movement over at Hing-chung-wo?'

'Not at the moment, though I've spoken to Intelligence, and they'll let us know if anything crops up.' Ah Gut scratched at his cheek. 'Prevention is better than cure. If we can get both sides to hold their fire, or if we can swoop in and arrest the lot at the first sign of violence, that'd be best.'

Lok nodded. Ah Gut was a veteran on the Yau-Tsim Crime Unit, and his work was excellent. Having such a subordinate gave Lok a little relief from the hot potato he'd just caught.

'Actually,' said Ah Gut thoughtfully, 'given Yam Tak-ngok's personality, it's unlikely he'll pick a fight directly with Boss Chor. He seems to be pulling back from the scene, and Hing-chung-wo has lost so many men that Hung-yi is sure to win anything they start.'

'But will he be able to stomach his own son being humiliated like that?'

'It's hard to say. Back when Boss Chor kicked Yam aside, the old guy just took it, for the sake of keeping the peace.' Ah Gut gestured at the photo of Uncle Ngok on Lok's noticeboard. 'This dude's an old-school gangster, not an upstart like Chor.'

'Even if he can swallow it, his gang might feel the need to take revenge on behalf of their boss.' Lok jerked his thumb at the photos below Yam's.

'Possible. Harder to prevent than street fighting. And what if...'

'What if someone does attack Boss Chor, and innocent people get dragged in?'

Ah Gut nodded. 'No matter who wins, as soon as there's public violence, we're in trouble. Boss Chor swans around as the head of an entertainment company. If he gets openly assaulted and we're not seen doing anything about it, people will say the police must be useless against the Triads.'

'I'll formally notify Intelligence. Open a file for this case, and tell Mary that you and she will be keeping tabs on Hung-yi and Hing-chung-wo, as well as verifying that rumour. Hopefully this time we'll get a jump on them.'

'Yes, Commander.' Ah Gut stood a little straighter to accept the order. As he turned to go, he suddenly thought of something else. 'Even if we don't manage to stop them, and some Hing-chung-wo lowlife strikes first, that might still be good. We can't deal with Boss Chor anyway; why not fight evil with evil? We get a freebie, and everyone's happy.'

'Ah Gut, I'd love to see Boss Chor get torn limb from limb, but if we went down that route, what kind of police officers would we be? Besides, if it came to a gunfight here in the city, I don't think I'd ever forgive myself if some child got caught in the crossfire.'

'Yes, Commander, you're right.' Ah Gut stood at attention again and raised his hand in a salute before departing.

There was a thick layer of mud at the bottom of the lake; best not to stir it, to keep the water as pristine as possible. Scoop away the muck very carefully, a little at a time. Too much and you'd foul the whole lake, destroying its ecology.

The following day, Intelligence confirmed that Eric Yeung had indeed been ambushed the day before, and that he had harassed Candy Ton two weeks previously. The most important fact – his parentage – was also verified.

Lok got the detailed report from Ah Gut. Eric Yeung was twenty-two years old. Brought up by his mother, a nightclub mama-san named Yeung, he seldom saw his father. Yam Tak-ngok had never used his underworld connections to give his son a leg up in showbiz – so few had known of their relationship. A year ago, Eric Yeung had got a lot of public attention for playing the hero's sidekick in a film, and hadn't stopped working since. With only four movies under his belt, he was already considered a rising star.

After the attack, neither Hung-yi nor Hing-chung-wo acted any differently. Informants reported only that Uncle Ngok had issued instructions that he would personally sort out the matter of his son and Boss Chor, and his gang should stay out of it – it would be disrespectful to him if they retaliated on their own. It was as Ah Gut said: Yam Tak-ngok was very patient, for a Triad leader.

Sonny Lok opened the next folder to read about Candy Ton. She'd joined Starry Night three years ago, and after a massive publicity campaign last year, her sweet voice and attractive looks had propelled her into the limelight. The case file didn't mention her relationship with Boss Chor, but in Lok's eyes, she was no different from any low-ranking member of the underworld. Petty thugs worked themselves to the bone for the organization, smuggling drugs, starting fights, pimping, all in order to climb up the ranks, with no idea of how they were being exploited. Candy Ton was offering her body and youth to Boss Chor in exchange for fame – but she was merely a money tree to him. She and the gangsters would end up in the same place by different paths.

Four days after the attack – 20 January – Intelligence had nothing new to report, while the gossip magazines murmured that Eric Yeung had been beaten up. Of course they didn't dare use Boss Chor's name, saying only that Yeung 'might' have offended 'someone' powerful, and that he only had himself to blame. Lok breathed a sigh of relief that they all failed to mention the likeliest source of conflict – Eric Yeung's parentage.

Even with neither Triad making a move, Lok couldn't relax. He decided to give his mentor a call.

'Hi, Sonny, I'm surprised you have the time to chat,' came Kwan Chun-dok's voice.

'A little.' Lok kept his voice light. 'I was calling to ask how you were, and to see if you had time next week for a meal.'

'I'm tied up with this Wan Chai prostitution ring. They're connected to a group that traffics young girls from the mainland. I won't have time next week... but aren't you occupied with the case of Yam Tak-ngok's son?'

Lok was momentarily stunned, not having expected his mentor to cut straight to the chase like that. Since the subject had come up, he decided to ask his questions directly.

'That's right. Sifu, have you heard anything new? Like who was responsible?'

'Almost certainly Boss Chor,' said Kwan simply.

'I'd guess so too. And now there might be open conflict between them. I don't want assassinations or gang brawls happening on my turf.'

'You don't need to worry about that. Yam Tak-ngok's not going to send his men to their deaths just because of his son, and if it came to the crunch, Hing-chung-wo would be outnumbered ten to one.'

'Sure he won't send anyone to confront Boss Chor?'

'He's in the same position as us: unless anyone could get rid of Chor's entire gang by the roots, how would any of us dare touch even a hair on his head?'

'Sifu, I've got a question. Could Boss Chor have known from the start that Eric Yeung was Uncle Ngok's bastard son?'

'Chor's never given two hoots about other people's families. Besides, why pick on a rival's son?'

'Reduce the other side's power? Attack their reputation?'

'Eric Yeung isn't part of Hing-chung-wo, so hurting him won't help Hung-yi. Besides, it was Yeung who started it by harassing Candy Ton. This is just business as usual – someone insults a Starry Night client, Boss Chor sends thugs to "teach them a lesson".'

Lok thought his mentor had a point, but still felt uneasy. 'Do you think we ought to leave things here?'

'Well, I won't lie to you, HQ Narcotics is investigating Yam Tak-ngok – they have lots of proof they can use directly against him—' An electronic beep cut in. 'Ah, call waiting. Let's stop there. Call me another time about dinner.'

'Sifu—' But before Lok could say any more, his mentor had hung up.

Kwan's last words made Lok nervous. Was this new drug investigation supposed to deal with Uncle Ngok? Was it taking advantage of Hing-chung-wo's state, weakened by Hung-yi and ripe for the picking? A quick strike might make the police look good. Yet if Hing-chung-wo were disbanded, wouldn't the main beneficiary still be Chor Hon-keung?

Lok shook his head and dismissed the thought. The Crime Unit wasn't Special Duties nor Anti-Triad. Whether or not Hing-chung-wo was annihilated, their job was to tackle crime, to prevent further disruption to the lives of ordinary people. As for getting rid of drugs and dealing with the swaggering Triad bosses, that was for their colleagues. They had to trust their fellow officers.

But on 22 January, six days after the attack on Eric Yeung, Sonny Lok's fears that this incident would have further repercussions came true.

3

'COMMANDER, WE'VE GOT a suspicious package.' Ah Gut rapped on Lok's open door.

'What's it say?' Lok looked up from the document he was studying.

'Um, I think it's best if you see it for yourself.'

In the main office, Lok's team were huddled around Ah Gut's desk, on which was a pile of letters. The top one was a manila envelope, about eight inches long, with 'Inspector Lok, Yau-Tsim Crime Unit' scrawled on it in marker pen.

'No postmark – it didn't come in the mail,' noted Ah Gut.

No one here would treat an unknown item lightly. The thinness and size of the envelope suggested it wasn't a bomb, but Lok was still extremely careful as he slit the tape, in case it held razor blades or anthrax. But no, there was nothing except a CD, in a cardboard sleeve.

On the card, in the same writing as the envelope, was a message seemingly scribbled in haste: 'I'm just a cowardly reporter, scared of getting into trouble.'

'An anonymous tip-off?' said Mary, squinting at the writing. Mary was the only woman on Lok's team; a staunch feminist, she more than held her own in the male-dominated environment.

'Looks like it.' Lok pulled out the disc and examined both sides. It was a standard writable CD, unmarked, its surface wiped clean of fingerprints.

'Ah Gut, you're better with computer stuff.' Lok handed the CD over.

'There's just one file.' Ah Gut pointed at the folder that appeared on his screen. The file was called 'movie.avi', created that day at 6.32 a.m.

'Open it,' said Lok.

Ah Gut started the player and dragged the file into it. The indicator showed the clip was three minutes twenty-eight seconds long.

A pitch-black screen, then after two seconds, a street. Nighttime. No one around, just boarded-up worksites and streetlamps. Not even a single car, and just one pedestrian, seen from the back.

'Looks like Jordan Road, near Ferry Street,' Mary said, indicating a corner of the screen. West of Jordan Road was the Kowloon West reclamation project – a massive public works undertaking to create almost a thousand acres of new waterfront property. Numerous construction works were in progress at the moment, and it was predicted that when complete, these would turn Kowloon West into a bustling district. In front of the reclamation project was Jordan Road Ferry Pier, once Kowloon's busiest transport hub.

'No sound, Ah Gut?' asked Lok.

'Image only.' Ah Gut clicked on 'About this document' to show it had no sound files.

The camera was following the walker, a woman in a voluminous jacket, shouldering an enormous bag. Long black hair flowed from underneath her woollen cap. She wasn't very tall, and walked slowly. Yellowish streetlight made it impossible to tell the colour of her clothes.

'What is this, amateur porn?' joked Cheung, a young officer.

Lok was about to snap at him when the woman on the screen

suddenly stopped and looked nervously to her left. She seemed startled by some sound.

Seeing her profile for the first time, Lok felt a rush of blood to his head. He suddenly realized what he was about to see.

'That's Candy Ton!' Ah Gut had recognized her too.

Now everything started happening very fast. Candy Ton began running, disappearing off the right side of the screen. The camera operator seemed agitated too, and the frame wobbled before moving to the left, where four men in masks, baseball caps and heavy-duty gloves were pursuing Candy, wielding metal pipes and cleavers. They sprinted across the screen from left to right. The camera paused a second, then jolted around as it tried to catch up with them.

Rounding a corner, the four men were closing on Candy. The shortest one was also the fastest, and got to her first, reaching out to grab her collar. Unexpectedly, she lashed out and caught her attacker right in the face with her fist. The short man slumped on the ground, clutching his nose. Candy got away, but now the other three were just a few metres behind her.

The camera showed that there was no one else around, and the sidewalk ahead led only towards a high footbridge. Candy rushed towards it. The camera was some distance away, but happened to be at just the right angle to capture her expression as she glanced back in terror. She clambered up the stairs, her face twisted in the fear and panic of someone facing death. She almost fell but managed to grab the handrail. Her shoulder bag had disappeared – she must have dropped it, but there was no time to think of that, because in those few seconds, the men had arrived at the stairs too.

All five people now disappeared behind the bridge railings, so Lok and his team could only watch agitatedly until the cameraperson got there too – but the image stopped at the stairs, instead of climbing them.

'Why's he stopping?' cried Mary.

'I think... he got distracted by something?' Ah Gut didn't take his eyes from the screen.

The camera now swerved to the side – and what came next terrified all of them.

Something lay on the sidewalk by the bridge. The watchers couldn't tell what it was at first. They didn't connect this thing to the idea of 'Candy Ton', because it was splayed at such an odd angle, arms clutching weirdly at the ground, one leg twisted up to the waist. The head, still in its woollen hat, hair straggling all over, was twisted to one side, and a dark liquid was oozing from it.

Most terrifyingly, that broken body spasmed a few times before finally growing still.

'Did... did she fall?' gasped Cheung.

'Maybe she was pushed?' Ah Gut spoke slowly, trying to hide his unease.

The bridge was about three storeys high, and to fall head first from it would mean almost certain death.

Now the camera turned upwards, and two figures came into view over the railings, one of them clutching a metal bat. The other one turned to look straight into the lens.

'That's done it,' muttered Ah Gut.

The image started shaking violently, jerking between sky, ground, streetlamp and bridge. The watcher was running for his life, not even stopping to turn off the camera. About half a minute later, the camera was inside a car – he'd made it.

And with that, the screen went dark. Three minutes and twenty-eight seconds.

'Candy Ton... killed?' Mary stammered.

'Ah Gut, notify the uniforms to seal off the overhead bridge at Jordan and Lin Cheung Road, and send a forensics team to the site. Mary, stay in the office – you'll be in charge of comms. Everyone else, come with me.' Lok had to suppress his rage to give these orders calmly. He hadn't felt so angry in a long time. Although he couldn't stand celebrities like Candy Ton, no defenceless person deserved to be murdered by four thugs like that.

It wasn't far to the scene, and they arrived a few minutes later.

In the car, Lok tried to clear his mind and focus on the investigation.

'The cameraman was probably some paparazzo,' said Lok. 'Following her in the hopes of digging up more dirt about Eric Yeung.'

'And he witnessed a murder instead, but didn't want to get involved, so just sent us the footage?' said Ah Gut.

'Probably.' Lok wrinkled his brow. 'No sound, so I'd guess print media. He'd have hoped a few freeze frames might be worth some cash.' Something along the lines of 'Eric Yeung beaten up while sultry Candy Ton smirks' or 'Candy Ton and Boss Chor's secret rendezvous' would do wonders for sales.

'Mary says no one in the mail room remembers when this came in,' reported Cheung, coming off the phone.

'It might be one of those journalists who're always outside the precinct trying to get a scoop,' said Ah Gut. 'They could have asked a crime reporter to drop it off, or maybe someone who'd recently transferred from crime to entertainment.'

'We can look into that later. IDing the cameraman isn't a priority,' said Lok.

'No one's phoned in a report – so did they move the body?'

'No idea. But if they've covered their tracks, that'll make things harder for us...'

The look on Candy Ton's face in the video had given Lok a bad feeling. Yam Tak-ngok had given orders for his men not to do anything, because he'd take care of this on his own – was he thinking: 'You've beaten up my son, so I'll take it out on your girl?' Attacking this singer would have meant Uncle Ngok could keep his dignity and settle the score without provoking a direct conflict with Boss Chor.

But murder was another matter.

Had the attack gone wrong? Maybe the intention had only been to scare her, but she'd panicked and leapt over the railing.

The team arrived at the deserted site. An assault vehicle and eight uniforms had arrived and were securing the area, even though there was no one around.

Lok glanced at his watch. The incident had taken place twelve hours ago at most. There might still be some evidence left.

He and Ah Gut walked to the spot where the corpse had lain. No obvious traces of blood, but if someone had swabbed the area with water, it would have dried in a few hours in the windy weather they'd been having. He ordered forensics to investigate, then started climbing – nothing out of the ordinary on stairs or bridge. The two men walked to the spot they guessed Candy Ton had fallen from, looking for blood or other marks on the railing.

'The criminals were wearing gloves, so probably no fingerprints,' said Ah Gut.

Lok knelt to examine the underside of the railing. 'Candy wasn't wearing gloves, and if we can find her prints, we'll know if she jumped or was pushed – the difference between murder and manslaughter.'

Leaving an evidence marker, Lok continued to the other end of the bridge. He couldn't think of any reason for her to jump, unless her pursuers had caught up with her, or if she'd been surrounded. The sidewalk ended at the bridge, so they'd have known she'd go up – and if they'd set others in wait at the other end, she'd have been trapped.

'Commander! They've found something!' shouted one of the forensics officers from below.

When Ah Gut and Lok got back down, the officer was pointing at the ground. 'Blood traces – lots of them.'

They'd sprayed luminol across the ground, revealing a patch roughly fifty by thirty centimetres, just where you'd expect from the video.

'So much blood – she must have been badly injured. If she fell from above, there's probably no hope that she survived,' added the officer.

'See if you can find other bloodstains. I want to know where the victim was moved – whether she was alive or dead,' said Lok.

'Commander.' Cheung approached. 'We retraced her steps, and found something.'

Lok followed him to the first street corner the camera-person had tailed her to. There was a construction site to one side, and some roadworks surrounded by barriers and steel boards.

'Here.' Cheung pointed into a hole about a metre deep. In a corner, next to some water pipes and electric cables shrouded in canvas, was a shoulder bag, the colour of tea. It looked exactly like the one in the video.

After photographing it in situ, they hauled it up. The bag contained make-up, snacks, a notebook, some clothes, a cellphone and a wallet. Lok opened the latter and found an ID card with Candy Ton's name and photo.

'I guess the roughs didn't notice she'd dropped her bag,' said Ah Gut. 'It probably slipped off her shoulder as she turned the corner, and she didn't have time to stop to get it back.'

'Or she may have thrown it off to run faster,' said Cheung.

'However it happened, at least we've confirmed the victim's identity.' Lok stuffed the wallet back into the bag, and looked at the phone. Her last call had been received at 10.20 p.m., from 'Office', lasting a minute and twelve seconds. Every call before that was from either 'Agent' or 'Office' – the only two numbers in her address book. There were no saved texts.

'Ah Gut, check this call log with the provider.' Lok handed over the phone.

'Since the last call's from "Office", why not just go straight to Starry Night?'

'What if she deleted other call records?'

'Are you saying...'

'Just in case.'

What Lok couldn't understand was why Candy Ton had been here in the first place, in the middle of the night. Jordan Road was a construction site, and there were no nightclubs around here, nor even any proper transport. As a public figure, she could have got anywhere she wanted by cab, or had her agent drive her, yet she had been walking alone in this desolate landscape. Lok suspected she'd been summoned to some kind of secret meeting – which meant she might have got a call beforehand.

For there to be only two numbers in her phone, Candy must have been very isolated, or else in the habit of erasing her call log. Entertainment reporters had been known to steal stars' phones to glean what they could from the calls and texts: affairs, arguments, all could be stir-fried into articles. It wasn't unusual for a cautious celebrity to make sure their phone didn't give anything away.

Who'd summoned Candy Ton to a midnight meeting? One that turned out to be a trap.

The answer flashed into Lok's mind: Eric Yeung.

But if he'd asked her, would she have come? Surely she'd have been more careful than that, especially knowing her boss was responsible for him being beaten up.

Unless she was being threatened, and had no choice.

Lok shook his head and stepped back from that line of thought. He'd gone too far into his own mind. There was limited information at his disposal, and he needed to analyse it more deeply before drawing any conclusions.

After a thorough search, the Crime Unit returned to the office and got to work investigating the persons involved, as well as searching for potential witnesses, starting at Jordan Road and working outwards. Lok personally visited Starry Night, where Candy Ton's agent said he hadn't heard from his client that day, and that she was probably resting at home. After trying her home number and getting no response, and then identifying the bag Lok held as Candy's, he grew anxious. They headed to Candy's apartment in Kwun Tong, which was small enough that Lok could see at a glance nothing was out of place. The bed and empty bin suggested she hadn't been home that night, though the agent said he'd driven her home around eleven.

'Did you actually see her enter the building?'

'Well, no... I dropped her off at the car park and left.' He furrowed his brow, as if he was realizing what trouble he was in.

Lok didn't tell him about the video. He felt this man was probably more worried about explaining himself to Boss Chor than about Candy's safety.

Lok went to the building's management office and requested security camera footage of the main entrance and elevator, but a quick scan showed no sign of Candy. If the agent was telling the truth, that meant she hadn't gone home after getting out of his car, but had headed straight for her appointment on Jordan Road.

So she didn't want him to know about this meeting? thought Lok.

The agent said that Candy had seemed perfectly normal last night. She was quite a taciturn character and didn't show much emotion – the sort of star who kept her head down and worked hard.

'She's down-to-earth, not like most girls her age, dreaming of stardom,' he added.

'And her family?'

'I don't think she has one,' said the agent vaguely.

'None at all?'

'Candy never talks about her personal life, only that her family's all gone.'

'Then who was her guardian? She joined Starry Night three years ago, when she was just fourteen. She'd have needed an adult's consent.'

'I... I don't know. Sir, I just work here. The boss asked me to be her agent, and I didn't ask too many questions.'

So that's how it was. Inspector Lok understood this man's predicament. Candy Ton might have been a runaway, and Boss Chor didn't seem like the sort of chap who'd bother with red tape.

Having found no clues at Candy's apartment, Lok returned to the police station. The press had only been told that someone had fallen from a bridge at Jordan Road the night before, that Triads might be involved and investigations were under way. Forensics said Candy's fingerprints weren't on the railing, so she might have been thrown over. And the blood traces stopped abruptly at the side of the road, suggesting the criminals had taken away the corpse – or the dying woman – in a car.

'Why move the body?' asked Mary. 'Triads murder in order to intimidate – they don't usually try to conceal their killings.'

'That means they had a different motive,' said Cheung. 'Maybe the boss only told them to "send his regards" to Ms Ton, but the ruffians got carried away and accidentally killed her?'

'Even if it was a mistake, why take away the corpse?'

'Because they knew they were in trouble,' answered Ah Gut. 'Think about it, Candy Ton was quite possibly Boss Chor's mistress. If Uncle Ngok wanted revenge, it'd be along the lines of kidnapping her and taking nude photos, that sort of thing. Murder is different – there's no coming back from that. In the underworld, if your men accidentally kill one of my people, then it has to be a life for a life. Those thugs would have feared getting killed in turn, but if they concealed the body, then she'd just be "missing", and there'd be no death to be avenged, and Hung-yi would have no reason to demand their heads from Hing-chung-wo.'

'But someone taped the whole thing...' mumbled Mary, still trying to think it through.

'In any case, this isn't going to be easy,' said Ah Gut.

Inspector Lok listened in silence to his team's discussion. Ah Gut's view was logical, but something about it felt wrong.

'Commander, big trouble,' said Ah Gut the next morning, striding agitatedly into the inner office, where Lok sat staring at the photographs and relationship webs on his noticeboard. He was pointing outside, towards the main office.

Once again, the entire team was gathered around Ah Gut's desk, animatedly discussing the video of Candy Ton's attack which was playing on the screen.

'What's up, did you find something new in the footage?'

'No,' said Ah Gut, gesturing at the images. 'This isn't the CD we got yesterday. Someone's put the video on the web.'

4

THE FOOTAGE FIRST surfaced on one of Hong Kong's anonymous chat boards. Someone posted a link that led to a free web-hosting service with the video on its server.

The initial responses were 'What kind of trailer is this?', 'Isn't that Candy Ton?' and 'What a disgusting film.' But when someone pointed out that a variety show Candy was due to guest-star on had been cancelled at the last minute, people began to realize this might be the real thing. Some still insisted it must be a promotional stunt, but others retorted, 'Candy Ton's always been a terrible actress – remember how that three-year-old was better than her in *Autumn Sonata*? If she could pull something like this off, she'd have won an award by now.'

This point of view received widespread support. The woman running for her life in the video was clearly not faking it. Some people recalled seeing Ms Ton at an event that weekend wearing a jacket and hat just like that, and so the online discussion moved on from 'Is that really Candy Ton?' to 'What happened to Candy Ton?' Many of the participants were worried fans. Meanwhile, the video became generally accepted as genuine after the chat board's moderators deleted the entire thread. Of course, by this time the video had been downloaded multiple times, and reposted on other sites.

Sonny Lok received word at 11 a.m. that there'd been four-teen crime reports, all from concerned citizens who'd seen the video online. The police hadn't released any information the pre-vious day because there was a chance Candy Ton was still alive, and, however slim that might be, going public with the news too early might endanger her life. But now that the recording was out in the open, they had to make a statement to attempt to calm the situation.

'Hong Kong Police have confirmed that a seventeen-year-old female has gone missing,' said Inspector Lok at the press confer-ence. 'A video of unknown provenance suggests that this woman was attacked by four criminals on a Jordan Road pedestrian bridge. The whereabouts of the victim are not known at pres-ent. The police are taking a serious view of this case, and the Crime Unit is investigating. As the case is ongoing, we are unable to release more information at present, but hope any witnesses who walked or drove past Jordan Road or Lin Cheung Road on the night of the 21st to the 22nd will get in touch if they saw anything out of the ordinary. In addition, the police urge the individual who shot the footage, or anyone who knows them, to come forward. We will guarantee their safety.'

'Was the injured party Candy Ton?' asked a reporter.

'Police investigations are ongoing.'

'I've heard that police secured the crime scene yesterday. Did you already know about this case then?'

'We did have a report, but can't say any more than that.'

'Have you got any firm suspects?'

'No comment.'

A journalist resembling a fox, his eyes pressed into a line, raised his hand. 'Inspector Lok, does this case have anything to do with the Hung-yi Union and Hing-chung-wo Triads?'

'We haven't excluded underworld involvement.'

'What I mean is, could Candy Ton's murder be related to Eric Yeung being Boss Yam Tak-ngok's illegitimate son?'

Dammit, cursed Lok inwardly. As the saying goes, you can't hide fire with paper. The fact he'd most hoped to conceal had been sniffed out by these feral dogs.

'I have no comment to make.' He maintained his poker face. Nonetheless, he could see that all the other journalists were agog at this revelation.

'This is tough,' said Lok, loosening his tie back in the office. 'One drop of blood and those sharks surged towards it.'

'Commander, I've pulled Candy Ton's phone records,' said Ah Gut. 'The last call was the one from her office – there weren't any others.'

'Nothing?' Lok was startled.

'Nothing. So she hadn't been erasing her call logs. Maybe she had two cellphones, and this one was just for work stuff.'

That was possible, thought Lok. But then the other phone was probably in her pocket, and the criminals would dispose of it together with her corpse – assuming she was dead.

'I've also traced this morning's post.' Ah Gut flipped open his notebook. 'I got in touch with the chat board and the web host, and got the IP addresses of whoever posted the message and uploaded the video. The first was from the University of Basel, and the second from Mexico City.'

'Switzerland and Mexico?' This was even more perplexing.

'Probably someone hacking their network to mask their real IP address. We could crack that and find the real location, but that'd take time, and if they looped it via five or six places round the world, we could be searching for weeks.'

'Mm, let's leave that line of inquiry for now, then.' Reporters have a wide circle of acquaintances, and Lok guessed whoever posted the video might happen to know a hacker who'd devised this convoluted method of spreading the news. If not for the fear of Triad reprisals, he thought, this person would probably have sold the video to a TV station for a tidy sum instead.

'Mary's looked into the family background,' continued Ah Gut, flipping several pages forward. 'Candy Ton's parents were unmarried. Her mother, Tang Pui-pui, passed away ten years

ago, and her father, Ton Hei-chi, died five years ago. They lived
in Sham Shui Po. So she wasn't lying when she told her agent she
had no family.'

'What did they do?' asked Lok casually. His initial thought was
that at least, since she was an orphan, the police wouldn't have
the unenviable task of delivering news of her death to her parents.

'A bartender and a waitress at a Yau Ma Tei bar.' Ah Gut
looked up from his notebook. 'Mary asked around where they
used to live, and the neighbours said the parents were both very
young – not a "proper family".'

Or, Lok thought, these neighbours were probably elderly, and
might have been biased against the young couple who left for
work in the evening and returned in the small hours.

'I'm heading off now to retrace her steps that night. I'll start
around her apartment building.'

'No, send Mary to do that. You come with me – there's something more important.'

'More important?'

'We're going to invite Uncle Ngok to help us with our investigation.'

'But Commander, we have no proof.' Ah Gut's face had gone
pale.

'I know,' interrupted Lok. 'We have no evidence to show he
has anything to do with this. But I'd like to see his reaction.'

Ah Gut knew the police were within their rights to interrogate
anyone associated with a case, but when the person in question was a Triad boss, this was reckless – especially as they only
had guesswork to go on at this point. If Uncle Ngok was the
mastermind, then he'd know they were on to him and would
have time to take precautions, such as fleeing overseas; and if he
wasn't, then the Triad would retaliate in some way, to remind
the police to treat others as they'd like to be treated. The last
time a gangland boss had been brought in for questioning, the
regional police station had found itself besieged by more than a
hundred thugs.

In fact, Lok hadn't initially intended to confront Yam Tak-ngok. A day earlier, the culprit wouldn't have been aware that the police had the video. That meant the ball was in Lok's court. But now the whole thing was exposed, he'd decided on a risky gambit, bringing the biggest fish back to the station and seeing if they could destabilize his position.

Because he was questioning Yam as a witness rather than having him arrested, Lok worried something might go wrong. If Uncle Ngok didn't play nice and this escalated, there'd be more problems down the road.

In the end, reality exceeded his expectations.

Lok and Ah Gut arrived at the enemy camp – Hing-chung-wo's legal shell company, Hing-ngok Finance – and while the stern, murderous-looking 'employees' weren't particularly friendly, the company's 'chairman', Yam Tak-ngok, seemed delighted to see them. He happily accompanied them to the station.

'Far too many people here – better to talk at your office,' said Uncle Ngok.

This was Lok's first meeting with Yam Tak-ngok. From the pictures and reports, he'd expected a dour Triad boss, only to find himself facing a man who could be any ordinary old uncle. The only unusual thing was that Uncle Ngok's eyes were far more piercing than the average person's, not containing the slightest hint of a smile even when he was beaming.

Uncle Ngok and one of his black-suited associates rode back to Tsim Sha Tsui police station in Inspector Lok's car. Every officer looked on in amazement as the boss of Hing-chung-wo arrived.

'This way, Mr Yam.' Lok opened the door of an interview room on the third floor.

'Ah Wah, wait here for me,' said Uncle Ngok to the suited man.

'But Big Brother—'

'Call me "Boss".' Uncle Ngok's face sank for a moment, but he soon resumed his normal expression. 'I'm just going to talk alone with these two officers. We're in the police station – surely you don't think they'll torture me as soon as that door is shut?'

Lok noted the veiled threat in his words, a hint that they'd better not try any little tricks. He thought Uncle Ngok would find it easy to lead an inexperienced officer by the nose.

In the room, Lok and Ah Gut sat on one side of the table, facing Yam Tak-ngok.

'Mr Yam, we've asked you here today to talk about the Jordan Road...' Lok began.

'Is this the Candy Ton murder?' Uncle Ngok didn't beat about the bush.

'You know that Candy Ton was killed?'

'My guys showed me the video today. To fall from such a height – she must be dead.'

'Why are you so sure it's Candy Ton? It could just be someone who looks like her.'

'I wasn't sure to start with, but since you've come looking for me, I thought it was certain—' He coughed. 'Because my idiot son got beaten up, you suspect I set someone on that woman in revenge.'

'So Eric Yeung really is your son?'

'Mr Inspector, let's not play around.' Uncle Ngok smiled unpleasantly. 'The police must already have established Eric's relationship to me. Let's be clear – even though it was that woman who led my son on before changing her mind and running to Boss Chor, I want you to know I didn't send anyone to take care of her. That's what you wanted to ask me, isn't it?'

Lok hadn't expected him to guess the police hypothesis so completely.

'When you say "deal with", do you mean "threaten" or "murder"?' Lok deliberately raised his voice on the last word.

'I didn't send anyone after Candy Ton – she's got nothing to do with me.' Uncle Ngok's expression hadn't changed one bit.

'You said she led Eric Yeung on? According to whom?'

'That's what Eric said. Mr Inspector, you can choose not to

believe him, but I don't think my son would lie over something
so trivial.'

'But if he was drunk?' Ah Gut cut in.

'Okay, fine, perhaps that woman didn't exactly "lead him
on", but I don't think the word on the street is entirely accurate.
Eric might have been a tiny bit keen – but then women are like
horses, you have to break them in before use.'

Lok and Ah Gut both thanked their lucky stars that Mary
wasn't in the interview room. She'd have started yelling at the
Triad boss for being a chauvinist pig.

'You say you didn't send anyone to deal with Candy Ton. But
Eric Yeung was ambushed and assaulted – aren't you even a little upset about that?'

'If I said I wasn't furious, you wouldn't believe me,' said Uncle
Ngok calmly. 'Which father's heart wouldn't ache to see his son
get beaten up? But you can't just lash out in anger. You have to
look at the big picture.'

'What big picture?'

'Mr Inspector, let's be frank. You run the Crime Unit, you
know very well the balance of power in this region. In two years
at most, the name of Hing-chung-wo will vanish from the underworld. I'm getting tired of this endless back-and-forth, anyway.
I've done plenty of bad things in the past, too many, and if you
want to pin this one on me, fine. I'll probably spend the rest of
my life in Stanley or Shek Pik Jail, but I don't want to take my
gang down with me, and I particularly don't want Eric, stupid
as he is, to take the same road I did.' Uncle Ngok paused. 'The
world of entertainment isn't straightforward, but at least it's
law-abiding. If I'd hurt even Candy Ton's little finger and word
got out, wouldn't that just damage Eric's prospects?'

Lok was taken aback by this. He'd never expected the 'big
picture' to be Eric's future in the entertainment industry.

'Mr Yam, you're openly admitting to being part of a criminal
gang – aren't you afraid I'll charge you?' Hong Kong law was
clear: to even proclaim oneself a Triad member was a crime.

'You're dealing with Candy Ton's case right now. What good would it do you to arrest me?' Uncle Ngok grinned. 'Besides, your drug guys already have that fellow Chiang in their hands, you don't need to come after me too.'

Lok remembered what Kwan Chun-dok had said – that the Narcotics Unit had enough evidence to charge Yam Tak-ngok. 'That fellow Chiang' was probably some witness. Lok didn't know the details, but he could guess. By the sound of it, Uncle Ngok was mentally prepared to do jail time.

Nothing in his words gave Lok an opening. Either he was a crafty old fox, or it was all true.

'Mr Yam, let me ask you one more time.' Lok looked him straight in the eye. 'Did you or didn't you send someone to attack Candy Ton? If one of your men accidentally killed her, the sooner he turns himself in, the more likely it is he'll get away with a manslaughter charge. I don't need to tell you how much lighter that sentence would be than for murder.'

'I didn't order anyone to harm a hair on her head,' said Yam Tak-ngok, no longer smiling. 'Just as I said earlier, I'd never do anything that might damage my son's career.'

'In that case, Mr Yam, is it possible that your subordinates are deceiving you? Wanting to take revenge for your son, and attacking Candy Ton behind your back?'

Uncle Ngok was silent, and for just a second Lok saw his brows contract. After some time, he said slowly, 'I trust them. They've obeyed my orders all these years.'

'Perhaps, knowing their Big Brother was going inside soon, they wanted to do something to help you?'

'Not possible. No one in my gang would be so dumb. Besides, Candy Ton is outside the organization, and you know we believe wives and children shouldn't be touched.'

Uncle Ngok's words were firm, but Lok and Ah Gut could see he was wavering. The human heart is unknowable, and even his right-hand men couldn't be guaranteed not to go against orders.

Lok knew he wouldn't get a name out of Uncle Ngok that day,

so he let him leave, after remarking that they might look him up again for further assistance with their inquiries. He hoped that this meeting would send a clear message – that if a Hing-chung-wo member had accidentally killed Candy Ton, surrendering himself would be the best option, firstly to show Hung-yi that the death wasn't intentional and thus prevent an all-out gang war, and secondly as grounds for a reduced sentence. Rather than waiting in fear for Boss Chor's retaliation, it'd be better to put everything out in the open.

Still, Lok was hardly naive enough to pin all his hopes on this elderly gang leader. He asked his Intelligence Team to find out what every member of Hing-chung-wo was doing on the night of the killing, as well as to check if anyone in the gang had suddenly vanished since the incident. Guys on the outer fringes of the organization were often happy to turn informant, and while there was a risk that they were double agents, they were the most reliable source of information. There'd been at least four assailants, which meant four mouths rather than one to keep shut – if they had come from Hing-chung-wo, the culprits might have bragged about it afterwards, or else got frightened and confessed to their colleagues.

Still, four days went by with no new reports. There were attempts at retaliation by low-ranking Hung-yi Union thugs who were unhappy that Hing-chung-wo had apparently attacked someone outside their organization, but these were isolated incidents. There was absolutely no movement from the upper half of the hierarchy. No witnesses had turned up either – no one even seemed to know how Candy Ton had travelled from Kwun Tong to Jordan. A night bus passed along that stretch of road at half-hour intervals, but none of the drivers remembered seeing anything out of the ordinary, including a chase, an attack, the moving of a casualty or the road being hosed down. If they were telling the truth, the criminals must have studied the bus timetables and the pattern of routine police patrols, in order to make sure the whole incident took place unobserved.

Entertainment circles were abuzz with the news, with many voices raised in sympathy or denouncing the attackers, but others hinting that Candy Ton had got exactly what she deserved. Reporters tried to interview Boss Chor, but a Starry Night publicist told everyone he was away on business for a few days.

Five days after the press conference, Ah Gut took a phone call and rushed over to Lok. 'Commander, a female corpse has been found in Castle Peak Bay.'

'Candy Ton?' said Lok, immediately alert.

'Don't know. A police patrol boat dredged her up. She'd been submerged a few days, and her face is gone. A long-haired woman, between fifteen and twenty-five.'

'Clothes?'

'She was naked,' said Ah Gut. 'Want me to go take a look?'

'I'll go with you.' Lok grabbed his suit jacket from the back of his chair.

Lok and Ah Gut got to the Kowloon Public Mortuary in Hung Hom, only to find the body hadn't arrived yet. In the waiting room, both men were uneasy, half hoping this was Candy Ton, because her body would provide more clues, but also hoping she was alive and well despite everything that suggested otherwise.

'It's here,' called a worker, summoning them into the morgue.

As Ah Gut said, the body was not in good shape. Not only were its features swollen from days in the water, the body itself was damaged all over – impossible to say if fish had been nibbling or if it had got entangled with boat propellers. Fortunately the fingertips seemed all right, so they should be able to identify her from her prints.

The pathologist arrived while they were still looking at the body. He seemed surprised that the police had got there before him, but after hearing that Inspector Lok was in charge of the Candy Ton case, understood why they'd were anxious.

'A detailed autopsy will take time – I'll do a quick examination first,' he offered.

According to the pathologist, the cause of death was drowning. There were many broken bones, with visible wounds to the skull, all inflicted before death. This would be consistent with what they had seen on the video.

'I'll let you have the fingerprints, and you can run them through your system.' He lifted the corpse's right hand, and very carefully dried the fingertips before dabbing them in ink and taking the prints.

They thanked the pathologist and left the morgue.

'Commander, do you think that's her?' asked Ah Gut.

Before Lok could answer, a familiar figure appeared before him. 'Sifu?'

Sure enough, Kwan Chun-dok was talking to a mortuary worker.

'Ah, Sonny, are you here on a case?'

'Yes, the body in Castle Peak Bay. We came to see if it was Candy Ton.'

'And?'

'We don't know yet. She was in the water too long.' He patted his briefcase. 'But we managed to get some prints, and they ought to give us some answers. Sir, what brings you here?'

'Same as you, the floating corpse.'

'Oh?'

'That Wan Chai sex trafficking case. A plea-bargain witness told us three prostitutes had been tortured to death, and one of the bodies is still missing.'

'So we each hope this one belongs to our case,' sighed Lok.

'It's our job to deal with other people's misfortunes,' Kwan smiled grimly. 'I won't take up any more of your time, I need to go have a chat with the pathologist too.'

Lok said goodbye, but he'd only taken a few steps before Kwan called him back.

'Hey, I have some free time this week – come look me up, I'll be home every evening.'

On their way back to Tsim Sha Tsui station, Ah Gut asked,

'Commander, who was that older guy in the baseball cap?'

'That was my superior when I was in Intelligence, former Superintendent Kwan Chun-dok.'

'Kwan the genius detective?' gaped Ah Gut. 'The man who never forgets a place, and can identify a suspect just from the way he walks? The "Eye of Heaven"?'

Lok smiled inwardly. His mentor's nicknames seemed to have spread throughout the entire policing world.

At the station, Lok handed the fingerprints over to the Identification Bureau. Their report came back at half past five that day.

The fingerprints of the corpse matched those of Candy Ton.

Once news got out that Ms Ton's corpse had been found, the whole of Hong Kong was in an uproar. This was now officially a murder investigation. The nation's eyes were on them, but the Crime Unit had nothing to report. Some thought Headquarters was going to intervene any day now, and since this looked like it might be an underworld revenge killing, the Anti-Triad Task Force might get involved too. Yet no officer ever wanted an active case to pass into someone else's hands, because that would look like they couldn't handle it themselves.

The following day, morale was low in the Crime Unit. As soon as he got off work, Lok drove towards Mong Kok, calling his mentor from the car. 'Hello, sir? I'm on Nathan Road, heading towards your place...'

'Ah, that's unfortunate, I'll be home late tonight. Why don't you wait for me there? My wife is in, though she has a mahjong date at seven.'

Lok parked the car. Thinking it had been a while since he'd seen Mrs Kwan, he stopped by a patisserie and bought her half a dozen exquisite fruit tarts, then remembering her fondness for Mont Blanc, added a piece of that. Mrs Kwan was happy to see him – they hadn't met since he visited the family home for a meal when he got his promotion, more than a month ago. She accepted his gift with pleasure: a treat for her mahjong buddies. Lok knew she didn't have a particularly sweet tooth; her joy was at being able to show the other women how this young man was like a son to her and her husband, how much he cared for them. The Kwans were childless, and they really did treat Sonny like their son – and in return, he saw them as more or less his godparents.

After Mrs Kwan departed, Lok settled in to wait for his mentor. Kwan Chun-dok might be a retired superintendent, but his penny-pinching streak meant he and his wife still lived in a five-hundred-square-foot apartment. He had asked several times why they didn't move to a larger place, but Kwan always answered, 'A small place is easier to clean, not to mention keeping our electric bills down.' Lok also admired Mrs Kwan for being willing to lead such a simple life despite her husband's lofty position – but then if she'd been a materialistic woman, his mentor would hardly have married her.

As Lok sat on the sofa, his brain was busy with details of the Candy Ton case. The longer he sat there, the more frustrated he felt. Standing, he paced around the living room several times, and then went into Kwan's study – the only other room in the flat apart from the bedroom. It contained a desk, two armchairs, a bookcase and a computer. Here Kwan would sit reading case files, combing them for clues before coming to his conclusions.

Lok looked listlessly at the large and small files on the shelf, then sat in his mentor's chair. The wall was covered in framed photos, many of them faded, quite a few in black and white. The oldest one was by the window, showing Kwan Chun-dok in his twenties – Sonny knew this had been taken in 1970, when his mentor was in England for training. It was said that his outstanding performance in preventing a bomb blast during the '67 unrest had caught the attention of his British superior, and that started him on his career as 'genius detective'. Yet Lok had never heard Kwan mention those riots – in fact, he always avoided the subject. Lok guessed that his mentor didn't like to brag, especially about an episode in which many officers had lost their lives, not to mention innocent civilians. Those who'd lived through it probably didn't like to look back.

Kwan's desk was covered in random objects, a confusion of documents and notebooks. The living room was impeccably neat, yet this place was as messy now as it had been a decade ago. Mrs Kwan had told him that her husband forbade her to touch anything here, and she wouldn't want to anyway, lest she unwittingly prevent him from solving a case. And so the chaos remained year after year.

The clutter was unimaginable. Apart from the papers, there were pill boxes, a fountain pen, photographs, slides, a desk lamp, a magnifying glass, a microscope, test tubes, lock picks, finger-print dust, pinhole cameras, a recording device disguised as a ballpoint pen, putty for copying keys... It might seem more like the set up of a private detective or spy than a police investigator, but knowing his mentor's unconventional methods, it all seemed perfectly ordinary to Sonny.

In his mentor's chair, Lok crossed his legs, imitating the position Kwan assumed when he was thinking. Picking up a glass vial, he played with it idly, again just as his mentor did. The vial held a single bullet, no doubt a souvenir of some case. Bullets were restricted items and shouldn't be stored in this manner, but for someone as untroubled by rules as Kwan Chun-dok, that was a mere detail.

As Sonny rotated the vial, the bullet tinkled clearly against the glass walls. His gaze drifted aimlessly across the mess on the desk, but was abruptly arrested by the name on a manila folder, which pulled him back to full attention: 'Yam Tak-ngok'.

Kwan Chun-dok's file on Uncle Ngok, right there on his desk.

Although nosing around in his mentor's papers would prob-ably earn him a scolding, Lok didn't think twice before flipping open the folder, intent on reading every word. Yet after only half a minute, he closed it again in disappointment. This was just a copy of Uncle Ngok's official file. Lok had the exact same file in his briefcase.

He set aside the folder and was about to lean back in the

chair, when six words in red caught his eye.

Below Uncle Ngok's folder lay an envelope stamped 'Top Secret: For Internal Circulation Only.'

He reached out for it and saw it was unsealed. Unable to bear the curiosity, he pulled out the papers inside.

Sonny had expected this to be classified material about Uncle Ngok, but a quick look showed it was something else altogether. This was something to do with the Witness Protection Programme – copies of letters between that office and the Immigration Department. Sensing that this was sensitive information, Lok was about to replace everything when a name caught his eye: 'Chiang Fu'.

An unfamiliar name, except that it reminded him of Yam Tak-ngok's words: 'Your drug guys already have that fellow Chiang in their hands, you don't need to come after me too.'

This document was stacked together with Uncle Ngok's folder – that was no coincidence. Sonny pulled it out again and scanned it quickly. The letter said someone named Chiang Fu was entering the Witness Protection Programme, and would need the Immigration Department to provide him with a new identity – the Police Commissioner and Chief Executive had already approved it. One of the pages was a response from the Immigration Department with a list of five names – four Chiangs and one Lin, probably all the same family – followed by different names in both English and Chinese.

'Chiang Fu became Kong Yu, Lin Zi became Chiu Kwan-yee, Chiang Guo-xuan, Chiang Li-ming and Chiang Li-ni became Henry Kong, Holly Kong and Honey Kong...' murmured Inspector Lok.

Then the sound of a key turning in the front door. Lok hurriedly stuffed the documents back into the envelope.

'Sorry for the wait, Sonny,' said Kwan Chun-dok.

'No, no worries.' Lok hurried out of the study.

Kwan looked narrowly at his protégé as he hung up his hat and stick, then bent to take off his shoes. 'It's fine if you've looked at the papers on my desk, just don't say anything to anyone.'

Lok froze. Had he already given himself away?

'You haven't eaten, have you? Where shall we go? Ming-kee at the street corner has a special on roast goose. Or shall we call for takeout? I'm not overly fond of pizza, but I've got a Domino's coupon that expires this week, it'd be a shame not to use it.'

'Sifu, are you investigating Uncle Ngok?'

'I've already told you I am. HQ Narcotics want to deal with him. He's been trafficking huge quantities for the last decade or two, but they never had anything on him. Then last year, a witness agreed to testify against him. Looks like all our hard work finally paid off...'

'And that was Chiang Fu?' The name from that Top Secret document.

Kwan raised an eyebrow. 'Yes. He's Vietnamese-Chinese, involved in the South-east Asian drug trade, then turned state's evidence. If the dealers in Vietnam find out he's switched sides, his days will be numbered, so he and his family have been brought to Hong Kong and given new identities. I can't tell you much more than that – to be honest, I'm already breaking the law by saying this much.'

'Is Yam Tak-ngok worth this much effort? Even if you did nothing at all, Hing-chung-wo would eventually be taken over by Hung-yi Union.' Lok paused. 'Unless the witness also has dirt on Hung-yi... on Boss Chor's drug trafficking?'

'No, Chiang Fu's evidence is only good against Uncle Ngok. The other names he gave us were already deceased.'

Lok wanted to say this arrest would just be for show, to make citizens feel the police were doing something. It wouldn't help with the drug problem in Yau-Tsim at all. But he didn't dare mention this in front of Kwan – after all, the head of Narcotics was his mentor's old friend. Apparently the two of them had worked together in the 1970s, in the Kowloon Investigation Unit.

'Sifu, was it Uncle Ngok's men who killed Candy Ton?' Lok changed the subject.

'You've questioned him, haven't you? What do you think?' Kwan lowered himself onto the sofa.

'I believe he's not the mastermind. But I'm not sure he doesn't have subordinates stupid enough to seek revenge for their Big Brother, and end up accidentally shoving Candy off a bridge.'

'That would normally be a logical line of thought,' smiled Kwan. 'But if you still think that in the light of the facts already in your possession, you haven't done your homework.'

'What have I missed?'

'You know Hing-chung-wo is a splinter of Hung-yi Union, right?'

'Yes.'

'And as Hing-chung-wo's been getting swallowed up by Hung-yi in recent years, quite a few little ruffians have switched allegiance to Boss Chor, right?'

'Sure.'

'Uncle Ngok's son got beaten up, but he issued an order for his underlings not to retaliate. You saw that?'

'It was in the Intelligence report.'

'Put those three points together. How many people do you think there still are in Hing-chung-wo who'd disregard their boss and go off on their own? Firstly, the young toughs wouldn't have stuck with Uncle Ngok in the first place, they'd have gone with their kindred spirit, Boss Chor. Besides, anyone capable enough to organize this killing would have been poached by Hung-yi long ago. The remainder are surely fiercely loyal to their chief's every little command. Even if he did have subordinates who were out of control, they'd go after Boss Chor, not Candy Ton – she's nothing to them, and killing her just brings trouble to their organization and their boss. Hardly worth it.'

'But it may have been an accident? They might just have wanted to rough her up.'

'Then why were they armed with cleavers? Do you think they were planning to cut up some watermelons?'

Sonny recalled the flashing weapons in the video.

'From the footage, it's clear they were after her life from the start,' said Kwan simply.

'Then, sifu, do you think they weren't from Hing-chung-wo?'

'Sonny, I'm very tired right now, and there's not much more to be said about this case. Just get more usable clues, make the witnesses testify, and you'll be able to make an arrest. In these Triad cases, the mastermind is never directly involved, and you won't find any material evidence linking him to the crime. That's why you'll have to find a witness. Just be patient.'

'But, sifu...'

'You're an inspector now, there are some things you'll have to decide on your own, and stop relying on an old fellow like me.' Kwan smiled. 'Believe in yourself. You were promoted because those above were confident of your abilities. Just trust in yourself, and you'll be a good leader.'

Sonny started to say something, but sputtered to a halt, reluctant to ask more questions right after his mentor had effectively told him to stand on his own two feet.

Lok came away from the evening empty-handed. Kwan Chun-dok seemed largely uninterested in the Candy Ton case, and hadn't brought it up again. Instead, he'd talked about soccer, the economy, the situation in the Middle East, as well as recent rumors of a mysterious infectious disease in Guangdong Province. Sonny guessed he was being cautious. With Narcotics preparing a case against Yam Tak–ngok, if he let anything slip – such as the current whereabouts of the witness Chiang – that might jeopardize the whole operation.

Lok left around ten thirty – in the old days, he and his mentor would have chatted till one or two in the morning, but with a pregnant wife at home he didn't like to stay out too late. Before he went, Kwan patted his shoulder and said, 'Sonny, try to relax. Don't think about your cases all the time. Listen to music or watch TV after work – it'll help you do your job.'

Despite this advice, all the way home Lok's mind was still flooded with names: Candy Ton, Yam Tak-ngok, Eric Yeung, and others.

'Hey, you're still up?' He walked in to find his wife propped up in bed. The TV was on, though she was busily reading a gossip magazine.

'I was waiting for you,' Mimi said, pretending to sulk.

'It's not good for pregnant women to stay up too late,' he said, leaning in to kiss her.

'It's just eleven-something, how's that too late?' she teased him. The moment she'd told him she was pregnant, Lok had begun anxiously monitoring everything about her – her surroundings, food, drink, work and rest.

'Would you like me to warm you some milk?'

'I've had some, thanks,' said Mimi tenderly. 'You've been working hard all day, you should have a good rest. I've got your bathwater ready.'

Sonny shrugged off his jacket and glanced at his wife's magazine, the latest copy of *Eight-Day Week*. The cover story was on Eric Yeung, with some old pictures of Candy.

'If you keep reading such rubbish, it might affect the baby's development.'

'All my friends are talking about this. If I don't keep up I won't be able to join in,' she retorted. 'Poor thing, this girl, she was about to go work overseas, then all of a sudden something like this has to happen.'

'Going abroad?' Lok had been about to say she deserved what she got, but suddenly realized he hadn't heard this bit of news.

'That's right, my friend knows someone who's related to an entertainment reporter, and apparently some big Japanese company took a fancy to Candy. They were going to snap her up with an enormous salary and turn her into a megastar across the whole of Asia.'

'Doesn't she have a contract with Starry Night? How could she just go like that?'

'Oh? I don't know about that...' Mimi said thoughtfully.

Soaking in the bathtub, Lok thought about what his wife had

said. If Candy Ton had really had the chance to jump ship it could be significant.

Back in the bedroom, he found Mimi had fallen asleep in front of the TV. Carefully picking up the magazine she'd dropped, he reached for the remote, but an instant before he could press 'Off', he saw something on the screen that sent a shock through his brain. Forgetting his sleeping wife, he turned the volume up.

'... deeply grieved and outraged by Candy Ton's tragedy. The death of such a talented singer is a loss not just for Starry Night, but for music fans all over Hong Kong...'

On the screen was a stern-looking man in an immaculate suit, a dozen microphones shoved in his face. The caption read, 'Starry Night boss Chor Hon-keung returns to Hong Kong, speaks for the first time on Candy Ton's death.' Lok guessed this would have been a couple of hours ago.

'Starry Night Entertainment condemns the violent criminal who did this. We're furious that such a thing could happen, and urge the police to spare no energy in seeking the culprit. As for the rumours that Candy had been involved in some unpleasantness with Mr Eric Yeung, I'm not aware of this, but she was a simple, good-hearted girl, and I'm certain no blame could lie with her.' His voice was measured, every inch the respectable entrepreneur.

'Were you aware of the assault on Eric Yeung?' asked a reporter.

'I've heard a journalist friend say so. As for this recent spate of violent incidents, we at Starry Night share the feelings of our fellow Hongkongers, and hope the culprits are brought to justice as quickly as possible.'

He was talking as if none of this had a damn thing to do with him! Lok cursed silently.

'Will Candy Ton's album be coming out as scheduled?'

'This album represents Candy's sweat and tears. These ruffians wanted to prevent her fans from enjoying her music, and we're not going to let them get their way. The CD will be on shelves this week as planned,' said Boss Chor solemnly. 'The concert that would have accompanied the launch is cancelled, of course. Instead, we're organising a candlelit remembrance, with various singers performing. This is planned for the middle of next month...'

All of a sudden, Lok remembered Kwan telling him to 'listen to music or watch TV after work'. That wasn't fatherly advice; he'd been given a tip.

Lok realized he'd been looking in the wrong place all along. 'You have to be patient when you're angling for a big fish. If you can't get him on the hook right now, just still your heart and wait, and keep an eye on the surface of the water. You may only have an instant, when the opportunity arrives.'

His eyes remained on the screen, but he was no longer paying attention. His mind was now focused on that flickering moment of opportunity. A chance to charge Boss Chor with incitement and conspiracy to cause Candy Ton's death.

5

THE MOMENT Sonny Lok arrived in the office the next morning, his entire team sensed something odd. Even the usually oblivious Cheung could tell his commander had things on his mind.

'Commander.' Ah Gut rapped on his door. 'I've pulled the file of every low-ranking member of Hing-chung-wo, then compared their build against the four killers. I've got seven possible matches—'

'Don't bother, you won't find the culprits there.' Inspector Lok sighed deeply, and was silent for a moment. 'Ah Gut... do you think I'm fit to be your commanding officer?'

Uncertain what Lok was getting at, Ah Gut couldn't answer right away. 'Commander, I haven't worked under you for long, so I can't answer that. But you're always good to us, and when Operation Viper went wrong you didn't take it out on us. We all feel we can trust you.'

Inspector Lok smiled, seemingly pleased with this answer. 'So if I were transferred somewhere else, I could leave with an easy conscience?'

'Commander?'

'I'm taking sole responsibility for today's operation. If there's an inquiry, it'll all be on my shoulders.' He stood. 'Ah Gut, let's go arrest the mastermind behind Candy Ton's death.'

'Who's that?'

'Boss Chor.'

Ah Gut was stunned. 'Chor Hon-keung? Why would he want to kill Candy Ton? Commander, do you have any evidence?'

'No,' said Lok simply.

'In that case...' At that moment, Ah Gut understood why Sonny Lok was taking complete responsibility for whatever came next. Picking a fight with Boss Chor, without any proof to back you up, was sure to lead to all kinds of problems, especially when you were an insignificant commander of a little District Crime Unit. 'Commander, are you trying to lure him into a confession?'

'No,' smiled Lok grimly. 'An old crocodile like him won't be foolish enough to say anything incriminating. But it'd go against my principles to sit by and shut my eyes, to protect my career, when someone is blatantly breaking the law. Even if we can't bring charges against him, I still want Chor Hon-keung to know that he can't just do what he wants in Yau-Tsim District.'

Ah Gut wanted very much to tell Lok that if he were to ask his question again, the answer this time would be, 'You're more than fit, it's an honour to serve under you.'

Lok and Ah Gut headed to Starry Night to invite Boss Chor to assist with their inquiries. Outside the main entrance were throngs of reporters who'd been there since early morning.

'Inspector Lok, are you here to ask Boss Chor about Candy Ton?'

'Inspector Lok, do the police have any confirmed suspects?'

'I heard Eric Yeung's father, Yam Tak-ngok, has been arrested. Is Mr Yeung a suspect too?'

Lok didn't respond to any of these questions, instead asking the receptionist to inform Mr Chor that the police were here.

'Officer, do you need more information about Candy Ton? I'm only in charge of administration, I don't know if I can be much help.' Boss Chor wore a designer suit, his hair neatly parted, looking nothing at all like an underworld figure.

'Mr Chor,' said Lok, keeping his voice level, 'I'm Inspector Sonny Lok from Yau-Tsim District, and I'll have to trouble you to accompany us to the station. We suspect you may have something to do with a murder case.'

For just a second, Chor looked like he couldn't believe this was happening, but in the next instant he'd returned to his businesslike appearance, pasting a smile onto his face. 'In that case, I'd like to have my lawyer with me. Is that all right?'

'Go ahead.'

Chor spoke briefly into the phone, then followed Lok and Ah Gut out through the horde of startled reporters.

'I'm just helping the police with their inquiries, providing a few leads, that's all.' Boss Chor strenuously presented a relaxed front, but the journalists weren't going to miss an opportunity, and were already ferociously snapping away.

The three men reached Tsim Sha Tsui station to find Boss Chor's lawyer waiting for them. Once again, everyone in the precinct was shocked by Lok's tactics. Just a few days ago, he'd brought in the boss of Hing-chung-wo, and now the 'untouchable' Boss Chor was showing up here too.

'Mr Chor, please have a seat.' In the interview room, which happened to be the one in which they'd spoken to Uncle Ngok, Lok placed Chor and his lawyer on one side of the table.

'Inspector Lok, I don't understand why you'd waste my client's time by insisting he come here,' said the lawyer. 'If it's evidence you're after, he could just as easily have provided it in his office.'

'We believe Mr Chor is involved in incitement and conspiracy to murder,' said Inspector Lok, cutting straight to the chase. Chor raised his eyebrows but said nothing. His lawyer's hand was up anyway, indicating he should be quiet.

'Who's the victim?' asked the lawyer.

'A client of Starry Night Entertainment, Candy Ton.'

'Inspector Lok, this is ridiculous,' said the lawyer. 'Why would an entertainment company's boss want to hurt the most promising singer on his roster, the one with the most future earning power?'

'So according to you, the killer must be someone with a grudge against Starry Night or Mr Chor himself, seeking to hurt Candy Ton in order to damage his business?' Lok replied.

'I have no idea. We're the victims here. Catching criminals is the job of the police, not ours.' The lawyer's frosty glare swept across Ah Gut and the inspector.

'Can Mr Chor shed any light on the attack on the actor Eric Yeung?' Lok changed the subject suddenly.

'I've only heard about it from a reporter friend – that was the first I knew of the incident.' More or less the same response he'd given at the press conference the day before.

'Do you have any guesses, Mr Chor? Why Eric Yeung was attacked, for instance?'

The lawyer was about to answer when Boss Chor raised a hand to stop him, and said, 'As a private citizen, I'm guessing it was because he misbehaved on a regular basis, making enemies and bringing punishment upon himself. I've heard his father was the Triad figure Yam Tak-ngok. So the attack on him might have something to do with gang activity – but the police would know far more about that than an ordinary citizen like me.'

What a bastard, thought Lok.

'How about the director Leung Kwok-wing, the actress Shum Suet-sze, or the TV host Jimmy Ding? Do you know them?'

'Of course I've heard their names. I might even have met them at some event, I can't remember.'

'Leung Kwok-wing was beaten up three years ago. Last year, Shum Suet-sze and Jimmy Ding were separately dragged into vans, held for five hours and threatened by thugs. All these incidents happened after the individuals made remarks about Mr Chor or Starry Night performers. What do you have to say about that?'

'These two things aren't connected,' interjected the lawyer. 'Before Jimmy Ding was attacked, he slammed the Hong Kong government several times on his radio programme. Have the police brought the Chief Executive in for questioning?'

'Naturally, I'd regret it if fans were to take the law into their own hands in retaliation for their idols being insulted,' smiled Boss Chor.

Inspector Lok realized there was no need for the lawyer to be there – Chor was perfectly capable of brushing every speck of dirt off himself. He'd asked for the lawyer purely so that he himself could go on the attack and mock the police.

'Mr Chor, you mentioned earlier that Eric Yeung's attack might have been due to his father being a Triad figure, but now you've just said it might be fans taking the law into their own hands. Isn't that contradictory?'

'Those are different possibilities – I'm just guessing here.' Boss Chor smiled again. 'The performers we work with appeal to different levels of society, and if some of their fans are Triad members, that's not something I can control.'

'Mr Inspector,' said the lawyer, the other half of the double act, 'you keep bringing up matters that have nothing to do with Mr Chor. I can't imagine what evidence you have connecting my client to Candy Ton's death. If you carry on like this, I'll consider making an official complaint. You invited Mr Chor to come to the station, and tomorrow that'll be all over the news media – a PR blow for Starry Night. We have the legal right to pursue this.'

Shaking his head, Lok decided to plunge the knife straight in.

'Before this, I'd thought Candy Ton was killed by Hing-chung-wo thugs,' he said. This sudden change in direction left Chor, his lawyer and even Ah Gut baffled.

'Then—'

Lok put out a hand to shut the lawyer up, and went on, 'Ms Ton was insulted by Eric Yeung, after which Mr Yeung received a punishment beating from underworld thugs who were unaware his father was Hing-chung-wo's boss, Yam Tak-ngok. According to this theory, Mr Yam or his underlings had ample motivation to seek revenge on Candy Ton.'

'Then you ought to go arrest this Mr Yam,' chuckled Boss Chor.

'But Mr Yam couldn't have ordered this attack. The criminals were surely Triad members, but not from Hing-chung-wo. They were Hung-yi Union men – that is, your subordinates, Mr Chor Hon-keung.'

'Officer, what you've just said is defamation against my client's reputation,' threatened the lawyer, standing suddenly and placing both palms on the table.

'Hang on, let him continue,' said Chor suddenly. Ah Gut could see the lawyer hadn't expected this move, and was looking warily at his client.

'First of all, I'd like to talk about what happened on the night of the 22nd,' Lok said at a leisurely pace. 'That evening, Candy Ton was driven home by her agent, but didn't actually enter the building, because Mr Chor Hon-keung had arranged a secret meeting with her. I'm not sure what excuse he used, but he was her boss, and had just taken revenge on Eric Yeung on her behalf, so she had no reason not to keep the appointment. But it was a trick to lure her into a trap, because Mr Chor himself didn't show up. Waiting instead at the location were some low-ranking thugs from Hung-yi Union, sent there by Big Brother Chor himself.'

The lawyer had several objections to this, but each time he looked at Chor and, seeing no signal, allowed Inspector Lok to continue.

'The scene was perfect for an ambush. Few passers-by, no homes or businesses in the vicinity, and most importantly, nowhere for the victim to escape except up the bridge.' As Lok spoke, he kept his eyes fixed on Chor's. 'Put one or two men on the bridge, and the prey would find herself surrounded.'

'Inspector Lok,' Boss Chor grinned suddenly, 'are you feeling quite all right? Nothing you've just said makes any logical sense. Even if I were a Triad leader, as you claim, why would I kill the employee with the highest earning potential? That's already hard to understand, let alone why I'd lure her to a public place so she could be ambushed by my "thugs". Why not just kidnap her? I'm sure she'd get in any car I asked her to, and then she'd be mine for the taking. Both motive and method are full of holes – even a complete outsider like me can see that.'

'Let's talk about motive first.' Lok's tone remained exactly the same. 'True, Ms Ton is Starry Night's highest-earning singer for now, but she was about to jump ship. Once she signed with her new agency, she'd be of no value to Starry Night, and everything you'd invested in her wouldn't just be wasted, it'd become the property of your rival.'

The inspector knew how much market share meant to Chor. The way he was intent on expanding Hung-yi's territory showed how focused he was on getting as close to a monopoly as possible.

'Inspector Lok, I don't know where you heard this rumour,' retorted the lawyer, 'but Candy signed a ten-year contract with Starry Night. She couldn't have left for another seven—'

'What if the contract was invalid?' said Lok coldly. From the expressions on the faces of Chor and the lawyer, he knew he'd scored a point. 'According to Hong Kong law, minors below the age of fifteen need the permission of a parent or guardian to work. Candy Ton joined Starry Night at the age of fourteen, which means the contract she signed isn't legally recognized. When the Japanese agency that wanted to poach her learned this little detail from Candy's own lips, they knew it was the loophole they needed. It was too late by the time you discovered this – knowing she had the opportunity to develop her career with a bigger company, she naturally wouldn't be willing to sign a new contract with you.'

'The Japanese company trying to poach her is just industry gossip, there's no evidence for it,' said the lawyer. 'And even if there was, it's ridiculous to slander my client in this way – to suggest he'd commit murder over this.'

'That's just the first motive, I haven't come to the second and third,' Lok went on. 'Losing the goose that laid the golden eggs was now inevitable, and simply cutting his losses and parting ways might have seemed like the best plan, but Mr Chor is a crafty businessman, and even with a dead goose, he'd be sure to use every scrap of its flesh. There's no better PR than the death of a star – as long as you have the rights to her work, you could make enormous profits. But crucially, the death would need to be eye-catching enough for maximum publicity, turning the deceased into a "fallen star" – that's how you hit the big sales.'

This theory had occurred to Lok the day before, when Boss Chor had mentioned Candy's forthcoming album at the press conference.

'So not only did you plot to have Ms Ton attacked in a public place, you also tipped off some paparazzo so he'd follow her – basically, you arranged for the assault to be filmed. You hoped the bloody attack would be on the cover of every magazine, only the journalist wasn't quite as conscience-free as you'd expected – his first response was to send the footage to the police.

'This little show killed two birds with one stone,' Lok continued, before the lawyer could butt in. 'You may already have known that the police had their eye on Yam Tak-ngok, which meant this would be a good time to wipe out Hing-chung-wo – but if Mr Yam had named a successor, that'd be a variable you hadn't accounted for. When Ms Ton was murdered, anyone who knew of Eric Yeung's relationship to Mr Yam would put the blame on Hing-chung-wo, and Boss Chor would have an excuse to do whatever he wanted to Hing-chung-wo in return, without breaking the Triad code of honour or provoking intervention from other districts. The underworld is like a battlefield, and all you've lacked so far was an excuse to go to war.'

'My client will not be responding to any of your conjectures,' said the lawyer, furrowing his brow. 'Everything you're saying is completely unfounded. If you do have evidence, please produce it now.'

'True, I don't have any evidence, but one of your underlings

made a mistake.' Inspector Lok kept his tone neutral. 'At first
I guessed it was Hing-chung-wo thugs who moved the corpse
because they'd murdered her accidentally and were panicking,
afraid that Hung-yi Union would take revenge. Then I found
out the body was naked, and I understood the real reason.
It wasn't the corpse that had to be removed, but its clothes. Mr
Chor, have you seen the video of Ms Ton being attacked?'

'I have. So what?'

'No one would have expected tiny, delicate Candy Ton to lash
out at her attacker the way she did. That punch landed pretty
hard, and caught him right in the face. Even with a mask on,
you'd expect a nosebleed or a tooth knocked out, wouldn't you?'

In the video, the man she'd punched had immediately clapped
his hand over the lower part of his face.

'That thug would have realized his face was covered in
blood, and that some of it might have stained Ms Ton's clothes.
Gang killers aren't usually that fussy about staying anonymous,
but this was different – the whole plan hinged on conceal-
ment, not of the killers' own identities, but of which Triad they
belonged to. If the police caught the gangsters and used DNA
evidence to prove their guilt, it would be clear they were from
Hung-yi rather than Hing-chung-wo, and that would wreck
Boss Chor's scheme. There wouldn't have been time to strip the
corpse at the scene, so they could only move the body and deal
with it elsewhere.'

'If it happened the way you say, wouldn't that just mean
there was no evidence?' said Boss Chor coldly, looking distinctly
uncomfortable.

'The clothes are gone, but the blood wasn't necessarily on the
clothes.' Inspector Lok produced some photographs of the stairs
leading to the bridge, taken from different angles. 'The Identification Bureau has searched every inch of the railing, and found
traces of blood in the exact spot touched by the man who was
punched by Candy Ton. That video recorded the whole incident
– that's indisputable proof. So now, we just need to find who the

blood came from. So, yes, I have no evidence right now that Mr Chor ordered the killing, but the testimony of the diminutive killer should do.'

'And you've caught him?' Chor said in a low voice. Although his suit remained expensive and crisp, his posture no longer resembled that of a respectable businessman.

'Our colleagues are pursuing inquiries. We should have our target by tomorrow.' Lok turned to him with a meaningful smile.

'Then you still don't have any evidence right now?' said Chor. 'Everything you've said is conjecture. John, did you take note of how many things Inspector Lok just said that constitute defamation?'

The lawyer froze momentarily, not having expected to be called on. He stammered, 'Um, yes, if these words were heard by the public, that'd be grounds for a lawsuit.'

'Inspector Lok, you still want to play? I'll meet you every step of the way,' grinned Chor slyly. 'Go ahead and detain me for forty-eight hours. But if you don't get anything on me, be prepared for an avalanche of lawsuits as soon as I get out.'

'I have no plans to detain you. This time tomorrow, I'll formally arrest you. I only came to find you today to tell you something important.' Inspector Lok stood. 'I don't care whether you're a Triad boss or high-class entrepreneur, whatever it is, I'm not buying it. My colleagues might be afraid to bring you back to the station, but I'm not. Don't think you're free to do as you like.'

With that, Inspector Lok flung open the interview-room door and indicated that the two men were free to leave. Boss Chor looked like he'd never been so humiliated. Without another word, he stalked out, the lawyer behind him, glaring at Lok as he left.

'Commander, so there was blood on the railing? I don't remember seeing that in the report,' said Ah Gut in the corridor.

'No, that photo was faked.'

'Oh?'

'Ah Gut, tell the uniforms and Surveillance that it's a full alert tonight for Hung-yi Union, especially their armed units in charge of operations. I've set the bait; let's see if Chor will take it.'

'Take the bait? You mean he might try to get rid of those four killers tonight?'

'Right. I set him a deadline because I wanted him to be anxious – he'll deal with those four before tomorrow. No matter what happens, we have to keep at least one of them alive, so he can testify.'

Lok remembered his mentor's words: 'In these Triad cases, the mastermind is never directly involved, and you won't find any material evidence linking him to the crime. That's why you'll have to find a witness.'

'Yes, Commander.' Ah Gut nodded and returned to the outer office.

Lok might have put up a show of bravado, but in truth he wasn't feeling certain of victory. His entire future and career were riding on this gamble, and he knew the odds were only fifty–fifty.

'Not bad.'

Lok hadn't realized someone was behind him, but the voice didn't startle him too much. Kwan Chun-dok was hobbling towards him, his short walking stick in his left hand.

'Sifu? Why are you— Oh, you mean the Chor Hon-keung case?' Lok had been about to ask his mentor why he was at the station, but decided against it.

'Of course.' Kwan pointed at the interview room, which was fitted with surveillance apparatus. 'I saw the whole thing.'

'But we still don't know whether Boss Chor will give himself away...' Lok sighed.

'Come on, Sonny, let's go outside. We'll have a walk. Your subordinates can take care of all this, you don't need to waste your energy.'

'Outside? Where to?'

'To solve the case,' Kwan Chun-dok smiled enigmatically.

6

SONNY LOK FOLLOWED his mentor to the station car park.

'Give me the keys, I'll drive,' said Kwan. He had a licence, but no car of his own – he was fond of saying that it cost too much to own a car in Hong Kong, what with gas and parking, so why bother driving, especially when public transport was so convenient? That said, he was always getting lifts from colleagues or subordinates, and Lok often ended up serving as his personal chauffeur.

'Hmm?' Lok handed over the keys, uncomprehending.

'It's simpler than trying to explain the route to you.'

Pulling out of Tsim Sha Tsui station, the car headed in the direction of the Cross-Harbour Tunnel.

'Where are we going?' asked Lok.

'Sheung Wan.' Kwan clutched the steering wheel, glancing at Lok. 'By tomorrow, you'll be the talk of the town, the new commander who brought in Yam Tak-ngok and Boss Chor for questioning. Both sides will be calling you a hard-boiled detective.'

'If we don't find evidence of Boss Chor's guilt tonight, this hard-boiled detective is going to be put out to pasture.'

'Well, Sonny, to be honest, you've underestimated Boss Chor,' said Kwan. He might as well have stabbed Lok in the thigh. Lok turned to stare in agitation at his mentor.

'I've underestimated him?'

'You've learned some good tricks from all your years with me. This one, "luring the snake from its hole", would work on most criminals. But Chor's a deep one. He might see through you.'

'You mean, he might sit on his hands, and not strike against Candy Ton's killers?'

'Chor is different from the other Triad bosses, more far-seeing.' Kwan steered the car into the tunnel. 'Think about it. After seizing control in Hung-yi, he spent the next five years steadily usurping Yam Tak-ngok's power. He might seem rough and vicious, but underneath all that is some very intricate planning. There was a flaw in your tactics earlier, and an opponent like Chor would be sure to detect it.'

'A flaw?'

'You couldn't explain why you brought him in so publicly today,' Kwan said. 'If the police really did have a piece of evidence as important as the killer's blood sample, you'd already be looking at a suspect, so why tell him all this instead? Just for the sake of playing detective?'

'He might have thought I was a rookie, just trying to assert my authority.'

'If you really were that useless, you'd never have been able to deduce all those details. Your conjectures told him you were an accomplished gambler, but out of chips. To alert your opponent before the final battle – that proved you were all noise and no action.'

Lok opened his mouth but said nothing. He wanted to insist there was still a chance Chor might fall for it, but he knew his mentor was probably right.

'Sonny, you won't solve the Candy Ton case, because your opponent is too wicked.'

As the car pulled out of the tunnel, late afternoon sunlight flooded its interior, but Lok saw only darkness. Kwan's words were like a judge's sentence. Yet, unexpectedly, he wasn't worried about his own future at all, but anxious at the thought of a criminal evading the law.

After a long silence, he asked disconsolately, 'Sifu, can you think of a way to catch Boss Chor?'

'Of course!' chuckled Kwan. 'Why else would I bring you out here?'

'What are we doing in Sheung Wan? Chor's influence hasn't extended to Hong Kong Island, has it?' Lok peeked out the window. They were turning into Queen's Road Central.

'We're going to see someone named Chiang. Ah, no, I should say Kong now.'

'Oh?' This was unexpected. The drugs case witness. 'Didn't you say Chiang Fu's testimony didn't relate to Boss Chor?'

'That's right, he's only a witness in the Yam Tak-ngok case.'

Lok had no idea what his mentor was up to, but not wanting to appear foolish, he kept his mouth shut. In a short while, Kwan parked the car by the roadside. 'We're here.'

Climbing out of the car, Lok looked around. They were near Bridges Street in Sheung Wan. Although relatively close to Central, there were a number of tenement buildings in this area, destined for demolition and rebuilding in the near future.

'This way.' Kwan walked in front, until they got to the entrance of a five-storey building with a dilapidated exterior wall on Wing Lee Street. Lok guessed it must be a Witness Protection safe house.

The two men walked up the stairs to the third storey. There was only one apartment on each level, with flimsy metal gates in front of each front door. Kwan Chun-dok pressed the doorbell, but there was no sound at all within the flat. Just as Lok was wondering if the bell was broken, the wooden door swung open. Standing behind the gate was a plump woman in her forties, dressed casually in an orange T-shirt with cartoon characters on it. She looked nothing at all like a Witness Protection police officer.

The woman's face didn't change when she saw Kwan, as if she'd been expecting him. She let the two men into the apartment.

'Sorry to trouble you, young Miss Koo,' said Kwan. Lok was startled by this form of address, but perhaps his mentor had first known her twenty years ago, when the lady would indeed have been a 'young miss'.

'I'm a little busy today, sir, so I'll have to leave the two of you to it.' Miss Koo closed the front door, then walked into a room to the right of the sitting room, and shut the door on them. The apartment was not what Lok had expected – he'd envisioned a Hong Kong flat from the sixties or seventies, but instead the living room was exceedingly contemporary, with shiny wooden floorboards, chairs and tables designed with fluid outlines, a fifty-inch TV in front of a genuine leather sofa, and elegant recessed lights in the ceiling. Such sumptuous furnishings made Sonny gape – who'd have thought the police would spend that kind of money?

'This isn't a safe house,' Kwan smiled, guessing what Lok was thinking from his expression. 'It's Miss Koo's home.'

'And who's Miss Koo? She's not from the force, is she?'

'Of course not – she's as far from the police as you could possibly get. You might say she's a criminal,' said Kwan, deadpan.

'A criminal?' gasped Lok. Was Miss Koo another informant, then?

Kwan Chun-dok grinned but said nothing, instead walking over to a door on the left of the sitting room and knocking. In a moment, the door clicked open.

'Hello, Superintendent Kwan.' Lok saw the speaker was a young woman with a ponytail and glasses, extremely deferential towards his mentor.

'Sonny, let me introduce you. This is Honey Kong.'

Lok stuck out his hand. Honey hesitated, but after a moment reached out to shake it. If he remembered right, her real name was Chiang Li-ni, and she was the daughter of that Yam Tak-ngok witness—

'Isn't Chiang Fu in?' Lok stuck his head into the side room. It was spacious, but it was obvious at a glance that no one else was there. Honey looked uncomprehending at his question.

'Of course he's not in,' answered Kwan.

'Aren't we here to see Chiang Fu?'

'No, we're here for Chiang Li-ni.'

'This girl?'

'That's right.'

'Why?'

'Chiang Fu, his wife Lin Zi, and their son and daughter – the whole family of four – have enrolled in the Hong Kong Police Witness Protection Programme,' said Kwan.

'I know. I've seen the document.'

'You weren't listening carefully. I said "family of four".'

Lok saw the discrepancy. 'But doesn't Chiang Fu have three children? Chiang Li-ni, Chiang Li-ming and Chiang Guo-xuan...'

Kwan didn't answer, only gestured at Honey Kong's – Chiang Li-ni's – hair. She let down her ponytail, pulled off the glasses and looked up, sweeping her long hair to one side.

Lok didn't understand what this meant, but just as he was about to ask, something about her expression tugged at his memory – and then the pieces fell into place with a shock that was like a rush of blood to the head.

'You're... you're Candy Ton?' he stammered.

Honey Kong nodded, smiling bashfully.

Lok could barely see the resemblance in this plainly-dressed girl with no make-up. She seemed a completely different person from the sultry siren on magazine covers.

'Why's Candy Ton here? Isn't she dead? Didn't we find her body?' Lok flung out one question after another. Candy rising from the dead completely overturned his understanding of the case, filling his mind with contradictions.

'Sonny, this case is ten times more complicated than you think.' Superintendent Kwan patted his protégé's shoulder. 'Let's sit down, we can talk it over slowly.'

Lok and his mentor sat on the sofa, and Candy brought them tea before settling herself into the armchair. As she set down their cups, Lok kept his eyes fixed on her face, trying to work whether or not she was the real Candy Ton.

'Sonny,' Kwan sipped his tea, 'you've been in charge of the Candy Ton murder case, but in truth, that case has never existed. It's just one link in the chain of an operation.'

'What operation?'

'To catch the "Giant Deep Sea Grouper".'

'Boss Chor?'

'Of course.'

'Sir, you mean Candy Ton's death was completely manufactured? A fake case to fool the courts into convicting Boss Chor?'

'It's true Candy Ton's murder never happened. We weren't trying to frame anyone, though. That sort of thing might have gone on in the bad old days of the seventies, but we'd never get away with it now.' Kwan chuckled. 'Like I said, Candy is just one link in the chain of the operation. This all began far earlier than you imagine.'

'From the attack on Eric Yeung?'

'No, from the preparations for Operation Viper.'

Lok was stunned. 'But that was last November!'

'That was a link in the chain too,' smiled Kwan gently.

None of this made sense to Lok. He felt he'd been plunged into thick fog.

'Let me start from the beginning.' Kwan put his feet up. 'Sonny, you remember me saying that the only way to catch a crafty old fox like Boss Chor is eyewitness testimony? But none of his underlings were willing to betray him, and even the informants who gave us snippets were mostly eliminated. His regime was almost watertight.'

'So no one was willing to testify.'

'You're mixing two things up.' Kwan waggled a finger at him. 'Boss Chor's underlings didn't dare to testify – it wasn't that they weren't willing. Outside Hung-yi, it was the other way round: we found people who didn't want to testify, although they wouldn't have been afraid to.'

Lok was muddled at first, but after thinking through it, he realized who his mentor was referring to.

'Yam Tak-ngok?' he said suspiciously.

'Precisely.' Kwan nodded, apparently pleased. 'Yam Tak-ngok was in Hung-yi Union for more than forty years. He watched Boss Chor enter the underworld, and knew his operations inside out. The problem was, no Triad leader would co-operate with the police. Yam Tak-ngok is old-school, the sort who values his code of honour more than his old life. There's no way he'd rat on Chor Hon-keung. Sonny, do you know about the Prisoner's Dilemma?'

'Yes, it's one of the basics of game theory.'

The Prisoner's Dilemma was a scenario in which two criminals were arrested, kept separate, and told that if neither betrayed the other, they'd each be sentenced to a month in jail; if they both betrayed each other they'd each serve one year; and if only one betrayed the other, the betrayer would be instantly released, while the betrayed would serve ten years. The best outcome for them both would be to remain silent and serve the shorter sentence, but they'd have no way of knowing if they were being betrayed. In order to avoid the long sentence, they'd both choose to betray the other, and each would have to serve a year. This exercise shows that the rational choice for an individual doesn't always lead to the greatest good – and may produce perverse outcomes.

'The Prisoner's Dilemma falls apart when it comes to Chor and Yam,' said Kwan. 'Yam Tak-ngok knows very well there's a good chance he'd be betrayed, but would still choose silence – making Boss Chor the big winner. Meanwhile Chor is completely certain Yam won't betray him. Yam isn't trying to protect Chor, only this "honour" he so believes in – Chor's counting on that, which is how he was able to seize power five years ago, and has been gradually increasing his influence since.'

Kwan paused, then went on, 'So the simplest way to deal with Boss Chor was to shatter Yam Tak-ngok's conception of underworld honour. If Uncle Ngok no longer stood by his faith, the balance between the two of them would fall apart, and Chor's line of defence would be gone. Uncle Ngok turning state's evidence would surprise Boss Chor's underlings. They'd think he was finished, and rush to join Uncle Ngok in denouncing him, to protect their own positions. Outlaws are the same the world over, especially the lower-ranking ones. Very few of them would actually put their lives at risk for their bosses. This operation to encircle Chor was intended to create a Prisoner's Dilemma. Make each isolated prisoner think he's about to be betrayed, and teach him that only betraying in turn can bring the greatest benefit.'

'I don't understand what any of this has to do with Candy Ton's fake death.' Lok turned to look at her, uncomprehending. 'And who on earth is she, anyway? Is she an undercover cop?'

'Last month, Interpol sent us a report that a South-east Asian drug ring's accountant was about to switch sides,' said Kwan, ignoring Lok's questions.

'Chiang Fu?'

'Right. But HQ Narcotics discovered that Chiang Fu's evidence and testimony would only put Yam Tak-ngok behind bars. Knowing that Hing-chung-wo was likely to vanish from Yau-Tsim before too long, putting Yam in prison seemed to be letting Chor off too easily. So they sat on the information. Then in October, Benny Lau got hold of Candy Ton, and the operation finally started moving.'

'Superintendent Lau?' Sonny hadn't expected his superior's superior to suddenly crop up in the conversation.

'Yes, the Commander of West Kowloon Regional Crime Wing. But you know which department Benny used to run?'

'Wasn't it HQ CIB Division A? I was in Division B at the time, working under you.'

'Sonny, what is Division A in charge of?'

'Surveillance, and also making contact with and buying off informants.'

'Candy Ton's father was an informant, in charge of providing reports on Hung-yi's drug dealing,' said Kwan dispassionately, looking at the girl.

'Really?' Lok hadn't expected this at all. But then he remembered Ah Gut saying that Candy's father, Ton Hei-chi, had been a bartender at a bar in Yau Ma Tei, within Hung-yi's turf. And those guys meet all kinds of people. It would make sense for them to be police informants.

'But Candy...' Lok looked at her, wanting to ask about her father, but not knowing where to start.

Candy had shuddered when she heard her father's name. She turned her head beneath Lok's gaze, as if trying to avoid the question. But seeing Kwan nodding gently at her, she gained courage and met his eye, speaking the words she'd kept unsaid for years.

'Daddy was murdered five years ago.' Her voice was slow, and thick with anger.

'Murdered?' exclaimed Lok.

'The hospital said it was a ketamine overdose, but Daddy was no druggie. He'd never touched the stuff.'

'Wasn't there a police investigation?'

'No! The cops said there was nothing suspicious. They were biased! Because Daddy worked in a bar where drugs were sold, they assumed he was one of those scumbags.'

'The regional police didn't have the full story,' said Kwan. 'At the time, Boss Chor had just taken charge, and eight-tenths of Benny Lau's Hung-yi informants were killed off. Everyone in CIB knew something was wrong. Informants are a sensitive area, and Intelligence didn't want to let the other departments see their data, so had to carry out their own investigation. But the mastermind had been clever, and none of the deceased showed signs of having been murdered – they died in their cars, or at home, or at work.'

'Daddy was forced to take those drugs. That day, on my way home from school, I saw five men pull him into a car...' Candy's eyes grew red as she spoke.

'Didn't you tell this to the police?'

'They didn't believe me. I was only twelve. Daddy died in the back room of the bar he worked at, so they all said there was nothing suspicious.'

'Those five men must have been Boss Chor's thugs. They'd have paid the bar owner hush money, making it look like Ton Hei-chi died of an overdose,' said Kwan.

'I'll never forgive those bastards!' Candy spat out, rubbing at her reddened eyes. 'I found Daddy's diary later. He wrote how he'd turned informant, with a whole list of names, but I didn't want to ask the police for help again. I decided I'd take revenge my own way.'

Lok was startled by her attitude, though the situation was starting to make sense. 'And so you joined Starry Night, in order to... kill Boss Chor?'

Candy shook her head. 'Killing that scumbag wouldn't bring Daddy back to life. I wanted to expose all his crimes, to give Daddy back his reputation.'

'You were just a girl. How would you expose Boss Chor's crimes?' How naive, Lok thought.

'People said Chor was a lech, so I figured if I slept with him, I'd get close enough to dig up some evidence.'

Lok gaped. That was a new one, that a girl, just fourteen at the time, could already have had such cold determination. She hadn't used her body for fame, but for vengeance.

'And so... did you?'

'I didn't even get to see him that often, never mind seducing him,' said Candy, despairingly. 'The first two years I was with Starry Night, it was just some agent setting up a few small jobs for me. I only got to see him in my third year there. My agent said the boss wanted to give me a boost, and I thought the old perv must have finally noticed my body, but each time I saw him, he only wanted to talk about official business. I never had a private meeting with him.'

'You underestimated Boss Chor,' interjected Kwan. 'He's not actually a womanizer at all – those are just rumours he planted.'

'Rumours?'

'I've told you before, Chor Hon-keung is a crafty bastard. He's laid down red herrings all over the place. In order to hide his true weaknesses, he's manufactured false ones. Think about it, Sonny. If some underworld upstart decided to attack his floozy as a way to get at him, or if the police tried to recruit the female star we'd heard he was intimate with, how would that actually affect him?'

'Not at all?' Lok was beginning to realize where this was going. So a starlet could have an 'accident', and Boss Chor would be unmoved; the police would take her on as an informant, but that'd be a waste of time – they'd be looking for evidence in the wrong place. And this provided him with a screen behind which he could watch and see what happened to his female stars, in order to know what his opponents were up to.

'You judge a system not by its strongest point, but by its weakest link. Boss Chor understands this very well, and so he lays down false weak links to confuse his enemies,' said Kwan. 'And to keep up the smokescreen, singers or DJs who "accidentally" mention his supposed indiscretions are severely punished. This has three functions: firstly, it makes the deception more convincing; secondly, it creates the impression that he's impulsive and vicious; and thirdly, it increases the respect his thugs have for him. But much stronger than sexual lust is his thirst for power. This fellow is a seasoned gambler, and it's impossible to tell whether he actually has a good hand or is just bluffing.'

'You mean Boss Chor has never actually cared whether he or his stars have their reputations damaged?'

'Correct. These distraction tactics have prevented the police getting any dirt on him, making it possible for his Triad leadership to be an open secret – they couldn't arrest him without evidence – but they've also created the impression that even the law is on his side and the police are helpless against him. And as long as the police hesitated to bring him in, he'd find it easier to control his gang, whilst keeping himself separate from his illegal activities. Only today, when some newly appointed "hard-boiled detective" dared to beard him without any evidence whatsoever, was this legend finally shattered.'

Lok didn't react, uncertain whether his mentor was praising or making fun of him.

'One of the reasons Benny Lau was transferred to West Kowloon Crime was so he could eliminate Boss Chor,' Kwan continued. 'But he couldn't find a single point of attack. Then last year he began to suspect that Starry Night's new singer, Candy Ton, was the daughter of a deceased informant. He investigated and discovered she was Ton Hei-chi's child. This might have been a coincidence, but he was afraid Candy was trying to get close to Boss Chor for some reason – and he was right. After all those informants died mysteriously, he was naturally worried about Candy's safety.'

'When Superintendent Lau found me, I pretended he had the wrong person,' added Candy. 'I wasn't about to let anyone interfere with my plan, and anyway I thought the police were all untrustworthy.'

'So Benny asked me for help.' Superintendent Kwan sipped his tea.

'Asked you for help? So were you the commanding officer of this op?'

'What commanding officer? I'm just a consultant,' beamed Kwan. 'But as a consultant, I could do exactly what I wanted, including some tricks you guys would never dare to pull. To start with, I looked up Candy Ton and told her she was wasting her energy. Even if she did manage to get close to Chor, he'd never trust her. Boss Chor might not pay much attention to other people's family relationships, but if you went too far, even he would start to take notice.'

Lok realized that when his mentor had told him before about Chor being indifferent to families, he'd been referring to Candy rather than Eric Yeung.

'Superintendent Kwan told me that as long as I played along, we'd expose Boss Chor once and for all.' Candy's expression was fierce, far more so than you'd have expected from a seven-teen-year-old. 'Not only would I be part of the scheme, he'd give me a lead role. So I really would be able to take revenge with my own hands.'

Lok looked at his mentor, who was smiling faintly. Kwan was a sweet talker, and could see right into the human heart – he always hit on your vulnerable point. Candy Ton wanted vengeance, and she wanted to bring it about through her own efforts, so this was what he offered her, in order to complete Benny Lau's task.

'I said from the start that as long as we could get Yam Tak-ngok into the witness box, Chor's defences would collapse, so that became the point of this exercise,' Kwan went on. 'Chi-ang Fu was the first condition for subduing Yam Tak-ngok; once he was in police custody, Yam would know his days of freedom were numbered. Then we'd have to find a method of forcing Yam to abandon his underworld code of honour, and so our next step was Operation Viper.'

'But Operation Viper failed,' protested Lok.

'It was designed to fail.'

'Designed to fail?' Lok stared at him. 'You're saying that Kow-loon West mobilized more than two hundred people, and knew all along that the op would fail?'

'They mobilized, all right, but only Benny and I knew what would happen.' Kwan's lips curled up on one side. 'Why do you think Fat Dragon was able to escape? Because someone leaked the plan – but no one would expect the commanding officer to do that.'

Lok was on the brink of jumping up to yell at his mentor. After all, he was the one who'd had to sit through that inquiry, endur-ing the scathing comments of his senior colleagues. But then he remembered that Benedict Lau had not said anything neg-ative, and perhaps that ought to have told him something was up. 'Why design an operation to fail?'

'We had to put on a show for Yam. All the underworld bosses

know we barge in every now and then for a "clean sweep", as inevitable as the seasons changing. If such a large-scale drug bust didn't affect Chor at all, Yam would start to think his rival was untouchable. And Chor wouldn't suspect anything – his underlings would just take all the credit.' Kwan glanced at Candy. 'While you were preparing for this failed mission, I gave Ms Ton a few tasks.'

'What tasks?'

'First, to let slip to the media that she was being poached by a Japanese company,' said Kwan. 'There was no such company, but the journalists wouldn't care. We just needed the word to spread. And secondly, we needed Candy to make an enemy of Eric Yeung.'

Lok saw the connection. 'To increase the friction between Chor and Yam?'

'Correct. We knew of the relationship between Eric Yeung and Yam Tak-ngok, but Yeung wasn't involved with the Triads, and Yam was never our primary target, so we didn't make anything of it. But with this plan, he was a good catalyst. I told Candy to flirt with him at a party, and then turn on him when he tried to take things further. Boss Chor often used insults to his clients as excuses to deal with someone, so I beat him at his own game. Once he made a move, I had my connection with Yam Tak-ngok.'

'But how did you ensure the incident would reach Chor's ears?'

'Sonny, do you think the *Eight-Day Week* reporter just happened to be there? It was a private party, and naturally someone needed to bring her in.' Kwan glanced again at Candy, and Lok finally understood that she'd scripted the whole scene. He was impressed.

'But in the end, even I got fooled by Superintendent Kwan,' grimaced Candy.

'Fooled?'

'He told me that Eric getting beaten up would create a grudge between Yam and Chor. But I didn't know that was just the first step. No one told me I'd have to die.'

Lok looked at the two people before him, confused.

'You have to lie to your own people first, before you can deceive outsiders,' shrugged Kwan. 'Even after his son was assaulted, Yam wouldn't abandon his golden rule of non-betrayal. After so many years as a Triad leader, he has a good sense of what really matters. No, Eric Yeung getting beaten up was just a prelude – to Candy Ton's death.'

'So, sifu, was it you who sent those men after Candy?'

'You could call them associates. Just like young Miss Koo, they're the cream of certain shady professions. Of course, their lips are sealed. They'd never let slip a word to either the police or the other side.'

'That evening, Superintendent Kwan told me to go alone to Jordan Road and walk in the direction of Lin Cheung Road. I had no idea why,' Candy explained to Sonny. 'After I'd been walking for half an hour, those four masked men charged towards me. I thought Boss Chor had learned about my plan, or that Eric Yeung's dad was settling accounts. I ran for my life, towards the bridge, and there was Superintendent Kwan. As soon as he saw me, he said, "Well done," and pulled me to safety at the other end of the bridge. He only told me why later on, and that was the first I learned of this part of the plan.'

'Sir, does this mean the video was all faked?'

'That depends on your definition of "fake",' smiled Kwan. 'Of course Candy didn't actually get murdered – the "corpse" below the bridge was someone else. We knew what Candy was wearing, and got one of my female "associates" to dress like her. When the cameraman came to the dead end, our fake Candy was lying there covered in fake blood. That's also why there was no soundtrack – no thud of a body hitting the road. But that little pause in the picture would make people imagine there'd been one.'

'And the man Candy punched ...' Lok suddenly remembered.

'That was a surprise to us too. His nose was bruised for a

week,' chuckled Kwan. 'But that was great, it made the film even more believable.'

'Sir, wasn't this much too risky? What if a passer-by had seen you?'

'Sonny, you've got it the wrong way round. It was because there were no witnesses that we went ahead with the plan. Besides, your team weren't even able to figure out how Candy got to the scene from her apartment, were you?'

'Did you drive her there, sifu? Wait, you said you only saw her on the bridge.'

'I got a taxi to Jordan Road, then walked to the scene,' Candy cut in.

'But when the news of this "murder" was everywhere, why didn't the cab driver step forward?'

'Haven't you guessed yet, Sonny? You got the video on the 22nd, but that doesn't mean it was filmed the night before. In fact, we did it just two days after Eric Yeung got beaten up – that is, on the 18th. Remember, a CD only tells you when it was burned, not when the actual recording was made.'

'What?' Lok looked at his mentor, baffled.

'Candy's "murder" took place on the 18th, but no one knew about it. After I'd filled her in about the plan, she went back to her regular life on the 19th. Then on the 21st, she made sure to wear the same clothes she'd worn three nights before, and went "missing" after her agent drove her home. No cab-driver witness to deal with. In the small hours of the 22nd, we did two simple things: we sprayed blood where the "corpse" lay in the video, then hosed it away, and we dropped Candy's handbag into the hole by the side of the road. That just took a couple of minutes – much less stressful than that whole production on the 18th.'

Lok laughed silently. So Candy was no victim, but a conspirator. The crime scene and sequence of events had been doctored beyond recognition. And he had to laugh again when he remembered what his mentor said to him in the car: 'Sonny, you won't solve the Candy Ton case, because your opponent is too wicked.'

'And I suppose on the morning of the 22nd, you were the one who slipped the CD into the police station?' Lok grumbled.

'No, that was Benny. And that was his handwriting on the envelope.'

Lok had thought nothing his mentor said would ever shock him again, but he was astonished to hear the commander would do such a thing.

'And the body we found in Castle Peak Bay?'

'It was actually one of the prostitutes from the sex-trafficking case I was telling you about.'

'But the fingerprints...'

'A little switcheroo.' Kwan spread his hands wide. 'You told me the pathologist had given you the fingerprints, so I went straight to the Identification Bureau and swapped Candy's prints for the ones you'd handed in. You know how easy it is for me to do that sort of thing.'

Lok smacked his forehead.

'I was going to find some other way to cook up a body, then one came along ready for use. No one would notice anything as long as I falsified the records after the body was cremated. After all, we're talking about a nameless corpse, someone who entered the territory with false documents. It'll probably take us several years to uncover her real identity.'

'All right, so now I understand the whole business of Candy's "murder". But I'm still not sure what the point of all this was?'

'To get you to step forward.'

'Me?'

'Yes. In this whole operation, you and Candy are the two main figures.' Kwan pointed at Lok. 'And there's no one better suited than you for this role.'

'What role?'

'A stubborn, hot-blooded man who doesn't cave in to shows of strength on his way to solving a case. A hard-boiled detective.'

Lok remained confused.

'Everyone assumed Candy's murder was Yam Tak-ngok's

revenge for the attack on his son, but Yam himself would know very well he wasn't the culprit. We needed a police officer to point out that Boss Chor must be the real murderer. Even if he wasn't completely convincing, that'd be enough to make Yam suspicious. The Japanese company supposedly poaching her, the attackers coming armed with cleavers, Chor's calm reaction to the news – all this was to make you believe in Chor's guilt. You couldn't obtain the evidence you needed because it never existed – Chor never sent anyone after Candy Ton. Knowing he was innocent, he didn't need to take any action – he could just sit back and wait for you to humiliate yourself. But I used the point to make Yam believe that Chor wouldn't even flinch from murdering an innocent teenage girl. As soon as Uncle Ngok hears of the accusations you flung at Chor today, he'll start to wonder whether he's been wrong about his code of honour. And if he believes your version of events, he'll worry about what he might suffer under Boss Chor, and whether Eric Yeung will be implicated in the future. In the Prisoner's Dilemma, if someone believes he might be betrayed, he'll choose to betray the other person first.'

'But why did I have to do this? Just because you're my mentor?' said Lok, after a long silence.

'No, because you have two particular characteristics – you're willing to step up to the plate, and you have excellent deductive abilities. The fewer people who knew about the real plan, the better – that was the only way to keep it a secret from two old hands like Boss Chor and Yam Tak-ngok. Only someone with your skills would deduce the "truth" about Chor's guilt from the faint clues I laid. And only someone with your courage would stand up to him. It's not easy to find someone like that. The police force today is full of timid fellows who only care about their careers. God knows what'll happen when they're in charge, whether all the hard work my generation put in will be wiped away. When that time comes, brave idiots like you will be in for a lot of trouble...'

Once again, Lok had no idea if he was being praised or made fun of.

'Uncle Ngok will have heard about your little chat with Boss Chor by tonight,' grinned Kwan. 'Tomorrow he'll hear that Chor Hon-keung wasn't arrested after all, and he'll think that once again Chor has pulled some strings to get off the hook. When that happens, if someone glib enough explains what's in it for him, he'll turn into the prisoner who betrays his fellow.'

Lok was about to ask who this glib fellow might be, when he realized it would surely be his mentor himself.

'Then earlier, when I brought Chor to the police station, he must have thought...'

'He must have thought you were about to frame him – to use fake evidence to force him to confess,' Kwan finished his protégé's sentence. 'He must have thought it was someone from Hing-chung-wo who killed Candy, or else some other gang who had a grievance against him. He might even have wondered if it was some of his own men acting independently, for the reason you suggested – to give Hung-yi an excuse to go after Hing-chung-wo – or even to land him in trouble. He knows he's innocent, but he'll have started wondering if he's been deceived by his lieutenants. Clever Boss Chor wouldn't say any of this out loud, but he'll go back and quietly investigate them one by one. Still, as I said, I think he'll see through your bluff, and you won't get a rise out of him in the next few days.'

Lok shook his head with a grimace. He'd never have thought even his own deductions were part of his mentor's plan. In front of this man, he appeared no more than a high-school student trying to show off.

He suddenly remembered the other thing that was puzzling him. 'Right, so why has Candy Ton turned into Chiang Fu's daughter?'

'Candy had two choices after her "attack" – she could let everyone think she'd been dragged away by the thugs, only to be miraculously rescued after Boss Chor had gone down for trafficking drugs and conspiring to kill informants; or she could do what she's doing now, which is to vanish completely.'

'Yes, that's what I chose,' said Candy. 'I don't miss my old self – I was willing to give everything up, for the sake of revenge. And I never liked the entertainment world.'

'Of course, the fact that Candy's death was faked won't appear in the report, so we might as well let her start life again with a new identity.' Superintendent Kwan shook his head admiringly. 'Chiang Fu was instrumental in delivering Uncle Ngok to us, and he in turn is going to finger Boss Chor. We had no choice but to take the entire Chiang family into Witness Protection, so I slipped Candy's information in with theirs. There was never such a person as Chiang Li-ni. Chiang Fu doesn't know anything about this either. And so I've been able to get Candy a new legal identity as Honey Kong. Two layers of false identity should be enough to make Candy Ton disappear from the face of the earth.'

'Sifu, there's still one thing I don't understand,' said Lok, brow wrinkled. 'Was it also you who released the video on the internet?'

'Of course. If the news hadn't gone viral, the plan couldn't have gone ahead. Images are far more powerful than words – Uncle Ngok would have to see it for himself.'

'Why give me the CD a day before that?'

'Sonny, you're my protégé,' said Kwan tenderly.

Inspector Lok understood. His mentor could easily have put the video out in the world right away, but that would have left the Crime Unit dealing with media inquiries, investigating and gathering evidence, all at the same time. By giving him the CD ahead of time, Kwan had bought them a day's head start – a breathing space.

'Sifu, I give up – you've had me in the palm of your hand all along,' sighed Lok. Then he smiled. 'Ah, and where did you find a hacker good enough to post the video from Switzerland and Mexico?'

Kwan winked at the closed door behind him. 'Just don't ask how she made the money which bought this Italian sofa your bum is resting on.'

*

'Sifu, what should I do now?' Kwan and Lok were back in the car, heading to the station.

'Your team should keep a close watch on Boss Chor's gang – just continue with your plan,' said Kwan from the passenger seat. 'I'll look up Uncle Ngok tomorrow. I've got it all prepared. Just wait and see what a chef like me makes out of these ingredients.'

'But sir, didn't you have any other way of getting Yam Tak-ngok to do what you wanted? Why such an elaborate scheme? Candy Ton's murder will wind up as an unsolved case, which makes the police look bad.' And me as well, he added silently.

'Because I wanted to get Candy away from Boss Chor as quickly as possible,' replied Kwan. 'Every day she spent in Starry Night put her in more danger of being found out. Fortunately, Chor didn't notice Benny had contacted her, but if her father's identity had come to light, it's a sure thing he wouldn't have let her off. Never mind that she was his highest-earning star, never mind that she's just seventeen – he'd snuff her out regardless. As well as bringing Boss Chor to justice, this was also a rescue mission. The police force exists to protect citizens, and even if she was willing to sacrifice her life, I wasn't going to stand by and see a teenage girl go to her death.'

Lok felt a sense of release at this response. His mentor was happy to use all kinds of underhand tactics to get to his goal, but he valued every single human life.

Events played out exactly as Kwan Chun-dok said they would. Two days later, Yam Tak-ngok voluntarily provided the police with vast quantities of information about Hung-yi Union, including evidence of Boss Chor's drug dealing. In order to secure immunity, Chor's foot soldiers then lined up to give away their boss. There wasn't enough evidence to prosecute them all, but the police had more than a good haul. Apart from Boss Chor, several of the Hung-yi top brass were arrested, including Fat Dragon, the dealer who had evaded Inspector Lok before.

Candy Ton's case was suspended because of insufficient evidence, but public opinion was that Boss Chor must have been the mastermind. Lok knew Chor was innocent, but was happy with this result. *He's escaped punishment for many lives he did take, so let him have the blame for one he didn't*, he thought.

Three months later, Lok and his mentor went back to Miss Koo's apartment to see Candy Ton. As Lok pressed the doorbell, Kwan explained that the front door was fitted with a camera, and his face would have appeared on her screen right away. Lok wondered if her room was fitted with a self-destruct mechanism – something to wipe her computers at the touch of a button.

'You're... Candy Ton?' Lok could barely recognize her, with her hair cut short and dyed brown.

'I'm Honey Kong, Inspector,' she corrected him.

'Ah, yes, Honey Kong, Honey Kong...' he repeated.

'Just call him Sonny, Honey. Honey and Sonny – a perfect pair,' teased Kwan.

'At least call me Brother. If I were a few years older, I could be your fath—' He stuttered to a halt.

'It's fine. I'm happy that Daddy's case has been reopened – and it's all thanks to you. Brother Sonny, you don't need to worry.'

'What are your plans?' asked Lok.

'I'm just waiting for the moment when Boss Chor gets found guilty. After that, I'll think of something. Newton's very good to me – she's letting me stay here for free. I help with the housework, and sometimes step in as her assistant.'

'Newton?'

'Miss Koo. "Newton" is her handle on the net. Pretty cool, don't you think?' interjected Kwan.

Lok was about to advise Candy not to get too close to Miss Koo, because after all hackers operated outside the law – but then thought she might be eavesdropping on them that very minute, and bit his tongue.

'There's some sort of infectious disease spreading, and the government's urged everyone to stay home. This virus – I think it's called SARS – seems to be spreading quite fast, especially in Kowloon, and people are afraid to go out. I guess the Hong Kong economy will be tanking for a while. But let's take the risk and go to a restaurant for dinner. Honey, you don't get to leave the house very often, do you?'

Candy shook her head delightedly. Sonny realized the way she was now, open and frank, was the real Candy Ton.

'Isn't there a danger someone will recognize her?' Lok looked her up and down. Her hair had changed, she was wearing glasses and no make-up, and a decidedly unglamorous cardigan and sweat pants. It seemed unlikely anyone would notice her, but still he worried.

'Just hide behind this.' Kwan plucked the baseball cap from his own head and popped it onto hers. She pulled the brim down a little and smiled bashfully from underneath.

At the gate, as Candy kicked off her house slippers and pulled on sneakers without bothering to put socks on first, Lok noticed something odd. 'Honey, why have you only painted three of your toenails? And why black?'

'After Daddy's case was reopened, it came out that apart from the five men who took him away, the bar owner and Boss Chor, two dealers and a bar worker were also involved,' she said. 'Only Boss Chor and the dealers have been arrested so far. The other seven men are still on the loose. I've painted my toenails black to remind myself of unfinished business. As each killer is brought to justice, I'll paint another nail...'

Lok could see in her eyes that this battle for revenge was only just beginning. He hoped he'd be able to catch the remaining culprits before too long, to finally release Candy from this war. After all, the people battling evildoers should be the police, not victims' families.

He wanted to promise Candy he'd do this for her, but said nothing in the end. Because Inspector Lok knew that justice consists of actions, not words.

III

THE LONGEST DAY:

1997

1

To most Hongkongers, 6 June 1997 was perfectly ordinary. Two days previously, there'd been heavy rainstorms and some localized flooding, but things were back to normal now. The weather was sultry as always – even though the sky had been hazy since morning, with occasional showers, and the temperature showed no sign of dropping. Fire broke out in a West Point apartment block in the small hours, and a truck full of chemicals overturned during the morning rush hour, creating a serious traffic jam on Des Voeux Road in Central, but for most people, 6 June was just a normal Friday.

For Kwan Chun-dok, though, it was anything but normal. This was his last day of service.

He'd been on the police force for thirty-two years, and now, aged fifty, Senior Superintendent Kwan was preparing for a glorious retirement. His time actually ran out in mid-July, but he'd accumulated a month of leave which, according to police regulations, he'd have to take before departing. Just as well – if he were still on duty come July, the force would have to give him a whole new appointment letter and uniform badge. After the handover on 1 July 1997, the Royal Hong Kong Police Force would become simply the Hong Kong Police Force, the St Edward's Crown on its crest replaced with a purple bauhinia flower. It wasn't that Kwan was particularly attached to the word 'Royal', it just seemed a waste to go to all that trouble for something he'd use for less than a month.

Kwan Chun-dok had been working at the Criminal Intelligence Bureau for the past eight years as Commander of Division B, which was in charge of analysing intelligence materials such as surveillance videos and wiretap recordings. His team members were at less physical risk than other members of the force, for example their colleagues in Division D, tailing suspects who might be armed and violent, or Division A, who went on stakeouts and handled informants whose loyalties were always in question, or even thenewly-established 'Hit Team', which carried out arrests. Yet the psychological pressure on them was higher, because they were aware that every single result of their analysis could be responsible for the success or failure of an entire operation. They'd all seen examples of intelligence going wrong – underestimate criminals' firepower, and cops would lose their lives as a result. The slightest oversight, even of a seemingly insignificant detail, could have tragic consequences. Frontline officers could adapt to a situation and make decisions in the heat of the moment, but Division B had to make all its choices ahead of time, and afterwards could only reflect on its errors – which it would never have the opportunity to correct.

Kwan Chun-dok both loved and hated his position. This unit had given him a chance to explore all his strengths. At the heart of Police Intelligence, he had a finger on the pulse of every case in Hong Kong. His insight helped other departments succeed and saved frontline lives. Still, Kwan didn't like that he had to rely on others passing intel to him. Before this, he'd been with regional Criminal Investigation Departments and Crime Units where he could operate on his own, searching for clues at the scene, getting first-hand testimony and evidence. During his eight years in Intelligence, he'd sometimes had doubts about the interview transcripts handed in by other departments. Why hadn't the officer pursued a particular line of questioning? Why hadn't they investigated this or that corner?

'Am I better suited to being at the scene?' he wondered from time to time. But he knew this was wishful thinking – especially after the age of forty-five, when his body wasn't as nimble as it used to be. Being on the front line meant confronting criminals directly, and he was very aware he no longer had the energy for that. It was better that he put his brain power to use instead.

Besides, he was too high-ranking to be allowed anywhere near the front line. Only inspectors and junior police officers actually carried out operations. Anyone with a gazetted rank – from superintendent up to commissioner – would instead be in charge of planning, deployment and so on. Kwan knew he'd taken on too much in Division B, and in recent years had tried his best to delegate to his team, only intervening at key moments to point out gaps in their analysis. To his eyes, most clues were fairly obvious, but his subordinates always gaped at him until he explained his reasons – or confirmed his 'conjectures' after the event – when they'd happily agree with his logic.

This was another reason why Kwan Chun-dok was retiring at the age of fifty. He could have stayed on for another five years, till compulsory retirement age, but he knew remaining in Intelligence would hinder the growth of his subordinates. Intelligence was at the core of the force, and if Division B couldn't function without him, they'd endanger the entire police body.

'... and that was the report from customs.' It was half past nine in the morning, and Chief Inspector Alexander Choi of Division B Team 1 was updating Superintendent Kwan in his office. Division B was split into four teams, each with an inspector at its head, and Kwan allocating their duties. Team 2 had the day off, Team 3 was assisting the Commercial Crime Bureau on a case of insider trading, and Team 4 was working with the Organized Crime and Triad Bureau on an undercover operation to stop West Kowloon secret societies from infiltrating schools. Team 1 had just concluded an op two days previously, breaking a smuggling ring together with the Customs and Excise Department.

'Good.' Kwan nodded, satisfied. Alex Choi was in line to take over when he retired, an appointment Kwan was pleased about – Choi was methodical in his management of personnel, and had a warm relationship with his counterparts in other departments.

'Team 1 is following up on reports that two Big Circle Men entered the territory illegally four days ago.' This was a common phrase in Hong Kong meaning outlaws from Mainland China. Choi handed over a folder containing two blurry photographs of the Big Circle Men in question. 'Informants indicated they might have concealed firearms, and might be planning to strike during the Handover, when we will be at our busiest. Background reports show both men have prior convictions for armed robbery, and their target is likely to be a jewellery or watch shop. Initial investigations have ruled out the possibility of terrorism.'

'That's an unusually small number of people,' commented Kwan.

'Yes, we suspect someone else is masterminding, or else that local organizations are involved, and these two are just mercenaries for hire. They probably don't know we're watching them.'

'Do we have a location for them?'

'Yes, they're at Chai Wan, probably the industrial area near the cargo docks.'

'Nothing more precise?'

'Not yet. There are too many empty buildings around there, and ownership is a big mess. Looking into every suspicious venue will take some time.'

Stroking his chin, Kwan said, 'Move quickly. I'm afraid they won't wait till the end of the month.'

'You reckon they'll do something in the next couple of weeks? But tourist season doesn't hit its peak till July, and shops will be holding much more cash then—'

'But I can't ignore that there are only two of them,' Kwan cut in. 'If one of them's the mastermind, he wouldn't have brought just one other person to Hong Kong with him. He'd need a driver and two more accomplices, at the very least. Mainland gang leaders never arrive here without a full team – they don't recruit locally. Whereas if they're hired muscle, then the mastermind must be a Hongkonger – but he wouldn't have summoned them unless the plans were all laid and ready. Something must be imminent.'

'Ah, that makes sense,' replied Inspector Choi. 'Let me talk to Division D – I'll get them to send a dog team to Wan Chai.'

'Are there any other open cases?'

'No... Oh wait, there's still the "acid bomb" case from before, but we haven't had any new leads, and I'm afraid we'll have to wait for them to strike again,' Choi sighed.

'True. This sort of case is the hardest to deal with.'

Half a year previously, there'd been an acid attack at Tung Choi Street in Mong Kok, a market street with many open-air stalls selling clothes, jewellery and toiletries. Also known as Ladies' Alley, it was a famous tourist destination. On either side of the road stood old-fashioned buildings, making it one of Hong Kong's most characteristic streets. These buildings lacked security features – quite a few of them didn't even have a main gate, so anyone was free to walk in and out. A criminal took advantage of this, entering one of these five- or six-storey buildings around nine o'clock at night, opening a bottle of drain cleaner and flinging the concentrated sodium hydroxide down onto the street. Weekend evenings were when the market was at its busiest, and several stall owners and shoppers suffered chemical burns from the corrosive liquid. Another Saturday night two months later, a similar incident happened at the other end of the market, when two bottles of the same brand of drain cleaner fell from the sky. Even more people were hurt this time, some almost blinded after direct hits to the head.

The West Kowloon Regional Crime Unit started investigating, but were completely unable to identify any suspects. The rooftops of the neighbouring buildings were all connected, so the culprit could easily have escaped from the scene of the crime.

After the first incident, the police urged residents to increase security, but it was unclear who would be responsible for this in shared buildings, and in any case both landlords and tenants reckoned there was no point – it had already happened; why mend a fence after the sheep had escaped? And then came the second case.

West Kowloon Regional Intelligence asked the CIB to go through surveillance footage from hundreds of local shops, plus ten roadside cameras, looking for anyone suspicious. After sifting through and cross-referencing huge amounts of material from the time of both events, they identified a plump man about five foot two, his face hidden beneath a black baseball cap. The police put out a bulletin on him – as a witness, not a suspect – but nothing turned up.

Fortunately, there'd been no further incidents in the four months since then. Perhaps black baseball cap was their guy, and he'd given up because he realized they were onto him. Or perhaps the business owners had finally been willing to fork out for proper gates and security guards. In any case, no more innocent people were hurt on Tung Choi Street.

The only problem was, their investigation was now stalled.

'Let's focus our energies on the Big Circle case, then.' Kwan closed the folder.

'Yes, Commander.' Alex Choi stood, then changing his tone, added, 'This is probably the last time I'll be reporting to you?'

'That's right. Next week you'll be in my place, listening to someone else's report.'

'Commander, we're all very grateful for your leadership these last few years. We've learned so much.' Chief Inspector Choi opened the door as he spoke, motioning to whoever was outside. 'We got this to show our appreciation.'

Kwan Chun-dok hadn't expected the whole of Team 1 to be standing outside, one of them bearing a cake iced with 'Happy Retirement!' They walked in, all smiles, everyone clapping. The man with the cake was Sonny Lok, who'd only joined Division B at the start of the year. Kwan often chose him for tasks, as if he were his personal assistant, and so his colleagues had given him the job of 'cake ambassador'.

'You shouldn't have!' smiled Kwan. 'We've already arranged to go out for a meal next week. Why the cake as well?'

'Don't worry, Commander. Everyone will have a share – not one speck of buttercream will go to waste.' Choi was well aware of his superior's frugal nature, and had made sure not to get too large a cake. 'It's your last day here, and we couldn't let you go without marking the occasion.'

'Well, thank you all. It's only just after ten, are you hungry for cake?'

'I skipped breakfast today,' someone yelled.

'Everyone's busy in the afternoon – it was hard to get the whole team together,' Choi explained.

'Happy retirement, Commander!'

'Don't forget to come visit us!'

'Quick, get a knife and cut Commander a slice.'

'Hey, what's going on here?'

At those words, everyone froze except Kwan Chun-dok. Standing behind the crowd was Chief Superintendent Keith Tso, his suit perfectly pressed, not a hair out of place, his face stern. Chief Superintendent Tso, four years Kwan's senior, was the Director of CIB. He hardly ever smiled, and his brow was creased for roughly twenty-three hours of every day. Everyone in the bureau treated him with fear and respect. Choi and his team hadn't expected their ultimate superior to suddenly show up in Division B's office, and they hastily stood to attention. Sonny Lok was in the most awkward position, momentarily unable to find anywhere to put the cake down, yet frantic to salute the Chief Superintendent.

'Were you looking for me, sir?' Kwan said calmly, standing. 'My team got a cake to celebrate my retirement.'

'Ah. Shall I come back a little later?'

'No, no,' said Chief Inspector Choi quickly. 'We'll leave you two to talk.'

Chief Superintendent Tso nodded as if nothing could be more

natural, and Team 1 hurried out of the office, the last person carefully shutting the door without a sound.

After they'd all gone, Kwan chuckled, 'Keith, you gave them such a fright.'

'Only because they're cowards,' shrugged Tso, settling himself into a chair. He had known Kwan Chun-dok for many years, and he'd never put on airs around an old friend – not even if he was that old friend's superior.

'Is it anything urgent?' Every CIB division commander and deputy commander had a weekly meeting, but these took place in the conference room. Keith Tso very seldom put in a personal appearance in the Division B office.

'You're leaving today, of course I had to come by.' Tso pulled a small box from his pocket. Opening it, Kwan found a silvery-white fountain pen. 'Old farts like us still prefer the traditional ways, even though reports all have to be on the computer these days.'

'Ah... thank you,' Kwan said, although he was happy with any pen as long as it could write, and an exquisite instrument like this felt like a waste to him. 'To be honest, I don't know how often I'll need to pick up a pen after I've retired. Or are you hinting I should write my memoirs?'

'Apart from this little memento, I'm also here to ask about your plans.' Chief Superintendent Tso leaned forward, looking straight into Kwan's eyes.

'Keith, you're wasting your breath. You know I've made up my mind.' Kwan shook his head, smiling.

'Are you sure I can't persuade you? Whether we're going by track record, ability or human connections, you're the best in the department. I'm leaving next year, and the CIB won't be left with any top-notch commanders. Ah-dok, you're still young. Recontract and take my seat for the next five years. Number One himself will be overjoyed.' The Police Commissioner was often known as 'Number One', as the license plates of his official car bore no other number.

After retiring and starting to draw their pension, Hong Kong police officers have the option of coming back to the force on a contractual basis, with a limit of four terms of two-and-a-half years each, after which they'd get a cash bonus. Even so, this tended not to happen for anyone over the age of 55, with an exception made for high-ranking individuals, such as gazetted officers, because their experience was irreplaceable.

Kwan knew very well that Chief Superintendent Tso would be retiring in a year's time. Tso's family had already migrated to the UK, like many Hongkongers who were wary of what would happen after the handover of sovereignty, but he had chosen to stay behind and continue to serve in the force. Although the British government had decided against giving blanket permission for Hong Kong citizens to emigrate in their millions, they had allowed eligible public servants to apply for residency; the existence of this escape route meant they were more likely to remain in Hong Kong, preventing a mass exodus from the civil service. Meanwhile, their families made new homes in the UK or other Commonwealth countries, while their children inevitably chose to go to university abroad, and then never returned.

'No thanks, let someone else have a shot at it,' said Kwan. 'Benny's very suitable for the job, and he's younger than me. Even if I came back for five years, at the end of that we'd be left with the same problem of succession. Why not nip that in the bud by letting younger folk learn on the job?'

'Benny isn't bad, but he's too led by his emotions.' Benedict Lau was the Commander of Division A. 'Ah Dok, you know very well that the head of CIB needs a crystal-clear mind, as well as eyes and ears in all directions. Benny's better suited to regional work.'

'Keith, stop trying. I've only ever enjoyed deduction and analysis, and you're asking me to go into planning. There's no way I'd be able to put up with it. Don't you know this? It was your idea for me to stay in charge of my division after I was promoted.'

In Intelligence, most division leaders were regular superintendents, with a senior superintendent serving as deputy director.

After Kwan rose in rank to senior superintendent some years previously, he had remained at the head of his division – a special arrangement Tso had made after weighing up his strengths.

'Fine, I give up.' Keith Tso's brow settled into its habitual furrows. 'Can I at least tell you about our Plan B?'

'What Plan B?'

'You recontract for a new post, but don't take my chair.'

'Then what am I meant to say to Alex? He's all set to take over my job.'

'No, you won't be staying where you are either. I've talked it over with Commissioner Hung – we'd keep you on as a special consultant. Officially under Intelligence, but you'd be free to step into any case you like – naturally, only where the department's asked for help. We wouldn't want to interfere where we're not wanted, it would be bad for morale.'

'Oh?' Superintendent Kwan's deductive abilities were extraordinary, but he hadn't expected his superiors would make such an unusual proposal to him. The man Tso had mentioned was Senior Assistant Commissioner Daniel Hung, Director of the Crime and Security Department, which the other bureaus came under. Daniel was only forty-one, but being a university graduate, had been on the inside track from the moment he joined the force – a very different breed from Keith Tso or Kwan Chun-dok, who'd started as lowly constables and worked their way up.

'This was the best plan I could come up with. I'm not going to force you, but have a think about it. After July, who knows what new challenges we'll face – your experience will certainly come in handy.'

Kwan was silent for a while. This was an attractive proposition. He'd be able to return to frontline investigation without worrying about the burden of his ageing body – probably the best possible compromise. Still, Kwan was a meticulous thinker in life as in his job, and wasn't going to give an answer until he'd considered every angle.

'Let me turn it over in my mind,' he said. 'When do you need an answer?'

'Before the middle of July.' Tso stood. 'You're not officially retiring till then, anyway. Just let me know.'

Kwan walked him to the door. Tso added, 'Ah Dok, whether or not you agree to this, I'm going to wish you a happy retirement now. In this line of work, making it safely to pension age is something to be celebrated.'

'Right you are, Keith. Thanks.' Kwan shook his hand, and held the door open for him.

Outside, the officers of Division B were busy at their desks, some speaking on the phone, their faces grim, others leafing through documents. Kwan expected them to drop the act as soon as Chief Superintendent Tso was out of sight, but they carried on, and he realized this tense atmosphere wasn't just put on for Tso's benefit.

'Commander, something's come in.' Inspector Choi hastily filled him in. 'Hong Kong Island Regional called – another acid attack. Their Crime Unit is looking into it. To think we were just saying we couldn't proceed without more evidence, and now this.'

'Hong Kong Island?' Kwan frowned. 'Not Mong Kok?'

'In our neighbourhood this time – Graham Street Market in Central. For now we don't know whether this is the Mong Kok perp or a copycat – we've sent someone for details.'

'Good, let me know if there are any updates. If we find the same suspect, we'll have to inform Kowloon West.' Kwan patted Choi on the shoulder. Whatever happened next with this case, Choi would be in charge – Kwan was leaving tomorrow, and wouldn't be giving any more orders. Yet even as he went through his final batch of op reports, Kwan kept an eye on Team 1. In the rise and fall of their voices as they spoke on the phone or chatted amongst themselves, he gleaned the first bits of info about the case – that at 10.05 a.m. four containers of drain cleaner had been flung from the roof of an old building, hitting the market stalls on Graham and Wellington Streets. Graham Street was the oldest open-air market in Hong Kong's history, selling fresh food as well as other items, and people who lived nearby often went there for their daily needs, alongside the tourists. Thirty-two people were so far known to have been injured, three of them seriously – hit in the face or head by the corrosive liquid.

Half an hour later, Alex Choi rapped urgently on Kwan's door.

'What's up? Did one of the casualties die?' asked Kwan.

'No, no, Commander, this report's much worse – a convict has managed to escape while being treated at the hospital.'

'Where? Queen Mary?' This was where Stanley Prison sent its convicts when necessary, a public hospital in Pok Fu Lam on Hong Kong Island.

'Yes, yes, Queen Mary,' stammered Choi. 'But the problem isn't where, it's who – the escaped prisoner is Shek Boon-tim.'

Kwan Chun-dok froze at this name. Eight years previously, on his very first day in the CIB, he'd been roped into an operation against the Shek brothers, Boon-tim and Boon-sing, who'd occupied the first and second places on the Most Wanted list that year. Boon-tim, the older man, was cunning and knowledge-able, while Boon-sing would kill a person without blinking. The younger brother died in a gunfight during that operation. Boon-tim got away – until the police uncovered his hiding place a month later, and took him into custody. And the person who'd managed to piece together the fragments of evidence to make that arrest was Kwan Chun-dok himself.

2

AN HOUR AFTER Choi's report of Shek Boon-tim's escape, Division B felt like they'd been on a rollercoaster ride, dizzy from the ups and downs.

To start with, they only heard of the incident by chance. Alex Choi had dispatched an officer to the Command and Control Centre to get incident reports on the latest acid attack. That officer happened to arrive as someone from Correctional Services was requesting urgent help because Shek Boon-tim had just fled from the hospital. The Control Centre's director immediately put out a call for all Emergency Units, mounted police and patrols to assist.

According to the initial report, Shek Boon-tim ran from Queen Mary Hospital and jumped into a white Honda Civic parked close by. As soon as he was in the back seat, the car zoomed off, crashing through the flimsy railings and speeding northwards along Pok Fu Lam Road. Because of disruption resulting from the fire in West Point that morning and the traffic accident in Central, patrol cars weren't able to intercept it.

When Alex Choi got that initial information, which he passed on to Kwan at eleven o'clock, that was the state of play. What he didn't know was at that very moment, an Emergency Unit car had spotted the target vehicle at West Mid-levels. Following

radio instructions, they drove ahead to place a road block at the
junction of Pok Fu Lam Road and Hill Road. But before they'd
finished setting up, the white Honda charged towards them,
smashing their barricade to smithereens. The squad car chased it
down Pok Fu Lam and onto Bonham Road, driving dangerously
fast. Near Honiton Road, the Honda swerved to avoid a goods
truck and crashed into a lamppost.

This was where the trouble started. The five officers in the
squad car hadn't expected the suspects they were pursuing to
be heavily armed. Before they could even disembark, a dense
swarm of bullets came towards them. The commanding officer quickly activated the vehicle's MP5 sub-machine gun and
Remington shotgun, exchanging fire. In an instant, bullets were
flying and the street had turned into a battle zone. Neither police
nor criminals could advance or retreat, but fate was smiling on
the cops, and another Emergency Unit showed up in the nick of
time, firing on the Honda from the other side. After heavy fire,
the three criminals lay dead, and only five bystanders and officers were injured – a bit of relative good fortune amongst the
bad. Fifteen minutes later, officers from the Crime Unit showed
up, and uncovered an astonishing fact.

Of the three deceased, not one was Shek Boon-tim.

In the chaos of the gunfight, the convict could have jumped
from the car and got away – no one from the police vehicles
could swear that they hadn't been tricked by a decoy, watching the man with the gun while the escapee dashed out the other
side of the car, blending into the crowd of fleeing civilians. It was
also possible that Shek Boon-tim had already left the vehicle by
the time they caught up with it, switching cars or even hopping
onto public transport, again disappearing into the crowded city.

'Organized Crime is formally taking over the Shek Boon-tim
case. We just got a request for report analysis.' It was noon, and
Alex Choi was just opening the official briefing. While officers
gathered information on the front line, CIB had only a short
time to put reports in order, sort out lines of inquiry, and work

out the basic shape of the case. In this instance, every minute they delayed was another minute Shek Boon-tim had to run, increasing the diameter of the search area by a hundred metres.

In the briefing room, Division D's second team commander and an investigator from Organized Crime had joined Division B. They would be working together, with Division B not only analysing the reports but also coordinating the other departments, ensuring that information flowed smoothly between them. Kwan sat beside Choi. While he'd handed full responsibility over to the younger man, he still wanted to be present – he was, technically, still in charge.

In truth, everyone in Division B very much wanted Kwan Chun-dok to give his opinion. Apart from his crime-solving skills, he also had the advantage of being the only officer in the department who'd been up against Shek Boon-tim before. The two men had never met, but Kwan could be said to know Shek's personality inside out.

'Shek Boon-tim, forty-two years old. Sentenced to twenty years on charges of armed robbery and kidnapping, eight years ago.' Choi pressed the slide projector button as he spoke, bringing up an image of the man. 'Between 1985 and 1989, he and his brother Shek Boon-sing were the two most wanted men in Hong Kong. Boon-sing carried out the heists, while Boon-tim was the brains. In 1988, businessman Lee Yu-lung was kidnapped, with Shek Boon-tim secretly contacting his family to demand a ransom of four hundred million Hong Kong dollars. This fellow doesn't operate with guns or knives – his weapons are his brain and tongue.'

This was the hardest sort of criminal to deal with, thought Kwan. The photo on the screen had been provided by Correctional Services, taken just a month ago. Shek's features were as he remembered – the same rectangular face, thin lips, close-set eyebrows and black-rimmed glasses – but he was thinner than before, and there were wrinkles by the corners of his eyes and streaks of white in his short hair. Prison life seemed to have aged him.

'This morning, around nine o'clock, Stanley Prison inmate Shek Boon-tim claimed to be experiencing abdominal pains. The prison's head doctor gave him an injection of painkillers, and when the ache continued, Correctional Services arranged for a detailed examination at Queen Mary Hospital.' Inspector Choi paused to sweep his eye across the assembled officers before continuing, 'Because Shek Boon-tim's prison conduct had been good so far, no special measures were taken, just two officers guarding the felon, and a single pair of handcuffs.'

Everyone understood what Choi was letting go unsaid. The Shek brothers had been a cancerous growth in society and given the police years of trouble. No one in the entire force believed such human trash could ever change for the better. Correctional Services was clearly to blame here, having relaxed their vigilance just because of a little good behaviour.

'The correctional officers and Shek arrived at Queen Mary at ten thirty-five. About twenty minutes later, Shek asked to use the restroom. As the ground-floor Emergency Room was full of victims from the West Point fire and the Central acid attack, along with other patients, Shek's escorts took him to a bathroom upstairs. He then took advantage of a moment's inattention to leap from the window, escaping to his colleague's car, which rammed the hospital's electronic gates and headed towards West Point along Pok Fu Lam Road.' Choi indicated the direction on the projected map with a marker pen.

'At a minute past eleven, Emergency Unit Car 2 had a visual on the target vehicle at the Hill Road junction.' The tip of his marker pen moved over the map. 'The suspects continued down Bonham Road, until they had a collision near King's College. The officers in Car 2 exchanged fire with the suspects, while Car 6 approached from the west. Under fire from both sides, three suspects were hit and died at the scene.'

Click. Three photographs flashed up on the screen.

'Regrettably, Shek Boon-tim was not one of the three. He remains at large. Identities of the three deceased have been verified. The first is Chu Tat-wai, nicknamed Little Willy, formerly Shek Boon-tim's subordinate. Ten years previously, he was sent down for assault and battery, and released five years ago. The other two are Big Circle Guys who recently entered the territory. We'd received intelligence suggesting that they were planning something, but there was insufficient information for us to have predicted this.'

Two of the three faces on the screen were the ones in the report Choi had given Kwan earlier that day. Just as Kwan had predicted, they hadn't waited till the end of the month to strike.

'The deceased had with them a Škorpion vz. 61 sub-machine gun, two Type 54 Black Star pistols and almost a hundred bullets. I believe this amount of firepower couldn't have been intended solely for Shek Boon-tim's escape. Going by the backgrounds of the two Big Circle men and Shek himself, it's likely they were preparing for a major heist following the prison break. This accident has bought us some time to investigate their associates and plans, but the greater question is the whereabouts of our suspected mastermind, Shek Boon-tim.'

Next, some photographs of the scene. The number of holes and bloodstains on the white body of the car showed how vicious the gunfight had been.

'We found another set of car keys on Little Willy's person, which we believe indicates the suspects had planned to change vehicles. On the back seat were a prison uniform with the numbers torn off, and a pair of broken black-rimmed glasses. Expect Shek Boon-tim to now be in civilian clothing, and wearing contact lenses.'

Choi walked up to the map. 'Our Emergency Unit colleagues were unable to confirm whether Shek made his escape before or during the exchange of fire. If he blended into the crowds during the fight, then his present location is very likely to be in Sai Ying Pun.' He circled the location of the gunfight. 'Our colleagues in the Western District are currently sweeping the area and collecting eyewitness testimonies. We have no further information at present.' The marker pen moved down. 'However, if Shek Boon-tim made his escape *before* the gunfight, then we have a bigger problem. Between the car leaving the hospital and its encounter with Car 2 on Hill Road, we have five or six minutes of blank space. According to his record, Shek is a cunning criminal. Most people would flee with their associates after a prison break, but he might have instead used them as bait, buying more time for himself. If this really was the case, he may well have left the Honda at Smithfield, and merged with the crowds at the western edge of West Point. Shek's photograph has been circulated, and patrol officers will be on the lookout for him. In addition, the relevant images have been circulated to the media, in the hopes of obtaining more information from the public.'

Kwan knew that hoping civilians would provide usable leads was like climbing a tree to catch a fish. Shek Boon-tim was no ordinary criminal, and if he really had slipped away before a shot was fired, he'd certainly have prepared some impenetrable disguise.

'Our position was initially passive, but fortunately we have since received a report giving us a line of attack.' Choi walked back to the screen, pointing at the two Big Circle men. 'We'd heard that these two Mainlanders were concealing themselves in the industrial zone near Chai Wan loading docks. We now have reason to believe that their hideout was also Shek's base. Shek couldn't have expected that Little Willy and the others would be shot dead by police – and as the getaway car driver, Little Willy was an important figure in his escape plan. With him and the other two dead, Shek's mind must be racing. After so many years in prison, he may no longer be familiar with the environment outside. It's likely he's lying low, waiting for the heat to die down. We've had our colleagues in Division D set up a twenty-four-hour stakeout in Chai Wan, paying particular attention to Fung Yip and Sun On Streets.'

The Division D Tracking Team leader nodded.

'Our colleagues in Organized Crime will continue to work on the three deceased, using the items found on them and evidence from the car to narrow the scope of the inquiry.' Choi nodded at the representative from Organized Crime, then turned to his own team. 'Ah Ho, you'll be in charge of following up with O-Crime; Kwong and Elise, analyse the crime reports and collate the statements from our colleagues who were involved in the gunfight; Bob, get in touch with Division A, see if their informants have any inside info; the rest of you, check the surveillance cameras along Pok Fu Lam and Bonham. I want to know whether Shek Boon-tim left the car during those five minutes. Any questions?'

Silence.

'Okay, get to work. Dismissed.'

The team scattered. The Division D Commander spoke a little further to Choi before leaving, documents in hand. The Organized Crime investigator also wanted to clear up some details before going, her face sour. This close to Handover, O-Crime had their hands full preventing Triad activity, and now Correctional Services' slip-up had increased their workload.

'Commander, what do you think?' The briefing room now contained only Alex Choi and Kwan Chun-dok.

'My view is... for the moment I don't have one.' Kwan shrugged. 'I do have one suggestion.'

'What's that?'

'Have lunch now. In half an hour, when the witness statements and security camera footage arrive, you won't have a second to spare. You'll probably be busy till nightfall.'

Choi smiled grimly, but accepted the suggestion and went to the canteen for a boxed lunch. Kwan watched him go, his relaxed expression concealing a hundred emotions.

Eight years ago, Shek Boon-sing had lost his life during a gunfight. A number of innocent people had also died – something Kwan would rather not remember. Today, Shek Boon-tim had escaped custody, and once again shots had been fired. It seemed Kwan's eight years in the CIB were to be marked with a gunfight at either end. A cruel coincidence.

Perhaps events had their own way of ordering themselves,

perhaps beginnings and endings always had coincidences no ordinary person could penetrate. In the flood of time, human beings were no more than flecks of grit, borne along by the flow.

Eight years ago, Kwan had been able to take matters into his own hands, arresting Shek Boon-tim after he slipped through the net. But today, he was out of time.

'Some things can't be forced,' he muttered to himself. He'd decided this case was out of his jurisdiction, and Inspector Choi would be in charge.

A thought flashed through his mind – if he accepted Keith Tso's proposal, he could stay on in the role of a consultant, and continue his pursuit of Shek Boon-tim.

No, that's no basis for making a decision, he thought.

By 1 p.m., the office had turned chaotic. Every desk was piled high with incident reports and witness statements. The notice-boards were covered in photographs of the crime scene and territorial maps covered in lines. Most of Division B were staring hard at their screens, viewing chunk after chunk of video footage. The search area stretched south of the hospital, taking in the Chi Fu Fa Yuen housing development and Wah Fu Estate. As Shek Boon-tim had quite possibly switched to a car travelling in the opposite direction, Choi's orders were to sift through everything the traffic cameras along those roads had captured. But the team had no idea what they were looking for. They were like hunting dogs who had no idea what rabbits actually smelled like, scampering here and there after random scents, hoping to find a trace of something.

After a report came in that 'a suspicious individual was hiding in West Point', a sense of panic descended on the incident room. A member of the public had called to say that around 12.30 p.m., they'd spotted a man behaving suspiciously near Building C of the Kwun Lung Lau public housing estate. Western District police quickly sent armed officers to carry out a search. The estate contained more than two thousand apartments, housing more than ten thousand residents. A thorough search would be near-impossible, and Shek Boon-tim was likely to be armed, so the police had to operate with great caution.

'This might be a false report. I want you all to go on working full steam – keep searching for traces of that bastard,' ordered Choi. It had been an hour since the search began, with virtually no progress. The white Honda had been spotted on camera at a gas station near the junction of Pokfield Road and Pok Fu Lam, but between the hospital and that point there was still no sign, no way of knowing whether Shek Boon-tim had left the car during those three minutes. And there were no reliable reports as to whether the vehicle had three or four people in it at the moment of the accident.

Dammit, this won't be over any time soon, thought Inspector Choi. He turned to ask the officer in charge of witness statements if anything had turned up, only to see Kwan Chun-dok standing before a noticeboard, coffee cup in his hand, studying photographs of the gunfight.

'This fellow.' He pointed at someone with a gunshot wound to the chest. 'His hairstyle is different in this photograph.'

Choi drew closer. It was one of the Big Circle men.

'Sure, but it's definitely the same person. Ignore the hair – his features, build, even the scar on his left cheek all match.' Choi pointed them out on the mugshot. In the picture from a few days earlier, the criminal's hair was parted to one side, but the more recent picture showed him with a crew cut.

'True, even a pair of twins wouldn't have matching scars.' Kwan sipped his coffee.

Choi looked at his commanding officer, uncertain what he was getting at. Before he could ask, Sonny Lok arrived with a document.

'Headman, Organized Crime just sent over the statements from Shek's Correctional Services escorts,' said Sonny. Choi was known as 'Headman' to his subordinates, a common nickname for team leaders.

'Okay... but didn't I put Ah Ho in charge of following up with O-Crime?'

'Ah Ho's swamped. I'm helping him out.'

Choi grimaced. 'Sonny, you have bars on your shoulders now. You don't have to run errands for Ah Ho.'

Sonny Lok had been promoted to sergeant the month before, and now had three chevrons on his sleeves. He outranked Ah Ho, but being ten years younger and only six months into his CIB stint, not to mention never spending time with his colleagues outside work hours, he was susceptible to the older man pulling seniority on him.

'What I'd like to know is, how could these two guards have been so careless as to let Shek run off like that?' Kwan suddenly blurted out.

'Commander, is that important?' Choi turned back to him. 'Now isn't the time to assign blame.'

'I'm just curious, that's all,' said Kwan, flipping through the document Sonny had brought.

'Commander...' Lok paused, as if wondering whether it was appropriate to speak directly to Kwan, going over Choi's head. 'Apart from the written statement, O-Crime's also got the interview on video. I've got it on my desk, if you'd like to see it.'

'Even better.' Kwan shut the folder.

Noting Kwan's response, Choi asked cautiously, 'Commander, do you really reckon there's a clue in the way Shek escaped? We already have a rough idea of the circumstances, and surely the manhunt is more important.'

'There might be a clue, there might not be.' Kwan shrugged. 'But when you're dealing with a mastermind as crafty as Shek Boon-tim, you can't afford to pass over a single detail.'

Choi followed Kwan's gaze to the picture of Shek on the noticeboard.

'Of course,' Kwan added, 'you have full responsibility for this case. If you think it's a waste of time, I have nothing to say.'

Sonny arrived back with the video tape.

Alex Choi looked quickly around the office, all his subordinates glued to their screens and documents. 'Okay, Commander, you have a point. But no one else has the time – let's take a look ourselves.'

Kwan's lip curved up slightly, and he swivelled to indicate they should all go into his office – Sonny too. Choi had a sneaking suspicion that Kwan just wanted a look at the two guards. He'd been instrumental in capturing Shek in the first place, and probably now wanted to see which two idiots had ruined this achievement on the eve of his retirement.

3

– **Please state your name, age, rank and department.**
Ng Fong, forty-two, Assistant Officer Class 1, Correctional Services Department, Escort and Support Group.

– **Describe the events of this morning, Friday 6 June 1997.**
Around ten o'clock this morning, I received an order to escort a male convict to Queen Mary Hospital for an examination. This was prisoner number 241138, Shek Boon-tim, an inmate of Stanley Prison. Assistant Officer Class 2 Sze Wing-hong and I were in charge of guarding him. The ambulance set off at 10.05 a.m. We arrived at Queen Mary at 10.35.

– **Was it just the two of you in charge of this convict?**
Yes.

– **Shek Boon-tim's record shows he's a dangerous felon. Why not request police back-up?**
241138's conduct in prison has been exemplary. In all these years, he's had no infractions, and has taken part enthusiastically in rehabilitative programmes and activities, earning many commendations. The duty supervisor saw no need to go beyond normal restraints.

– **What happened at Queen Mary Hospital?**
241138 was sent to the Emergency Room, where a triage nurse determined he was a low-urgency case, and he was sent to wait. Sze and I sat beside him. During this time, he kept complaining of stomach pain. Around 10.50, he said he needed a crap. Sze and I decided to take him upstairs to the bathroom.

– **Why not the one on the ground floor, by the waiting room?**
There were a lot of patients in ER that morning, and civilians were going in and out constantly. We didn't want to get in anyone's way. We had to prevent him interacting with anyone else, and clear the bathroom before he entered, making sure there were no other people, nor anything that could be used as a weapon.

– **So you went up and inspected the bathroom?**
Yes. The first floor is used by the Medical Social Services Unit, so there were relatively few people. We chose the bathroom in the east wing. There were only three cubicles. Sze guarded the convict while I went in. There were two glass bottles and a mop, which I removed; I made sure all three cubicles were empty, including one which was shut, with an Out of Order notice on the door.

– **And the window? Didn't you think the convict might escape through the window?**
Um... I did. So we took measures to prevent that. Only... those measures failed.

– **What were the measures?**
After I'd inspected the bathroom, Sze and I escorted the convict in. I stood by the closed window while Sze stood behind the prisoner. The convict indicated he couldn't go with the handcuffs on, so Sze released the left side and closed it around the handrail – the one for infirm patients. I allowed the convict to close the door halfway, and stood just outside the cubicle, while Sze stood guard in the corridor to prevent anyone else entering.

- **So how did Shek Boon-tim escape?**
About a minute after the prisoner had entered the cubicle, I heard a commotion outside the bathroom. When the disturbance continued, I made sure he was firmly secured to the handrail, then went outside to lend assistance. A long-haired man was yelling at Sze Wing-hong. He said we had no right to keep him out of the bathroom, and attempted to barge his way in. We both tried to prevent him. I shouted that we were carrying out official duties, and could charge him with obstructing us. Hearing this, he finally gave up and went down the staircase, cursing us all the way. This took no more than a minute. When I went back inside the bathroom, 241138 had freed himself from the handcuffs and fled the scene.

- **Please go into more detail.**
I walked back into the bathroom. First, I saw the cubicle door wide open, and no one inside. Then I noticed the window was open, and the handcuffs were on the floor in front of the window. I rushed to the window and saw the prisoner sprinting towards a white car. I shouted at him to stop, but he ignored me, and there were no police officers or hospital guards nearby to assist. Sze heard me yelling and rushed inside. He climbed out the window and told me to take the stairs. I rushed down, but by the time I got out of the building, the car was already moving. Sze was standing some distance away. I think he'd tried to chase the vehicle on foot.

- **What did you do next?**
I called in the incident at once, then asked the guards at the gate for the licence number.

- **Why did you leave Shek Boon-tim's side, giving him the opportunity to escape?**
I... It was a moment of carelessness. I did make sure his handcuffs were secure before stepping outside, and we'd searched

him thoroughly before setting out, to make sure he didn't have any tools on him that could be used to pick a lock. My attention lapsed for less than a minute, but that was enough for him to break free and jump out the window. I hadn't expected him to have so much resourcefulness, or physical strength...

— **This hairpin was found at the scene of the crime. Do you remember seeing it?**
No, not at all. I'm certain he wasn't carrying anything on his person at all. Before we left the prison, I even looked inside his mouth.

— **In that case, he must have picked the hairpin up inside the bathroom?**
I... I don't know. I searched the entire room beforehand, and found nothing out of the ordinary.

— **During the time you were escorting Shek, did you notice anything suspicious?**
Now that I think about it, I'm sure he was faking the stomach ache. But apart from that, there was nothing at all unusual about yesterday's assignment. Even while we were in the waiting room, no one approached the prisoner, or so much as exchanged looks with him.

— **Please state your name, age, rank and department.**
I'm, I'm Sze Wing-hong, twenty-five this year, Escort and Support Group...

— **And your rank?**
Assistant Officer Class 2.

— **Describe the events of this morning, Friday 6 June 1997.**
Um, yes. This morning, Brother Fong and I got an order to deliver

that prisoner, Shek Boon-tim, to Queen Mary. We left at ten-something. Shek kept moaning in the vehicle, like his belly was on fire or something.

– **'Brother Fong' is Assistant Officer Class 1 Ng Fong?**
Yes, yes, that's right.

– **What time did you arrive at the hospital?**
I... I don't remember. Around half past ten.

– **And then what happened?**
Shek Boon-tim kept screaming that his stomach hurt and he had to take a shit. But the ER was so full, we took him to the men's room upstairs. It was chaos there, all the smoke inhalation victims from that fire, and I heard there was some people got splashed with acid. It was so crowded that—

– **What happened in the bathroom?**
Brother Fong made sure there was no one inside, and nothing that could be used as a weapon, before we let Shek go in. I hand-cuffed him to the railing, because he said he couldn't shit with his hands together.

– **Are you certain it was securely locked?**
Yes, I'm sure. Brother Fong can confirm that.

– **And then you and Ng Fong remained in the bathroom guarding Shek?**
Brother Fong stayed inside, and I stood in the corridor outside. But not long after I went out, some guy with long black hair and a red T-shirt came over and wanted to go in.

– **And you prevented him?**
Of course. But this guy wasn't happy about it, he said he had the right to use the bathroom and I was abusing my authority.

I tried to reason with him, but he wouldn't listen. After a bit, Brother Fong came out. He's been doing this job much longer than me, so he knows how to deal with this kind of bother. I've escorted prisoners to the hospital before, but nothing like this ever happened—

— **And so the man was sent away by Ng Fong?**
Yes, Brother Fong said he'd call the police to arrest the man, so he thumbed his nose at us and walked off with a face like thunder.

— **Then you discovered Shek Boon-tim had escaped through the window.**
Um... So Brother Fong went back into the bathroom, and a few seconds later, I heard him cursing and shouting, and rushed in to assist. He was standing by the window, pointing out. I went over to look. It was Shek Boon-tim in his brown prison uniform, sprinting towards a white car. I told Brother Fong to run down the stairs, and climbed out of the window myself.

— **But you couldn't catch up with him.**
No, I wasn't fast enough. When I got to the driveway, Shek was already in the car. I ran, but they were too far ahead.

— **You and Ng Fong contacted your department next?**
That's right. Ugh, we're in so much trouble... but I'm not to blame, am I? I didn't do anything wrong. I followed all the rules and procedures. Ng Fong's an old hand, he'll be fine, but I've only been working here a few years. Sir, please put in a good word for me when—

— **Mr Sze, we're only in charge of the inquiry. What happens within Correctional Services is your own affair. The police don't have the authority to interfere.**
Oh... but won't my boss want to look at the police report? I'm

begging you, please don't turn me into the scapegoat, I can't afford to lose this job...

- **Let's get back to the case. When you jumped out of the window, did you notice a pair of handcuffs on the ground?**
Huh? Oh, probably, I don't remember.

- **We found this hairpin at the scene. Do you think Shek Boon-tim might have used it to pick the lock?**
I... I guess so. I don't know. I'm sure the key was in my pocket all along. Our handcuffs are the normal sort, so if Shek was able to bust them with a hairpin, that wouldn't surprise me...

- **Could this hairpin have been concealed on Shek Boon-tim's person?**
I don't think so... Brother Fong searched him.

After they'd watched both videos, Alex Choi stood up, grumbling, 'So that was just the same as the report.'

'Not at all.'

Choi and Sonny Lok stared at the commander in his office chair, fingers laced together, his face perfectly calm.

'Not at all?' queried Choi.

'Their oral testimony provided a very obvious lead.'

'What's that?'

'The long-haired man in the red T-shirt,' said Kwan nonchalantly. 'He's a co-conspirator.'

'A co-conspirator? But he might just be a regular civilian...' protested Choi.

'So you're saying Shek Boon-tim took advantage of an unexpected coincidence to escape? It's possible the guy wandered by at exactly the right moment just by chance, but there are two things that make it unlikely. Firstly, the disturbance lasted not more than two minutes, and Ng Fong was outside for just one.

To make his escape in such a narrow timeframe, Shek must have been prepared. If this was opportunistic, he'd have had to come up with a plan and decide to go through with it in under sixty seconds. And if he failed, he'd have thrown away his reputation as a model prisoner who didn't need special restraints – his greatest advantage here.'

Kwan glanced at Choi and Sonny, and seeing that they had nothing to add, went on.

'Secondly, wasn't that man's behaviour just a little too odd? Sonny, let's say you needed the bathroom urgently, but someone prevented you going in. What would you do?'

'Uh... run to the next one, I guess.'

'That's right. But this man stayed put, arguing with two uniformed guards for a full two minutes. A normal person, even if he didn't know it was an offence to obstruct public servants in the course of their duties, would still be careful around uniformed security officers. If they'd been in plain clothes, then maybe, but it was obvious this was official business. Either there's something wrong with him, or he'd been planted to create a diversion and give Shek the chance to get away.'

Choi was forced to agree with Kwan's reasoning. 'Then we should...'

'Go through the hospital's security footage and find that long-haired man. He could be in disguise – the long hair might be a wig – but the time is precise enough to keep the search narrow.'

'Right. And should we get an ID from the escorts? They ought to remember his face.'

'The older one, Ng Fong, should be enough,' said Kwan. 'That Class 2 boy is too green, don't waste your time on him. After he's done the identikit, circulate it to the teams on Chai Wan. They should keep a lookout for this guy along with Shek Boon-tim.'

Before Choi could leave to disseminate these orders, two officers knocked on the door.

'Headman, new findings from O-Crime,' one said. 'They found a receipt in the getaway car from a convenience store at

Bonham and Park, timestamped 6.00 a.m. They've also searched the area around that store, and found a vehicle that matches the keys Little Willy had on him. A small black van, in a parking lot by Babington Path.'

'The second vehicle was at Mid-levels? I'd thought he'd planned to go down Hill Road to Sai Ying Pun before changing cars, and only the Emergency Unit prevented that. So they were headed towards Mid-levels...' Choi rubbed his forehead, trying to work out where the investigation should go next.

'Why would they make things difficult for themselves?' Sonny interrupted. 'Wouldn't it have been much easier to park the second vehicle in Sai Ying Pun rather than Babington Path? From there, they could have gone along Des Voeux Road or Connaught Road, and then down the Eastern Corridor all the way to Chai Wan. If anything went wrong, they could still escape to Kowloon via the Cross-Harbour Tunnel. The roads in Mid-levels are narrow, and there aren't many junctions – they'd find it hard to get away if there were a road block.'

'There'd been an accident on Des Voeux – traffic was chaotic in Central. Mid-levels might have seemed the better choice,' interjected the officer who'd brought the report.

'Send someone to get all the surveillance tapes from around there, especially from the convenience store,' Choi said. 'If we can understand what Little Willy and the Big Circle guys were up to this morning, we'll know where their hideout was.'

'We've already put someone on that.'

'Good.' Choi nodded, then turned to the other officer. 'And you? What have you got?'

'Nothing, Headman,' was the shamefaced reply. 'I wanted to tell you that Hong Kong Island Crime Unit called. They want the report on the Mong Kok acid attack, and info on the Graham Street incidents.'

Choi furrowed his brow and waved away the request. 'We're in the middle of tracking down an escaped convict. Tell them we can't spare the manpower right now.'

'But Inspector Wang is on the line...'

Everyone followed his gaze to the phone on Kwan's desk, and the blinking red light showing he had a call on line 3.

Choi sighed. Just as he was wondering how to mollify his counterpart, Kwan suddenly picked up the receiver and pressed 3.

'This is CIB Senior Superintendent Kwan Chun-dok.'

This startled everyone present, though Wang at the other end of the line was probably even more shocked.

'Right, yes. Division B has a lot on its plate right now. I do apologize,' smiled Kwan. Choi guessed the other man must be apologizing too. 'The teams are all tied up. Team 2 just finished a big case, so they're on leave, but even if we recall them urgently, they won't be able to help till tonight... And it's always been Team 1 dealing with the Mong Kok acid attacks, but they're all tracking down Shek Boon-tim right now... Oh good, I knew you'd understand.'

Hearing this, everyone thought Inspector Wang had given way to the higher-ranking officer. Just as they were breathing a sigh of relief, they heard Kwan go on, 'We'll send a... no, two investigators to assist with the acid case. It's not very much, but at least with their knowledge of the similar case in Mong Kok, they'll be of some assistance. Yes, yes. No, that's quite all right, we're all part of the same force, of course we ought to help each other. Maybe the CIB will need to rely on you for some intel before too long – I hope you won't let us down then. Bye!'

Kwan put down the receiver and looked up to a row of startled expressions.

'Commander, do we really have to send someone to deal with the acid attack?' asked Choi anxiously. 'We've got our work cut out for us here – looking for the long-haired man, and then there's all that footage to go through for the cars...'

'Don't worry. I don't think losing Sonny will affect you too much.'

'You're sending Sonny? But he's—' Choi was about to protest that Sonny Lok was new. In fact, having joined the CIB only after the first acid attacks, he hadn't even been a part of that investigation.

'I don't have a car, you see,' said Kwan, standing up.

'Oh...' Choi realized. 'Commander, you're dealing with the acid case yourself?'

'There are already too many clues to do with Shek Boon-tim. You just have to keep at it, and you'll eventually find that Chai Wan hideout – then he'll be yours for the taking. The acid-attack case is still at the needle-in-a-haystack stage. If I don't seize the moment, the investigation might drag on for months.' Kwan grabbed a few folders from his desk, then reached into a drawer for his holster and revolver. 'Besides, this way I'll see if I can still cope with frontline investigation. Call it an experiment.'

Alex Choi and the other three officers looked mystified, not having been privy to Kwan's conversation with Keith Tso earlier that day.

Kwan tapped Sonny lightly on the head with a folder. 'What are you waiting for? I'm retiring in a few hours, we need to make the most of the time.'

4

Sonny Lok followed Kwan Chun-dok out of the office to the main entrance.

'Commander? My car's parked over—' Sonny turned towards the parking lot on their left, but Kwan was heading straight for the main gate.

'Graham Street is just ten minutes away on foot, we'll walk there.'

'But you said you wanted me to drive?'

'That was just an excuse.' Kwan glanced back at Sonny. 'Or do you mean you'd rather be back there, being used as a runner?'

'No, no, of course I'd rather be here assisting you, Commander.' Sonny walked faster to catch up with Superintendent Kwan. In the last half year, Kwan had often picked him to run errands, but he had no complaints. It was a wonderful opportunity to spend time with the finest brain in the police force, watching him analyse and solve real cases. Sonny didn't know what Kwan saw in him – perhaps it was just that his previous assistant had been transferred elsewhere, and Sonny had arrived at the right moment to take his place.

Graham Street Market was just a few blocks from Central Police Headquarters, and it took hardly any time for Kwan and Sonny to arrive at the scene of the crime. The closer they got,

the more media vehicles they saw parked by the roadside. Sonny
guessed these journalists were betting on this case being sensa-
tional – even the gunfight at West Mid-levels hadn't drawn their
attention over there.

'Inspector Wang must be nearby,' said Kwan.

'Oh?' said Sonny, a little surprised. 'He's at the scene?'

'I heard a lot of background noise on the call earlier – he's definitely not at the station,' said Kwan, looking around. 'Besides,
he bypassed Regional Intelligence and called in person; that's
serious. I can't blame him – it's been four hours since the incident, and if he doesn't say something to the press soon, these
little tyrants might revolt. He can't hide behind "investigations
are ongoing" forever... Ah, I see him.'

Sonny followed his commander's gaze. Standing inside the
police line was a balding man in a grey suit, his forehead crinkled, looking ghastly. This was Senior Inspector Wang Yik-chun,
leader of Hong Kong Island Crime Unit Team 3, currently saying something to a subordinate.

'Inspector Wang, long time no see.' Kwan clipped his police
badge onto his lapel, signalling the uniformed officer guarding the
cordon to let him and Sonny in. Wang turned around and froze
for a moment before recovering and walking towards Kwan.

'Superintendent Kwan, how...' he began hesitantly.

'Team 1 was too busy, so I've come in person.' Kwan gave
him the files. 'Rather than fax these, I thought I'd just hand
them over.'

Inspector Wang almost asked how Kwan had known to look
for him at the scene, then remembered he was talking to the 'Eye
of Heaven', Kwan Chun-dok of the CIB.

'So sorry to have troubled you,' he said, shooing his subordinates away. 'I understand Shek Boon-tim's case is important,
but we can't ignore what's going on here. It's similar to the two
Mong Kok incidents, but far more serious. The culprit flung four
bottles of corrosive liquid – we're lucky no one's died from their
burns, as of now.'

'Same as in Mong Kok, Knight Brand Drain Opener?' asked Kwan.

'Yes, exactly the same, though we haven't been able to determine if it's the same person or a copycat. We'll have to rely on the CIB to...'

'We haven't said anything yet, so you can't go blabbing to reporters.'

'Ah... right.' Wang looked a little embarrassed.

Kwan understood the unspoken agreement between the departments. If Inspector Wang made any public statement before receiving the CIB's analysis, the Hong Kong Island Crime Unit would bear full responsibility. If he made a guess and his conjecture turned out to be wrong, he and his subordinates would be in for some harsh criticism from the top brass, but if he equivocated, the public would think the police were powerless, and the morale and reputation of the Crime Unit would take a hit. If he had the backing of the CIB, however, it didn't matter whether he got it right. As long as the Crime Unit presented a unified front, any fallout would land on the CIB.

'Have you determined where the suspect was standing?' Kwan asked.

'We're fairly certain. This way, please.' Inspector Wang led Kwan and Sonny to a tenement building at the junction of Wellington and Graham Streets.

'It seems two bottles were first thrown from here towards the stalls on Graham Street.' Wang pointed at the tenement roof, then at the road, where his officers were busy searching for evidence. 'The crowd naturally ran in the opposite direction, but he was waiting for them – two more bottles were flung in the direction of Wellington Road.'

'All from the same rooftop?' Kwan looked up at it, five storeys above.

'We believe so.'

'Let's have a look.'

The three men trooped up the stairs to a roof terrace painted

mud-yellow. This building had lain empty for two years. Previously, it had been an apartment block, with a well-known
provisions trading company operating on the ground floor. A
property developer had acquired it, but hadn't yet managed to
buy the old buildings on either side. The ultimate plan was to tear
all three down and put up a thirty-storey skyscraper in their place.

Kwan Chun-dok stood at the edge of the roof, looking at the
two streets below, then walked to the other side and stared at
the neighbouring buildings and roofs. He went back and forth
several times, spoke for a few minutes with the investigators who
were gathering evidence, then carefully inspected the tags they'd
placed on the ground, finally walking slowly back to Inspector
Wang without a word.

'What do you say, Superintendent?' asked Wang.

'It completely fits,' said Kwan. Sonny realized that although
Kwan was giving Wang a straightforward answer, there was
something nuanced about his expression.

'It's the same culprit as Mong Kok?'

'Seventy... no, eighty per cent certain.' Kwan looked around
once more. 'The two incidents in Mong Kok also involved buildings like this, with connected rooftops and no security. The
second case in particular was like this one – the culprit chose
a corner building, attacked one side first to create chaos, and
then the other. The media only reported that "two bottles of acid
rained from the sky", and didn't mention the details – yet this
modus operandi is exactly the same.'

Kwan pointed at a canvas covering that had clearly been
seared by the liquid. 'This happened last time too – throwing
an open bottle onto a stall's awning so it bounced and sprayed,
causing even more damage.'

'Which means this fellow's come to Hong Kong Island to
make mischief,' sighed Inspector Wang. 'Probably after they
increased security on Ladies' Alley, he couldn't operate there any
more, so we have a change of location.'

'The case file I just gave you contains a few video stills,' said

Kwan. 'You might already know that our suspect in the Mong Kok case is a plump man. We've put out a call for him as a witness, but he's likely to be our guy. CIB doesn't have the manpower at the moment, but you could look through the security footage from around here, see if you can spot him.'

'Understood, Superintendent.' Wang opened the folder and glanced at the images.

'What's the latest figure for casualties?'

'Thirty-four, three serious – one still in ICU, the other two probably requiring surgery. Minor injuries for the rest – they were mostly splashed on the arms and legs, and discharged after treatment... though they'll be mentally scarred.'

'Who are the three seriously wounded?'

Wang scrabbled for his list of names. 'The one in ICU is Li Fun, an old guy – he's sixty – who lives alone on Peel Street, round the corner. He was at the scene to buy groceries, and got hit directly in the face. He'll probably never see again. He already had high blood pressure and diabetes, so the prognosis isn't optimistic.'

Wang flipped a page and went on. 'The other two are stall owners, both male. Chung Wai-shing, thirty-nine, known on the street as Brother Wai. He runs a small plumbing and electrical business. The other is Chau Cheung-kwong, forty-six. He sells flip-flops from his market stall. Both were direct hits, like Li Fun – injuries to the face, neck and shoulders. Is this useful, Superintendent?'

'Might be, might not be.' Kwan waved his hands vaguely and smiled. 'Ninety per cent of the details in any incident are useless, but if you miss anything in the other ten per cent, you'll never crack the case.'

'I guess that's an article of faith for Intelligence?' Wang smiled back.

'No, just me.' Kwan rubbed his chin. 'I'd like to walk around, is that all right? I won't get in the way of your team.'

'Of course, go right ahead!' Wang could never say no to someone so many ranks higher than himself. 'I have to get ready to read a statement to the press. Can I say the CIB believes there's a good chance this is the same perp as Mong Kok?'

'Sure.'

'Great, thanks.' Having gained Kwan's consent, Wang began running through what he might say to the assembled journalists. Kwan walked back outside, with Sonny following closely behind.

The police had sealed off thirty metres each of Graham and Wellington Streets. Apart from the investigators assiduously gathering evidence, the scene contained only the carnage of that morning. Overturned stalls, vegetables trampled into mush, and black spots where acid had scorched the pavement. Sonny imagined the scene hours ago, and thought he could still detect the acrid stench of drain cleaner, the malevolent chemical smell seeming to spread nauseatingly all around them.

Sonny thought Kwan wanted to have a closer look at the damage to the stalls, but was surprised to see his superior heading straight for the police line.

'Commander, don't you want to inspect the scene?'

'I saw enough from the roof. I'm not looking for evidence. What I need is the Intelligence Unit,' said Kwan, not breaking his stride.

'The Intelligence Unit?'

Kwan stepped outside the cordon and looked around, then said to Sonny, 'There, found it.'

Following Kwan's line of sight, Sonny saw a cheap clothing stall. Outmoded women's fashions dangled all over the counter, and a rack of hats in various colours and styles stood nearby. Three women sat on folding stools in front of it, chatting away. One of them, in her fifties, had a money pouch around her waist and was probably the proprietor.

'Good afternoon,' said Kwan to the trio. 'Police. May I ask you some questions?'

Her two companions looked alarmed, but the woman with the money bag remained calm. 'Officer, your colleagues came by ages ago! I guess you want to ask if I've seen any suspicious strangers? I don't know how many times I have to tell you, this is a tourist area, we see strangers all the time.'

'No, I wanted to ask if you'd seen some unsuspicious friends.'

The woman was stunned into silence, then burst into howls of laughter.

'Ah, Mr Policeman, are you serious? Is this some kind of joke?'

'Actually, I meant the victims. Three of them are in a serious condition – two stall owners and a resident. I'm asking around the area to see if anyone knows them.'

'Then you've come to the right place. I've had a stall here twenty years, I can even tell you which high school Porky Wing from the corner's son got into. So I heard the serious cases were Old Li, Brother Wai, and Boss Chau with the slipper shop. A bolt from the blue – they were perfectly fine this morning, and now they're lying in the hospital,' she sighed.

She'd got all three of them right away – no wonder the super-intendent called her the Intelligence Unit, thought Sonny. There's always a gossip queen in these marketplaces, sitting in the same spot morning and night, nothing to do as she tends her stall but people-watch and chat with customers and neighbours.

'So you knew all of them— Oh yes, what should I call you?' With a show of familiarity, Kwan pulled up a chair and sat down.

'Call me Auntie Soso.' She pointed at a sign nestled amongst the gaudy clothes and hats: 'Soso Fashion'. 'Old Li and Brother Wai have been here more than ten years, but Boss Chau I only met recently. The slipper stall owner before him emigrated to Canada, and Chau took over just a few months ago.'

'Old Li was sixty-year-old Li Fun?' Kwan said, for the sake of confirmation.

'Yes, Old Li from Peel Street. I heard he was buying some vegetables from Fatt Kee when he got it right in the face. Horrible...'

'Hey, I don't want to talk behind his back,' interrupted the woman to Auntie Soso's left, 'but if Old Li wasn't such a lecher, he wouldn't have been flirting with Fatt Kee's wife while Fatt

Kee was busy elsewhere, and then he wouldn't have got hit with the acid.'

'My goodness, Blossom, don't talk like that in front of the officer! Old Li was a randy old goat, but you can't actually think he and Mrs Fatt Kee had a thing going on,' Auntie Soso scolded, only half joking. Sonny thought this Li Fun must have been quite a womanizer to be dallying with younger women in the market-place. He probably didn't have a good reputation.

'Li Fun was a regular? He came here every day?'

'That's right, rain or shine, Old Li would be here getting his groceries. We've known him at least ten years,' replied the third woman.

'Do you know if he has any vices? Or if he's had any money issues, grudges, that sort of thing?' asked Kwan.

'I haven't heard anything like that.' Auntie Soso tilted her head to one side and thought about it. 'He's been divorced a long time now, and doesn't have any kids. He might dress shabbily, but he owns several apartments and earns more than enough in rent. As for grudges, he's always chatting up Fatt Kee's wife, so Fatt Kee can't stand him, but I don't know if you could call that a grudge.'

'Do you also know the other victim, Chung Wai-shing?'

'Sure, Brother Wai, he's the handyman on the corner.' Auntie Soso gestured towards the cordoned-off area. 'He wasn't at his stall often, mostly he was out making house calls. Who'd have thought the one day he happened to be here, some psycho would fling acid at him. The best laid plans...'

'Brother Wai's a nice guy, I hope he gets out of the hospital soon! His wife and kid must be so worried,' chimed in Blossom.

'You've known him long?'

'Pretty long. Brother Wai's been on Graham Street more than ten years now. He's good at what he does and doesn't charge too much. If anyone in the neighbourhood has an odd job, like changing a tap, putting in a water heater, fixing a TV aerial, they look up Brother Wai. I think he lives in Wan Chai, and his wife works part-time at the supermarket. Their son's just started high school,' said Auntie Soso.

'Sounds like Brother Wai was popular.'

'Yes. No one cared much when they heard about Old Li, but when word got out Brother Wai was in the hospital, the whole neighbourhood was on edge.'

'Which means Brother Wai was an upright citizen, with no dark secrets?'

'I guess... not,' Auntie Soso stuttered, exchanging glances with Blossom.

'So there's something?' Kwan looked curious, as if gazing straight into Auntie Soso's heart.

'Well... Officer, this is just a rumour, take it with a pinch of salt. Brother Wai's a nice guy, but I heard he's been to prison. It seems in the past he was involved with those secret societies. Then when his father was on his deathbed, he turned over a new leaf.'

'He installed my air conditioning once,' said Blossom. 'It was almost thirty-five degrees that day, so he took off his shirt, and there on his back was a green dragon flashing its claws and teeth. It gave me a bit of a shock.'

'So he didn't mind other people seeing his tattoo,' said Kwan.

'Um, I guess not.' Auntie Soso dismissed the suggestion. Sonny thought Brother Wai probably didn't care who knew about his past, and it was these three gossips who were prejudiced.

'And finally, Chau Cheung-kwong...'

'So that was Boss Chau's full name?' interrupted Blossom.

'I think so,' said Auntie Soso. 'I seem to remember it was something Kwong.'

'I guess you don't know Boss Chau very well.'

'We haven't known him long, that doesn't mean we don't know him well,' snapped Auntie Soso, as if he'd impugned her professionalism. But then, reflected Sonny, gossip more or less *was* her profession, and selling clothes just a pastime.

'Boss Chau's spot is just beside mine.' She leaned forward

and pointed to her left. Sonny and Kwan glanced over at a little stall covered in flip-flops in a multitude of styles and colours.
'I believe I know him better than anyone else on Graham Street.'

Kwan had to suppress a laugh before he could ask, 'And you
said Boss Chau has only been here how many months?'

'He started this March, I think. Boss Chau's a solitary one.
He says hi and bye, but never comes over for a chat.'

'I bought a pair from him once. Asked if he had them in
a smaller size, and he had the nerve to tell me to go look for
myself,' said Blossom. 'His assistant Moe seems more like the
boss – I heard he was a nephew of Chau's who couldn't find a
job and ended up helping out with the stall.'

'Had Moe recently graduated?'

'Not by the looks of him. He's a shrimp, but has to be in his
late twenties, maybe thirties. I bet he was fired by his last boss
and had to scrounge a job from a relative.'

'Is Boss Chau often not around?'

'I wouldn't say that, he's here almost every day. But it's Moe
who opens and closes the stall, and Boss Chau only shows up for
two or three hours. Sometimes Moe doesn't show up, and then
the stall stays shut all day,' said Auntie Soso.

'My guess is Boss Chau's the same as Old Li, a landlord with
rent coming in. His market stall is just to pass the time.' Blossom sucked her teeth, contemptuous of rich and poor alike.
'He disappears on race days – he's quite the gambler. And the
day before, he'll be too busy clutching his form to pay attention
to anyone.'

'Oh, even when there isn't a race on, he still ignores everyone!' jeered Auntie Soso.

'Hang on,' Sonny asked abruptly. 'How was Boss Chau hurt?
His stall's over here, but the attack was on the other end of the
market.'

'He and Moe were fetching a delivery. Trucks can't drive
through the market, so we have to fetch everything from the
road in handcarts. The trucks park either on Wellington or

Hollywood.' Auntie Soso pointed in both directions. 'I said hello to Boss Chau and Moe just this morning. They said they were going to move some stock, and next thing you know, disaster struck!'

'And Moe hasn't been back?' Kwan asked Auntie Soso, eyeing the neglected flip-flop stall.

'Blossom saw him get in the ambulance with Boss Chau. I guess there wasn't time to pack up the stall. We're all neighbours, so I'll do it for him later on, but to be honest, there's not much worth stealing at a little stall like that.'

'And you? Did you see the incident take place?' Kwan turned to Blossom.

'You could say I did. I was in the dry goods store on the corner, chatting with the shopkeeper, when suddenly there were two enormous crashes outside, and then people screaming in pain, rushing into the shop demanding water. We filled some basins and handed out bottles to everyone coming in. Their arms and legs were covered in the stuff, it burned right through their clothes. When it quieted down, I summoned my courage and stepped outside. There was Old Li, lying by the side of the road, and Fatt Kee's wife pouring water over his face.'

'Did you see Brother Wai and Boss Chau?'

'Yes, yes, I turned the corner, and saw the whole scene. Brother Wai and a few others were hiding in the incense store, and when I got closer, there was Boss Chau coming from the other direction, leaning on Moe, screaming for help. He and Brother Wai were in terrible shape, and there was weeping and wailing all around. It was hell on earth, truly hell on earth.' Blossom spoke with animation, waving her hands around.

'That sounds bad...' groaned Kwan.

'Officer, are you going to ask if anyone had a grudge against Boss Chau?' Auntie Soso raised one eyebrow. 'I don't think so, but if you're going to ask about bad habits, I really can't say. Do the police think someone had it in for these men? I'm good at keeping secrets, you can tell me, I won't breathe a word.'

Again, Kwan had to suppress a chuckle as he placed his index finger against his lips. 'Thank you for your report. We have to continue with our investigation now.'

Kwan and Sonny walked away. The three women began muttering to each other before they were out of earshot.

'"Good at keeping secrets." Unless she turns mute, I don't think she'll ever be good at that, not in this lifetime. No, even if she couldn't speak, she'd gossip in writing,' laughed Kwan, once they were back inside the police cordon.

'Commander, why're we trying to find out about the three victims? Shouldn't we be looking for suspicious individuals?' asked Sonny.

'The three victims are the main point,' said Kwan. 'Sonny, go back to the station and fetch the car, I'll wait for you at Queen's Road.'

'Huh? Where're we going?'

'Queen Mary Hospital. If we want to crack this case, we'll have to start with the wounded.'

'Why? Wasn't this a random attack?

'Random? Not at all.' Kwan stared up at the rooftop from which the culprit had flung his missiles. 'This was carefully planned, and there was most definitely a target.'

5

Sonny returned to the station and started his blue Mazda. At the junction of Graham Street and Queen's Road Central, Kwan stood clutching a small purple plastic bag and waving. When Sonny pulled up, he climbed into the passenger seat.

'Queen Mary Hospital,' he repeated. Sonny stepped on the accelerator.

Pulling on his seat belt, Kwan said, 'I went to tell Wang we were leaving. Turns out he just got an order to follow up on this morning's fire in West Point too. Investigators think it's suspicious, so the case has been handed over to the Hong Kong Island Crime Unit. It seems more than twenty residents have been hospitalized. The team's just been at Queen Mary to take statements from the Graham Street victims, and now they have to stay to talk to the others. At least it'll save them a trip. Hey, Sonny, are you listening?'

Sonny started. 'Ah, um, yes, sorry, Commander, I was thinking about what you said earlier. That the acid-thrower must have had some kind of plan, and a particular target.'

'Yes.'

'Why?'

'To begin with, I thought this was a copycat crime,' said Kwan.

Sonny looked doubtfully at his commanding officer, wondering what this had to do with his question. 'A copycat crime?'

'On the face of it, the Graham Street case was fundamentally different from Mong Kok. At the scene, I was still full of confidence in this hypothesis at first,' said Kwan slowly.

Sonny understood now why Kwan had looked so dubious when he told Wang 'it completely fits' – the environment had given him a completely different answer from the one he expected.

'Why fundamentally different? Both open-air markets, drain cleaner flung from a rooftop, large numbers of injuries...'

'The Mong Kok cases took place on weekend evenings. This was a Friday morning. Doing it by daylight would be far riskier – you might be seen by people in neighbouring buildings, so you'd have to spend as little time as possible up on the roof. Even when leaving, you might be recognized by a passer-by, or captured on a security camera.'

Sonny got it. They'd jumped straight away to the similarities between the cases, rather than considering how they differed, and why.

'Also,' Kwan continued, 'Graham Street on a Friday morning would never be as busy as Ladies' Alley at the weekend. If the culprit really is a madman who gets his kicks hurting other people, he picked the wrong time and place this time. If he'd waited till the weekend, he'd have had even more prey, and created a bigger commotion. Or he could have picked somewhere with more surrounding buildings to make his getaway easier, somewhere like Jardine's Crescent Market in Causeway Bay or Tai Yuen Street Market in Wan Chai.'

'So these were two different people?'

'No. The evidence at the scene suggests it was the same person, or at least the same gang. And that contradiction gives us a motive.'

'What motive?'

'Sonny, haven't you ever read one of those serial-killer novels? If the culprit isn't some psycho who just enjoys murder, what's his usual reason?'

'... To hide who his real target is?' As the answer came to Sonny, a chill of fear ran through him.

'Exactly. I believe this case follows that pattern. Our perp started out in Mong Kok for two reasons – firstly, to create a history of cases, in order to "hide a leaf in the forest"; secondly, for practice. In Mong Kok he learned how to fling the stuff to create maximum damage, how to get away, how to observe the police investigation afterwards, and so on. When I thought this was a copycat, I assumed the imitator just hadn't planned as well as the Mong Kok guy. But the methods are so similar that I believe it's most likely the work of one person, which means Mong Kok must have been a rehearsal.'

'Couldn't Graham Street be a rehearsal too?'

'No, too risky. Even if it had to be here, you'd pick Saturday or Sunday. More people would mean more chaos, and you'd get away more easily. This was the real thing, and so we ought to look at the most seriously wounded.'

Sonny looked enlightened as he realized why his commander had asked Auntie Soso all about the three victims. Mong Kok had been the scene of trial and error, to see if the drain cleaner would do enough damage. The first time was a failure, which is why he tried the two-bottle method the second time, the first as a feint, the second to create chaos. Once he'd perfected his method, he struck. As it was morning, he used four bottles to create even greater confusion. Old Li, Brother Wai and Boss Chau – one of them must be the real target.

Who was most likely? Sonny pondered. The practice run in Mong Kok had been six months before, so the target couldn't be Boss Chau, who'd only taken over the stall three months ago. Brother Wai was well thought of in the neighbourhood. He might have been involved in secret societies as a young man, but had left the underworld to work in the marketplace a good decade ago. Even if he'd left bad blood behind him, no one would wait this long for vengeance. The most likely target was Old Li, also the most seriously wounded, now hovering between life and death – perhaps because the criminal had flung the acid directly at him. No one around here seemed to like him much, and it could well be a jealous husband deciding to teach him a lesson – though starting six months beforehand seemed too pre-meditated for a crime of passion.

'Hey, drive carefully.' Superintendent Kwan's voice brought Sonny back to the present. He'd been carried away with his thoughts, and forgotten he was speeding down the highway with his hands on the wheel.

'Right, right.' Sonny brought his attention back to the road. They'd just passed the University of Hong Kong's Haking Wong Building, meaning they were minutes away from Queen Mary Hospital.

'Commander, what's in your plastic bag?'

'Oh, I bought this from Auntie Soso back on Graham Street.' Kwan pulled out a brand new baseball cap. 'She wanted thirty dollars, but I bargained her down to twenty – not bad. This'll come in useful when I go walking in the countryside after retirement.'

'But black absorbs heat – you might find it uncomfortable on hot summer days.' Sonny eyed the cap, just coarse black material with no words or pictures, though on the right side of the brim was a grey arrow about the size of a coin, trying to imitate a famous fashion brand, but unable to hide that it was just a cheap knockoff.

'Hot? Well, it might be.' He returned the cap to the bag.

Sonny couldn't understand how Kwan had time to go shopping at this critical juncture, but in the past half year he'd learned that this commander liked to do things his own way.

A few minutes later, the car turned into the entrance of Queen Mary, the biggest public hospital in Hong Kong, with half a century of service behind it. It had a full set of facilities, from the Emergency Room to various specialists and a psychiatric ward, whilst also being the teaching hospital of the University of Hong Kong. It consisted of fourteen buildings, the size of a smallish neighbourhood.

'Building S,' said Kwan on getting out of the car.

'Huh?' Sonny had been about to head towards the ER, in Building J. 'Don't we want to speak to one of the Emergency Room workers?'

'The Orthopaedics and Trauma Unit would deal with chemical burns. It'd be simpler to just ask at reception there.'

At the Orthopaedics and Trauma reception, Kwan flashed his badge at the duty nurse and asked how the three victims were doing.

'Mr Policeman, didn't I just tell your colleague? Doctor says the patients can't answer questions right now,' the young lady said rudely.

'I'm sorry, that must have been a different department,' Kwan replied equably. 'Is their condition bad?'

'Li Fun in ICU is in critical condition, but his life isn't in danger.' Seeing that Kwan wasn't going to lean on his authority, the nurse softened. 'The other two, Chung and Chau, were hit in the face. Forcing them to talk now might stop their skin healing, and getting them agitated won't help their recovery at all.'

'Oh, in that case... Can we ask their doctor a few questions?'

The nurse reluctantly picked up the phone and said a few words. A short while later, a tall, good-looking man of about thirty, wearing a white coat, strode over from the far end of the corridor.

'Dr Fung, these two officers want to ask about the three acid victims.' With that, she lowered her head and promptly went back to her work.

'Call me Kwan.' The superintendent shook the doctor's hand. 'So we can't ask the victims any questions?'

'That's right. From a medical standpoint, I can't permit anything that might worsen their condition. I hope you understand.'

'That's fine. Could I ask you a few questions instead?' smiled Kwan.

Dr Fung didn't seem to have expected this, but said, 'If I can help, just say.'

'How serious are Li Fun's injuries? I heard he might have been blinded.'

'Yes, the liquid went into both his eyes. When he's stabilized, I'll ask my colleagues in ophthalmology to take a look.' The doctor shook his head. 'His left eye is more badly hurt, and there's probably no hope. But I'd say we had a sixty per cent chance of saving the right.'

'What about Chung Wai-shing and Chau Cheung-kwong? Were their eyes hurt?'

'No, that's the one good thing in all this. Chung was hit on the shoulder, and it splashed onto his lower face. Neck, mouth and nose are all badly damaged. Chau was struck full in the face, but fortunately was wearing sunglasses, so his eyes were spared.'

'Any injuries to their limbs?'

'Yes, but only mild burns on arms and legs. Chung's left arm and leg were hit, while with Chau it was both his hands – he must have tried to wipe the stuff off his face, so both palms are burned too.' Dr Fung placed his hands over his own face to show what he meant.

'Will they be in the hospital for long?'

'It's hard to say for now, but I think two weeks is a reasonable prediction.' Fung glanced at a wall calendar. 'I've planned for all three to receive skin grafts tomorrow. Chau will have to go first. The responders didn't do enough for him, so although his injuries weren't any worse than the other two, his skin's the most damaged.'

'Didn't do enough?'

'I'm talking about how quickly the ambulance crew was able to wash the acid off, neutralize what was left on the skin, bandage the damaged areas to prevent infection, and so on. My colleagues in ER said they only discovered how bad his condition was when they examined him, so even triage must have dropped the ball there. But there was so much going on this morning, I can't really blame them. First the fire, then this attack, and finally an escaped felon – they had their hands full.'

'This morning was truly terrible,' Kwan nodded.

'It was the same in our department.' Fung smiled grimly. 'There were already several burns victims from the West Point fire, then the wave of acid victims came. Fortunately that truck accident didn't cause any casualties, otherwise I'd still be working on patients now.'

'You mean the accident this morning on Des Voeux Road?'

'Yes, I was telling an officer how busy today had been, and he said if the truck in the Central accident had been carrying something corrosive, rather than just a harmless emulsifier, the hospital would have exploded from overcrowding. Though it's pretty much exploding now. And actually, if not for the traffic jam in Central, some of those thirty-plus acid cases would have been sent to Tang Shiu Kin Hospital in Wan Chai, and our ER wouldn't be quite this busy.'

'I wanted to ask – who did the paperwork for these three men's admission?' Kwan dragged the subject back to the matter at hand. 'If we can't talk to the patients, I'd like to have a chat with their families.'

'Now you bring that up, we did have some trouble there.' Dr Fung looked frazzled. 'Li Fun has no immediate family, and we haven't been able to get in touch with any of his relatives, so there's a lot of forms waiting to be signed.'

'And the other two?'

'You just missed them, Superintendent. Chung Wai-shing's wife was here earlier, and Chau Cheung-kwong was accompanied by a family member – I think also his assistant. Visiting hours are over, so they've gone now. They should be back at six.'

'Then we'll have to wait,' said Kwan. Sonny looked at his watch – it was only 3.30, two and a half hours still to go.

'I have to go on my rounds. Excuse me.' The doctor nodded to the two policemen.

'Oh, one more thing, which wards are Chung and Chau in?' asked Kwan.

'Ward 6, third door on the left. They're in the same room.'

After Dr Fung had departed, Sonny whispered, 'Commander, are we going to sneak in and talk to them when no one's looking?'

'Even if we did that, they might not be willing to speak to us,' said Kwan breezily. 'Let's just wait. A couple of hours will go by very fast.'

He settled himself into one of the waiting-room sofas, while Sonny remained standing, puzzled. Who'd have thought Superintendent Kwan would pick this moment to start obeying the rules?

He sat next to Kwan, feeling helpless. Just as he was about to ask how they'd ever find clues to the culprit's identity from these three victims, Kwan began talking a blue streak about chemical burns, everything from emergency treatment to antibiotic medication and non-steroidal anti-inflammatories, chatting artlessly about skin grafts and how artificial skin helped heal wounds. Sonny thought the people around them must imagine Kwan was some kind of specialist, explaining a course of treatment to a relative.

'Commander, I'm going to the bathroom,' interrupted Sonny, just at the point when Kwan was explaining that burns victims' skin was constantly losing moisture, so it was important to keep them hydrated. Sonny needed to get away from this bombardment.

'How on earth does the commander know all this?' wondered Sonny as he followed the signs to the bathroom. On his way back, he was heading towards the waiting area when a sign caught his eye: 'Building J – This Way'.

Building J housed the Emergency Room, which Sonny had no interest in, but he was enticed by the bathroom upstairs in its east wing. The bathroom whose window Shek Boon-tim had escaped out of.

Although he was here with his commander to look into the acid case, he was still an investigator. Shek Boon-tim was public enemy number one, and if Sonny had the choice, he'd definitely go after Shek than probe some small-time acid attack.

'I might as well have a look,' he thought, glancing at his watch.

At the other end of the walkway to Building J, he found himself in a stairwell, with signs pointing towards the various departments. Just as the prison officer had said, the first floor was Medical Social Services, with the Emergency Room downstairs. On the eighth floor was a ward reserved for Correctional Services, where they could detain unwell suspects or bring convicts in need of treatment.

If those two officers had been a bit more cautious, and taken Shek to the eighth-floor bathroom, he'd never have escaped, thought Sonny.

Following the staircase, he made his way to the scene of the escape. The bathroom was in a corner of the east wing, with no offices or wards nearby – the whole place had a deserted look about it. Sonny thought it was no wonder they'd brought Shek here. There were no police officers around, but they'd probably unsealed the room after gathering evidence. Keeping watch on the place now wouldn't help capture Shek Boon-tim.

The bathroom was bigger than Sonny had expected. Three cubicles on one side, a urinal trough and long sink on the other. There was no door – instead, it was shielded from outside by a wall immediately within the entrance. Walking in, you found yourself facing a large window.

Sonny inspected the cubicles first of all, hoping to find some clue others had missed. Only the wooden door with the 'Out of Order' sign was half closed. He pushed it open, to see the toilet seat had come off and the chain for the flush was snapped. Otherwise, it was exactly the same as the other two. All three cubicles had metal handrails, though after studying them for several further minutes, Sonny still couldn't tell if Shek had been handcuffed in the second or third cubicle. He'd expected the handrail to show some signs of his hasty escape, but he seemed to have left no marks at all.

With nothing gained from the cubicles, Sonny turned his attention to the window, which gave a clear view of the driveway outside Building J. Looking out, he guessed Shek's accomplice must have had the car waiting about thirty metres away. The drop to the ground was about four or five metres, but there was a shallow ledge outside the window, with numerous pipes to the left. A man could probably climb down them safely if he were careful. In fact, if he were agile enough, even leaping straight down to the ground might be okay.

Sonny had now spent twenty minutes in the bathroom without uncovering even a whisper of new evidence. He left dejectedly, and was about to head back to Building S, when he suddenly recalled his commander's words: 'Go through the hospital's security footage and find that long-haired man.'

Why hadn't the long-haired man escaped together with Shek?

Walking down the staircase, Sonny noticed a window that gave the same view as the one in the bathroom. It had metal bars across it. He tugged them, but they didn't move, and on closer inspection were covered in dust. He continued downstairs and walked along the corridor, round the corner, until he was beneath the bathroom window. This took him about half a minute.

'If I were an accomplice, why not just leave in the getaway car?' he wondered. 'He couldn't have gone through the stairwell window, but even running this way, and then the thirty metres to the car – he could do that in twenty seconds, at a sprint. Was he afraid the hospital guards might stop him? But the bad guys had sub-machine guns – even if things went wrong, firing a few rounds should have been enough for them to get Shek out anyway.'

In order to escape, a convict needs to get out of his hand-cuffs and evade his guards. Shek had already done these two things when he leaped from the window, and if Long Hair was his accomplice, then his job was already done. There'd be no more need to keep a low profile, so why not just run?

Sonny couldn't put his finger on it, but something about this case wasn't right. Shek Boon-tim was a famously merciless felon, and he might be a brainbox, but his followers were a bunch of desperadoes. Look at the way they started a gunfight with the police after the accident – it was clear they had no compunction or respect for the law. Given that, why didn't Shek's escape take an even easier form – have the long-haired guy shoot the two prison officers dead, then escape together?

Why had Shek chosen such a roundabout method? Did his conscience act up, making him reluctant to kill? Or was he uncertain whether the officers escorting him would be armed, and an exchange of fire might have caused the plan to fail?

Sonny thought hard, but couldn't come up with a plausible explanation.

As he stood on the driveway, an ambulance drove past and he returned to the present. Looking at his watch, he realized he'd been gone a full half hour and rushed back to the reception area, trying to think how to explain himself to the commander. He hoped the older man hadn't given up and wandered off.

Back in Building S, he was surprised to see Kwan leaning against the front desk, laughing and chatting with the nurse at reception. She was beaming too, a completely different person.

'Sonny, there you are. You took your time in the bathroom.' Kwan turned back to the nurse. 'I won't take up any more of your time. Nice talking to you.'

'Commander, what were you chatting about?' Sonny asked curiously, as they returned to the sofa.

'Nothing much, health tips and that sort of thing.' Kwan smiled, then lowered his voice. 'Also about Dr Fung – his interests and hobbies, and so forth.'

'Is he a suspect?' asked Sonny anxiously.

'Of course not, but I noticed his watch, the calluses on his left fingers, his shoes, and the pen in his shirt pocket, so I know he enjoys diving and playing guitar, and has a fondness for British products, plus he's frugal. That was enough to start a conversation with the nurse.'

Sonny looked confused.

'Ah, you still don't understand,' chuckled Kwan. 'The lady has a romantic interest in the good doctor.'

'Really?'

'Sonny, you have to learn to pay more attention to the details of how people react. Every move and gesture speaks volumes, unintentionally. When she phoned for Dr Fung, and when she spoke to him in person, there was a significant difference in her expression.'

'So it's the nurse who's a suspect.'

'No, I was just passing the time.' Kwan suppressed a laugh at Sonny's wild ideas. 'Not everything is connected to the case.'

Sonny scratched his head, puzzled by Kwan's behaviour. They had a pile of difficult cases before them, and here he was merrily chatting about this and that. But maybe this 'genius detective' had never found himself in such a difficult situation.

'Commander, I thought of something earlier on.'

'About the acid case or Shek Boon-tim's escape?'

Kwan's question told Sonny that he had worked out the reason for his half-hour disappearance.

'Um... the Shek Boon-tim case.'

'Let's hear it.'

Sonny had expected a scolding for losing focus, and was pleasantly surprised by his commander's breezy reaction. He explained his doubts to Kwan, one by one.

'The movements of the long-haired man make no sense at all,' he finished.

'That's true, your questions are all very logical.' Kwan smiled with satisfaction.

'What do you think, Commander?'

'Me? I'm here to investigate the acid attack. I'm setting aside Shek Boon-tim for now.' Kwan spread his hands wide.

'Huh? Commander?'

'Let's deal with one thing first, before we move on to the other. Haven't you heard the English saying about a bird in your hand being better than two in the forest? Or the Japanese one, that if you chase after two rabbits you'll probably catch neither? But feel free to use this time to think, and you may come up with a conclusion.'

Sonny remained baffled, but as his commander seemed to have made up his mind, it wasn't his place to question.

'It's true, genius is hard to understand,' he reflected.

In the next hour, Kwan didn't subject Sonny to any further facts about chemical burns, nor did he attempt another conversation with the nurse. Instead, he sat quietly on the sofa, watching people go by. Sonny rested his chin in his hands and kept pondering the circumstances of Shek Boon-tim's escape, but it was as if the commander had cursed him, and each time he thought about the long-haired man's route, the image of Auntie Soso discussing the three victims popped up in his head. His thoughts were a hunting dog caught between chasing the fox in the forest to his left, or rooting out the wild boar in the grove to his right.

When the clock's hour hand finally reached the 6, the corridor suddenly grew busy. Some people hurried by, their faces pinched with worry, whilst others strolled along unconcerned.

'Should we go to the ward and wait for Chung's wife and Moe there?' asked Sonny.

'Don't worry, we can sit a little longer.'

Visitors filed past one by one. Five minutes later, Kwan stood abruptly and said, 'We can go in now.'

Sonny obediently stood and followed his commander. Suddenly, he noticed Kwan was no longer holding the purple plastic bag, but when he looked back, it wasn't on the sofa either. He started to call his chief back, not wanting him to lose his newly purchased cap, but then decided not to distract him from the job in hand.

The two officers walked into Ward 6, which contained four beds. Nearest the door on the left was an elderly man missing one leg, while the other bed was empty. On the right side were two patients with their heads swathed in bandages, mummy-like, and tubes poking into their arms. The one closer to the door also had bandages on his arms, and Sonny guessed that this must be slipper-selling Chau; sitting next to him was a young man of medium build, probably Moe, in a blue jacket and carrying a brown sling bag, speaking in a low voice into the patient's ear. Next to the bed by the window were a woman in her thirties and a little boy in school uniform clutching the patient's right hand – this must be the Chung family.

'Is your name Moe?' Kwan and Sonny had walked up to the man in the blue jacket, who looked suspiciously at them. Sonny remembered him from a moment ago – he was one of the anxious-looking visitors who'd scurried past them.

'We're from the police.' Kwan flashed his ID. 'You're Mr Chau Cheung-kwong's nephew Moe?'

'Right, yes, I am.' Seeing the badge seemed to pull Moe to attention. 'Did you want to ask about what happened today? I've already told the other officer...'

'No, that's fine, I already know about that,' smiled Kwan. 'You look much thinner than in your picture. Can't have been easy to lose all that weight in such a short time.'

Sonny, standing behind Moe, had no idea what nonsense Kwan was spouting.

'Officer, what are you talking about?' Moe looked equally confused.

'You can stop pretending. We've got hard evidence.' Kwan produced a clear plastic bag from inside his jacket, in which was a flattened black baseball cap. 'Isn't this what you wore, the third time you did it? You dropped your cap on the rooftop, and my identification team picked it up.'

'That's impossible—' Moe's face changed. He reached quickly for his shoulder bag.

'Ah, so it's in your bag?'

Before Kwan had finished speaking, Moe made a run for it, but Sonny was standing right there, and before Moe knew what was happening he'd been caught. Everyone else in the room watched in shock as Sonny wrestled Moe to the ground.

'Commander, is Moe...?' Keeping the suspect immobilized, Sonny patted him down for weapons and handcuffed him.

'He carried out all three acid attacks: six months ago, four months ago, and this morning.'

'How did you know it was him?'

'Like I said, every move and gesture reveals volumes. Everyone has a unique way of walking. When I saw him go by in the corridor, I knew he was the fatty from the video footage of the Mong Kok attack. I've seen those clips more than a hundred times, and despite his weight loss I'd know that walk anywhere.'

Sonny gaped. Identifying a perp by his *walk* seemed a little arbitrary, even impossible. But Moe's reaction proved Kwan correct.

'What happened?' The nurse from reception rushed into the room.

'The Royal Hong Kong Police Force is arresting a suspect,' answered Kwan calmly, showing his ID. The nurse stood petrified. 'Please inform the hospital guards and ask them to assist.'

Still stunned, the nurse nodded vacantly, then rushed off.

'All right, Sonny, we've solved one case, now we can transfer our attention to the other.' Kwan turned to face the bed-bound patient. 'So, finally we meet, Mr Chau Cheung-kwong... No, I should say, Mr Shek Boon-tim.'

6

SONNY FROZE, THINKING he must be hearing things. The man in the bed was Shek Boon-tim? Although he was still occupied keeping Moe pinned to the floor, all his attention was now on the man with the bandaged face, only his eyes, nostrils and mouth showing, like a movie monster.

'Commander, you mean to say... this is Shek Boon-tim?' stammered Sonny.

'That's right, this is the escaped convict Shek Boon-tim,' said Kwan implacably. The patient made no response, but moved his eyes frantically from left to right.

Sonny pulled Moe upright and shoved him into the chair by the bed, then looked more closely at the man who might be Chau or Shek. The man opened his mouth a little, as if he wished to speak, but nothing came out.

'Are you going to claim I'm wrong?' asked Kwan. 'Mr Shek, if we wanted to confirm your identity, the police have many methods, such as testing your DNA or matching your dental records, all acceptable in a court of law. But I'm very much afraid you won't have your day in court. In fact, if I hadn't exposed your plan, you might not have survived until tomorrow.'

The man stared directly at Kwan, a film of doubt now in his eyes.

'Your scheme was ingenious, but you lack specialized medical knowledge, which is how you've created a life-threatening situation. I do mean "life-threatening", by the way – you might actually die,' said Kwan nonchalantly. 'Do you know what the point of triage is, when you first arrive at ER? Apart from deciding how urgently the patient needs to be seen, it's important to note if he has any drug allergies, and what treatment has already been administered. Skipping this step is more serious than you imagine. This morning in prison, you pretended to have a bad stomach ache and the doctor gave you a painkiller, yes? That was intravenous aspirin. And flowing into your veins now is an anti-inflammatory called ketoprofen. If the doctor had known you'd already had an aspirin injection, he'd never have used ketoprofen, which relies on the liver for metabolizing, whereas aspirin halts the liver's metabolic function. Your liver and kidneys will now have ketoprofen damage, and if not treated within twelve hours, will fail altogether. By the time the patient experiences abdominal discomfort, the liver has already lost eighty per cent of its function. If you don't get a transplant it's too late.'

Even before Kwan had finished, the man in bed sat up abruptly, clawing at the tube in his arm. Because both his hands were bandaged, he had to snatch awkwardly a few times before he managed to get it out. Sonny noticed his eyes were no longer hesitant but full of fear and hatred, and rage directed at the two officers. There was now something altogether different about this man. His expression reminded Sonny of a wounded wild beast, showing cunning and anger even in the moment of its defeat. No one in the ward made a sound. It was as if they'd all been flung into an alternative reality.

Hurried steps broke the silence. Two uniformed guards followed the nurse in.

'Superintendent Kwan Chun-dok, CIB.' Again the ID badge was flashed. 'And this is Sergeant Lok.' Seeing that they were outranked, the two uniforms hastily stood at attention before asking for details.

'This fellow is a suspect in this morning's Central acid-attack case,' said Kwan, indicating Moe. Then, pointing at the bed, 'And this is the wanted criminal Shek Boon-tim. Place them in the holding ward upstairs for now. I'll inform colleagues in the relevant departments to come get them.'

The uniformed officers stared dumbly. Sonny shoved Moe in front of one of them, at which they finally responded, the other briskly cuffing both of Shek's hands to the bed before turning to summon help. Attendants arrived three minutes later and shifted him onto a stretcher. One of them noticed his drip tube had come out, and was about to reattach it when Shek batted her away.

'No... don't...' he gasped feebly.

Kwan walked to the bedside, pressed down on Shek's hand-cuffed right hand and nodded at the nurse, indicating she should proceed. 'Mr Shek, I was lying to you earlier. You're not about to die at all. That's just a hydration tube. You had your ketoprofen injection ages ago – aspirin and ketoprofen are both non-steroidal anti-inflammatory drugs, and mixing them doesn't cause liver damage. At the very worst, they might give you a mild gastric ulcer. It's true that a blood test or dental record check could have confirmed your identity, but I wanted you to confess so I could be satisfied.'

Shek's eyes bulged, glaring at Kwan with shock and loathing. But before he could take a second look, the hospital staff had already pushed him out of the ward.

After quickly wishing Chung and his family well – they were still trying to work out what had just happened – Kwan and Sonny went up to the eighth-floor ward. The director there was astonished that Shek Boon-tim had been recaptured. He'd never expected this escaped convict to be hiding out in the hospital itself, in the building next to the detention ward.

Sonny expected his commanding officer to call Inspector Wang immediately, not to mention notifying Organized Crime and Intelligence to stop their search for Shek Boon-tim, but

Kwan instead dragged his protégé to the room where Moe was being held.

'While the two of them are separated, there's just one thing left to do,' said Kwan.

Moe was sitting dejectedly in a chair, hands secured behind his back, watched over by one of the hospital guards. When Kwan and Sonny entered, he glanced briefly at them, then lowered his head and resumed staring at the floorboards.

'I want the address of your hideout,' said Kwan, in the tone of a command.

Moe didn't respond.

'Don't get me wrong, I'm not asking you to confess.' Kwan's voice was dry. 'But I do need you to be clear what your situation is. Your boss Shek Boon-tim is definitely going back to prison, Little Willy and the two gunmen from the mainland are dead, and most of your other gang members are done for. You're lucky: the acid cases are serious, but no one has died. Li Fun is the most badly wounded, and the doctor says he'll probably survive. You'll be inside for more than a decade, but I imagine you'll be out even before Shek. If your colleagues kill that poor bastard, though, you'll be charged with conspiracy to murder. You're not yet thirty, are you? Ten-odd years living at the tax-payer's expense, and you'll still only be in your forties when you get out. If you live till eighty, that's four more decades of freedom. But if you get a life sentence, your next fifty years will be in a cell no bigger than this room, eking out day after day, waiting for death.'

At least there was some reaction to this – still no words, but Moe looked up at Kwan with a conflicted expression.

'The dog team are camped out in Chai Wan, and we'll find your lair sooner or later. What I'm hoping won't happen is that we find a corpse there, and while the real killers have got away scot-free, the blame falls squarely on your head.'

'I...' Moe seemed unable to make himself speak.

'I know how important honour is in your line, but I'm not

asking you to betray anyone, only to spare an innocent life. You shouldn't have to take responsibility for a crime you didn't commit, especially something as big as murder. Besides, you've been living with that poor devil for quite some time now; you don't want to see him get killed over nothing, do you?'

'Gloria Centre on Fung Yip Street in Chai Wan. Room 412,' Moe spat out, then sullenly lowered his head again.

Kwan nodded, and left the room with Sonny. First, he phoned Alex Choi to let him know Shek had been captured, and the whereabouts of his hideout. Next, he called Inspector Wang to report that the acid attacker had been arrested.

'Commander, whose life were you talking about saving?' Sonny asked, when they were outside the ward.

'The real Chau Cheung-kwong, of course,' said Kwan.

'Why's he in danger? No, I mean, is that really Shek Boon-tim in there? Then who is Chau Cheung-kwong?'

'Let's find somewhere to sit down, then we can talk,' said Kwan. He told the ward director they'd be waiting downstairs, and instructed him to keep a close watch on his prisoners. Sonny didn't understand why they couldn't stay on the eighth floor, but if the man with the explanation was going downstairs, so was he.

They took the elevator down, and Kwan walked out of the building to look at the darkening sky. The lobby, at the opposite end of the building from the Emergency Room, was comparatively so quiet it seemed a little unreal. Kwan sat on a stone bench by a planter and indicated that Sonny should join him.

'Where to start...' Kwan stroked his chin. 'Ah, let's talk about the photos of those two Big Circle men.'

'What about them?' Sonny hadn't thought there was anything noteworthy.

'After the noon briefing, I didn't have a clue, to be honest. Inspector Choi thought Shek might have slipped away during the gunfight, or else changed cars during the five minutes between leaving the hospital and being spotted by the Emergency Unit.

I thought the latter was more likely – Shek was exactly the sort of criminal who'd know everyone expected him to go north, so instead he'd escape in the other direction and hide at the southern end of Hong Kong Island, or else get on a boat to one of the smaller islands. But when I saw pictures of the scene, something caught my attention.'

'Pictures of the gunfight?'

'It was the bodies of the Big Circle guys.' Kwan tapped his own forehead. 'One of them had changed his hairstyle, and looked different from his photo of just a few days before.'

'So what? Criminals disguise themselves all the time.'

'No, be precise. Criminals often disguise themselves *after* a crime. But you don't often see them do it *beforehand*,' said Kwan with a smile. 'It makes perfect sense that he'd do it afterwards. Say he was afraid of being identified by a witness, so he'd change his hair to make himself less recognizable. Before would be possible if it meant something like putting on a wig for the duration of the crime, then resuming his normal appearance afterwards. But here, I couldn't find any reason at all why he'd go from parted hair to a crew cut.'

Sonny thought again of the two pictures on the noticeboard.

Kwan went on, 'Those two had no way of knowing they'd already been spotted by Intelligence – though we didn't know very much, in truth – so that person had no reason to cut his hair short. If he wanted to conceal his identity, he'd get a haircut after rescuing Shek – but there's no way back once you've had a crew cut. When I first saw the photo, I even wondered if we'd mistaken him for someone with similar features, and the deceased wasn't actually the Big Circle man at all – but the scar on his left cheek matched exactly. Twins with identical scars? Too farfetched. So why the haircut, before rescuing Shek?'

'Maybe because... the weather's hot?' Sonny felt this was a stretch, even as he said it.

'That's possible. But I thought of something else. The crew cut was a disguise.'

'But Commander, you said changing his appearance before the crime wouldn't help him evade capture.'

'So he wasn't trying to evade capture,' chuckled Kwan. 'Sonny, what sorts of people usually have crew cuts?'

'Police recruits, soldiers... ah! Convicts!' Sonny shouted, as he saw the answer.

'Correct. When I noticed that, I wondered whether we'd been misled by appearances – what if the man who ran from the hospital to the getaway car wasn't Shek Boon-tim, but one of the Big Circle gangsters? Because it all happened so quickly, as long as the running man had a crew cut, black-framed glasses and a brown prison uniform, every eyewitness would assume it must be the prisoner Shek Boon-tim escaping.'

Sonny recalled the photo of Shek during the briefing, in which his hair was closely cropped – just like the dead Big Circle man's.

'After the gunfight, O-Crime found a prison uniform in the getaway vehicle, with the number tags removed. I wondered about that. Of course an escaped convict would change into civilian clothes, but why rip off the numbers? If it was to destroy evidence or cover his tracks, he'd just burn the whole thing. Besides, only one person escaped from jail today, so we'd know the uniform was his in any case. Unless, of course, it wasn't Prisoner 241138's uniform at all, but a prop used by the false Shek.'

'And that's why you wanted to know exactly how he got out of the bathroom,' said Sonny, thinking of the moment he'd arrived with the report for Inspector Choi.

'That's right. What I said was just one possibility, but the prison officers' statements made me think my hypothesis was almost certainly right.'

'And the long-haired man?'

'An important clue, though there was even more obvious evidence. But I hadn't sorted through all my ideas, and to avoid confusing Alex and his team, or accidentally alerting the criminals, I ordered him to go after the most certain, concrete lead – track down the long-haired man.'

'More obvious evidence?'

'Incredibly obvious!' Kwan laughed. 'You, Alex, whoever interviewed the prison officers, and everyone who saw those testimonies – all of you missed it. Should I be worried? Maybe you were all distracted by the gunfight, and the investigation would have had to hit a dead end before you examined the other evidence and saw it then. The handcuffs by the window – didn't they strike you as odd?'

'In what way?'

'One of Shek Boon-tim's hands was fastened to the cubicle handrail. In order to escape, he had to either release that hand, in which case the cuffs would have been left dangling from the rail, or else open the other side and run off with them round his wrist. What kind of criminal would be stupid enough to waste time opening *both* sides of his handcuffs, and then drop them before escaping?'

Sonny rapped his forehead. How had he not thought of this himself?

'So... Shek Boon-tim didn't escape then?'

'Correct. He used the handcuffs to entice the guard over to the window, from where Shek's stand-in could be seen running towards the car, thus creating the illusion that the convict had got out that way. I'm guessing Shek was actually hiding in the "Out of Order" cubicle. Ng Fong said he'd gone into the bathroom beforehand and pushed that cubicle door open, and he'd naturally have pulled it shut again afterwards, creating an excellent blind spot for Shek.'

'Commander, you're saying... Shek was hiding behind a half-closed wooden door, listening to two Correctional Officers going after him? Wasn't that risky?'

'Not really, if one of the officers was on his side.'

'Huh?'

'A turncoat in the prison itself,' said Kwan, lowering his voice.

Sonny stared at the superintendent, uncertain whether to believe him.

'You mean... Ng Fong, the older one?' whispered Sonny. He understood now why they'd had to leave the eighth floor – nothing they were saying could be overheard by Correctional Services.

'No, the young one, Sze Wing-hong.'

'But he was only keeping watch outside.'

'That's the genius of it,' said Kwan earnestly. 'This inside man didn't directly use his position to help Shek escape, he only created a series of conditions that would facilitate it. This made it unlikely the blame would ever be pinned on him. I'm betting it was Shek rather than Sze who came up with this plan. I hate the bastard, but I have to say I rather admire him too.'

'What conditions?'

'Let's reconstruct the escape. This is all conjecture, but should be ninety per cent accurate. Sze Wing-hong knew of the plan all along, so when Shek asked to use the bathroom, he suggested the one upstairs. Sze had just joined the service, so the more experienced Ng Fong would want to inspect the toilet himself. That left Sze alone with Shek, allowing him to pass over a hairpin, which Shek would have hidden in his trousers or on his collar – this is the hairpin our investigators found later.'

'And Shek used this to pick the lock?'

'I don't think so. It was a red herring.' Kwan shook his head. 'Ng Fong came back out, then he and Sze took Shek into the bathroom. Sze released the left handcuff and fastened Shek's right hand to the railing. At the same time, he slipped the key into Shek's right palm, while pretending to return it to his own pocket. The hospital cubicles are a little larger than usual, but it'd still have been easy to block Ng from seeing this move. Besides, Ng would only have been concerned about making sure the cuffs were secure. You don't need a key to close handcuffs, so Ng would never have suspected it was in Shek's hand.'

Sonny listened dubiously. Was Kwan fabricating an explanation out of thin air?

'This is all guesswork, but if I were Shek Boon-tim, that's how I'd have done it.' Kwan seemed to read Sonny's mind. 'If Ng

Fong hadn't pulled that cubicle door half shut, Sze would have found some excuse to re-examine it, maybe pretending to have seen something dangerous in there, and then closed the door himself. And then, while Ng was watching Shek inside the room, Sze's co-conspirator appeared, and they went through their scripted quarrel until Ng Fong was lured out. Right away, Shek undid the handcuffs and flung the window wide open, dropping the cuffs on the floor just inside. Then he threw the key outside and darted into the "Out of Order" cubicle. I'm saying he used the key, because with so little time available, he'd have gone for the most efficient method. The long-haired man hurried away and gave some kind of signal, and the Big Circle guy disguised as Shek, waiting beneath the window, started running towards the car.'

Sonny thought of the window he'd seen in the stairwell. It'd be easy to reach between the bars and signal to someone outside. The long-haired man must have gone down the stairs and waved to the car; Little Willy, behind the wheel, waved to Big Circle under the window – and the stand-in, pulling off the coat that had kept his uniform hidden and stuffing it down his shirt, would have started running towards the car.

'This was the boldest part of the plan.' Kwan glanced at Sonny. 'Shek was just hiding behind a door, and if Ng Fong had stayed calm, he'd have been trapped. But what Sze did next upset his older colleague's judgement – he climbed out of the window. Naturally Ng had to assist his partner, rather than letting him chase a felon on his own – that's part of the discipline of any uniformed organization, or you could even say it was instinct. Ng's conditioned reflex to help a fellow officer overrode his observation and focus, and just like that, Shek slipped away from under his gaze.'

'Just now you said Shek threw the handcuff key out of the window. Sze would have picked it up?'

'Yes, though that's just an educated guess,' Kwan nodded. 'Sze could also have made a duplicate key, but using the same one

23266636

was simpler, and eliminated the risk of being caught making a copy. As long as he got the key back and ran for a while after a car he knew he'd never catch, he'd have amply fulfilled his duties.'

Sonny recalled Kwan's instruction to Inspector Choi, only to ask Ng Fong to help with the identikit picture. That made sense now – talking to Sze would have alerted him that the police were on the trail of the long-haired man.

'Commander, wouldn't a person have to be pretty foolish to put himself in this position? Letting a convict escape on his watch – he'd be sure to get into trouble. Besides, how are you so sure it's Sze Wing-hong? Even if everything took place exactly as you said, Ng Fong could still be the inside man.'

'That why I said Shek's plan was masterful. He made sure Sze's role was smaller than Ng's. And would Sze care if he got into trouble? Both officers would have to take responsibility, but anyone looking at the matter would conclude Ng was more culpable, because he was the one who left the convict unguarded. Sze followed protocol every step of the way, and even selflessly chased after the escapee,' Kwan said sardonically. 'As to why I'm certain Sze was the turncoat, just look at how his testimony was different from Ng's.'

'I didn't think they contradicted each other?'

'They didn't, but their attitudes had an obvious disparity.'

'You mean how Sze kept asking if he was being investigated?'

'No, it's the way they referred to Shek. Ng Fong kept saying "the convict", but Sze used his name. Ng Fong saw Shek as just another prisoner, same as he encountered all day long, but to Sze he was an individual with a name. This detail, plus all the circumstantial evidence, is enough to convince me Sze Wing-hong is the inside man.'

Sonny thought back through the two videos, and realized Kwan was right.

'Then Shek Boon-tim ran off as soon as Ng Fong went down the stairs?' he asked.

'Instead of "ran off", you might as well say he walked casually away.' Kwan smiled bitterly. 'He dropped the hairclip to explain how he'd opened the handcuffs, then went off with the people who'd come to meet him.'

'What people? The long-haired man?'

'The long-haired man, Moe and Chau Cheung-kwong.'

Sonny stared dubiously at Kwan, waiting for him to explain.

'When I learned from Ng Fong's testimony that the handcuffs had been left in front of the window, I realized my earlier hypothesis was wrong,' said Kwan. 'I'd initially guessed he'd used his henchmen to create a distraction while he escaped to the south. But the handcuffs told me that he didn't actually jump from the window, because then he wouldn't have wasted time unlocking both sides. So that created an interesting problem. If he just wanted to confuse his pursuers, it'd have been far easier to switch cars after escaping, and head south. Instead, he went to a lot of trouble to have a body double act as a decoy. Choosing a difficult path over an easy one suggests other motivations. As you asked an hour ago, Sonny, why not just massacre anyone in his way? Have his men show up with enough firepower and bust Shek out that way? But think about it: if he wanted to deceive people into thinking he'd fled, then he must still have been in the hospital. Why would an escaped convict not get as far away as he could at the first opportunity, but stay at the scene?'

'Because... he wanted to impersonate Chau Cheung-kwong?' Sonny jumped straight to the conclusion, although he had no idea how to get there.

'Exactly.' Kwan nodded sagely. 'But I didn't think of this right after watching the videos. It wasn't until O-Crime found the second getaway vehicle at Babington Path that I had the next idea.'

'What was suspicious about that?'

'O-Crime found a convenience store receipt in the first vehicle, used that to narrow their search area, and so found the second car at West Mid-levels.'

'Right?'

'And you raised a good point then.' Kwan looked approvingly at Sonny. 'You said parking the car there would make things needlessly difficult for them, and wouldn't it have been easier to escape from Sai Ying Pun?'

'Yes, that's right, but didn't we find an answer? Traffic in Central was chaotic after a rush-hour accident, so West Mid-levels became the more sensible route to their destination, Chai Wan.'

'The time on the receipt was six in the morning – the accident hadn't happened yet.'

'Oh...' Sonny saw the problem.

'That was strange. Did Little Willy and the others have a premonition about the traffic jam and change the location of their second getaway vehicle? Or it could have been happenstance; but Shek Boon-tim is such a meticulous planner, if he deliberately selected a narrow road where he could easily be trapped or ambushed, there must be some reason behind it. And then I thought, what if the accident in Central was actually part of Shek's scheme, the very first step in this whole plan?'

'But what's the use of creating a jam in Des Voeux Road? To delay the police and help Little Willy get away?'

'No; if that was his goal, an accident on a main road in Central wouldn't help much. We'd just send officers from the Western District station instead. If Shek really wanted to slow us down, the accident should have been at Sai Ying Pun, and later on – as it is, the one at Central was two hours before his escape.'

'That's right, so what happened in Central was useless to him.'

'You're wrong. The accident in Central wasn't useful in his *escape*. Because the second car was found at Mid-levels, we knew the criminals intended to travel via Central, and we tried to connect the "accident" with the "escape". But that was a mistake. Another word floated up in my mind, and it wasn't "escape".'

'What was it, then?'

'"Hospital".'

'Hospital?'

'You forget, I'd already noticed there was something fishy

about those handcuffs and deduced that Shek was still at the hospital. Once I'd linked "hospital" and "slow traffic in Central", the picture became clearer. There are three public hospitals on Hong Kong Island with twenty-four-hour Emergency Rooms: Queen Mary in the Western District, Tang Shiu Kin in Wan Chai, and Pamela Youde Nethersole in the east. When there's an accident in the Central or Western District, the casualties are sent to Queen Mary – though when the Queen Mary ER approaches capacity, ambulances are diverted to Tang Shiu Kin instead. But if there was some chemical spillage in Central and the roads needed to be sealed off and cleaned, traffic in those parts, already slow at the best of times, would become completely paralysed. The ambulances would have no choice but to keep going to Queen Mary.'

Sonny recalled Dr Fung complaining how bad traffic had meant the acid-attack victims couldn't be transferred to Tang Shiu Kin that morning. And then, like electricity shooting through him, he suddenly understood why Kwan Chun-dok had got involved in this investigation.

'Commander, do you think Shek Boon-tim was also behind this morning's fire at West Point?'

'Yes.' Kwan's lip curled a little, as if satisfied that Sonny had finally caught up. 'If he crashed a chemical truck at Des Voeux to overwhelm Queen Mary's ER, then the increased number of patients probably wasn't a coincidence either. Shek Boon-tim was the mastermind behind the fire, the overturned truck and the Graham Street acid attack.'

Sonny thought of how Inspector Wang had said the West Point fire looked suspicious and the Crime Unit was taking over the investigation. So the arsonists must have been—

'Little Willy and the two Big Circle men set the fire at five in the morning, then drove the car, no, two cars to Babington Path, bought breakfast at the convenience store, then waited to stage the getaway at the hospital?' Sonny worked it out as he spoke.

'More or less.' Kwan nodded, his fingers interlaced over his knee. 'We don't have any evidence for this, only logic and deduction, so I didn't say anything to Alex, but decided to head to Graham Street and see the scene of the acid attack for myself.'

'And that's why you first said Graham Street was the work of a copycat?'

'Right, I thought at the time that Shek might have taken advantage of the situation, and sent someone to imitate the Mong Kok incident to create chaos and distract from whatever he was up to at the hospital. But when I saw how exactly the methods lined up, I thought this was neither coincidence nor opportunism but a carefully laid operation that they'd started preparing for six months ago. If Graham Street had been a copycat, that could simply have been Shek's way of sending more people to the hospital, making it even more overcrowded, but if it were that simple, he wouldn't have struck at Mong Kok once before, let alone twice. There must have been some other reason – and that's when I came up with the hypothesis that Mong Kok was a rehearsal.'

'But Commander, didn't you say the culprit wanted to ambush an enemy?' Sonny asked, remembering their conversation in the car.

'Ambush what enemy?'

'You mentioned novels about serial killers, and I said one reason was to conceal the true target of their murder...'

'Why do you have to be so literal?' laughed Kwan. 'The key word was "conceal", not "murder". Did you really think I was investigating the three wounded men to see if they had any enemies? I wasn't looking for a victim, but an accomplice.'

Sonny smacked his head, cursing himself.

'But sir, how did you guess one of those three was an accomplice?'

'Put these things together: Shek Boon-tim lured his pursuers away while remaining in the hospital himself. He overfilled the Emergency Room with patients, causing chaos. And a plan was brewing half a year, to injure large numbers of people with acid. The most logical conclusion is that Shek took advantage of the confusion to impersonate someone else. He'd arrange for an ordinary person to be admitted, and then swap places with him. Afterwards, he'd simply take over that person's identity, and live out in the open, while the police would never find the vanished Shek Boon-tim. Continuing down this line of thought, I knew one of the victims must be working with Shek – and that turned out to be the slipper salesman, Boss Chau.'

'Hang on. Do you mean to say Chau Cheung-kwong was pretending to be injured?'

'No, that had to be real. There'd be no way to fool the paramedics.'

'Huh? But you said this whole thing was planned by Shek Boon-tim, so if a victim was also an accomplice...'

'He deliberately splashed acid onto his own face.'

Sonny stared at Kwan in horror. 'Chau Cheung-kwong did that?'

'Of course it would have been Moe who actually threw the acid.' Kwan paused, then added, 'But Chau was a willing participant.'

'Willing?'

'I'd guess he must have owed a lot of money. One of Shek's henchmen – maybe Little Willy, maybe Moe, maybe the long-haired man – scoped out one of their debtors about the same build and age as Shek himself, then threatened and bribed him into co-operating. Many people in that position would go along with it. And so they made the necessary preparations for Shek to assume Chau's identity. Moe carried out the attacks in Mong Kok to lay a false trail, and then found a plausible way for Chau to start working on Graham Street, while getting ready to wipe out his face.'

Now Sonny grasped why Kwan had asked Auntie Soso if the three victims had money troubles or anything like that. Not to see if they had enemies, but to find out if they had weaknesses which might be exploited.

'This morning, following the plan, Moe and Chau used the

excuse of moving stock to head to the abandoned building at the corner of Graham and Wellington Streets. Chau might have waited in the stairwell, or else pretended to be moving boxes in front of the building, actually keeping a lookout while Moe threw the drain cleaner off the roof. After that, back in the stairwell, came the most important and boldest step – flinging the corrosive liquid directly at Chau's face and hands. I'd guess this was a lower concentration, but it still caused second-degree chemical burns. Or else Moe had water ready, and washed the acid off as soon as he thought Chau's skin was sufficiently damaged. In any case, Chau put himself through that willingly.'

Sonny swallowed hard, imagining the moment.

'When the paramedics got there, they quickly cleaned and dressed his burns, then Moe and Chau both got in the ambulance to Queen Mary Hospital. End scene.'

'Commander, when were you certain that Chau Cheung-kwong was the one who'd changed places with Shek? It could have been Li Fun or Chung Wai-shing too, couldn't it?'

'After my chat with Auntie Soso and her friends, I was, oh, eighty or ninety per cent sure.'

'That was when you knew?'

'First of all, Li Fun's too old for Shek to convincingly take his place. Besides, the doctor said both his eyes were damaged, so he probably was injured for real.' Kwan lifted one finger. 'That left Chung Wai-shing and Chau Cheung-kwong. They were both possible, but Chung was less likely, because he had a tattoo, which would make changing places with him harder. Chau was most suspicious, because he'd worked the shortest time on Graham Street, and because his behaviour in the marketplace was so odd, not at all like a trader. Also, his eyes weren't affected.'

'That's not a reason,' interrupted Sonny. 'The doctor said it was because he was wearing sunglasses that kept the acid out of his eyes.'

'Wrong again. It was the doctor's words that actually convinced me Chau must be the accomplice. Since that storm a couple of days ago, it's been consistently hazy and grey. Why would he need to wear sunglasses?'

Sonny thought back. It was true, there'd been no sun for a few days now.

'The victims were brought to hospital, and at the same time Shek faked abdominal pains to get sent here. Next came that little piece of theatre, the "escape".' Kwan looked back in the direction of the Emergency Room. 'Chau's injuries weren't as serious as Li Fun's or Chung Wai-shing's, so after triage he was placed behind them in the queue for treatment. With so many patients waiting and the ER in such a mess, Chau would have easily evaded attention and left his place, carrying out the rest of the plan. We've already said what Shek, Sze and the long-haired man were up to in the bathroom. At the same time, Moe would have helped Chau to a nearby place to wait – maybe another bathroom, or a storeroom. As soon as the prison officers left, the long-haired man would have returned to the bathroom to fetch Shek, and they'd have gone to the agreed meeting place for Shek to change places with Chau.'

'So Shek put on Chau's clothes?'

'No, not clothes. Chau's clothes were taken off after he was injured, and he'd have been wearing a hospital gown, or maybe he was shirtless. They'd have had to repeat a step from earlier on, and pour acid onto Shek Boon-tim's face and hands.'

Sonny took a deep breath. 'Commander, can it be... Shek was willing to endure such enormous pain, just to escape?'

'Yes. If he skipped this step, he wouldn't be able to get past the doctors and nurses.' Kwan's voice remained level. 'Shek ruined his face, then washed off the acid with water and bandaged his head. Then he went back to the ER with Moe and lay on the bed previously occupied by Chau. And Chau would have changed his clothes – probably putting on a windcheater with a hood – and gritted his teeth against the pain, leaving together with the long-haired man. The hospital was in upheaval because of Shek's escape, so they wouldn't have attracted much notice, even though Chau was still wrapped up like a mummy – patients get discharged all the time with bandages on. The long-haired man had a car ready, and the pair of them left in a leisurely manner. They'd have planned to meet Little Willy and the others at the hideout in Chai Wan.'

'So when Dr Fung said "Chau Cheung-kwong" was miscategorized by triage, the person he was referring to hadn't actually received any first aid at all!' Sonny realized.

'Shek's plan went very smoothly there. Yet however clever he might be, he couldn't have predicted the result of the car chase. Little Willy crashed the car, they got into a gunfight, and all three died. Long Hair and Moe would have gotten very agitated when they heard the news, but their mastermind was stuck in hospital and Moe couldn't get further instructions from him until six in the evening. They must have been completely at a loss, even postponing the next step of murdering the real Chau Cheung-kwong.'

'Murdering Chau?'

'I imagine Moe told Chau that after the swap, Boss Shek would get an underworld doctor to fix him up, then smuggle him to the mainland or South-east Asia to start a new life. But Shek wouldn't actually have done anything like that. A low-value chess piece like Chau is, to Shek, only worth using and throwing away. Done and dusted.'

'Commander, did you really recognize Moe as the Mong Kok perp from the way he walked?'

'Of course I recognized his gait, but I wasn't using that to discover the criminal, only to verify my own hypothesis. After talking to Dr Fung, because all the objective evidence pointed to the same conclusion, I was virtually certain that Chau Cheung-kwong was Shek Boon-tim, and Moe the acid attacker. I just needed to be sure. While I was waiting for you to bring the car round I thought of how to make Moe give himself away, and bought that black baseball cap. Next, I just had to wait for someone with the same way of walking as the Mong Kok fatty. If such a person appeared and went to visit "Boss Chau" in Ward 6, that would confirm my suspicion. What I didn't expect was that Moe would have lost so much weight. No wonder the police haven't been able to track him down.' Once again, Kwan pulled out the baseball cap in its transparent bag.

'How did you know Moe wore that cap during the attack?'

'It was broad daylight, and without a cap he could easily have been recognized. I'm guessing he also had a jacket on, and maybe even a mask. Besides, he knew the pictures of him in the cap were circulating, and that's who the police were looking for, so he *had* to wear it. That way, if he was seen, it would immediately link the Graham Street and Mong Kok cases.'

'Why tie the cases together? Why not just let people think it was a copycat?'

'Sonny, I'm going to send your question back to you – why didn't Shek Boon-tim just use brute force, and shoot his way out of that hospital?'

'Um... he was afraid of complicating the situation?'

'He even had an inside man in the prison. He could have handled that.'

'Uh... his conscience hit him, and he didn't want to hurt any more people?'

'Yes, and maybe the sun will rise in the west.'

'Okay, I really don't understand. Why use such a complicated method to escape?' Sonny shook his head in defeat.

'Sonny, escaping from prison is like committing murder – it's actually very simple,' explained Kwan slowly. 'If you want to kill someone, a single bullet or a quick knife slash, and it's done. Jailbreaks are the same. If you have enough manpower and firepower, you can blast a hole in the most secure prison to get your guy out. The hard thing isn't the process, it's what happens afterwards. How do you evade the law after committing murder? How do you stay free after you've fled from prison? These next steps are the real difficulty.'

Sonny listened in silence, like a disciple absorbing wisdom

from his mentor.

'Shek Boon-tim could get away easily enough, but once he was out, he'd have to hide in darkness, because the whole of Hong Kong would know this most wanted man was hiding among us, and the police would put everything we had into the manhunt. He'd be exchanging one prison for a slightly larger prison. Shek's not stupid. He'd want complete victory. In a city like Hong Kong, it's hard to get a new identity, unless it's under the Witness Protection Programme, which needs the Governor – ah, no, after the handover it'll be the Chief Executive – to approve it. All your records would need to be changed. But Shek chose an unexpected method – destroying his own features and fingerprints, and taking over someone else's life and identity.'

'But he could just have done that – got Moe to splash Chau Cheung-kwong with acid – without this whole plot, leaving dozens of people injured.'

'If this were an isolated case, the victim and attacker would come in for a lot more police attention. Even if the switch were successful, they might still let something slip during the investigation. There are hardly any cases of people having their face and fingerprints destroyed in this way, so the police would treat it as a targeted crime. But a series of attacks seemingly motivated by pure malice would help conceal the true objective – giving Shek Boon-tim a new identity. "Chau Cheung-kwong" would be just another wounded person in a crowd of victims. Best of all, even if the attacker was caught, Shek wouldn't be affected – everyone would just assume Moe was a psycho. So Shek actually hoped the police would think the Graham Street and Mong Kok cases were the same perp. That's why Moe had to wear the baseball cap.'

If they were all chess players, Sonny thought, Kwan Chun-dok and Shek Boon-tim would be grand masters, calculating with every move, weighing the opponent's plans and strategies, while he, Sonny, was just a novice, only seeing one move ahead. Kwan's explanation was slowly making clear to him every detail that he'd seen or heard earlier, such as his commander's quip to Auntie Soso about seeing 'unsuspicious friends' – because he knew the criminal must have been planted in the marketplace for some time, rather than being a stranger around there. And how Shek told Moe to stage the attack on Graham Street, rather than in Wan Chai or Causeway Bay, to ensure the victims would be sent not to some Eastern District hospital but to Queen Mary, where all the Stanley Prison inmates were taken. The first floor of Building J was Medical Social Services – and Shek used the fire and the acid attack to create large numbers of victims, so all the social workers would be busy downstairs counselling patients and their families, ensuring the area around the bathroom would be even more deserted, reducing the likelihood of someone stumbling upon their plans.

If Shek's plan had worked, he'd have had a brand new face after reconstructive surgery, erasing his past and starting a new life as Chau Cheung-kwong. And all the while, he'd be planning a new crime spree. Sonny thought it was unlikely he'd have returned to Graham Street. Moe would probably have told the locals that Boss Chau needed time to recuperate, sold the stall lease and vanished from their lives. Ironically, it would be a public hospital providing the surgery – with taxpayers funding his change of identity. If Kwan hadn't seen through the plan, Shek's victory would have been complete.

'I even had to ask the nurse at reception for this plastic bag – I didn't have any evidence bags on me,' laughed Kwan, placing the baseball cap on his own head.

'Commander, why did you want to scare Shek Boon-tim? Lying to him that his life was in danger from the medicine?'

Kwan snorted. 'Shek Boon-tim is human trash. His younger brother Boon-sing was garbage too – once he calmly killed five hostages in the course of an escape – but still the less heartless of the two. Shek Boon-tim had no regard for anyone but himself, and was perfectly content to sacrifice other people's lives for his petty little goals. To him, it was no big deal to burn down an entire apartment building, create a huge public panic with acid attacks, and involve dozens of people, maybe more than a hundred, in his scheme. In my whole life, I've never hated anyone more than selfish bastards like him. Even after this defeat, he'd probably go back to his cell without once thinking what he'd done was wrong. My bluff was a little warning, just to let him know there's at least one person on earth who can see right through him. I wanted him to realize he's no criminal genius, but just a regular scumbag who lost to an elderly policeman.'

Sonny had never seen such fury in his commanding officer, but the rage was quickly quenched when Inspector Wang and the Organized Crime investigator in charge of capturing Shek arrived together.

'Superintendent Kwan, we've apprehended two suspects at the address provided. One has serious chemical burns to the face, and has been admitted at the Pamela Youde Nethersole hospital,' the O-Crime officer reported. 'We also found two AK-47 assault rifles, numerous handguns and a vast quantity of ammunition. Looks like we were just in time to prevent an armed robbery.'

Kwan nodded in satisfaction. He'd predicted this too.

After they were done with the paperwork and had talked through the rough outlines of the case, Kwan handed over the two suspects from the eighth-floor ward to Wang and the O-Crime officer. Sonny followed him back to the parking lot. The sky was almost completely dark now – it was seven in the evening.

'Commander, are you heading home?' asked Sonny. He'd driven Kwan back to his Mong Kok apartment on several occasions.

'No, let's go back to the office.'

'Huh? Are you keen to finish your report, so you can retire in peace?'

'Not at all,' smiled Kwan. 'I want to catch the team before they leave, so we can all eat that cake together. I'd hate to waste it.'

★

The following morning, Sonny Lok went back to the Division B office. Inspector Choi had given the whole of Team 1 the day off. There was only paperwork left, anyway. Sonny could have stayed at home, but he wanted to take advantage of the weekend to tidy the place up, before taking his girlfriend on a countryside drive that afternoon.

'Ah, Commander, you're back?' Sonny noticed Kwan in his office, sorting through personal documents.

'Is that you, Sonny?' Kwan glanced up from beneath his baseball cap, then went back to the papers. 'I could have delayed this a few days, but I wanted Alex to get his office as soon as possible – he's the new commander, you know.'

'But didn't you write up the investigation yesterday?' Sonny thought this case was so complicated, only Kwan would be able to produce a report that made any sense.

'I'll do that at home, in my own time.'

'Oh, right.' Sonny suddenly thought of something. 'Yesterday, O-Crime said they'd arrested two people in Chai Wan – so that's the long-haired man and the real Chau Cheung-kwong. But what about Sze Wing-hong? I didn't see any news about him being caught.'

'He wasn't arrested,' said Kwan simply.

'But why not? He's just as guilty.'

'Benny will deal with him.'

'Benedict Lau? Superintendent Lau from Division A?'

'Yes, I told him to send someone to talk to Sze, and force him to turn informant.'

Sonny stared in confusion at Kwan. Just when he thought he had a handle on this case, this turncoat was being given a free pass.

Looking at Sonny's expression, Kwan explained, 'Sze Wing-hong is an inside man, but he's not the only one in Correctional Services. Arresting him alone wouldn't do any good.'

'You think there are others?'

'Sze's duties didn't normally bring him into contact with Shek.

There must have been a whole network for them to get in touch, which means Shek has other stooges amongst the guards. Sonny, do you know how I was so sure there was an inside man?'

'Wasn't it Sze Wing-hong's video evidence...'

'Not just that. It was the time.'

'Time?'

'The acid attack took place at five past ten, at exactly the same moment Ng Fong got the order to send Shek Boon-tim to hospital. That's too much of a coincidence. The prison authorities might not have allowed Shek to go to hospital at all, and even if they did, it would have been hard to say when. So it must have been someone on the inside who waited till that order came, then sent the signal for Moe to go into action, thus ensuring the victims would reach the hospital at the same time as Shek. If anything had come up, the Graham Street plan would have been aborted and kept in reserve for another time. The West Point fire and Central traffic accident would have been child's play for Shek to arrange, it was just the acid attack that they had to be careful about.'

'Ah...' Sonny ran through the timings of this case in his mind.

'And frankly, that cubicle being out of order was suspicious too. Without that, Shek's plan couldn't have worked. But if they'd faked the sign, we would have known at once that something was up. In other words, the damage was real, which means someone must have arranged it. That wouldn't be too hard to do, but without attracting attention? And making sure it'd still be awaiting repairs at that time? So there must have been a plant in the hospital too, waiting for the right moment to sabotage it and report it to the maintenance department.'

'The hospital too? Someone's paid off the doctors and nurses?' gasped Sonny.

'A hospital has more than just doctors and nurses. Don't forget – Building J has a detention ward too.'

'What! The detention ward?'

'I'm afraid that over the last few years, Shek Boon-tim has

used his powers of persuasion to pull a number of Correctional Services officers over to his side.' Kwan continued to tidy up as he spoke. 'A jail is cut off from the outside world, and its guards can easily get drawn into a close relationship with the inmates. Any young officer might fall into the psychological trap of a devil like Shek Boon-tim, and become his accomplice. Sze Wing-hong was just one of them. After all, it was management who decided which guards would accompany the prisoner; it'd be too risky for Shek if Sze was his only inside man. It'd be easy for us to charge Sze, but Shek would still be back in prison, hatching a new scheme. He likes to use turncoats – so let's give him a taste of his own medicine.'

'So that's how it is,' Sonny murmured. Although he knew Division A got reports from informants, he'd only just this minute realized how important that was.

'Commander, can I give you a lift anywhere?' He nodded at the heavy cardboard box on Kwan's desk. 'I'll be passing by Mong Kok later, I can drop you off. I'm meeting my girlfriend at noon, we're planning to drive around Sai Kung.'

'Ah, that'd be great. I thought I'd have to take the MTR,' said Kwan. 'I hope I can count on you for a ride in the future, whenever it's convenient?'

'In the future? Commander, aren't you retired?'

'I am, but I'm going to be a consultant, so I should be in and out of the office.'

'Great!' Sonny was overjoyed that he'd still be able to learn from Kwan's investigative skills. 'Of course, no problem! Just tell me what to do, Commander!'

'I'm no longer your commander,' smiled Kwan.

'Oh yes... Superintendent Kwan? No, former Superintendent Kwan?' Sonny said awkwardly.

Kwan broke into a grin at Sonny's embarrassment. 'If you don't mind, just call me Sifu, as in mentor. From now on, you can be my disciple.'

IV

THE BALANCE
OF THEMIS:

1989

KWAN CHUN-DOK STEPPED out of the elevator and into the murky corridor. A light fitting, grey with dust, dangled from the ceiling, its blinking bulb illuminating a cracked, pitted brick floor and white walls marked with unidentifiable stains and graffiti. The officers' footsteps and voices from the intercom echoed disorientingly off the bare, windowless walls. All down the corridor were silent doors, each protected by a stern, imposing steel gate, as if in rebuke at the inadequate security of this building. It all seemed to proclaim that any resident imprudent enough not to take anti-burglary measures was inviting thieves to their door – which was in fact the case.

All the residents on this floor had been evacuated just minutes before, ushered down the stairs by the police. Kwan knew that the most dangerous time was over, and emptying the building now was like mending a fence after the sheep had all been killed. Still, they had to follow protocol. And of course, if concealed explosives were to blow up now and injure an innocent civilian, the police would have to take responsibility – and they were already in enough trouble.

If I were the commander, I might well have done the same, thought Kwan.

Kwan Chun-dok was the highest-ranking officer present, but

he wasn't directing this operation. He could have stayed in the command centre, or followed Keith Tso back to HQ, but he'd chosen to go to the scene instead. Why had he followed his colleagues into this building? Perhaps instinct, developed over more than twenty years as a frontline investigator.

Kwan was very clear what his position was. His rank meant his suggestions would be heeded, but that would undermine the independence of this regional investigation. So he'd do nothing, and just observe.

Now he wanted only to go to the stifling, airless space of the crime scene, and see for himself what his former subordinate must have seen.

A few minutes previously, Kwan had seen that subordinate in the lobby. The man had never reported to him directly – he was a junior investigator who had been assigned from another department to operations Kwan had directed. Still, his courage and judgement back then had left a deep impression.

He'd left this courageous individual lying helplessly on a stretcher, receiving treatment from paramedics.

Their eyes had met, and Kwan had been about to say 'Well done,' but then thought this might come across as sarcastic. Instead, he patted the officer's uninjured shoulder, nodded slightly and walked to the elevator.

Standing in the corridor, Kwan seemed to feel the pressure of some time ago, of being on the line between life and death. Turning a corner, he passed through a wooden door and noted the clustered bulletholes in the wall. Two investigators were gathering evidence, meticulously examining and recording every mark.

Kwan continued on to the brightly lit scene of the crime.

Even without the headache-inducing flicker of the corridor lights, the atmosphere was hellish. The air reeked of gun smoke and blood. The floors, walls and furniture were all stained red and riddled with bullets.

Most unsettling were the bodies – lying on the floor, their skulls shattered, half their brains blown away, grey-white matter

leaking out and mingling, murky pink, with the crimson rivu-
lets of blood.

The investigators stood around one corpse after another, recording every detail they could. No one dared look directly at the
victims' faces. Not because of the gory expressions, though these
were indeed grotesque.

They averted their eyes out of guilt.

All these shattered faces and broken bodies were an indict-
ment of the Royal Hong Kong Police Force's impotence.

Every officer present knew that out of all these slain, only one
person deserved to die.

1

'EDGAR, THIS IS Superintendent Kwan Chun-dok, the new commander of CIB Division B.'

Chief Inspector Edgar Ko hadn't expected Superintendent Tso to show up without warning, let alone accompanied by the legendary Kwan Chun-dok. The officer in charge of a command centre never wants anyone higher-ranking there, just as generals commanding an army aren't pleased when the king or his ministers turn up at the front line – in the thick of the action, 'higher-ups' is just another word for trouble. When Edgar Ko shook hands with Kwan Chun-dok, he worked hard to disguise these thoughts, but suspected the other man, known for his deductive skills, had already seen right through him and was now only smiling out of politeness.

'Superintendent Kwan, how do you do,' said Ko. For the last few years, Kwan had been in charge of the Hong Kong Island's Crime Unit, attracting the admiration and envy of colleagues in other districts after solving a string of major cases. When Ko was promoted to the equivalent position in West Kowloon, many of his colleagues began secretly comparing him to Kwan. Never mind how glowing his past record was, how many drug factories he'd shut down or fraud rings he'd busted, he'd always be number two next to a freak like Kwan Chun-dok. Ko was only three years younger than Kwan, but in his eyes the older man was impossibly far ahead, a target he'd never catch up with.

Deep down, Ko believed he'd been doomed to failure from the very beginning. Apart from Kwan's superior abilities, what set him apart was being one of the first Chinese officers to make it to the elite. Kwan had applied to join the force in the 1960s, when all top-ranking officers were white, and locals only hired for grunt work. Yet he was among a select few to be sent for a two-year training stint in England. He returned to Hong Kong in 1972, just as the force was being restructured, and was immediately promoted to inspector. This was the era when British training was essentially a guarantee of promotion, a mark of exceptional status like the Emperor's gift of a yellow mandarin jacket. Ko had heard that Kwan had helped resolve some matter during protests in 1967, thus gaining the favour of a British inspector. After that, it was all smooth sailing. Edgar Ko had had no such opportunities to show his mettle.

'After Superintendent Kwan heard about this operation, he came over specially to say hello, with good wishes for your future collaboration,' said Superintendent Tso levelly. He was the Deputy Commander of CIB, a solemn man with a capable manner, considered by everyone in the force to be a sure thing for the CIB leadership.

'I understand. The Shek brothers have information about many criminal gangs – I guess they'd be a gold mine to CIB?' Ko deliberately kept his voice casual.

Kwan nodded. 'If we can get them to confess, at the very least we'll be able to plug four channels that have been pumping illegal firearms into the city.'

Shek Boon-tim and Shek Boon-sing occupied the top two spots on the Hong Kong Police's Most Wanted list. They'd started their spree four years ago, in 1985, which included the robbery of four jewellers on Nathan Road that year, the car-jacking of a money transfer van the following year, and the kidnapping of wealthy businessman Li Yu-lung in 1988. The brothers were

still on the run, and police believed they were connected to organized crime in both China and Hong Kong, leveraging these con-
tacts to acquire firearms and muscle, fence stolen goods and find
overseas hideouts. The police had launched numerous investigations, none successful. At best they had netted some accomplices,
but never the masterminds themselves.

Then, a few days previously, they had got news of the two
men by chance.

In response to rising crime rates in the Mong Kok district, the
Crime Unit there had devoted its resources to rooting out drug-
lords, robbers, murder suspects, Triad leaders and other criminal
elements. Investigators often ended up exchanging fire with the
suspects, and their departments frequently lacked the resources
to send adequate back-up, leaving officers to risk their lives for
those arrests.

In the midst of these operations – which now seemed routine,
day after monotonous day – the Mong Kok District Crime Unit
Team 3 encountered something out of the ordinary. On 29 April
1989, a Saturday, they were preparing to arrest a suspicious
character at Ka Fai Mansions, a housing complex on Reclamation Street, having received a tip-off that someone connected to
a car theft case was hiding out in Unit 7 on the sixteenth floor.
The division chief immediately posted a sentry, who observed
the suspect in the company of an unidentified man. A plan was
made to sweep in the next evening. At dusk on the 30th, just
as the team was preparing to move in, they received an abrupt
order to halt – the case was being taken over by the West Kowloon Crime Unit, with team 3 relegated to back-up.

The reason for this, it turned out, was that unidentified man.

'The Mong Kok squad was originally after the car thief known
as "Jaguar".' Ko indicated a photograph on the corkboard. 'But
then we spotted this other guy, and handed over the picture to
see if he was connected to any other case.'

'That's Shum Biu – Mad Dog Biu – Shek Boon-sing's right-
hand man,' Kwan interrupted. 'I've seen the report.'

Ko nodded, somewhat abashed, and continued, 'The bank heist at the end of last year – Mad Dog Biu's a suspect, along with the Shek brothers. He vanished at the same time as them. Now he's resurfaced, which could be a sign they're preparing for another big score. Unit 16-07 was only rented last month, probably as a hideout. As long as we keep up this surveillance, we should have a chance to nab our top two suspects.'

'So, any results from the last five days?'

'Yes.' Ko grinned triumphantly. 'The younger brother, Shek Boon-sing, put in an appearance.'

Kwan Chun-dok raised an eyebrow.

Ko had kept this news to himself partly to avoid any possibility of a leak, but more for his own advantage. If he'd told HQ the number one most wanted criminal had shown his face, Organized Crime would have stepped in, and even if the arrest was successful, the glory would no longer be his; it wouldn't be great for his squad's morale either. He had ample reason to suppress the news of Shek Boon-sing's reappearance, on the grounds of protecting the operation that was under way. It was a sign of his confidence that he revealed it to the two CIB officers now.

'The day before, we saw a bald man arrive in a Jaguar.' Ko pointed at an underexposed photo showing two men walking towards one of Ka Fai Mansions' entrances. 'We've analysed this, and although his appearance has changed a little, it's definitely Shek Boon-sing.'

'Yes, the scar on the back of his left hand. From the shoot-out four years ago.'

Ko felt a chill. He and his men had only noticed this detail after many hours of scrutiny, and Kwan had spotted it at a glance.

'From past experience, Shek Boon-tim wouldn't leave his brother to run the show solo, and there are only three people in the apartment – not enough for a big heist,' said Ko, bringing the focus back to the case. 'We've had intel that Boon-tim will show himself tomorrow. It's likely he's hired two or three guys from Mainland. As soon as he appears, we'll move in.'

'What's your source?'

Ko smiled to himself. 'We've got quite a few of Jaguar's pager numbers.'

'Really?'

'We nabbed a druggie a while back. He admitted to registering five pagers on behalf of Jaguar. And we know Jaguar's tight with the Sheks, so these are probably the ones they'll use on this job,' said Ko with a smirk.

In Hong Kong at the time, getting a pager required registering with an ID card. No intelligent criminal would want to leave that kind of trail, so they'd usually lean on some thug or drug addict to get hold of a few devices, and use those for communication within the gang.

'Just yesterday, we got this message.' Ko walked to a screen and nodded to a subordinate, indicating he should bring up the message. A row of green numerals flashed across the black screen.

042.623.7.0505

'The phone company wasn't too keen, but we had a warrant, so they had to let us intercept this. These numbers mean that—'

'Shek Boon-tim will show up on 5 May,' said Kwan Chun-dok.

'Uh, yes... Oh right, it was CIB that broke this code, naturally you'd have heard about it.' Ko smiled through clenched teeth, smoothing over the awkwardness.

Pagers first came to Hong Kong in the 1970s, but in the early days they only beeped and flashed, and you had to phone an operator to retrieve your messages. They'd now evolved to have LCD screens that could display numbers. The telecommunications companies came up with a code system to send messages with these numbers, relayed via the operator. For instance, the surname Chan was designated as 004, so the message '004.3256188' told you to call your friend Chan on that telephone number. 'On my way' was 610, 'traffic jam' 611, 'date'

was 7 and 'time' 8 – so '004.610.611.8.1715' meant Mr or Ms
Chan was calling to let you know they'd been held up by traffic
and would not arrive until 5.15 p.m. There were also codes for
places and landmarks such as 'Central', 'Jordan', 'Ocean Terminal' or 'New Town Plaza', and for common words: 'restaurant',
'bar', 'hotel', 'park', etc.

During their many previous attempts to capture the Shek
brothers, the police had sometimes found pagers left behind by
their henchmen, but the messages seemed to be garbled nonsense. Yet CIB was able to deduce from this scant information
that the Sheks had come up with their own version of the code:
623 was now 'gather' instead of 'mahjong'; 625 was 'start moving' instead of 'have a meal'; and 616 was 'get away' instead of
'cancel appointment'. Comparing pager records against actual
events, they were fairly certain that 042, originally the name
Lam, was now the handle of older brother Shek Boon-tim.

In other words, Shek Boon-tim only had to tell the operator,
'My surname is Lam, the message is: "Let's play mahjong on
5 May,"' for the pager to show '042.623.7.0505', which actually
meant 'Number One wants everyone to gather on 5 May.'

At this point, the police had the upper hand. To make sure
Shek Boon-tim didn't get wind and change the codes, this information was only made known to those of inspector rank and
above, within the CIB. Yet Ko was aware that Shek was a cunning adversary, and would surely have a back-up plan. They
hadn't managed to intercept many messages over the last few
days, and at the very least had missed one about Jaguar bringing Shek in, which meant the gang probably each carried several
pagers that they used in rotation. That way, even if some messages leaked, the police still wouldn't have the full picture.

Kwan and Tso both understood the significance of
'042.623.7.0505'. The police had hitherto only been able to
decipher these messages in the aftermath of a crime. Now, for
the first time, they'd intercepted one ahead of time.

'Do you have enough officers?' asked Tso. The Shek brothers

were vicious criminals, and each previous case had involved copious firepower, leading to quite a few casualties.

'It's a little tight at the moment, but we've notified SDU' – Special Duty Unit, the elite paramilitary squad – 'and as soon as Shek Boon-tim shows up, they'll activate and be here within half an hour.'

'But they aren't actually on standby here, so if things kick off without warning, you're still on your own,' observed Kwan, looking around the command centre – a second-floor tenement apartment across from Ka Fai Mansions. Apart from Chief Inspector Ko himself, the small room held three other officers: one monitoring pager messages, one liaising with the on-site teams, and one as a runner. The window faced the southern exit of their target building – though Ka Fai's layout was adding to the squad's difficulties.

Ka Fai Mansions was built in the 1950s, an eighteen-storey building with thirty apartments on each floor. At one point it attracted quite a few middle-class families, but from the 1970s, development moved away from the area and the building started showing signs of age. About three-tenths of the apartments were now put to non-residential uses, from tailors' shops, traditional medicine clinics, hair salons and trading companies to nursing homes and even Buddhist temples. There were also massage parlours, various clubs and associations, small-scale hotels and one-woman brothels – none of which were particularly good for public order.

A place like this was a nightmare for the police. The ground floor of Ka Fai Mansions had three exits to the street – at the north and south ends, and in the centre – as well as six elevators and three staircases. The main passageways had few windows but numerous corridors and corners, meaning many places from which criminals could ambush their pursuers. With so many units turned over to commercial purposes, security was lax and visitors went in and out unquestioned. The suspects hiding out here could certainly make use of this environment to evade pursuit

– even if they didn't leave by one of the three exits, they could leap from a second-floor window. The north and south ends of the building were a full hundred metres apart, and any kind of police search would require a great deal of time and manpower.

'There's a dozen officers outside. Unless there's a head-on confrontation, we should be able to cope.' Ko jerked a thumb at the window. 'If this was a regular building, with this number of people we could take the whole place. But it had to be Ka Fai Mansions.'

'You've split them into three groups, one per exit?' asked Kwan.

'Basically, plus another lot on the top floor of the building across the road. They can observe the target apartment's corridor from there, and just about carry out surveillance through the window.' Ko gestured at the map on the noticeboard. He guessed Shek Boon-tim had chosen this apartment because the surrounding buildings were not as tall, so there was no way to see inside. Even the distant perch only gave a partial view of the corridor. Ko had considered posting a sentry outside, but didn't want to take risks dealing with the Shek brothers. It might end up costing a subordinate his life, while the suspects got spooked and fled.

'Did you deploy two teams?' asked Kwan. Without back-up from CIB surveillance nor Regional Ops, the twelve officers outside and four in the command centre would make up two teams from Regional Crime Unit.

'No, only Team 1; everyone else was out on a case. The others are from Mong Kok District Crime Unit.'

'The ones who originally wanted to arrest Jaguar?'

'That's them.'

'Are they getting on all right?' asked Kwan.

'Of... of course they are.' Ko had not expected the other man to be this direct.

'Mong Kok Crime Unit Team 3 – that's TT's men, isn't it?' Kwan smiled.

Edgar Ko looked at Kwan's grin, decided he wasn't trying to

cause trouble, and let out a breath. 'So you know this Tang Ting fellow too?'

'He was at Wan Chai Crime Unit five years ago. I bumped into him quite a few times on one op or another.' Kwan chuckled. 'He's a clever man, quick on his feet too. Only thing is he's a bit hot-headed. He's put quite a few noses out of joint.'

Tang Ting's nickname didn't come from his initials, but from when a gun-loving officer had joked, 'You suit your name – you're like a TT handgun.' The TT (or the 7.62 mm Tokarev self-loading pistol model 1930, to give it its full name) was a Russian-manufactured semi-automatic, distinguished by its prodigious firepower and its lack of a safety catch, hence the joke against Tang Ting – that he was deadly but hard to control. Tang Ting, now thirty-three years old, often came in for criticism from higher-ups for taking too many gambles in his work, betting that his fast reflexes and superior marksmanship would allow him to tackle suspects without back-up. TT did not object to this nickname. He'd won the police shooting trophy for a few years in a row, and quite liked being named after a gun. Now superiors and colleagues were so used to calling him TT, some had forgotten his actual name.

'You said earlier the other team was the Kowloon West Crime Unit Team 1 – they're under Karl Fung. There's bad blood between him and TT – everyone in Wan Chai knew, back in the day. That's why I asked,' Kwan explained.

Ko reflected how difficult it was to pull the wool over Superintendent Kwan's eyes. 'Yes, he graduated from the academy the same year as TT. I'm not sure what happened between them, but there's certainly some kind of grudge. Still, we're all professionals, and no one's going to bring personal feelings onto the job. They've both done well with their reports, strategy and ops. I have complete faith in both of them.'

Kwan smiled faintly, not pursuing the matter. Karl Fung was a senior inspector, half a grade above TT, and in charge of a regional Crime Unit's team. If there were already hard feelings between the men, this difference in rank could only worsen the situation. If he were honest, Ko was uneasy about these two working together, which was why he'd posted TT at the north entrance and Fung at the south.

'At least TT will be a new man soon. Married men can't be impulsive – they have families to think of,' said Keith Tso.

'TT's getting married?' Kwan hadn't heard this bit of news.

'Oh yes. What's more, his bride is the Deputy Commissioner's daughter – Ellen, the one in the PR Branch,' Tso sneered, implying that a meteoric rise could well be on the cards for TT.

Kwan glanced at Ko who looked bored by this gossip. He changed the subject. 'We'll rely on you to get us Shek Boon-tim and Shek Boon-sing, Chief Inspector Ko. As long as you can take them alive, we'll get the information we need from them.'

'Don't worry, we're pretty confident we'll clip their wings this time.' Ko shook Kwan's hand once again.

'If CIB can do anything for you, just say the word,' added Tso.

'Of course, of course,' replied Ko.

Just as Tso and Kwan were preparing to leave, the walkie-talkie on the desk crackled.

'Water Tower to Barn, Water Tower to Barn, Sparrow and Crow have just left the nest, Sparrow and Crow have just left the nest. Over.'

'Water Tower' was the unit on top of the building opposite, 'Barn' was the command centre, 'Sparrow' and 'Crow' were Jaguar and Mad Dog Biu, who'd just walked out of the apartment. As for the ringleaders, 'Owl' was Shek Boon-tim, and 'Vulture' was Shek Boon-sing.

Given this sudden news, the two CIB men decided to stay where they were, watching events unfold.

'Attention all units, attention all units, Sparrow and Crow have left the nest, I repeat, Sparrow and Crow have left the nest. Be on full alert. Over.' At Ko's signal, the officer in charge of communications relayed the message. If the suspects left the building, they would be followed, and the remaining officers would have to reorganize themselves to make sure there weren't any gaps in the net.

Ko was worried that Shek Boon-tim might show up sooner than expected, in which case the gang might take off for their heist before SDU could get there. If that happened, he'd have to hope the sixteen officers now on the scene could delay them long enough.

2

It was 12.55 p.m. – Sonny Lok glanced at his watch, feeling that time was moving very slowly. He'd never thought that the job of investigator, one he'd been looking forward to, would be this dull. Ever since graduating from the academy, he'd spent his three years in uniform longing for a transfer to this department, though older colleagues had told him how hard life was in a Crime Unit – sometimes too busy to go home, even if you were passing right by your front door. Sonny knew he was able to endure hardship, and being very young, felt he might as well toughen himself up as soon as possible, to train himself into an outstanding officer, so he'd be ready when an opportunity finally arose.

What he wasn't prepared for was the boredom. For a guy who'd just turned twenty, this monotony was harder to get through than any amount of stress.

Because of his relentless work ethic and commitment, not to mention his outstanding grades at the academy, the top brass had sent Sonny to Crime Wing, freeing him from uniform. Mong Kong District Crime Unit happened to be a man short, and so he got his wish earlier than expected. In his two months here, he'd encountered quite a few investigative techniques and operations that were roughly what he expected – the opportunity to learn the skills he'd need. The problem was these things only took up a tiny proportion of his work hours, compared to lengthy stake-outs, searching with a fine-tooth comb for evidence that turned out not to exist, or interviewing hundreds of witnesses about things they turned out to know nothing about. An actual arrest operation could take only a minute, but the preparation before-hand and inquiries afterwards could take several days.

At this moment, he was engaged in just such a boring task.

'What's taking Headman so long?' hollered Sharpie, sitting next to Sonny. 'Sharpie' was the nickname of Constable Fan Si-tat, an officer five years older than Sonny who'd been in the Mong Kok Crime Unit three years now. He was the colleague Sonny was closest to – neither was much of a team player, which ironically brought them together.

'Hey, he's coming,' hissed Sonny, seeing TT striding down the hallway from his smoke break.

Sonny, Sharpie and TT had been stationed by Chief Inspec-tor Ko at a cooked food counter by the north entrance of Ka Fai Mansions. There were several shops in this lobby, some facing the street, others inwards, and a few corner units. The police had requisitioned the shop, so the owner had given his two employ-ees some time off, allowing the officers to take their places while carrying out their surveillance.

'Sharpie, your turn.' TT, reeking of smoke, tied on his apron and went behind the counter. Sharpie left the store, not even stopping to take off his own apron, and vanished towards the stairwell.

Long, open-ended surveillance operations were psycholog-ically wearing on officers, so they were always organized in groups – in addition to looking out for each other, this also enabled them to take breaks. Fifteen minutes ago, TT and his subordinates had taken turns to go to the toilet – there wasn't one in the shop, so they were forced to trek to the tenants' wash-room by the elevators. This also allowed nicotine addicts TT and Sharpie to indulge their habit. Although officers were generally free to smoke on stakeouts, the owner had warned them several times that it would be bad for business if they were to serve food with cigarettes dangling from their mouths.

'There's hardly any customers anyway. The food is disgusting. What business is he worried about...' grumbled Sonny to Sharpie, while the boss was busy in the kitchen.

Returning to his post, TT pulled out his pager and glanced at it again. Sonny had to chuckle. 'Preparing for a wedding isn't easy, I guess?'

TT smiled grimly. 'It's torture. Don't get married too soon, Sonny, and if you must, make sure you choose a time when there's no operations.'

That morning alone, TT's pager had beeped constantly, and he'd already had to go to the management office three times to make calls. They weren't allowed to use the phone at the takeout counter – the boss said he might lose business.

Sonny knew that although TT and Sharpie hadn't complained, they were both pretty dissatisfied with this stakeout. They'd been all set to move on Sunday and bring that car thief Jaguar, the Shek brothers' accomplice, back to the station, but someone at the top had pulled the plug at the last minute, and the case got snatched up by the West Kowloon Crime Unit. If that were all, Sonny might have sighed and dismissed it as bad luck, but what enraged the Mong Kok Crime Unit was that HQ had asked them to provide back-up, so they had to hang out like idiots with no say in the operation. The target apartment was in the south wing, and Shek Boon-tim went in and out of the south entrance. Of the six Team 3 officers on the premises, one was at the lookout point across the road and two were with the West Kowloon investigators at the main entrance, leaving the other three at this takeout joint, birds guarding an egg that would never hatch.

This was a form of professional revenge, thought Sonny. He'd learned from Sharpie about TT's antagonism with Inspector Fung, and seen for himself how the two men faced off at the command centre the day before. Even if the Shek brothers were successfully apprehended, West Kowloon would get all the credit, Mong Kok's hard work going unrecognized. Sonny guessed Chief Inspector Ko was cut from the same cloth as that hateful Fung. The pair of them were directly linked in the chain of command; of course they'd sing the same tune.

According to the original plan, Mong Kok's Team 3 would have arrested Jaguar and then ceased operations for a while in order to focus on interrogating the suspect and writing up the case report, handing over evidence and so on. That would have given them breathing space, and allowed their commander to focus on his wedding preparations. Instead, the whole team was left kicking their heels.

'Attention all units, attention all units, Sparrow and Crow have left the nest, I repeat, Sparrow and Crow have left the nest. Be on full alert. Over,' a message from the command centre suddenly came through all their earpieces.

TT pressed a button beneath his clothes and spoke into the concealed microphone in his collar. 'Scarecrow Roger. Over.' 'Cowshed', 'Millhouse' and 'Scarecrow' were Ka Fai Mansions' south, centre and north entrances respectively, while the three teams were known as A, B and C.

'This is Water Tower. Sparrow and Crow have entered the elevator. Over.'

Sonny's attention was caught, but he still thought this had nothing to do with him. They'd been at the takeout counter four days now, and there hadn't been one glimpse of the Shek brothers, or even their errand boy Jaguar. Instead, he felt he was rehearsing the role of takeout employee, learning to take orders, serve meals and ring up sales.

'Sonny, don't get too relaxed,' said TT. Taking heed, Sonny brought his attention back to their surroundings, looking out for suspicious individuals.

'This is Cowshed. Elevator is at ground level. Over.' Inspector Fung's voice, over the earpiece.

'Why isn't Sharpie back yet?' TT wrinkled his brow.

'Maybe he's had to take care of major business – he could be a while,' Sonny answered, trying to defuse the situation. The way Sharpie had rushed off certainly suggested a call of nature.

'Cowshed to Millhouse, Cowshed to Millhouse, Sparrow and Crow flying towards Millhouse. Over.'

This unexpected development left Sonny and TT open-mouthed. These few days, not once had Jaguar walked through the ground-floor lobby to the main exit.

'This is Millhouse. Sparrow and Crow sighted... Sparrow and Crow have not exited the building, they're continuing north. Both birds are flying towards Scarecrow. Over.'

'Scarecrow Roger. Over,' replied TT calmly. Knowing the criminals were drawing closer, Sonny couldn't help holding his breath, eyes fixed anxiously on the corner, waiting for them to come round the bend.

'Commander, they—'

'Shut up, don't give yourself away,' snapped TT in a low voice.

No sooner were the words spoken when the Shek brothers' henchmen showed up, walking straight towards them. They were dressed in T-shirts and jeans, Mad Dog Biu in sunglasses and Jaguar in a grey cap. They looked like ordinary people. Sonny glanced at TT and saw his commander's head bent over the display cabinet as he pretended to rearrange the beverages whilst keeping one eye on goings-on in the lobby. Imitating him, Sonny stirred the beef brisket stew in the countertop warming tray, whilst silently staring out of the corner of his eye at the two men.

'Hi.'

He jumped at the sudden sound.

'Hi!' Jaguar and Mad Dog hadn't walked through the exit, but stood at the takeout entrance. Only a counter stood between them and Sonny. It was Jaguar who'd spoken.

Sonny slowly raised his head, his eyes locking onto Jaguar's. In that instant, his mind went into panic, unable to decide how to respond now that they'd been exposed. Should he take cover?

Pull out his gun? Or first make sure to keep the civilians safe? He had no idea whether the henchmen's loose shirts concealed weaponry, as his did. The Shek gang all used Type 54 Black Star pistols, whereas the Crime Unit were only issued with .38 revolvers. The police were at a disadvantage in terms of both ammo and firepower, and once shots were fired, Sonny could only be on the losing end. How should they do this? Sonny could take on Jaguar, leaving the vicious Mad Dog for his commander...

'Hi! I'm talking to you!' Jaguar leaned forward, looking at the display of food. 'How much is the beef stew with rice?'

A great weight rolled off Sonny. They hadn't given themselves away. These fellows were just after some lunch.

'Fif... Fifteen dollars,' he answered.

'Give me two boxes of that.' Jaguar turned to Mad Dog. 'You're too fussy, always complaining no matter what I choose. So you pick something for yourself.'

Biu took a step forward, examining the warming trays.

'Is the fish in corn sauce fresh?' Mad Dog's voice was low, and as soon as he opened his mouth, Sonny could tell this wasn't someone you'd want to mess with.

'It's not bad,' he said, trying to tamp down the terror welling up inside him. As Mad Dog bent, he'd seen a bulge on his right side that was almost certainly a pistol.

'Hmm... no, the gravy looks disgusting. Give me some of that green pepper spare ribs in black bean sauce with rice.'

'Yes, okay.'

Sonny got three boxes out, first laying down a bed of rice and then ladling the other dishes in. His hands were unsteady. Gravy and beef slices tumbled onto the countertop.

'Hey, little brother, you're just giving me a box of carrots. There's only three pieces of meat in there,' grumbled Jaguar.

'Sor— Sorry.' Sonny nodded and quickly added more beef, but in his nervousness scooped up even more carrots.

'Hey—' Jaguar's voice broke off suddenly, and Sonny realized at the same moment that he'd made a big mistake – he'd turned while filling the box so the receiver in his right ear was fully visible. They were standing so close that Jaguar must have seen it.

In that moment, Sonny's mind emptied completely, leaving a perfect blank.

Smack! Something hit the back of his head. For an instant, he thought Jaguar had shot him, but the attacker was TT.

'Asshole! You shit for brains, listening to the radio when you should be working, look at the mess you've made. Did I hire you to drive my customers away? Fuck you!'

Sonny stood frozen, only realizing half a second later that he was being rescued.

'Get your ass out of my way!' TT snatched Sonny's earpiece. Sonny noticed the commander's own earpiece was safely tucked away.

'Gentlemen, I apologize for this idiot kid. Let me get you some free drinks – I hope you'll still consider coming here again. We have canned sodas and packets of iced lemon tea. What would you like?' As he spoke, TT grabbed the ladle and neatly finished filling the three lunchboxes, smiling ingratiatingly at Jaguar and Mad Dog.

'Coke is fine,' said Jaguar. His attitude had softened, and he even smiled back at TT.

'Forty-five dollars altogether, thanks.' TT placed the food, drinks and disposable cutlery in a plastic bag and handed it over. Jaguar paid and walked back into the lobby with Mad Dog.

Sonny was standing in a corner, like a child scolded by his teacher. An onlooker might have thought this was a worker sulking after getting told off by his boss, but he had actually noticed something else – Sharpie was just round the corner, pretending to be a passer-by looking in the window of a clothing store. Sonny guessed he'd probably heard the alert and rushed out of the washroom, only to find the two suspects already in the takeout, and was observing from nearby instead of entering and complicating matters further.

Once Jaguar and Mad Dog were far enough away, Sonny let

out a shaky breath and said to TT, 'Thanks for that, sir. I'm still new to all this.'

'Keep soaking in it, you'll adapt.' TT rapped on Sonny's head gently.

'My God, I was scared to death.' Sharpie walked back inside. 'Those two came in for food? Did they have to pick this place out of all the takeout joints?'

'At least nothing went wrong,' smiled TT. He popped his earpiece back in and said into the mic, 'Scarecrow to Barn, Sparrow and Crow bought some bird food, heading back to the nest now. Over.'

Sonny glanced at his watch. It was two minutes past one. The whole thing had only lasted a few minutes.

'This is Water Tower, Sparrow and Crow have returned to the nest. Over,' went the message to all officers, three minutes later.

'I guess the curtain only rises on the show tomorrow,' Sharpie half-joked, stretching.

Sonny nodded in agreement, but then a minute later the radio crackled, 'Water Tower to Barn! Urgent update! Three birds have left the nest! Sparrow, Crow and Vulture are all holding large suitcases. New developments. Over.'

At this news, Sonny's entire scalp went numb.

'Water Tower to Barn! Unexpected development. The birds didn't get in the elevator, they're continuing north along the corridor. Looks like they're retreating! Over.'

'Barn to Water Tower, keep observing! Other units, get moving immediately, prepare to apprehend suspects! Guard the lobby and exits! Report on elevator situation!'

Sonny's mind was scrambled. He worried that he had given away his true identity earlier, and this was all his fault. Sharpie smacked him on the back. 'Stop daydreaming, time to work.'

Sonny shook his head to clear his mind, then quickly pulled off his ridiculous apron and, gun in hand, followed TT and Sharpie towards the elevator lobby.

'Police operation! Don't come out!' Sharpie yelled at the staff

and customers curiously poking their heads out of neighbouring stores. Hearing this command and seeing three armed men,
they hastily complied and slammed the doors shut. The old guy
who'd been snoozing all morning behind the management desk
suddenly grew alert and hurriedly hid behind his counter.

'Cowshed reporting, both elevators are stopped at ground level.'

'This is Millhouse, one elevator coming down from level four,
the other remaining on ground floor.'

'Scarecrow calling Barn, one elevator stationary at ground
floor, the other going up from fifth... no, it's stopped,' said TT
into the microphone.

'All units remain in position, stand by to assist. Over.'

Sonny's heart beat faster as he crouched with TT and Sharpie
in a corner of the lobby. Each time civilians passed by or tried to
enter, they had to be stopped. Some public-spirited individuals
guessed that criminals were hiding out in the building, and took
it upon themselves to remain on the street, keeping residents and
shoppers out of the danger zone.

Ding. The elevator that had been on fifth returned to the
ground floor. As the doors opened, Sonny and the rest held up
their guns in readiness. There was only one woman inside, who
shrieked to see three armed men facing her. Sharpie quickly
grabbed her and shoved her to safety behind them.

'We can't go on like this,' said TT suddenly.

'What?' Sonny didn't understand.

'It's been too long. Shek Boon-sing will get to the second floor,
then jump out of a window and escape that way. It won't do us
any good to keep waiting here.'

'But the order was to stay put.'

'The sentry said they're carrying big suitcases – which means
they must have sub-machine guns or even AK-47s. Even when
the uniforms get here, we'll be outgunned. And those civilians
over there are going to get hurt,' TT said grimly.

Sonny and Sharpie understood what TT was referring to.
Once Shek Boon-sing had escaped a police siege by charging

onto a bus and taking everyone hostage. After getting away, he shot the driver and four passengers dead. The survivors testified that he'd had no reason to open fire, he was just angry that the driver hadn't gone fast enough, and the passengers had been crying and screaming too much for his taste.

'But, Commander, we only have eighteen rounds of ammo between us,' said Sonny timidly.

'There's three of them and three of us. We just have to hold them till SDU arrive.' As he spoke, TT checked his cylinder, making sure all six bullets were still there.

'I'd rather stay here, but Headman's right, attacking is our best defence,' said Sharpie. 'Who asked us to be the Royal Hong Kong Police? We have no choice but to put ourselves forward.'

Seeing that the other two were serious, Sonny took a deep breath and nodded.

'Hey, Pops!' TT called to the old man behind the counter. 'Got an elevator key?'

'Yes, here.' The old guy fumbled for his keys and, with TT and Sharpie covering him, walked into the elevator, pulled open the control panel, and killed the machinery.

'Now they'll have to come down the stairs.' TT gestured at the stairwell. 'If they try to get out by the south or central exits, they'll meet the other guys. We'll attack them from this side, and they'll be surrounded.'

TT studied the area for a minute. 'Pops, are there any business units above the eighth floor in this building?'

'I don't think... No, wait, there's a little guesthouse on the ninth floor, Unit 30. Ocean Hotel.'

'Dammit.' TT turned back to his men to explain, 'It's daytime, so there won't be many residents around they could use as hostages. But the hotel – the folks there might be in danger.'

Sonny knew what he meant. If Shek Boon-sing grabbed some people to use as human shields, there'd be nothing the police could do but stand by and watch as they got away. And then the hostages probably wouldn't have long to live. The Crime Unit had no formal combat training, but if they were going to act, it needed to be decisive.

'Let's take a gamble,' spat TT. He pressed the button on his radio. 'Scarecrow calling Barn, Team C now moving in via staircase. Over.'

'Barn to Scarecrow, please remain where you are, remain where you are. Over.'

'Ignore that.' TT plucked out his earpiece. 'We're on our own now. Let's go.'

TT pushed open the door to the stairwell, Sharpie and Sonny covering him from behind.

'We'll head straight up.' TT looked cautiously between the railings. 'From what the lookout said, if they took this route, they'd still only be at the twelfth or thirteenth storey.'

'What if they've doubled back on some other floor?' asked Sonny.

'If they'd got spooked and were trying to escape, they'd want to get to the second floor and jump out a window – not play hide and seek with us.' TT was already striding up as he answered. 'They didn't take the elevator, which means they know something isn't right. If it was just a meeting with Shek Boon-tim or an associate, they wouldn't have left by the corridor. They're all prepared, and they're taking an unusual route. That means they know they're in danger.'

'Dammit, everything seemed normal when they were buying lunch. It couldn't be something we did, could it?' Sharpie cursed behind TT. 'Or maybe old Fung and that lot did something wrong, and caught their attention. I hope nothing goes wrong, Lord preserve us so we all make it to Headman's wedding day.'

TT and Sonny didn't reply, and Sharpie stopped grumbling too, focusing on sprinting up the stairs.

At the eighth floor, TT suddenly stopped and indicated that the other two should be quiet. Sonny hadn't seen anything out of the ordinary, but thought his experienced commander must have surely noticed something.

They proceeded on tiptoe, sticking close to the wall. There wasn't much light here, just a small window every two floors.

Between the eighth- and ninth-floor landings, Sharpie and Sonny saw it too. Through a glass panel in the door that led to the ninth-floor corridor, Sonny could see a man's silhouette.

Was it a suspect or a resident? They bent low and kept moving. There were two doors leading to the ninth floor, an outer and an inner one, five metres apart. Residents used the space in between for their trash cans. When they got to the first door, TT peeped through the glass to see the person was now by the inner door, which was propped open by something, perhaps a wedge of wood or an old newspaper. Although the Fire Department was always urging residents to leave these doors shut to keep smoke out in an emergency, residents inevitably preferred convenience.

The glass panel was too dusty for TT and Sharpie to see if this was one of their targets. Sonny hung back in case it was a red herring. If they were ambushed now, they'd be sitting ducks.

TT gestured, indicating that Sonny should pull the door open for the other two to attack. 'Three...' he mouthed, counting down with his fingers, 'two, one, GO!'

Sonny yanked the thick wooden door open and TT and Sharpie charged through. The person by the door turned in shock. It was Jaguar.

Recognizing the takeout server, then seeing the weapon in his hand, Jaguar understood the situation at once. Sonny had expected him to surrender, given he had two guns pointed at him, but before TT could even shout a warning, he'd grabbed the pistol from his waistband.

Bang! Bang!

On the cusp of life and death, TT hadn't hesitated, but fired twice at his opponent. He was a sure shot, and both bullets went straight into Jaguar's chest, lifting him slightly off the ground with their force, tumbling to the ground before he could so much as pull the trigger. Bright blood flowed from the two injuries.

Just as Sharpie was about to exclaim in admiration, the real danger appeared, flashing through the door as Jaguar's body hit the ground: Mad Dog Biu, holding an AK47 in both hands.

Rat-tat-tat-tat-tat—

TT, Sharpie and Sonny instinctively flung themselves to the ground, but bullets were faster than their reaction speed. Sonny, at the back, managed to get himself to one side, but the only shelter for TT and Sharpie was a red plastic trash can. Sonny felt bullets passing over his head, the piercing sound as they ricocheted down the stairwell, the scent of gunpowder penetrating his nostrils.

In seconds, Sonny's instinct to hide was overridden by his police training – he had to assist his commander and Sharpie, even if it put him in danger.

Still on the ground, Sonny reached out to aim at the gunman at the other end of the corridor, but before he could fire, the figure crumpled onto its knees, the assault rifle crashing to the ground. Even in the dim light, he could see a black hole right between Mad Dog's eyebrows.

Before Sonny could react, he felt something tugging at his left shoulder.

'Pull back!' It was TT's voice.

Like waking from a dream, Sonny saw what had happened – two bodies in the corridor, Jaguar and Mad Dog Biu, TT crouching by him, and Sharpie still on the floor, breathing heavily.

Sonny and TT dragged Sharpie back into the stairwell and the safety door clicked shut behind them. Almost at once, another round of *rat-tat-tat* shattered the glass panel. Shek Boon-sing had arrived.

They had their guns out in readiness, but it would seem Shek wasn't as rash as his henchman, and in less than five seconds, silence resumed.

'Sharpie! Sharpie!' TT hollered, trying to bring him back to consciousness. Sharpie had been hit three times – in the left shoulder, the calf and, most seriously, in the neck, which was gushing crimson blood.

'Sharpie! Brother!' Sonny quickly pressed hard against the wound. He knew that once the carotid artery was severed, victims could bleed to death in a matter of minutes.

Sonny had never witnessed a colleague being wounded. As a uniformed officer, perhaps by good luck, he'd always managed to stop suspects in time to prevent serious injuries. There'd been cases involving death, of course – elderly people, or victims of car accidents – but he'd never experienced this sensation of being on the dividing line between life and death, his own actions able to pull a human existence this way or that, not knowing if he himself might be killed the next moment.

'We should... we should radio for back-up...' Pressing down on Sharpie's neck with his left hand, he reached for his earpiece – tugged out during the firefight – but his bloodstained right hand trembled so much he couldn't get it in. 'Calling Command Centre... why's there no sound...?'

He grabbed hurriedly for the walkie-talkie in his back pocket, only to find the outer shell was smashed and the buttons were unresponsive.

'Aah!' A muted scream of surprise from the corridor.

They turned cautiously towards the sound.

'Sonny,' said TT in a calm voice, 'leave Sharpie. We're going in.'

'Commander?' Sonny looked up wide-eyed, unable to believe the order he'd just heard.

'Leave Sharpie. Cover me.'

'Commander! If I let go, Sharpie will die!' shouted Sonny. He was kneeling on the ground, his trousers already soaked in Sharpie's blood.

'Sonny! We're police officers! Protecting civilians has to come before taking care of our colleagues!' Sonny had never heard his commander in such a rage.

'But... but...'

'Leave Sharpie for the rescue team!'

'No.' Sonny stayed put.

'Sonny! This is an order! Let go!'

'No! I refuse!' Sonny screamed hoarsely. He'd never imagined he'd dare disobey a direct instruction from his commander.

'Fuck you!' screamed TT, grabbing the revolver by Sonny's side, quickly counting the ammo, then bursting through the bullet-riddled wooden door in a half crouch.

3

WHEN THE FIRST gunshot sounded outside, Edgar Ko felt a chill down his spine.

Something had gone wrong.

The officers in the 'Barn' all knew gunfire when they heard it, even muffled like this. Especially when it was followed immediately by a louder stream of shots.

Passers-by outside seemed to sense something was wrong, some looking up for the source of the noise, others cautiously ducking beneath an awning or into a shop. It sounded like fireworks, burst after burst echoing through that vast concrete building, though no one could have said which floor or apartment it was coming from.

Edgar Ko didn't know the location either, but he could guess who was responsible. TT had radioed 'Now moving in via staircase', and not responded to any further messages.

That bastard – Ko cursed him several dozen times in the space of a few minutes.

When the sentry post had reported that Jaguar and Mad Dog Biu had gone back in with their lunch, everyone had let out a sigh of relief. Keith Tso and Kwan Chun-dok had been about to say goodbye. Then word arrived that all three men were armed and on the move.

'Are they preparing for a heist? Moving to a rendezvous with Shek Boon-tim? Did they receive any orders?' the officer in charge of comms had asked Ko.

'No new messages to the known pagers,' another officer reported.

'Maybe Shek Boon-tim's using a different pager? Our guys in the south and main lobbies haven't seen anything unusual. We shouldn't assume they're withdrawing just yet,' said Ko suspiciously.

'No, they're escaping,' Kwan interrupted. 'Even if they don't know about the ambush, they must have detected something, so they're withdrawing in haste.'

'How do you know?'

'If they were going to meet Shek Boon-tim, it wouldn't be that urgent. They could finish their lunch first. But for them to buy some food so casually, then dash out with their weapons just a minute later, not even taking the elevator, what else could that be but a retreat?'

Ko froze, then sent out the order to seal all exits and prepare to apprehend suspects. At this point, expecting Shek Boon-tim to walk into their trap was a fantasy, but if they could nab Shek Boon-sing, that'd still be half the battle. Knowing he didn't have the manpower to surround a rabbit warren like Ka Fai Mansions, Ko summoned the SDU and asked the station for back-up. Even if patrolmen or Emergency Unit officers couldn't match the Sheks' firepower, each additional officer meant one more handgun and a little more protection.

Just after TT had reported he was 'moving in', two Emergency Unit vehicles and three traffic cops on motorbikes had arrived at the scene, providing at least enough officers for them to surround the building. Still, Shek Boon-sing had heavy weaponry, and Ko was worried that he could easily overwhelm the police, not to mention taking hostages or hurting civilians. He could only hope the SDU would arrive as quickly as possible.

Those gunshots told him matters were only going to get worse.

The officers on the ground floor had all heard the sound and rushed to radio the Command Centre for guidance.

'Millhouse calling Barn, gunfire from upstairs, please instruct. Over.'

'Cowshed calling Barn, shots not coming from our direction. Over.'

Unable to verify the location, Ko could only instruct them to seal the elevators and take the stairs to investigate.

Less than half a minute later, Karl Fung's voice came over the radio. 'Team A Roger, elevators locked, now leaving Cowshed and beginning search. Over.'

The officer in charge of the main exit spoke next: 'Team B leaving Millhouse, now heading up.'

While uniforms were replacing TT's team in the north wing, the Crime Unit officers from the south and central wings moved in by two separate staircases, handing the ground floor over to the new arrivals. With gunshots echoing through the corridors and staircases, they didn't dare let down their guard – after all, even though the shots were far off, that didn't mean all the bad guys were in one place. What if Shek Boon-sing and Mad Dog had separated as they fled? An armed thug could be about to appear round every corner.

In the midst of all this, Edgar Ko snuck a glance at Keith Tso. Ko saw Kwan Chun-dok as a peer, even though Kwan had a higher rank. But Tso was undoubtedly a superior, the Deputy Director of HQ Intelligence, soon to be a major figure leading the unit. Who could say 'Superintendent Tso' wouldn't be 'Assistant Commissioner Tso' in a matter of days? If Ko looked bad in front of him, he'd be cutting off his own career. And even if Tso remained at CIB, Ko would still find it hard to explain matters to his own superiors and the Regional Director of West Kowloon.

He'd thoroughly messed this one up.

As the gunfire continued, an update suddenly came over their earpieces.

'Officer down. North wing, ninth floor. Send assistance! Over!'

The voice was TT's. Immediately after he spoke, a new volley of shots started up.

'TT! Report your location!' shouted Ko, grabbing the mic.

'Ninth floor, Unit 30 – Ocean Hotel. At the entrance. Jaguar and Mad Dog Biu are dead. Only Shek Boon-sing left. But he has an AK, there are hostages inside—' TT gabbled, panting hard, interrupted by yet more gunfire.

'TT, stay where you are! Back-up arriving soon!'

'No! That bas... bastard is killing people!' TT's voice was virtually obscured by gunfire.

'Don't do anything stupid! Back-up will be there in less than a minute!' screamed Ko.

'They're about to die! Fuck!' The speakers relayed TT's slurring words, and then silence. Meanwhile, loud shots continued to come from across the road.

'Attention all units, head immediately to north wing, ninth floor, Unit 30, Ocean Hotel,' Ko ordered.

'Team B Roger, presently at seventh floor. Over.'

'Team A Roger. Over.' Karl Fung's voice.

Ko leaned on the desk with both hands, clenching his teeth. The situation was now irretrievable.

After the teams reported back, more shots ripped through Ka Fai Mansions, but ten seconds later there was silence. Everyone braced themselves for the next round, but there was nothing. Through the windows of the command centre they heard only police sirens and traffic noise, roadworks and the normal babble of pedestrians. The piercing bangs of a moment ago could easily have been illusions.

Ko could only pray this wasn't the calm before the storm.

'Team B arrived at ninth floor, outside Unit 25. Ocean Hotel around the corner. Now moving in. Over.' This team was the four officers from 'Millhouse': two of them from Kowloon West, the other two TT's subordinates.

'Roger.' Ko waited for Team B to report further, but they transmitted nothing, and there was no more shooting.

After a while, the speakers came back to life. The officer sounded hoarse, his voice unsteady.

'Team B reporting... Request ambulance urgently. The scene... scene is clear, suspect is dead. But officer is down, many casualties. Over.'

Everything went black in front of Ko's eyes.

'Eddie, take over,' he said to the officer in charge of comms. 'I'm going to the scene.'

Looking back, he saw Kwan's brows knitted and Tso stony-faced.

'I'll head back to HQ now,' said Tso.

'You're not going to the scene?' asked Kwan.

'I'm not directing this op.' Tso couldn't stop himself glancing at Edgar Ko as he spoke. 'A situation like this, the higher-ups aren't going to be happy. I'll go back and work on a strategy. If Shek Boon-sing really is dead, O-Crime will want to take over pursuing Shek Boon-tim, and CIB will have to hand over huge stacks of paperwork.'

This was obviously aimed at Ko, the unspoken message being that he was dead meat. He took it in silence.

'I'll stay a bit longer. The scene might tell us something about Shek Boon-tim,' replied Kwan.

'Boys, please excuse me. I'll pass any information on to Superintendent Kwan.' Escaping the awkward atmosphere, Ko called an investigator to go with him and they left the command centre. Tso departed shortly after, leaving Kwan behind in the tiny room with a couple of the Kowloon West officers.

Edgar Ko crossed the road, his mind uneasy. Hurrying along, he passed the traffic police keeping order, went straight into the north wing lobby and ordered management to start the elevator again. Arriving at the ninth floor, he saw a scene of unparalleled carnage.

Shek Boon-sing was dead. He'd taken shots to the torso and head, and was lying in the middle of the hotel's reception area. And the person who had shot him was slumped by the counter, his face the picture of despair, his left wrist torn open by a rifle bullet: TT.

As for the civilians in the hotel, not one of them had survived.

The Ocean Hotel was an independent business, a small and seedy budget establishment. There were only four rooms, some occupied by guests in straitened circumstances or from irregular backgrounds. Mostly, though, it was prostitutes and their customers, taking advantage of rooms that rented by the hour.

The reception area was only seventy square feet. Apart from Shek Boon-sing, still clutching his AK-47, there were two other corpses, an elderly man who'd fallen in a corner and a middle-aged woman on a sofa. The lower half of the old guy's face had been completely smashed by a bullet, so his chin was hanging loose, his neck and chest nothing but gore. The woman was half leaning against the sofa, her eyes bulging, two bullet holes in her chest like crimson peonies embroidered on her white blouse.

On the threshold of the corridor leading to the bedrooms was a man whose skull had been pierced so brain matter spilled out onto the floor. Most of the bullets had gone in the back of his head and come out the front. He'd been shot in the back as well.

There were three other bodies in the hotel. At the end of the corridor, in Room 4, was a woman in her twenties, shot through the head. Diagonally opposite, in Room 1, was a young couple, the woman naked, lying across the bed, covered only by a white sheet, now mottled with red. The man was lying by the door, wearing only boxer shorts, two bullet holes in his bare chest. It was a scene from hell.

'The civilians are all dead,' reported Karl Fung, who'd arrived before Ko. 'Jaguar and Mad Dog Biu's bodies are by the stairwell. Two of the Mong Kok guys are there, one of them seriously wounded.'

'I... I missed... I didn't hit him...' TT seemed to realize Ko was standing next to him, lifting his head a little and speaking with difficulty. 'That woman... I could have saved her... I thought I could save at least one of them...'

Ko looked around, dizzy. This was too awful for words. Although TT had disposed of all three criminals, innocent citizens' lives had been lost too – and so many of them. This was the worst possible outcome. If Shek Boon-sing had survived, he could still have been interrogated and his evidence used to track down his brother. Now the trail had come to an end, and Shek Boon-tim might well be planning an even more horrendous crime to avenge Boon-sing.

An investigator burst in, yelling, 'Inspector Ko, sir, the paramedics are here.' Ko pulled himself together.

'Karl, bring a couple of paramedics to attend to the Mong Kok guy. I'll take charge here.' Ko turned to another subordinate. 'Go tell the uniforms to evacuate all residents above the eighth floor, and send someone to investigate Floor 16, Unit 7. I'm afraid Shek Boon-sing might have left a booby trap.'

Fung and the other officers rushed off to execute these orders, while Ko and the other paramedics examined the corpses, hoping for a miracle. But there were no signs of life. The police could only preserve the scene as far as possible and begin collecting evidence.

As he faced the bullet-riddled walls and furniture, the bloodstained floorboards, the wood fragments and bullet casings that littered every surface, Edgar Ko had a sense that none of this was real. TT and Sharpie were carried away by the paramedics, and his colleagues from the Identification Bureau arrived, and still Ko felt there was no point in his being at the scene. Anything they did now would just be official procedure, far too late to do anyone any good. Guilt and regret tore at his heart, and he kept asking himself what had gone wrong.

Was it TT?

He'd love to push the blame for this tragedy onto TT and his refusal to obey orders, but that would just be an excuse. Shek Boon-sing was a psychopath who could kill a person without blinking, and if he had got out into the street, there would quite possibly have been even more casualties. The moment Shek and his henchmen left the apartment was the moment the whole operation failed.

Rationally, Ko knew that he bore a far greater responsibility than TT. When TT reported that Shek was starting to kill people in the hotel, Ko had responded by the book, instructing him to wait for back-up. If he'd authorized TT to go in a few seconds earlier, would that short span of time have been enough to save one life? By not trusting his subordinate, he'd made the situation worse.

Ko told his team to record the evidence, and listened to their reports about evacuating the residents. He didn't even register when Kwan Chun-dok showed up. Apparently Kwan had learned of the tragedy from the other officers, and had seen TT.

'Inspector Ko, sir, the SDU wants to know if the op is cancelled,' an officer said from behind him.

'Yes, cancel it... cancel it...' He'd been about to add that they were far too late to do any good, but bit off the words. As the director of this operation, he had to maintain dignity even with the situation crumbling around him.

It had only been twenty-odd minutes since the gunfight, but Ko felt as though several hours had passed. The report came in that the hideout on the sixteenth floor contained no booby traps or hazardous items, so he sent investigators in. Officers came and went, while reporters began to gather, huddling round the various entrances to Ka Fai Mansions and snapping the police as they went about their work.

'Inspector Ko, I'm leaving now.' Kwan had stayed quite a while, walking around the scene and inspecting the environment, but it was only when he spoke that Ko remembered he was there.

'All right. If I find any leads on Shek Boon-tim, I'll pass them on to CIB,' said Ko with a forced smile. 'I'm sorry you had to see this, Superintendent Kwan.'

'This wasn't your fault. We'll always encounter situations like this, and there's no help for it.'

'Thank you. Take care.'

'Goodbye.'

As Kwan Chun-dok left Ka Fai Mansions, the journalists descended on him in a swarm. Surely the famous Superintendent Kwan was in charge of this case? But he only smiled grimly and shook his head, departing without answering a single question.

That day, the TV and radio news led with 'Most Wanted Criminal Shek Boon-sing Killed in Shoot-Out', describing the massacre of the residents and the haplessness of the police. The following day, newspapers printed more details, along with op-eds blaming the police for these civilian deaths.

On the surface of it, while Shek Boon-tim was still at large, the Shek Boon-sing case was now closed. No one knew yet that a new wave of trouble was just about to start.

Trouble that started with an internal investigation.

4

FOR THE NEXT few days, the media indulged in blanket coverage of the Ka Fai Mansions massacre. The headlines remained focused on the police killing of most wanted career criminal Shek Boon-sing, but the public were more concerned with details about the civilian casualties. For those interested in blood, gore and sex, the local news during this period was more enticing than the gossip rags. 'Innocent bystanders slaughtered by felon' was eye-catching enough, and the fact that most of the deceased were living on the fringes of society was exactly the sort of spice these ghouls sought out.

The man and woman who died in the hotel reception were the fifty-seven-year-old owner, Chiu Ping, and a cleaner, Lee Wan. Public sympathy was generally on their side, although some pointed out that by running such an establishment, Chiu was encouraging the sex trade. The other four victims were looked on less kindly.

The couple in Room 1 were a pimp and a teenage runaway prostitute. The man was Yau Choi-hung, aged twenty-two, a notorious figure of the red light district of Portland Street, Mong Kok, where his nickname was Well-hung. His handsome face and smooth tongue induced any number of naive young girls to start selling their bodies, one of whom was the naked girl in the bed. Fifteen-year-old Bunny Chin had left her home three months previously and met Well-hung while wandering the streets. He persuaded her into becoming one of the working girls under his control. A reporter sought out a fellow pimp who said Well-hung had told him he'd be meeting 'a new horse' to 'put her through her paces' – little knowing these would be his last words.

Room 4 held a woman in a similar situation, twenty-three-year-old Lam Fong-wai, a 'PR manager' – in other words, an escort – at the New Metropolis Nightclub in Tsim Sha Tsui, where she was known as Mandy. The nightclub madam guessed she'd had an appointment at the hotel before work – but ended up getting killed before the customer even showed up. Mandy's colleagues said she'd been telling everyone she'd found a good man, claiming she'd soon say goodbye to the seamy side of life and settle down to be a respectable housewife. She probably hadn't imagined this would be the manner of her leaving it.

These latter three victims were quickly turned into cautionary tales for teachers and parents to warn children about. Rationally, they must have been aware that these deaths had nothing to do with the deceased's professions, but the Chinese love stories of retribution. 'Dishonourable deeds destroy the doer,' the saying went, so they must have deserved their grisly fate. Like executed corpses displayed before the public, the bodies were now fuel for tabloid moralizing.

If the moral majority saw Well-hung, Bunny and Mandy as authors of their own misfortune, then the man whose brains Shek Boon-sing blew out in the corridor would be the most innocent – or so one would think. He was named Wang Jingdong, aged thirty-eight, a Mainlander from Hunan. Six months ago, he'd come to Hong Kong to stay with relatives, but after constant arguments with his cousin's wife, finally had no choice but to move out. This was only his second day at the Ocean Hotel.

Wang Jingdong was a hardworking man from a peasant family, not a nasty bone in his body – but the media chose to depict him as uncivilized, poor and ignorant. Just as Mainlanders saw Hong-kongers as money-grubbing and unscrupulous, Hongkongers painted Mainlanders as coarse and stupid. 'If he had stayed back home where he belonged, he wouldn't have died in that hotel,' people said, casting his fate as a different form of retribution.

And so the same reports appeared in the papers, day after day, until Kwan Chun-dok stopped noticing them. Then, at noon on Monday 8 May, he'd just concluded a meeting in the CIB Division B office and was preparing to go to the canteen, when a friend knocked on his door.

'Superintendent Kwan, do you have a minute?'

'Hi, Benny,' said Kwan, looking up and smiling to see Senior Inspector Benedict Lau. 'What wind blew you here today?'

'I've been busy for a few days now, but managed to find some time today to come see you,' said Benny warmly, as Kwan pulled on his jacket. 'I still haven't congratulated you on your promotion. Are you doing anything now? I'd like to take you out for a roast pigeon lunch.'

'I'd be honoured to join you.'

Benedict Lau was eight years younger than Kwan Chun-dok. He'd been in the Hong Kong Island Crime Unit from 1983 to '85, where his relationship to Kwan was like that of Karl Fung and Edgar Ko, team leader and director. Benny was a forthright, optimistic man who'd received good evaluations from every department he'd worked with. Only in his early thirties, he'd already been allocated to CIB Division A. All his colleagues believed the higher-ups wanted him to take over the management of informants and undercover operatives, and once he had a few years' experience under his belt, he'd probably be promoted to head the division.

The two men walked out of Police HQ in Central, chatting as they made their way to Taiping Restaurant. Apart from being Hong Kong's main business district, Central was also home to many tea houses and Western-style restaurants. Every gourmand knew which establishments along D'Aguilar Street provided value for money. Benny adored Taiping, not just for the great skill of the chef, but also for the generous spaces between tables, which meant less chance of being overheard.

After biting into the crispy-skinned, tender young pigeon, Benny chatted aimlessly with Kwan, and the conversation wandered from the Hillsborough disaster in Britain the month before, in which almost a hundred soccer fans had been crushed to death, to the tens of thousands of university students currently gathering in Beijing's Tiananmen Square to press for government reforms. Finally, the topic came around to the gun battle the previous Thursday.

'Superintendent, I heard you were on the scene?' asked Benny.

'Yes, I happened to drop by with Keith to say hi to Edgar Ko, and we saw the whole thing.' Kwan added two spoonfuls of sugar to the milky tea the waitress had just served.

'Oh.' Benny raised one eyebrow, looked around and said in a lowered voice, 'As you were there, I don't think there's any harm in telling you. Did you know Internal Investigations have got involved?'

'Really? Quite a few mistakes were made, and TT went rogue, so there'll have to be some sort of disciplinary inquiry, but Internal Investigations? What's there to investigate?'

'Naturally, it was an inside job,' Benny said, grimacing.

'An inside job?'

'Sir, you know how I keep my ears open.' Benny took a sip of his coffee. 'After I knew Internal was involved, I asked people in O-Crime and Kowloon West what was going on. Apparently, when Shum Biu and that guy Jaguar were on their way back to their hideout after buying lunch, Shum stopped at the south lobby mailbox to pick up some letters.'

'Letters?'

'Mostly fliers, takeout menus, that sort of thing. After O-Crime took over the case, that's what they found in the sixteenth-floor apartment. Because the neighbouring units all got similar things, we can be pretty certain that's what he brought up from the mailbox.'

'Was there anything unusual about these leaflets?'

'No, but investigators also found a piece of paper.' Again Benny looked around to make sure they weren't being observed. 'Three by six inches, on the table, six numbers written in blue ballpoint pen: "042616".'

Kwan's eyes opened wide.

'I see you get the meaning,' said Benny.

'Escape,' muttered Kwan. The pager code 616, which originally meant 'cancel appointment', now meant 'run for it'.

'According to reports from the scene, the three of them left in a great hurry. Two of the packed lunches on the table hadn't even been opened, and the third had only one bite taken out of it. Next to the food was the jumble of leaflets, and on top of them, that note.'

'So O-Crime thinks one of us gave Shek a tip-off?'

'To start with, they thought it might have been Shek Boon-tim getting word to his little brother, but Boon-tim would just have called the pager – there was no need for a middleman. In fact, on the day of the incident, Boon-tim did send his brother a pager message with the date of their rendezvous.'

Kwan recalled that Edgar Ko had mentioned this.

'That means someone other than Shek Boon-tim sent that note.' Benny rapped the tabletop. 'O-Crime thinks it must be an associate of the Shek brothers who had no other way of getting in touch with them – which must mean the traitor is someone from within Kowloon West Crime Unit. That's why that part of the case has been handed over to Internal Investigations.'

'Hang on, that doesn't stack up either,' protested Kwan. 'If Shek Boon-tim had someone infiltrating the Crime Unit, the insider could just call Boon-tim when he had a break or was changing shift, and get him to pass the message on to Boon-sing.'

'You're right, sir, which is why there's a third theory now.'

'What's that?'

'The person who wrote the note is from the Crime Unit, but not working for the Shek brothers.'

'Why would he sabotage the operation, then?'

'To stop a difficult colleague. Permanently.' Benny pursed his lips.

'A difficult... You mean TT?' Kwan hesitated. 'Then the prime suspect would be his nemesis, Karl Fung?'

Benny burst into laughter. 'Sir, your brain works faster than anyone else's. That's right, Karl's the main target of the internal investigation. Everyone knows TT's a real hothead, and if it looked like Shek Boon-sing was getting away, he'd definitely charge right in. Even if he didn't get himself killed, he'd still have disobeyed a direct order, and there'd be an inquiry afterwards. Besides, if the op failed, Edgar Ko would most likely be removed from his post, and his misfortune would be an opportunity for Karl to grab promotion. Two birds with one stone.'

Kwan pondered. 'Who supplied the evidence that it was Mad Dog Biu who checked the mailbox?'

'The Kowloon West constables stationed by the south exit,' said Benny, deadpan. 'The funny thing is, two of the three guys there mentioned this. Guess who didn't?'

'Karl Fung.'

'Right. He said he was worried that if they all focused on Jaguar and Mad Dog, they might miss something else important, so he was looking in the other direction – which could, of course, be the truth. Besides, I heard that a day before the incident, Karl and TT got into an argument in the command centre over who was stationed where. Maybe that lit the fuse on Karl's rage, and he decided to set a trap that would damn TT beyond redemption.'

This reminded Kwan to ask, 'How's TT now?'

'Been discharged and resting at home. Before Internal Investigations stepped in, the disciplinary inquiry was already looking bad. He might not actually have been demoted, but maybe would have been sent to some regional station to shuffle papers. But now it seems his left arm's broken, so who knows if he'll even be fit for work in the field after this.' Police departments had their fair share of administration and support work, such as applications for liquor licences, drafting internal strategies for workplace health and safety, maintaining police vehicles and firearms – all tasks, Kwan knew, that would be utterly incompatible with TT's personality.

'I heard – and this really is just a rumour' – Benny gulped down his last mouthful of coffee – 'during the incident, Karl

Fung's team deliberately slowed down, so they were only at the sixth floor when TT's men reached the ninth. You could say that's because Karl is cautious by nature, but it might also be that he didn't want to come to TT's assistance, hoping that if he stayed out of it, TT and Shek Boon-sing might destroy each other.'

Kwan Chun-dok was silent. A popular saying in the force was 'Anyone in uniform is family.' Kwan didn't want to believe it was possible that someone had hurt a fellow officer for selfish motives, but it couldn't be denied that Internal Investigations was right to look in this direction, based on the available evidence.

'Sir, you were at the scene, so Internal might ask you some questions down the line. You're much cleverer than those fellows, so I thought I'd give you a heads-up, and perhaps you'll dig up the truth sooner. The way things are in Kowloon West, if the Crime Unit is compromised, no one wins but the gangsters, which means all the more work for us in Intelligence.'

After saying goodbye to Benny, Kwan began pondering the question. Had Karl Fung really used such a despicable method to deal with TT?

Like TT, Karl had once been stationed at Wan Chai, and Kwan had a vague impression of him – a meticulous worker who undertook his duties scrupulously, unlike the slapdash TT. Unless Karl had undergone a radical personality change in these last few years, Kwan's instinct said it was unlikely that he'd ever do such an awful thing.

But Kwan also knew how preconceived ideas can affect one's deductions, so he didn't definitively proclaim Karl Fung innocent – or guilty.

In the afternoon, he pulled the relevant case files from Organized Crime and Kowloon West. Intelligence was supposed to be looking for clues to Shek Boon-tim's whereabouts, so no one would wonder why he wanted to look at the Ka Fai Mansions incident. He read through every officer's report, including one by Fan Si-tat, known as Sharpie, who'd spent half a day in surgery, barely emerging with his life.

It was all as Benny said, including the details about the mailbox and one division being delayed. The situation after TT's solo attack was the least clear, but as all three members of that group had survived, he was able to piece together the circumstances.

According to TT's statement, he'd charged out of the staircase door, requested back-up, then heard gunshots and screams from the hotel and knew Shek Boon-sing was 'thinning the herd' – he wouldn't need that many hostages. In fact one would be ample. Ko unsuccessfully ordered him to stand down, but TT fired twice into the room before running out of ammo. Shek Boon-sing was clutching the cleaning lady, Lee Wan, so TT tossed aside his pistol and put his hands up. In the instant when Shek Boon-sing moved the rifle away from the hostage to point it at him, TT whipped out his other gun, Sonny's pistol, and scored a direct hit. At the same time, Shek shot at him, hitting his left wrist. TT said his error was aiming at the torso, a larger target, rather than the head, which meant Shek survived long enough to pull out another pistol and fire off a few more rounds, killing Lee Wan. By the time TT got off a second shot to stop Shek for good, it was too late.

Sonny Lok, who'd just joined the Mong Kok unit, filled in some of the blanks. He described their encounter with Jaguar and Shum Biu. Even with TT charging ahead, this rookie insisted on staying with his fellow officer, disobeying a direct order and abandoning the possibility of saving even more lives. Kwan thought this Sonny Lok would probably get torn apart by the disciplinary committee, and with a mark like that on his record, could forget about ever getting promoted.

TT didn't explicitly say so, but strongly hinted that Edgar Ko hadn't acted logically or quickly enough. Team B arrived half a minute after TT had said he was going in, but by then it was already too late. TT believed that if the director had given the green light sooner, at least some of the hostages might have been saved.

Two days later, Kwan Chun-dok took advantage of a free moment to make a trip to the Identification Bureau. He was curious about that '042616' note, which hadn't been written about

much in any of the reports. Having broken many cases, Kwan
had been in and out of the Identification office numerous times,
and was familiar with the workings of the department. Inspector Szeto there was a friend, and he knew it would be far easier
to ask for a favour than go through official channels.

'Superintendent Kwan! Aren't you in CIB now? What are
you doing back here?' smiled Szeto, his moustache waggling
comically. He was right to wonder – as a division head, Kwan
shouldn't have to run around getting his own reports.

'I've got something on my mind I was hoping to have a chat
with you about,' said Kwan. 'A detail about the Ka Fai Mansions incident.'

'Are you after Shek Boon-tim?'

'No, I'm more concerned about the internal investigation.'

Inspector Szeto let out a whistle. 'You're involved in that too?'

'I happened to be at the scene that day.'

'Ah, in that case...' Szeto scratched his scalp, his hair as tan-
gled as a bird's nest. 'Of course, I know you'd never let anything
go if you had a doubt.'

'Is that note still here?'

'You mean the one with the code? Yes, with the other items. The
officers at the scene dumped a whole load of stuff on us, every one
needs to be fingerprinted and recorded. Where are we supposed
to get that kind of manpower? My colleagues have been glued to
their lightboxes all day long, staring themselves blind... Hang on a
minute, I'll get you the note.' Inspector Szeto shrugged and spread
his arms wide, a habitual gesture with him, then trotted into the
room next to the office, coming back with a cardboard box.

'This is it.' He pulled out a clear plastic bag. Inside was a sheet
of white paper on which was scrawled '042616'.

Kwan looked carefully at this piece of evidence from every
angle. It was roughly three by four inches, its edges smooth
on three sides and jagged on the fourth, probably torn from a
pad, the right side more roughly than the left, meaning it had
been done by a right-handed person. The paper was thin and

yellowish – cheap and unlined. Holding it up to the light, Kwan couldn't make out any marks from whatever had been written on the sheet above it.

The numbers '042616' were sloppily written, as if someone were trying to disguise their handwriting. Blue ballpoint pen, Benny had said. Kwan looked carefully and saw it was indeed the common sort, not a fountain pen or anything like that. Even the Identification Bureau would be at a loss when it came to differentiating the different models or type of ink of regular ballpoint pens. That would take a government lab to sort out.

'No prints on the note?' asked Kwan.

'Only the three suspects.'

Kwan stared some more at the note, flipping it back and forth, but it yielded up no further clues. He returned it to the box, where it lived together with a vast quantity of objects including the gang's pagers, a few notebooks, and business cards they'd found on the criminals' bodies. Then something grabbed his attention.

'Those are the leaflets they got from the mailbox?' He pointed to a few other evidence bags.

'Right, yes.' Szeto nodded, retrieving them and laying them out on the desk. There were three of them, a takeout menu for a restaurant near Ka Fai Mansions, a promotional mailshot from a big pizza chain – the envelope hadn't even been opened – and a black-and-white card advertising a removal business, with the company slogan under a drawing of an old man giving the thumbs up.

'There were quite a few prints on these, but they're probably all from the postman or whoever printed or delivered these. Internal Investigations wants us to go through them one by one, which is a waste of manpower and resources – we really have better things to do.' Szeto waved his arms before his chest, as if to ward off trouble.

'Only three?' interrupted Kwan.

'Yes, just these.'

'Sure there weren't others?'

'That's all we got. Something wrong?'

'Um... I just noticed.' Kwan didn't really answer the question, being unwilling to share his ideas until he was sure of them.

'Actually, the reason I asked earlier about Shek Boon-tim is Arms Experts found something that might not be a major clue, but you might "just notice" it.' Szeto mimicked Kwan's tone.

'Arms Experts?'

'Yes. Shall we go over there now and have a chat with Inspector Lo?'

The Forensic Firearms Examination Bureau, also known as the Arms Experts, were in charge of analysing evidence to do with weaponry and explosives – studying gun trajectories, examining bullets and so on. They also stored any firearms confiscated by the police in the course of their duties.

Szeto brought Kwan up in the elevator to the Arms Experts' office. Fortunately, Inspector Lo was free and could chat with them a moment.

'Superintendent Kwan, long time no see,' said Inspector Lo in English, offering his hand. Lo Sum was a strapping Scotsman, a long-serving member of the Arms Experts. After more than a decade in Hong Kong, he still hadn't mastered Cantonese, only knowing a few words and phrases. His actual name was Charles Lawson, his Chinese name being an approximation of his surname.

'Charles, you said there was something odd on Shek Boon-sing's body. Superintendent Kwan happened to drop in, and I thought he should come have a word,' said Inspector Szeto, switching to heavily accented English.

'Right,' Lawson nodded happily. He turned to pick up a cardboard box about the same size as Szeto's, but evidently much heavier.

'These were the pistols the gang had on them,' he said, pulling out four Black Stars and laying them out on the table. 'This one's Jaguar's, this was on Mad Dog Biu, and the other two were in the bag Shek Boon-sing had beside him.' Lawson pronounced the few syllables of those names awkwardly.

'These four show no sign of having been fired,' interrupted Szeto. Kwan remembered the reports – how Jaguar was hit

before he'd pulled the trigger, while Mad Dog was armed with
an AK-47, so the pistol must have been a spare.

'I remember TT's... I mean, Inspector Tang Ting's report said
Shek Boon-sing shot the cleaning lady with a handgun before he
died. Wasn't it one of these two?' asked Kwan.

'He was using this little number,' said Lawson, pulling a fifth
gun from the box.

'A Type 67?' exclaimed Kwan.

'You hardly ever see one of these, right?' Lawson smiled. 'That's
why we thought it might be connected to Shek Boon-tim.'

The Type 67 pistol was, like the Type 54 Black Star, a military-
grade weapon made in China. Type 67 was unique because of its
design – it was silenced, suitable for use on reconnaissance or nighttime assaults. During the Vietnam War, the Viet Cong had used
Type 67s to give the American troops a headache. In all of Kwan's
years in the force, this was his first time seeing one in real life.

Lawson flipped open the chamber and handed the gun over
to Kwan. 'We've already checked the bullets and compared them
with previous cases, and found one match,' he said. 'Superintendent Kwan, do you remember that lawyer, Ngai Yiu-chung, who
worked for all those Triad guys?'

'The one who got shot last February in Mong Kok – in the
alleyway behind the Blue Devil Bar?'

'Yes, that one. He was killed by this gun.' Bullets acquire dis-
tinctive markings from the barrel they pass through, so looking
at them under a microscope can verify if two bullets were fired
from the same weapon.

'Wasn't that the work of a hired killer? How are the Shek
brothers involved?' said Kwan curiously.

'That's the strange thing.' Lawson shrugged. 'The Shek brothers have never held back from armed robbery and kidnapping,
but they're not hit men. Still, the evidence doesn't lie. Maybe we
just got their business model wrong.'

Ngai Yiu-chung was still an open case, though many people – including rival gang bosses as well as the police – were

pleased that he was no longer around to defend underworld figures in court. The Crime Unit was still investigating his murder,
but there were countless murders in Mong Kok, and with so few
leads to go on, no one was particularly pushing this one.

'I don't think Shek Boon-sing killed that lawyer,' said Inspector Szeto. 'Guns circulate on the black market all the time. This
one might just have fallen into their hands.'

Kwan studied the pistol. 'In all of their bags, how much unused
ammo was there?'

Lawson grabbed a folder off the shelf and glanced at it. 'More
than three hundred rounds.'

'What kind?'

'Kind?' Lawson seemed surprised by the question, and had to
go back to the folder. 'Two hundred and two of the 7.62 x 39 mm
assault rifle bullets, and 156 of the 7.62 x 25 mm handgun ones...'

'That's strange,' said Kwan. 'No 7.62 x 17 mm?'

'Mm? That's right...' Lawson knew what Kwan was getting
at. The Black Star used a 25 mm bullet, but the Type 67 required
the shorter 17 mm ones.

'Actually, if you look at it another way, that makes perfect
sense,' said Szeto. 'They probably acquired the Type 67 serendip-
itously, and rather than get more ammo for it, figured they'd just
use what there was, then get rid of it. Though if he'd lost the Black
Star, he'd have been left with the Type 67 and a hundred useless
bullets – that would be dumb.'

Lawson shook his head. 'I still think the Shek brothers had something to do with Mr Ngai's murder. Now that this gun's shown up
by Shek Boon-sing's side, I don't think that can be a coincidence.'

'If he had a particular target, Shek Boon-sing would have used
the Black Star in his bag, not this Type 67,' argued Szeto. 'Besides,
he fired so many shots – wouldn't he have saved his ammo?'

'So many shots?' asked Kwan.

'According to the crime scene report, Shek Boon-sing was
alternating between the AK-47 and the Type 67,' explained
Lawson.

'More accurately, he was using them simultaneously.' Szeto struck a pose, as if he had a gun in each hand. 'We found his left-hand fingerprints on the Type 67 and his right on the AK-47.'

Shek Boon-sing had a history of carrying out robberies with two rifles. He had strong forearms, and by resting the rifle butts against his waist, could easily shoot from the hip.

'Has the Bureau reconstructed the killings from evidence at the scene?' asked Kwan.

'Yes, but what's the point?' asked Szeto. 'Only the coroner would be interested in that. We know who the killer was – what's it matter how exactly he did it?'

'Superintendent Kwan, I presume you intend to deduce from the sequence of events whether there was a particular reason for using this weapon, or if it's as you said and Shek Boon-sing just happened to have it by chance' said Lawson.

'More or less,' Kwan replied.

Lawson flipped open the folder again, and pulled out a stack of photographs showing the corpses at the scene from various angles.

'First of all,' said Szeto, 'after Jaguar and Shum Biu were shot dead by the Mong Kok team at the ninth-floor stairwell entrance, Shek Boon-sing returned fire with the AK-47, but with both his henchmen dead, he gave up this confrontation and headed for the Ocean Hotel, which was open for business. He headed for the farthest room, number 4, and burst in, we think hoping to escape from there. Because Unit 30 is the northernmost unit in the north wing, and the staircase was blocked, he was trapped.'

'He kicked open the door and killed Mandy Lam with the handgun as she sat on the bed,' said Lawson, showing a picture of the corpse. 'Because her wounds show more clotting than the other bodies, the forensic pathologist is certain she must have been the first victim.'

'Besides, we found Shek's footprint on the door. He was a strong fellow – those doors were pretty thick, and he kicked them open just like that,' added Szeto.

'After discovering there was no exit from Room 4, he quickly turned back. At this moment, Wang Jingdong came out of Room 2 to see what was going on, and when he saw an armed man, quickly ran for the exit. Shek opened fire with the AK-47 and blew off his head.' Lawson placed the gruesome photo next to Mandy Lam's.

'Shek Boon-sing walked over to Wang's body and did another sweep with the AK-47. At this point, Inspector Tang Ting must have been outside the lobby. These shots killed the hotel owner, Chiu Ping.'

As Szeto spoke, Lawson set down a picture of Chiu, his chin and jaw disintegrated. This was even more grisly than the last one, with bright red blood spattered across the walls and counter like a scene from a horror film.

'At this moment, Yau Choi-hung foolishly opened his room door. Shek Boon-sing happened to be standing nearby, so he quickly used the Type 67 to kill both the room's occupants.'

Lawson laid out pictures of Well-hung and Bunny Chin, the former hit twice, the latter with a bullet to the chest.

'Then he grabbed hold of the cleaning lady, Lee Wan, who must have been too scared to move, preparing to use her as a human shield.'

'And TT pretended to surrender and flung down his gun, and when Shek Boon-sing was drawing on him, pulled out his colleague's gun and fired on Shek,' finished Kwan.

'Yes, that's right, but Shek Boon-sing didn't die at once, he returned fire with the Type 67 and hit Lee Wan.' Lawson put down a picture of the final hostage.

'Wasn't there anyone in Room 3?' asked Kwan.

'No, I remember the investigators said it was vacant, and the register said so too.' Inspector Szeto seemed to remember something, and looked down at the pictures. 'Yes, look, behind Chiu Ping's body, you can see the counter. There's only one key there, the other three hooks are empty.'

Szeto indicated a corner of the photo. The sole key had a blue tag about half the size of a business card, on which was the hotel's name and a tattered sticker that said '3'.

'If it had been occupied, we might have had another corpse on our hands,' said Lawson.

'Superintendent Kwan, look at the way he used this gun – you can't think he was holding back ammo in reserve for any reason?' Szeto went back to the earlier topic. 'Even if we don't count the final return of fire, he'd already wasted four rounds.'

'No, no,' Lawson objected. 'They might not have had any seventeen-millimetre bullets on them, but that doesn't mean Shek Boon-sing wasn't holding some elsewhere.'

'That gun came to them by coincidence, but it did indeed have a special function.'

The other two would never have expected such ambiguity from Kwan. They stared at him doubtfully.

'Even if...' started Szeto, scratching his head, but he didn't continue.

'I'm not too certain either. I'll tell my team to look into this.' Kwan smiled and nodded, though the smile had some bitterness to it.

'I also wanted to ask,' Kwan turned to Lawson, 'have all the bullets in the victims' bodies been accounted for?'

'All the basics have been done, of course, and there's no issue there, every one of those bullets came from either the AK-47 or the Type 67 in Shek Boon-sing's hands. As to whether there are any open cases using these weapons...'

'And in the criminal's body?' Kwan interrupted.

Lawson found this question odd. 'Naturally those came from Inspector Tang Ting's gun, as well as his subordinate Sonny Lok's. Superintendent, you can't imagine a third party burst onto the scene and finished him off, and Inspector Tang is just taking the credit?'

'I just wanted to make sure.'

Kwan said goodbye to Lawson. In the elevator with Inspector Szeto, he said, 'Could I borrow that note with the code on it?'

Szeto frowned. 'I'm sorry, Superintendent Kwan, that's one favour I can't grant. It's a key piece of evidence.'

'Then could I make a copy?'

'Of course. That'd be no problem.'

Back downstairs, Inspector Szeto got the note out again and placed it on the Xerox machine. Just as he was about to press start, Kwan halted him.

'Put this on top of it.' Kwan handed over a notebook that was lying by the photocopier, the kind that had been used in every department for many years now, with black covers and a red border. Szeto found this odd, but did as Kwan directed.

Photocopy in hand, Kwan thanked Inspector Szeto and returned to Intelligence. As soon as he stepped through the office door, he gave an order to a subordinate.

'Get in touch with the phone company. I want the outgoing call records for 4 May from Ocean Hotel.'

'Is this an important lead?' said the officer, jotting down the instruction.

'Maybe, maybe not, I just want to make sure there aren't any irregularities.'

'Yes, Commander. Oh, I almost forgot, there was a call for you earlier.'

'Who was it?'

'Senior Inspector Benedict Lau from Division A. He said to call him back when you're free.'

Kwan did just that, back in his office.

'Benny, what's up?' said Kwan, staring at his copy of the note.

'Sir, has anyone from Internal Investigations been in touch with you?'

'Not yet. They're probably still completing their preliminary investigations. They'll want to check out everyone at West Kowloon Crime Unit before they get to me.'

'Then you haven't heard – it seems they've found the culprit. Someone's just been suspended.'

'Who? Karl Fung?'

'No. Edgar Ko.'

5

CHIEF INSPECTOR EDGAR KO's suspension sent shockwaves across the force. In less than a day, the news had reached every regional department. With the Ka Fai Mansions incident getting so much attention, even those who didn't know him would say, 'Ah, the director of the Shek Boon-sing op.' Still, because this was an internal investigation, there was no official statement, which meant the suspension was just a rumour, one that brewed and fermented in the various precincts and departments, no one certain how accurate it was.

Word of mouth was that Edgar Ko had given the criminals a warning, torpedoing the operation. He wasn't in the pay of the Shek brothers – had nothing to do with them – and didn't mind taking on the heavy burden of 'mission failed', wrecking his own career, all for one motive: to cause harm to the head of Mong Kok Crime Unit Team 3, Inspector Tang Ting.

'Operation director plots to kill frontline officer.' An unthinkable horror. During operations, officers entrusted their lives to their colleagues. The mindset of 'Anyone in uniform is family' came from this reliance. Once trust was lost, if everyone suspected everyone else, the organization would fracture.

Quite a few people had encountered Ko in the course of their duties, and most thought the rumours were baseless, or else that Internal Investigations was wronging a good man. Ko had always been loyal and dutiful, so mild-mannered it was hard to imagine him hating a fellow officer to the point of wanting to cause his death. But when they heard the purported motive, they had to admit, 'That's possible, I guess.'

When heroes reach the end of the road, there's only ever one reason: a woman.

Edgar Ko was pushing forty and still single. People generally reckoned he was too much of a workaholic to settle down, or else that he might be gay and staying closeted for fear of hurting his prospects. But the truth, which few people knew, was that he'd been in a relationship for some time; one that came to an end when the woman met someone else.

This woman was also in the police force, in Public Relations Branch. And she happened to be the Deputy Commissioner's daughter.

She was TT's fiancée, Ellen.

Ellen was a famed beauty within the force, and being very well-spoken, was often called upon to be the face of police press campaigns. Given her father's status, quite a few people secretly called her 'princess', and speculated which policeman would be lucky enough to become the 'imperial son-in-law'. Officially, of course, being married to the Deputy Commissioner's daughter didn't confer any actual privileges, and promotion would still be based on merit, but once your father-in-law was higher-ranking than the chair of any interview panel you'd face, as long as you didn't make any serious mistakes, your future would surely be bright.

Edgar Ko's secret relationship with Ellen had lasted three years. At the start, he'd just been promoted to probationary inspector, and didn't want to receive special treatment because of his girlfriend. By the time he'd made it to senior inspector, though, Ellen's affections had shifted.

TT's personality was the polar opposite of Ko's. He was brash and forthright, rebellious and unorthodox. To Ellen, who'd grown up under glass, this 'bad boy' was irresistible. TT knew Ellen had a boyfriend but still pursued her relentlessly, and even though Edgar's future was much more assured, she'd still chosen TT in the end.

After Ellen and TT had sent out their wedding invitations, Edgar Ko asked a close friend in the Traffic Branch out for a drink. After several beverages, he revealed that his 'mystery lover' from several years ago was the Deputy Commissioner's daughter. That night, Ko got extremely drunk and proclaimed he would disrupt the ceremony, then cursed Ellen for being too blind to choose the right man, insisting she was destined for an unhappy life. The friend didn't take these words seriously – until the Ka Fai Mansions incident.

When Internal Investigations began looking into the background of every officer involved in the operation that day, paying particular attention to anyone who'd had the opportunity to approach the south wing mailbox, Karl Fung was naturally their prime suspect, but they considered everyone else too, including Edgar Ko, the director of the operation, who'd personally inspected the south entrance. Once they called in the friend who'd spoken to Ko in the bar that night, he couldn't help thinking Edgar's words might have something to do with this case, and after repeated questioning, finally broke down and gave a full account of that conversation.

Edgar Ko was now the focus of the investigation. Ellen and the recuperating TT confirmed to investigators that four years earlier, the three of them had been involved in a love triangle. Ellen said that she'd met Edgar for a drink some time after the break-up, but they'd ended up fighting, and since then he'd been harassing her by phone.

Ko knew very well that if it looked like Shek Boon-sing was getting away, he'd only have to give TT an order to stay put for him to decide to charge in alone, leading to a face-off with vicious armed criminals – that was Internal Investigations' hypothesis. The motive had been verified, the method was plausible, and as director of the operation he could easily have destroyed any incriminating evidence, apart from that coded note, which Organized Crime had intervened too soon for him to retrieve.

Edgar Ko was temporarily relieved of his duties, to undergo a long period of interrogation and psychological torment. They wanted him to confess. On Friday 12 May, after a gruelling day of questioning, Edgar Ko was at home.

He'd taken his phone off the hook and turned off his pager, and was sitting alone in his room, unable to work out how he'd fallen this low. He didn't want to see or speak to anyone. He needed solitude.

He hadn't shaved for two days, his hair was a mess and his eyes were bloodshot. No one seeing him like this would have taken him for a man of heavy responsibilities, the senior inspector of a Crime Unit.

Or perhaps that should be: *formerly* a man of heavy responsibilities.

Ding-dong. The doorbell rang.

Edgar shuffled to the front door, grabbing his wallet from the coffee table on the way – he'd phoned the barbecue restaurant downstairs fifteen minutes ago and ordered some char siu pork and rice. He wasn't actually hungry, but knew on a rational level that human beings needed to eat.

'Inspector Ko.'

Edgar pulled the door open. Outside the metal gate, unexpectedly, was not the delivery person, but Kwan Chun-dok.

'What... what are you doing here?' Edgar made no move to open the gate.

'I need to speak to you.'

'I don't want to talk.' Edgar made to close the door.

'Wait—' Kwan reached between the bars to hold the door open.

'Please leave! I need to be alone!' Edgar shouted, pushing hard. As far as he was concerned, Kwan Chun-dok was the enemy, the person he least wanted to see him in this fallen state.

Kwan refused to retreat, pushing the door open just as hard as Edgar tried to shut it. This stalemate came to an end ten seconds later.

'Did... did someone order char siu rice?'

A young man in a white uniform, holding a plastic bag, stood timidly behind Kwan.

'Over here,' Ko sighed, cursing his bad luck, and had no choice but to open the gate. Without waiting for an invitation, Kwan seized that moment to walk into the apartment.

'Fine, Superintendent Kwan, say what you came to say, and then please leave.' Edgar pulled up a chair to sit opposite Kwan, who'd helped himself to the sofa.

'I want to know whether you did it.' Kwan came straight to the point.

'You all think I did! Just because of my relationship with Ellen, you believe I'd use such a low-down trick on TT? What's the use of me saying anything? Damn you!' Ko screamed in a single breath, venting all his anger at Internal Investigations on Kwan.

'You didn't answer my question. Did you or didn't you tip off Shek Boon-sing, causing him to escape and setting up the gunfight?'

'No! I didn't!'

'I knew it wasn't you,' smiled Kwan.

Edgar was stunned. 'You mean...'

'I knew you were innocent.' Kwan leaned back, relaxed. 'But I wanted to hear you say it, just to be sure.'

'Are you... are you interfering with the investigation?' asked Edgar. Everyone in the force knew Kwan Chun-dok was a crime-solving genius, and also a complete busybody.

'There's no "interfering" about it. Capturing Shek Boon-tim is one of the CIB's main tasks right now, and I came to look into this while on that investigation. We've got a lead from the weapons, and a location and list of Jaguar's associates from his pager messages. We'll find the guy somehow.'

Seeing that Kwan was happy to let him know where CIB was

at with their investigation, Edgar realized he really did trust him – trust that he wasn't the villain who'd tried to hurt TT, nor an insider for the Shek brothers. Kwan had brought these things up as a show of good faith.

'Then, Superintendent Kwan, why are you here? Did you just want to hear me say "I'm innocent"? Or do you want to know more about what happened that day? If you want to delve into that muddle of an operation, I'd suggest you go to O-Crime for a report, or head to Ka Fai Mansions and walk round the scene yourself, there might be more to see there.'

'I already went there this afternoon.' Kwan intertwined his fingers and placed them in his lap. 'I was there on the day as well, and I've seen more or less what I need to see. I came here today mainly to see how you're doing.'

'How I'm doing?'

'To wish you well,' Kwan smiled. 'It was your good friend who supplied Internal Investigations with info about your love triangle with TT and Ellen. I'm afraid you may not find a single person you can be open with. In the whole police force, only you, I and the real culprit know you're innocent. By the way, it took me quite a bit of effort to get your home address.'

'The real culprit? Who? It can't be... Karl?'

'Leave the investigation to me. I won't tell you any more, in case you can't resist letting it slip to Internal Investigations. Those fellows are too conservative, they only know the old methods, which makes it far too easy for the real culprit to find a loophole. Just keep telling them you're innocent. You'll be fine.'

Edgar nodded in understanding. He had no idea that Kwan Chun-dok had just lied to him.

'Now even HQ is talking about you, TT and Ellen. I heard Ellen's taken leave from work.'

'Then... I got her into trouble?'

'Do you still have feelings for her?'

Edgar hadn't expected that question. 'Superintendent Kwan, I believe you're married?' he asked in return.

'Yes, more than ten years now.' Kwan flashed the somewhat dulled ring on his fourth finger.

'Do you love your wife?'

'Of course.'

'If you knew she was about to do something foolish, and you couldn't stop her, wouldn't it make your heart ache?'

'You mean Ellen's marriage to TT is the wrong choice?'

Edgar nodded helplessly. 'When I heard they were getting married, I asked Ellen out for a chat. Before we'd been speaking five minutes, her face grew cold and she accused me of being childish.'

'She'd already made up her mind. How were you going to persuade her to take you back?'

'No! It wasn't like that!' Edgar grew agitated. 'You've misunderstood, just like she did! I wasn't stopping the marriage so she'd choose me instead. I just... just didn't want her to fall into marriage before seeing what TT was really like.'

'What TT was really like?'

'Colleagues say he's a playboy. The department he was at before, he cheated on a female officer.'

'That's it?'

Edgar's eyes grew wide. 'What do you mean, "That's it"? He's even willing to shit where he eats! God knows what kind of hell he's raising elsewhere. The worst kind of man – an unrepentant lecher. No woman is safe from him!'

Kwan thought Edgar was going over the top, but it seemed better to keep listening than to argue.

'True, I'm still fond of Ellen, but I know love can't be forced. If she was marrying someone who'd be good to her, I'd stay quiet and wish her well. But she's being tricked by that absolute bastard – I couldn't just stand by, could I?'

'They'd been together quite a few years. Why didn't you step in sooner?'

'I thought she'd come to her senses some day!' Edgar gritted his teeth. 'Even if TT was pretending to be devoted to her, I thought he'd show his true colours eventually.'

'Oh dear, Inspector Ko, your work is so outstanding – I hadn't expected you to be so slapdash in your personal life,' Kwan sighed. 'Once you've let go, you can't look back. Whether Ellen's choice was right or wrong, only she can take responsibility for that. You told her, and she wouldn't listen. You don't have the right to forcibly change her mind. If you claim to be her friend, all you can do is stand by her when she's alone and in need of help. The more you talk at her, the more stubborn she'll get. Speaking of which, have you ever made trouble for TT at work because of this?'

'Never. I keep my private life and work totally separate,' said Edgar seriously. 'I stationed him at the north wing that day because I thought his impulsive nature might put him and his colleagues in danger. If he'd been at the south exit, seeing the suspects walk in and out every day, God knows if he'd have suddenly snapped and done something stupid.'

'You thought too much about it.' Kwan shook his head. 'TT's personality isn't impulsive, it's unrestrained. He's arrogant about his abilities and has far too high an opinion of himself, that's all. He might enjoy taking risks, but he's not an idiot. If you'd put him in the south wing, he'd never have made that mistake.'

Edgar stared at Kwan, surprised at this speech.

'It seems you're not as good a judge of character as me or Keith Tso,' laughed Kwan.

Edgar thought to himself that that wasn't the only area where he'd lose to Superintendent Kwan.

Kwan glanced at the box of food on the table. 'You don't seem as despairing as earlier, anyway. I'll let you eat your dinner. We've been talking so long, it's probably cold.'

Edgar realized all of a sudden that his mood was better. Not only did the genius detective Kwan Chun-dok think he was innocent, but in this short conversation, he felt once more that he'd passed some sort of difficult test.

'Oh!' he suddenly exclaimed. 'That's right – with so many scandals in TT's past, perhaps the person who had it in for him was one of the women he cheated on? If any of my subordinates had something to do with these females, they might have taken advantage of the situation for revenge.'

'Inspector Ko, don't worry about this any more. I guarantee that by Monday, the whole matter will be resolved and you'll be back in your post. All right?'

'Are you serious, Superintendent Kwan?'

'Of course,' Kwan smiled. 'Take this weekend as a hard-earned break, and have a good rest. When you're back at work, we'll have many chances to talk again. Take care.'

Edgar said goodbye to Kwan, unspeakably grateful to the older man, although he remained doubtful as to whether even a genius detective could crack this case in just three days.

After leaving Edgar's apartment, Kwan didn't undertake any further investigations, but simply took the MTR home. Along the way, his brow was furrowed, and he didn't smile even once. What he hadn't told Edgar was that it had been a long time since a case had so frustrated him.

The following evening, Kwan went alone to Sham Shui Po, to the north-west of Mong Kok – a district of Kowloon with a great deal of history. Garment and fabric factories were once concentrated here, and even though many of these had moved away in recent years, many clothing distributors and fashion shops remained. Since the early 1970s, Apliu Street market had begun to gain a reputation for selling electronic spare parts, attracting nerds in search of the perfect spare part or the latest gadget. Kwan wove through the crowds of weekend shoppers and was covered in sweat by the time he saw his destination.

He was after an old residential building on Apliu Street.

TT's apartment was here.

Just as with his visit to Edgar Ko, he hadn't phoned ahead and didn't know if TT would be home – though he thought it didn't matter if he wasn't in, he could wander around nearby and try again later.

Unlike the clear tones of Edgar's doorbell, TT's was the traditional sort that let out a discordant buzz. Kwan thought he could easily have gone downstairs and selected one with a much more pleasing sound – that was just the sort of thing the vendors of Apliu Street specialized in.

'Coming,' called someone in the house.

The front door opened and TT stuck his head out. He froze when he saw Kwan Chun-dok – just as Edgar had – but then plastered on a warm smile.

'Super— Superintendent Kwan!' He stood at attention.

'We're not at work now, no need to stand on ceremony.'

TT ushered Kwan into the house. He lived alone in an apartment of about four hundred square feet, plenty of space for a bachelor.

'Would you like some tea? Or coffee?'

'Tea would be nice.'

TT went into the kitchen and emerged with a cup of pu-erh.

'Superintendent Kwan, did you need to speak to me about something?' he asked.

'How's your hand?' Kwan pointed at his left wrist, still swathed in bandages.

'The bullet shattered the radial bone, but the doctor said it's not a big deal, some physiotherapy and it should be as good as new. Fortunately it wasn't the right hand, otherwise all those years on the range would be wasted.'

'You'd be as sure a shot with your left hand inside of three years.'

'You're flattering me, Superintendent.' TT scratched his head, looking awkward. 'So sorry I couldn't speak to you that day, after I'd been injured... Oh yes, I heard you were a division leader in CIB now. What were you doing there?'

'I was just there with Superintendent Tso to see Inspector Ko. It was a coincidence.'

'If you'd been directing the operation, things might not have gone so badly,' TT sighed.

'No, even if I'd been in charge, the whole affair would have played out the same way.'

'Superintendent Kwan, you're famous for being a genius detective. With you overseeing things, how could the op have gone wrong?'

'No, I...' Kwan suddenly stopped. 'TT, let's skip the small talk.'

'Yes?'

'I want you to turn yourself in.'

The air seemed to freeze. TT looked at Kwan as though he couldn't believe his ears.

'TT, I know you were behind the plot to let Shek Boon-sing escape and wreck the operation.'

6

'ARE YOU JOKING, Superintendent Kwan?' TT sounded uncertain whether he should laugh or not.

'I know you were behind the coded message,' said Kwan simply.

'I couldn't have been – I never once went to the south wing. How could I have put it in the mailbox?' TT smiled. 'There's no way Karl Fung would've kept his mouth shut if I'd shown up anywhere within his team's surveillance area. I'd hardly be so stupid, asking for trouble like that.'

'The note wasn't in the mailbox. Mad Dog Biu found it in the takeaway bag.'

A faint tremor went through TT's body, but he kept the smile pasted on his face. 'That's just a hypothesis, though?'

'No, there's no way it came from the mailbox. You just got lucky there, when circumstances diverted suspicion away from you,' said Kwan, shaking his head. 'When the evidence team told me Mad Dog Biu only found three fliers in the box, I knew the note couldn't have been in there.'

'Why not?'

'If there'd been a stack of mail, he might credibly not have found the note till he and Jaguar got back to the apartment. But that's not possible with just three bits of paper. Anyone would have glanced through their mail while waiting for the lift, but if either one of them had spotted it then, they'd wouldn't have sauntered back to their hideout like they didn't have a care in the world.'

'Maybe they'd sensed danger, but were keeping a calm facade?'

'If that were the case, one of the meals wouldn't have had a mouthful taken out of it.'

TT was silent, his eyes fixed directly on Kwan.

'If they'd sensed danger, they'd have alerted Shek Boon-sing as soon as they got back, then grabbed their guns and prepared to flee. But they set the takeaway containers out on the table, and someone even started eating. Only one of the fliers was in an envelope, but that was still sealed. The logical conjecture is that the warning note was at the bottom of the plastic bag containing the food. Jaguar would have unpacked the bag and only found the note when all the boxes were out, at which point Shek Boon-sing gave the order to move out. According to your report, Jaguar complained that Mad Dog Biu was too picky when it came to food. He probably brought back the mail because it contained takeaway menus, which led the investigation down the wrong path.'

'Superintendent Kwan, you've just said yourself that this is a conjecture.' TT's expression was relaxed once again. 'In other words, the probability that the note was in the mailbox still isn't nil.'

Kwan shook his head and pulled a sheet of paper from his shirt pocket. It was a photocopy of the note, with the digits '042616' clearly visible.

'I suppose you're going to claim that's my handwriting?' smiled TT.

'The important thing isn't the numbers.' Kwan pointed at the upper edge of the note. 'It's the way it was torn.'

At Kwan's request, Inspector Szeto had placed a black notebook behind the note when photocopying it, so its outline was very clear on all four sides.

Now Kwan produced something in an evidence bag, and TT's smile vanished altogether.

It was a writing pad with half its pages ripped out.

'We got this yesterday from the takeaway where you were watching,' said Kwan solemnly. 'According to the owner, he took down orders on this notepad when a customer called or when the shop was busy. It lived near the counter. When I first saw the note, it reminded me of the kind of pad waiters use. Added to the details that didn't fit – the three fliers, the box of food with one mouthful missing – I knew where to go looking for evidence. When you rip off a sheet from this kind of pad it leaves a little strip still attached to the spine. If we took it to Forensics or ID, I'm pretty sure they'd find it's a perfect match...'

'Hang on, hang on!' TT interrupted. 'This must be a misunderstanding. All three kills were mine. Are you saying I disrupted Chief Inspector Ko's operation so I could tackle Shek Boon-sing on my own and steal all the glory? That's too crazy even for me. Some praise wouldn't be worth putting my life in danger for.'

'But covering up a murder might be.'

Kwan's calm utterance silenced TT, who stared at his opponent, complicated emotions flitting across his face.

'Of all the deceased,' Kwan fixed his gaze on TT's eyes, 'one was killed *before* the gunfight – and you hid the corpse amongst the other victims.'

Kwan placed two photographs on the coffee table. They were of the crime scene, showing the bodies of Mandy Lam and hotel owner Chiu Ping.

'I walked through the crime scene between forty and fifty minutes after the shoot-out. I didn't detect anything unusual at the time.' Kwan pointed at the photos. 'But when I saw these pictures, taken when the preliminary investigators went in, I realized something was wrong. Chiu Ping had been hit by an AK-47 – bright red blood spatter everywhere. Yet the blood from Mandy Lam's wounds was darker and thicker, with solid clots separating from the pale yellow serum. She was supposedly killed a minute before Chiu, but from the photo I'd put her stage of clotting at least ten minutes ahead of his. Naturally the difference became less pronounced over time: a forty-minute-old corpse has bloodstains virtually indistinguishable from an hour-old one. That's why I didn't spot this disparity at the scene.'

TT didn't make a sound. Kwan continued, still in a level voice. 'The ID team weren't clear on the exact sequence of events, so the gap of ten minutes didn't set off any alarms, and your average investigator isn't too knowledgeable about the stages of blood clotting. More importantly, because we were facing the prolific killer Shek Boon-sing, no one guessed that by "coincidence", an unrelated murder had actually taken place fifteen minutes before the gunfight.'

'You said it, Superintendent Kwan. Coincidence. This sort of guessing game is all based on assumptions – no one would believe it,' TT defended himself.

'A *seeming* coincidence. This was actually an act of desperation, a scheme dreamed up by someone backed into a corner.' Even when detonating these heavy words, Kwan's tone remained light. 'I've questioned the takeaway owner and Fan Si-tat, the hospitalized officer. You stepped outside at twelve forty on the day of the incident, for about ten minutes. Fan said you had to use the bathroom, and it was time for your break anyway, but I believe you weren't on any break. Instead, you made use of this small window of time to meet Mandy Lam at the Ocean Hotel.'

Kwan pulled out his notebook and flipped it open. 'I got the phone company to release the records of every number dialled from the hotel. Starting at eleven, five calls were made from Room 4, all to a pager. Two of them were "Miss Lam is waiting for you in Ocean Hotel Room 4," two were "Come to Ocean Hotel Room 4 quickly, urgent business to discuss," and the fifth was "Come to Ocean Hotel Room 4 within ten minutes or face the consequences." The last message went out at twelve thirty-five. When I asked who the pager was registered to, the answer was interesting: Miss Mandy Lam Fong Wai. That is to say, Miss Lam herself registered the pager, then gave it to someone else, suggesting this person was more than just a friend or client.

I believe this person was Miss Lam's fiancé, the man her colleagues mentioned. TT, it was you.'

'What nonsense is this?'

'Fan Si-tat told me you'd been leaving your post all morning to get your messages. Yet when I checked, your personal pager hadn't received a beep all day. Also, according to the records, all the calls to retrieve Miss Lam's messages were made from the payphone outside Ka Fai Mansions management office. You really shouldn't underestimate the CIB's ability to gather information,' said Kwan.

TT said nothing, shrinking slightly back as if trying to think of a response.

'My guess is that you and Mandy Lam had an intimate relationship, and she even believed you'd marry her, allowing her to quit her job at the nightclub. But then you broke up with her, or else she happened to find out about your upcoming wedding to a top brass's daughter, and she immediately went from pliant mistress to vengeful woman. For all we know, the hotel room was meant to be where she'd lure you back with her body. But you ignored her, until she made that impossible. I believe it was no coincidence that she picked Ka Fai Mansions for a rendezvous – she knew you were working there that day, which again shows how intimate the two of you must have been. The "consequences" she threatened presumably included wrecking your engagement, and possibly revealing other secrets that might cause you trouble.

'Around 12.40 p.m., you claimed you needed the toilet and to check your messages, and headed for the hotel. In her room, the conversation quickly grew heated, and Mandy Lam threatened to destroy you. You weren't able to placate her, and knew there'd be no saving the situation once she'd left the hotel. So you took the only chance you had, pulled out the Type 67 silenced pistol you'd concealed on your person, and shot her dead.'

'Where would I have got a Type 67?'

'God knows. But Mong Kok Crime Unit makes so many arrests – you must have fifty or sixty operations per year, including burglaries, drug deals and so on. It's not implausible that you'd come upon a rare gun like this and keep it for yourself instead of reporting it. After all, you love shooting and you're good at it, and it's not like you're some goody-two-shoes who follows regulations.'

'Even if *someone* took out that Lam woman beforehand and left the body in Room 4 of the Ocean Hotel, how would the murderer have made sure the gunfight took place exactly there? No one could have known which way the suspects would run. What if they'd headed for the other end of Ka Fai Mansions, or taken the elevator?'

'You told them where to go,' said Kwan simply.

'Why would Shek Boon-sing listen to me?' chuckled TT derisively. 'And how would I even have got in touch with them? Phone? Telepathy?'

'With this key.' Kwan pointed at a corner of the photo of Chiu Ping. 'All the Ocean Hotel room keys had their room number and the hotel name on their tags. After killing Mandy Lam, you locked the door, returned to your post and tried to work out how to lure Shek to the hotel. Just then, Jaguar happened to come in to place his food order, and you realized this was an opportunity you couldn't miss. As well as hiding the note in the takeaway bag, you also slipped in the key. When Shek saw them, he could only assume they were a cryptic warning from his older brother to relocate to Ocean Hotel Room 4. He'd never have guessed it was someone else using their code. Their only enemy was the police, and the police would never pointlessly throw their investigation into chaos. So Shek would have been sure this had come from his own side. He and his accomplices packed up and left for their new "hideout". You knew their destination, which is how you were able to pelt straight up the staircase, then suddenly slow down at the ninth floor and prepare to face them.'

TT didn't respond, just stared silently at Kwan.

'Shek had probably positioned his men in the corridor and by the stairwell outside the hotel, while he went personally to Room

4 to find out what was going on. You got there "just in time" and
accosted Jaguar. All three men had to die for your plan to work,
otherwise your murder of Mandy Lam would come to light anyway. You never intended to take them alive. TT, you compulsively
take huge risks in which there's only complete victory or utter
defeat. We've seen you venture alone into the tiger's den and take
on suspects one on one, using your own life as a gambling chip.
You might have been at a huge disadvantage when it came to firepower, but you'd guessed each of their positions and had faith
in your sharp shooting. And so you placed your stake – having
already killed Miss Lam, you didn't have many other options.

'You fired on Jaguar and Mad Dog Biu. Shek quickly came to
their assistance – I imagine he hadn't reached Room 4 yet. According to the reports of Officers Sharpie Fan and Sonny Lok, after
you'd killed his henchmen, Shek Boon-sing charged at the stairwell with an AK-47. The bizarre thing was that he didn't then flee
towards the other end of the corridor, but back into the hotel.'

'He wanted to grab a hostage to use as a human shield.' TT
spat out the words.

'No, that doesn't make sense. Taking a hostage at this point
would immobilize him – he could hardly walk down nine flights
of stairs whilst holding another person. He'd have sprinted down
the stairs first, and if he found no way out at the bottom, he'd
have barged into a shop or someone's apartment and taken a hostage there. He went back into the hotel because he expected Shek
Boon-tim to have left an escape plan in Room 4, or even that his
brother would be there in person. He rushed back in with his rifle
and kicked in the door – no time to use the key – only to see Mandy
Lam's corpse. That's when he knew he'd been tricked, so he set off
on a killing spree, having no idea which of the people around
him was dangerous or had a concealed weapon. That's how Wang
Jingdong and Chiu Ping ended up dead. Then you burst in, probably shouting and flashing your badge and gun. That left Shek
Boon-sing no choice but to grab Lee Wan, the chambermaid cow-
ering in a corner, and use her as a human shield.'

'All of this is just your imagination,' said TT indifferently.

'Imagination? TT, don't you have even a scrap of remorse?' Loathing showed on Kwan's face.

'What remorse should I feel?' TT's voice was cold.

'You bastard! You killed those hostages that could have been saved! You murdered all those innocent people to cover up your crime!' Kwan had been icily calm up to this point, but now rage suffused his features. 'You didn't take down Shek Boon-sing by pretending to surrender. Lee Wan took a bullet to the chest – no hostage would be stupid enough to run away facing their captor! You shot her with the silenced Type 67, distracting Shek enough that you could get him too. He'd never have expected a police officer to kill a hostage! You shot Lee Wan with the Type 67 in your left hand, before firing on Shek with the police revolver in your right. That's why you weren't as accurate as usual. You missed the first time, taking a bullet to your left wrist, and had to shoot him again in the head. In order to kill Shek Boon-sing, you used Lee Wan – no, in fact, from the very beginning, you didn't intend to leave a single living soul. You wanted to seal the mouth of everyone in that hotel!'

TT hasn't expected the normally placid superintendent to display such strong emotion, while he was the one with the poker face, staring coolly at the other man.

'Yau Choi-hung and Bunny Chin too! They were still alive at the moment of Shek's death. He didn't kill them, you did! No one would be such an idiot as to open their door when they'd heard gunshots, especially a Mong Kok pimp like Well-hung. There's only one reason he'd open his door, and that's if someone outside called out that it was safe and he'd better get away quick. That's how you got him to let you in, and then you shot both of them. You're a cold-blooded killer. In order to cover up your murder of Mandy Lam, you took the lives of a whole group of innocent victims!'

'So you think, after I'd killed everyone the way you described, I wiped my prints off the Type 67 and shoved it into Shek's hand, so it would look like he'd come out with both guns blazing? Superintendent Kwan, you've forgotten an important fact.' TT was relaxed again, smiling. 'Less than a minute after I entered the hotel – maybe forty seconds – the other team showed up. Do you think that was enough time for me to shoot Lee Wan and Shek Boon-sing, trick Yau into opening his door, shoot two more people, wipe the gun clean and plant it on Shek? Don't forget my left hand had been injured, and even if I'd been able to ignore the pain, it would still have slowed me down. Even supposing I could move as fast as that and was such a resourceful murderer, would I take the risk of doing all this, knowing other officers could appear at any moment? What if Yau had refused to open his door? I'd be sunk then.'

'You'd just need to do all this *before* you burst into the hotel.'

'Oh, so now I can split myself in two? Are you soft in the head?'

'What I mean is, you did all this before *claiming* to enter the hotel.' Kwan glared at TT as if seeing a monster. 'Instead of communicating with Chief Inspector Ko when you got there, you walked straight in, killed Lee Wan and Shek Boon-sing, lured Well-hung out of his room, dealt with him and Bunny, and only then did you radio in pretending to be outside, about to enter. Everyone was dead by then, and you knew your plan had worked. You picked up Shek's rifle and fired into the corridor, claiming that was the sound of him taking a captive for a stand-off. You told Ko you were going in to save the "hostage". Then you just had to fire a few shots to sound like a gunfight, wipe the prints off the AK-47, place it in Shek's hand, and sit tight waiting for "back-up". Forty seconds? Ten would have been ample.'

'You have no proof.' TT was no longer smiling.

'No concrete evidence, but discrepancies crop up as soon as you examine the whole sequence of events. When the first gunshot was heard from Ka Fai Mansions, Chief Inspector Ko gave the order to seal the lifts and head up the stairs, at which point you were already on the ninth floor. According to Sonny Lok's testimony, it was only ten to fifteen seconds from then to your retreating to the stairwell, then Shek returning fire, sweeping the stairwell for a few seconds before dashing back into the hotel. Shek shooting and running, you and Lok arguing over Sharpie in the stairwell – all of that can't have lasted more than fifteen or twenty seconds. If you'd really charged into the hotel right after those gunshots, calling the command centre for back-up, that would have been around forty seconds after Inspector Ko's order – but by then, the other team had arrived at the seventh floor. Yet while they were on the ground floor, they'd have waited for instructions after the first gunshot, then needed to order the maintenance crew to lock the elevators, which must have taken at least half a minute. If they'd run flat out, it's just possible they could have gone up seven flights of stairs in a little over ten seconds, but they were moving slowly and cautiously, afraid there was an ambush ahead. They sped up when they heard your radio message that only Shek Boon-sing was left, trapped in the hotel. So we have to conclude that when you ran in from the stairwell, you hadn't radioed yet, and when you did call for back-up, it was about two minutes after the exchange of fire at the stairwell. In this atmosphere of extreme stress, most people wouldn't have noticed the timings weren't quite right, especially as no one was certain where the gunshots were coming from. When we're under pressure, our sense of time is extremely unreliable. That's the blind spot you exploited.'

TT applauded, grinning widely. 'A most thrilling scenario! But Superintendent Kwan, no matter how gripping your tale, I still have to ask – where's your evidence?'

Kwan hadn't expected this volte-face from TT, and couldn't help frowning. 'I have the takeaway order pad.'

'You can't prove I wrote that note,' said TT calmly. 'If I were the criminal, I'd have ripped off a few pages to get to one with no indentations from above, and wiped the whole thing clean with my apron afterwards. If my fingerprints aren't on the note, you can't show that I'm the culprit. The killer could have torn off a slip of paper before or even during our shift. This piece of evidence also throws suspicion on Sonny Lok, Fan Si-tat, even the takeaway owner and his workers, not to mention all the customers who came in that day.'

'But you can't explain Lee Wan's chest wound, or why Yau opened his door, or Mandy Lam's blood clotting, or the mismatch in the time when you reported to Ko.'

'I don't need to explain any of those things. The only thing you can say is that they're unusual, but none of them *contradict* my testimony. Where did these discrepancies come from? How would I know? Forensics isn't my responsibility.' The corner of TT's mouth curled up slightly.

'You called the pager operator several times from the management office phone.'

'The manager was old and snoozed half the time. You think he'd remember who used his phone? I doubt it.'

'I've asked ID to check the Room 4 key for prints.'

'If I were the killer, do you think I'd have left prints?'

'I thought so too, but if they had Shek Boon-sing's prints...'

Kwan didn't go on, because he saw TT's smile holding steady. He knew then that even in the aftermath of the crime, TT hadn't forgotten to wipe Jaguar and Shek's prints off the key lying next to Mandy Lam's corpse. Perhaps he'd taken the key off Shek's body after shooting him, and planted it in Room 4 afterwards. It would be odd that there were no prints on the key, as Mandy would have had no reason to wipe it clean, but that fell into the same category as all the earlier discrepancies – TT was under no obligation to explain them.

'There's another route we could take to expose your crime.' Kwan's brow wrinkled. 'Motive. If we start with Mandy Lam, we have a sure way to show your guilt.'

'Superintendent Kwan, you can certainly try this method, but you'll be wasting your time.' TT's confidence made Kwan understand that this wasn't a sufficient threat. Earlier that afternoon, he had already been to the nightclub where Mandy worked, only to learn how tight-lipped she'd been, hadn't pursued that line of inquiry.

'In fact, Superintendent Kwan, you must be very brave.' TT's smile didn't reach his eyes, which were boring coldly into Kwan. 'If I really were the killer, wouldn't you be seeking your own death by coming here today? The piece of evidence most likely to cause me bother is that food counter notepad, and you've helpfully brought that along. Haven't you thought that the murderer might want to destroy the evidence, even if it meant knocking you senseless or taking your life?'

'You won't do anything of the sort. If you were capable of that, you wouldn't have gone to all this trouble to cover up Miss Lam's death. It's clear that you understand the *process* of killing someone is easy; the difficulty lies in disposing of the body and dispelling suspicion *after* the murder. After a death, as long as the police, doctors, family or friends have even a sliver of suspicion, in a city as densely populated as Hong Kong, you'd find it difficult to escape the attention of the law. Even if you could make a corpse vanish, the victim going missing would attract police notice. You knew that the simplest way to murder with no consequences was to find someone else to take the blame, but then the problem became how to silence your chosen scapegoat. And so you took the most evil route – pushing the guilt for Mandy's death onto Shek Boon-sing, and then killing Shek *by legal means.*'

TT smiled triumphantly. 'By the same token, it's far more likely that Edgar Ko was trying to push the blame onto me, and the Internal Investigation guys think he's guilty too, so they're hardly likely to admit defeat and accept your hypothesis. They're not going to budge unless you can produce hard evidence. You're just going to make a fool of yourself, going to them with your half-baked suppositions.'

Kwan realized how thoroughly TT had thought this through. What a shame he'd never used so much intelligence and ability in his detective work.

Helplessly, Kwan shook his head, and reached into his jacket pocket.

'Superintendent Kwan, you're not going to tell me you have

a concealed recorder, and our whole conversation is on tape? That wouldn't help you, because I haven't admitted to anything,' mocked TT.

'No, quite the opposite. If you'd been taping this, I'd be in more trouble than you.' Kwan produced a small glass bottle containing a single expended bullet.

'This is...' TT grew wary.

'If you want to talk dirty tricks, I have as many up my sleeve as you.' Kwan held the bottle up between his index finger and thumb. 'This is the bullet that Shek Boon-sing took to the chest.'

'Why are you showing me this?'

'I've swapped it,' said Kwan carelessly.

'Swapped it for what?'

'A bullet from that Type 67 pistol – the one that killed the crooked lawyer, Ngai Yiu-chung, last year.'

'You...'

'I've already left instructions for Arms Experts to re-examine the bullets from Shek, Jaguar and Mad Dog's bodies. Tomorrow's Sunday so they won't be in the lab, but when they get to work on Monday, they'll discover that there was an error in the previous report, and the first shot Shek sustained was actually from a Type 67 pistol. This "evidence" will conflict with your report, forcing the Internal Investigation guys to look at other possibilities, such as the "hypothesis" I've just told you about, the only difference being that you got flustered while shooting Lee Wan and Shek Boon-sing, accidentally using the wrong gun on Shek, which means the bullet found in his body doesn't fit with your version of events. That puts you under serious suspicion.'

'You... You falsified evidence!' TT stood up in shock.

'You're free to report me to Internal Investigations, but like you, I didn't leave behind a trace of my "crime". And you can try breaking into the evidence locker yourself, but Arms Experts holds a lot of weaponry; naturally, security is tight.'

TT sat again, his eyes darting wildly.

'Just give up. This is checkmate.'

Kwan had considered the possibility that TT, backed into a corner, would assault him, but that didn't seem likely. As soon as he struck the first blow, he'd be admitting failure. And TT was a gambler – he wouldn't give up as long as there was one day left in which he could try to turn the situation in his favour.

'That's all I have to say.' Kwan stood up, returning the photographs, bullet and notepad to his pocket. 'TT, if you run off or go into hiding, you've lost. If you want another throw of the dice, your best bet is to have your day in court. See if you can get away with a manslaughter conviction, or escape life imprisonment by pleading insanity. For that to work, you'll have to turn yourself in before the new evidence about the bullet comes back from Arms Experts.'

Kwan had reached the front door, and TT still hadn't moved a muscle. Kwan turned back. 'One last thing. If – just supposing, if – you were the culprit, how would you have lured Shek to the hotel, had Jaguar not come into the takeaway for lunch?'

TT looked up and blinked at Kwan, speaking slowly. 'I'd have said I'd spotted someone suspicious and needed to tail him, left Ka Fai Mansions on my own, and called one of Jaguar's pagers from the payphone. Afterwards, as long as I claimed the suspicious individual I was following had made a phone call, it would seem like one of Shek's underlings had warned him.'

'But how would you leave a message if they couldn't call the operator?'

'The standard code has "Ocean Terminal", "hotel" and "room number". You could cobble the message together out of those. Of course, they might misunderstand that as the hotel at Ocean Terminal rather than the Ocean Hotel, but the Terminal Hotel is posh enough that it wouldn't have room numbers with a single digit.'

'But the command centre was intercepting all the pagers, so Edgar Ko would have seen the same message. Wouldn't that have exposed the murder of Mandy Lam?'

'Not if the message said Room 3 instead of 4.'

Kwan recalled the empty Room 3, and without a further word, pulled open the door and left TT's home. TT still hadn't stirred, as if his mind was fully occupied searching for a way to reverse his fortunes.

Kwan Chun-dok walked down the street, rubbing shoulders with the throngs of tourists, his heart full of sorrow. TT was an intelligent man, and back when they'd worked together, Kwan had seen great potential in him. Yet he'd chosen a dark path. The day before, Kwan had been lying when he told Edgar Ko he wouldn't reveal the name of the suspect for fear of a leak from Internal Investigations. The truth was he'd wanted to give TT a chance to surrender himself. He was still anxious about whether he'd dealt with the matter in the best way, if he'd done everything he could to make TT give himself up. Kwan Chun-dok could be ruthless in pursuing criminals, but when it came to someone who'd once been an excellent subordinate, he was simply unable to go after them as harshly.

He reflected that there was no sadder sight than a fine example of a police officer turning to evil.

But this time, Kwan Chun-dok was wrong.

He got the news on Monday morning. Tang 'TT' Ting, leader of Mong Kok Crime Unit Team 3, had walked into the station, put the barrel of a gun into his mouth and shot himself dead.

'You mean to say, you didn't actually swap the bullets?' Keith Tso asked.

'Yes, I was just trying to scare him. Swapping a few documents in the Identification Bureau, I could maybe have managed. But pulling this kind of trick in Forensic Firearms Examination Bureau wouldn't be that easy,' said Kwan.

The day they got news of TT's death, Kwan went to Internal Investigations with his suspicions, evidence and data about the Ka Fai Mansions incident. The following morning, Tso turned up to see how he was doing, and Kwan told him everything.

'I discovered something else this morning.' Kwan flipped open an old case file. 'The lawyer who was murdered at the beginning of last year, Mr Ngai, was a frequent visitor at the New Metropolis – the nightclub Mandy Lam worked at. This could be a coincidence, but perhaps TT killed the lawyer too.'

'Really?'

'There's no concrete evidence, so this is just a hypothesis. I don't know how I'd ever prove it – after all, we have no way of knowing when TT acquired the Type 67,' Kwan shrugged. 'But if this were the case, then Mandy Lam may not have been killed for something as simple as threatening to stop TT's wedding. She might have been an accessory to TT's murder of Ngai Yiu-chung.'

'That's possible. She was willing to wait for him at Ka Fai Mansions, which means they must have known a fair number of each other's secrets.'

If TT really were Ngai's killer, Kwan thought, even he would never know if he'd done it to make his work easier, or if Mandy Lam had goaded him into it because of some dispute. Unless new evidence turned up, this would wind up a cold case, the truth never to be known.

'So instead of turning himself in, TT killed himself out of guilt,' sighed Keith.

'No, that bastard felt no guilt. He was making a big show to me – that I'd never beat him.' Kwan's brow was creased, unhappiness filling his face.

'Making a big show? Ah Dok, aren't you reading too much into this?'

'Keith, this fellow's aims in life might have been exactly the opposite of mine, but I can't deny that our brains worked similarly. To people like us, existence is also a sort of tool. I understand that each life is precious, and would risk my own to save another person, but he had no such restriction. For him, it was worth sacrificing his own life to gain a psychological victory.'

'So you're saying he's the real winner here,' said Keith despairingly. 'Campbell is pondering whether to make the matter public.' Senior Assistant Commissioner William Campbell – Kim Wai-lim in Cantonese – was the Director of Crime and Security.

'What's there to decide?'

'The higher-ups are thinking about covering up the whole thing, and pushing all the blame onto Shek Boon-sing. The official story will be that TT committed suicide out of depression at not being able to save the hostages.'

'What!' yelled Kwan. 'He's planning to lie to the public? Don't Lee Wan, Bunny Chin and all the other innocents deserve the truth?'

'Chief Superintendent Yuan from Internal Investigations has had a hand in this,' Tso explained. 'He said the incident would damage the force's reputation. After all, there's no definitive evidence to show TT was the killer, and the dead are beyond help. Putting the blame on the police won't bring them back to life.'

'And Campbell has actually agreed to this?'

'Ah Dok, you know how complicated the political situation is. Campbell's a Brit, and with the Handover just eight years away, he's obliged to pay more attention to what the Chinese say. I heard that when the Commissioner retires this year, he'll be replaced by a local. Our first Chinese Commissioner. The position of the Englishmen in the force is only going to get lower and lower.'

'Even so, isn't he hurting police morale with his actions?' Kwan's face was absolutely despairing.

'He says it's for "the greater good". If we lose the trust of the populace, that will only benefit the criminal element.'

'But we're shoring up their trust with a fiction. Does that trust still mean anything?' Kwan's fists were clenched.

'There's no help for it. The Ka Fai Mansions incident made us look so bad, the higher-ups don't think we can take another blow.'

Kwan rubbed his temples, and was silent for a long time. Eventually, he said, 'Keith, have you ever been in Statue Square, looked up at the Legislative Council Building?'

'I guess so?' Tso had no idea what he was getting at.

'And you know it used to be the old Supreme Court building, which was then taken over by the Council in 1978,' said Kwan slowly. 'Because it used to be a court, there's a statue of Themis above the porch roof, representing justice.'

'Ah, I know the one you mean, that Greek goddess with the sword and balancing scales.'

'Every time I walk past it, I look up at her. She has a blindfold over her eyes, to show that justice is blind, hence treating everyone fairly. The balance shows that the courts will weigh out responsibility in a just manner, and the sword is ultimate power. I've always thought that the police are that sword. In order to eliminate evil, we have to possess immense strength. But we're not the scales. We use everything we have to catch criminals, or to trick them into giving themselves away, but all I've ever done is present them to the scales, so that justice can weigh them and decide if they're guilty. We shouldn't have the power to decide what the "greater good" is.'

Keith Tso smiled grimly. 'I understand everything you're saying. But if Superintendent Yuan insists, what can we do?'

Kwan sighed. 'Yuan's reasoning is that the force has taken one too many beatings to withstand another scandal?'

'Right.'

'Then if we were to score a great victory, redeeming ourselves, and at the same time announce that we'd found a traitor in our midst, then good and bad would balance out. I guess the top brass could handle that?'

'Campbell would probably be all right with that.'

'Then please tell him that within a month from now – no, from the Ka Fai Mansions incident – I'll capture our most wanted criminal, Shek Boon-tim. And I'll get him alive, and make him spit out everything he knows about his criminal empire.'

'A month?' gaped Tso. 'Are you sure?'

'No, but even if I have to go without sleep or rest, chasing him to the ends of the earth, I'll still find Shek Boon-tim.'

Tso knew that once Kwan Chun-dok got serious, even an impossible task like this had a chance of success.

'All right, I'll talk to Campbell. I hope you give him a good show.'
Kwan nodded.

'Come to think of it,' said Keith, stretching in his chair,

'looking at the situation in Beijing now, who can say whether the Handover will go smoothly? For all we know, when the time comes, Campbell might end up remaining as our superior.'

Kwan understood what his friend was referring to – over on the Mainland, passions were riding high amongst the populace, with crowds in many cities cheering on the Tiananmen Square protesters – those students hunger-striking and calling for democratic reform.

'Or else the Communist Party might be on the brink of losing power, which would invalidate any agreement between China and the UK, meaning the British will be influential in the police force for quite a few more years,' Keith went on.

'I'm afraid of the opposite outcome – the protesters get violently suppressed, and we move backwards too.'

While Kwan spoke, his mind flashed back to the scene at Ka Fai Mansions.

That inhuman, bloody scene.

Just as Tso was about to leave, Kwan thought of something else. 'Oh, and do you know where that Sonny Lok ended up?'

'Not sure. Probably kicked back to uniformed patrol. Why?'

'I think it's a bit unfair for him to get punished over this,' said Kwan. 'He may have disobeyed an order from a superior, but his steadfastness in wanting to preserve the life he was certain he could save – I can't say that's wrong. If he'd gone by the book and blindly followed instructions, Constable Fan Si-tat would have bled to death, and Lok would have been shot dead by TT. Before we're police officers, we're human beings. By that measure, I think Lok showed some potential. Someone like that would only cause his colleagues trouble in the lower ranks, but if you placed him in a Crime Unit, he might excel.'

'In that case, I'll see if Campbell will give the rookie one more chance. It'd be awkward to leave him in Mong Kok. Maybe we'll transfer him to Hong Kong Island or somewhere like that.'

'I hope this time my feeling is right,' said Kwan Chun-dok with a helpless smile.

V

BORROWED PLACE:

1977

1

BRRRING...

Bleary-eyed, Stella Hill heard the telephone ring piercingly.

Brrring...

She rolled over and pressed a pillow over her ears. She didn't know how long she'd slept, only that it wasn't enough.

Brrring...

The phone was indifferent to Stella's feelings, like a loan shark come to collect payment.

'Liz... Liz...' Stella called for her son's nanny. 'Liz, could you answer the phone?'

Raising her voice for that last sentence, Stella's brain began to clear. She remembered the dream she'd been dragged out of – her husband and son were at their old home in England, watching a sci-fi programme, when the main character, 'the Doctor', suddenly leaped from the TV screen into their living room and began discussing the issue of debt with her husband. Just as he was saying the Martians could reduce the Hills' financial obligations, the doorbell rang – a bunch of lawyers sent by their creditor had arrived at the front door.

Of course, it wasn't the doorbell, but that relentless telephone.

'Liz! Liz!' she called, getting out of bed. It was after twelve, so Liz and the kid ought to be at home, but no matter how Stella shouted, there was no response. No movement in the air except that shrill ringing. No point yelling, she realized – if Liz could hear Stella's voice, she could certainly also hear that maddening bell.

Brrring...

Stella pulled on her slippers and opened the bedroom door. Striding out into the living room, she found it empty, as she'd thought. No Liz, and no sign of her son. She looked at the clock, which showed 12.46 p.m. Bright sun shot from the balcony into the living room. She snatched up the receiver anxiously.

'Hello?' she snapped.

'Are you a relative of Alfred Hill's?' It was a man speaking imperfect English – must be a local.

'Yes?' Hearing her son's name, Stella was suddenly wide awake.

'And this is Nairn House on Princess Margaret Road?'

'Yes... Why? Has... has something happened to Alfred?' With a lurch, she realized that her son and nanny being absent, and now this stranger's phone call, could mean a car accident. When she'd got home this morning, she'd bumped into Liz and Alfred on their way out. The school was no more than ten minutes away, and her husband said that ten-year-old Alfred should walk there and back on his own. But Stella was wary of this strange city, full of people with different-coloured skin speaking an unfamiliar language, and urged Liz never to leave her son's side. Alfred was in the fourth year of primary school, and only had classes in the morning. He normally came back with Liz at half past twelve, so finding him missing now, and this man on the phone knowing his name and address, Stella naturally imagined the worst.

'Are you Alfred's mother?' He ignored her question.

'Yes, yes. Is Alfred...'

'Don't worry. He's fine...'

Stella let out a breath, but didn't expect what came next.

'... but he's in my hands. If you want him to come home safe, you'll have to pay a ransom.'

Stella was frozen. These were nightmare words, spoken by kidnappers in movies or books, and for a moment she couldn't understand what they meant.

'What are you talking about?'

'I said, Alfred Hill is in my hands. If I don't get my money, I'll kill him. If you call the police, I'll kill him too.'

A cold shiver transfixed her heart, and her scalp grew numb. She couldn't breathe. Finally, the meaning of those words sank in.

'You – you have Alfred?' She turned back to the empty living room. 'Liz! Alfred!'

'Madam, please don't waste your energy. I need to talk to your husband – I assume he handles the finances? Please ask him to come home as quickly as possible. I'll call again at half past two. If he isn't back by then, don't blame me if I take it out on your son.'

'You're talking nonsense! My son isn't with you!' she screamed, trying hard to keep from trembling.

'Madam, I'd suggest you don't make me angry. If I'm not happy, it'll be your darling son who suffers.' The voice remained steadfastly calm. 'You're free to disbelieve me, but then you'll never see your child again... Ah, my mistake, I should have said you'll never see your child *alive* again. As a token of my sincerity, I've got a present for you – I left it by the streetlight outside the main entrance of Nairn House. It might help you to decide whether to call your husband.'

The line went dead. Stella's mind whirled with confusion. Flinging down the receiver, she rushed through the apartment screaming her son's name. She rushed into his room, which was empty, and then the bathroom, the storeroom, the study, the living room, the kitchen, Liz's bedroom – he wasn't in any of them. She was the only person in this huge apartment.

She looked at the clock. Little hand between 12 and 1, big hand on 11. At this time, her son ought to be sitting at the dining table, eating the lunch Liz had made for him. He was a reserved child, and barely smiled at his parents, but always ate his lunch with gusto. Stella and her husband had been in Hong Kong almost three years now, and still couldn't get used to Chinese food, but their son had adapted quickly. He was especially fond of the tofu soup Liz prepared. Staring at the desolate table, Stella felt something was out of sync, in a way she couldn't quite put into words.

Was this a prank?

Surely kidnapping was something that couldn't happen to her or her family. Returning to the phone, she picked up the receiver, flipped open the phone book and searched for a number she rarely used.

'Kowloon Tong British School Primary Section School Office...' she murmured, and then dialled the string of digits.

'British School Primary Section,' said a female voice in impeccable English.

'Hello, this is Alfred Hill's mother – from 4A.' She came straight to the point. 'Is my son still at school?'

'Hello, Mrs Hill. All the classes have been dismissed. Exam week is over, and today was extramural activities. Our students finished early, at eleven thirty. Is Alfred not home yet?'

'No... he's not.' Stella hesitated, uncertain what to say.

'Please hold on, I'll connect you to the 4A form teacher.'

As she waited to be transferred, Stella watched the living-room clock's second hand. It seemed to be ticking slower than usual.

'Hello, is that Mrs Hill? It's Miss Shum here.'

'When did Alfred leave?' asked Stella frantically.

'At eleven thirty. I saw him walk out the school gate. Isn't he home yet?'

'No,' rasped Stella. 'Did you see him with any of his classmates? Could he have gone off somewhere with them?'

'I remember a group of them talking to him, but he shook his head, and then they left. It looked like he was turning down an invitation.'

'And my nanny? She usually collects him. Was she there?'

'Mm? I think I saw her, although maybe I didn't...' Miss Shum paused, as if working hard to call the scene to mind. There was always such a crowd of people at the gate after school, it was hard enough to remember her own students, let alone any other faces. 'Could Alfred's nanny have taken him somewhere else?'

'No, she'd have told me, or left a note.' Because of work, Stella's schedule rarely matched her son's, so they communicated mainly through notes.

'If you're worried, should we give the police a call?'

With the man's warning ringing through her head – 'If you call the police, I'll kill him too' – she cried, 'No, no! That's... that's making too much of a fuss. It's only been an hour, after all. Maybe the nanny's been delayed by an errand. So sorry to have troubled you.'

'Ah, that might be it. If you need to, please feel free to call again. I'm at the school till six every day. You're at...' The sound of pages being turned. 'Nairn House. That's quite close to us. Let me know if there's anything I can do.'

Stella imagined she must be looking through the student records. In order to prevent Miss Shum from mentioning the police again, she mumbled something or other, thanked the teacher and hung up.

Replacing the receiver, Stella hesitated. She felt ashamed to have been so busy with work that she'd grown distant from her child. She hadn't even known it was extramural day! She felt completely adrift, uncertain what she should do next. Phone her husband? Call the school back and ask for help?

She thought back to earlier that day, running into her son in the vestibule. Alfred had seemed happier than usual – he was usually a little reluctant to go to school, sometimes outright rebellious. But this morning, he'd seemed livelier. As the name suggested, 'extramural day' was when students spent the morning not in class, but on the field or activity room, taking part in sporting competitions, film appreciation, music concerts and the like. Stella had never thought her son was interested in these things. Remembering how joyous he'd been, she couldn't help thinking she was no longer fit to be a mother.

Stella picked up the phone, but the man's parting shot sprang into her mind – a present by the streetlight—

Her fingers had dialled the first two digits of her husband's number, but she dropped the receiver and went out onto the balcony, which faced the main door – from here, you could see the parking lot, garden and fence, and the street beyond. If there was something by the streetlight, it would be visible too.

Walking out onto the balcony, she found the sun suddenly too bright to keep her eyes open. Only after a few seconds was she able to adjust to the glare. Clutching the balcony rail, she leaned forward and studied the streetlights. When her eye reached the second one to the right of the gate, she had to draw a deep breath.

At its base was a brown cardboard box.

Stella had still been clinging on to a shred of hope that this might be a prank, but that was now gone from her mind. Nairn House was in one of Kowloon Tong's fancier residential districts, and the streets had always been spotless. Since moving here three years ago, she hadn't seen a single person in this neighbourhood leaving trash in the street.

Throwing on her shoes, not even locking the front door, she rushed out, jabbing furiously at the elevator button and, when it failed to arrive quickly, sprinting down the stairs. The Hills lived on the sixth floor, yet Stella reached the street in under a minute.

The security guard eyed her as she passed the vestibule, no doubt wondering why her clothes were disordered and her hair such a mess, not to mention she was panting like an ox. Standing before the streetlamp, Stella looked at the box. It was between twenty and thirty centimetres square, large enough for a small football. It wasn't secured with tape, only the top flaps crossed over each other. She studied all four sides, but they were unmarked – just a plain cardboard box.

With trembling hands, she lifted the box, finding it surprisingly light, as if it contained nothing at all. This reassured her a little, and she boldly opened it.

She took one look at the contents of the box and plunged into hysteria. There were two things inside. Catching her eye first was a garment – a pale green shirt, covered in dirt and spattered blood droplets.

The uniform of the British School's Primary Section.

Above the crumpled shirt was a lock of bright red hair, tied with a string.

The exact same colour as Stella's hair.

Alfred's features and personality were very similar to his father's. Only the colour of his hair came from his mother, showing his Celtic heritage.

2

GRAHAM HILL ABANDONED his work and drove home, his mind uneasy.

He knew very well that his wife was a calm woman – as a nurse, she had to deal with patients without agitation, even if they were on the brink of death – so when he heard her howling and sobbing on the phone, saying something had happened to the child and he had to come home, he knew it must be serious. Normally, he'd have told his wife to wait, that he'd sort it out when he got home.

Graham had a strong sense of responsibility, a quality required in his job. He was an investigator in the Hong Kong Independent Commission Against Corruption.

Like many other British people, when he first arrived in Hong Kong, Graham Hill had acquired a Chinese name – Ha Ka-hon, the closest Cantonese could get to his name, surname first in the Chinese style. Some colleagues even started calling him 'Mr Ha' in English. He thought this was pretty funny, that he, a foreigner who spoke no Cantonese at all, should have a name in that language, while many Hongkongers were giving themselves English names, wanting to be fashionable. Take his son's nanny – she wanted to be known as Liz, but had no idea what that was short for. When she'd first started working for them, Graham often called her Elizabeth, to which she didn't respond. It took them a little while to clear that up. Hong Kong was peculiar like that, the colonials slowly turning local, while the colonized picked up the lifestyles and cultures of the incomers.

His wife's name was Stella, but she had ended up with the not particularly similar 'Shuk-lan'. Alfred became 'Nga-fan'. The person who gave them these names kept insisting they were beautiful and auspicious, which Graham didn't care about, not being a superstitious person. He thought all that 'feng shui' stuff was just unscientific nonsense.

He firmly believed that people needed to stand on their own two feet if they wanted to be happy.

Graham Hill was born in 1938, and was a child during the Second World War. After graduation, he trained as a policeman and worked in Scotland Yard. A colleague introduced him to Stella. They got married and set up home, and three years later had Alfred. The normal life of a British public servant. At the time, Graham had thought he'd go on working like this till he retired, then live out his last years with his wife in some quiet suburb, spending time with his son and grandchildren on holidays. But he was wrong.

Stella continued working as a nurse after their marriage – she was a strong, independent woman – but gave it up when Alfred was born. In order to give his family a better life, as well as to make up the shortfall left by his wife's unemployment, Graham invested his savings in the housing market, taking out a bank loan to buy a rental property. He calculated that if property prices continued to rise, he might even be able to retire early, and not have to worry about his son's university fees in the future.

The problem was, the British economy suddenly went into recession.

Four years ago, in 1973, British house prices started falling, putting banks at risk of collapse. At the same time, an oil crisis, stock-market crash and stagflation put the British economy beyond hope of revival in the short term. Graham had hesitated rather than quickly getting rid of the property; their tenant absconded, and the house was repossessed. Their investment had evaporated overnight, and they still had significant debts. Stella began working again, but with unemployment soaring, her wages were much lower than before. With prices rising all around them, they could barely support themselves after making their monthly repayments. The couple tried to support each other through this difficult time, thinking the situation would improve after a few months of hardship, but as time went on and they realized they would be in debt for the foreseeable future, they began to quarrel. Their six-year-old son sensed a change in the atmosphere and grew introverted, no longer smiling all day long.

Just as the couple felt they might lose their minds if this went on much longer, Graham saw an advertisement in the newspaper. The colonial government in Hong Kong was establishing a new law enforcement department – the Independent Commission Against Corruption – and experienced police officers were invited to apply. A Grade One investigator would receive a salary of six or seven thousand Hong Kong dollars, which was about £600 per month – more than he was currently earning – as well as attractive benefits and perks. After discussing it with his wife, Graham decided to try changing track. Thanks to his ample experience as an investigator at Scotland Yard, he got his letter of appointment just a few days after the interview, and the family of three set forth, leaving their familiar home for a strange city in Asia, prepared to work and pay off their debts.

The Hills knew nothing about Hong Kong to start with, only that it had been ceded to Britain for a hundred years. As he read up, Graham realized this 'colony' didn't belong entirely to the United Kingdom – Hong Kong Island and the Kowloon peninsula were British in perpetuity, while the New Territories were on a ninety-nine-year lease expiring in 1997. But it wouldn't be feasible for Britain to cut the territory in half after 1997, continuing to govern Kowloon and the Island whilst returning the

New Territories to China. The two governments had yet to come up with a solution to this problem. At this point, Graham felt that Hong Kong was just a borrowed place, and he would be doing the same as so many other British people had done, coming to scratch a living on someone else's land.

In June 1974, the Hills arrived in Hong Kong. In order to pay off their debts as quickly as possible, Stella found a job in Kowloon Hospital, where her experience was impressive enough for her to serve as a role model for local nurses, so they made her a good offer. The Independent Commission Against Corruption helped Graham negotiate the details of the move, most notably providing government accommodation for the Hills. Nairn House in Kowloon Tong was reserved for high-ranking civil servants, its spacious apartments designed to resemble high-class British dwellings, so European and American arrivals would feel comfortable. The surroundings were superb, security strong, and all the neighbouring buildings were occupied by important local businessmen, high-ranking employees of other companies, or foreign high fliers.

Their child's education was of the utmost concern to the Hills. When they first considered coming here, it was this point that almost deterred them. It wasn't a big deal for them to live abroad for five or ten years, but it would be a formative experience for their son. What if they couldn't find a good school in Hong Kong, or Alfred was unable to make new friends? Graham wrote to a friend in Hong Kong, asking about the quality and standard of education; the friend wrote back enthusiastically, enclosing a stack of school prospectuses. After reading through these, the couple felt more at ease, knowing the Hong Kong education system was modelled on the British one, and that several schools catered specifically to Western children, with textbooks, homework, lessons and even parental instructions all in English. They picked a school near Nairn House for their son. The premises weren't large, but the teachers and staff all spoke fluent British English and seemed passionate about their jobs.

For the last three years, the Hills had lived frugally. The benefits provided by the Hong Kong government were even greater than Graham had dreamed of. With overtime and Stella's salary, they were able to pay off their debts in two years. They'd even managed to save up a respectable amount in the last year, which was sitting in the bank, steadily earning interest.

Graham wanted to work in Hong Kong a while longer before returning to Britain, partly for the high pay, partly because of the economic situation back home. Reading the papers each day, he couldn't help shaking his head and sighing. Unemployment remained terrible, with more than a million people out of work, and labour strikes were constant. The country was now 'the sick man of Europe', brought so low it was mentioned in the same breath as the decline of the Ottoman Empire in the nineteenth century. Graham found this ridiculous, but still he despaired.

Of course, he was grateful for the opportunity this tiny Asian city across the ocean had offered his household. If they'd stayed in London, money problems might well have driven them to divorce by this point. Then again, a hefty salary is often the sign of a difficult job.

From his first day at the commission, Graham was startled by the scope of his work and the number of cases he faced. Daily they received a large volume of anonymous complaints, mostly about corrupt government officials. These weren't necessarily major cases involving huge amounts of money, but the scale and frequency of the incidents stunned him. Hawkers having to pay a few dollars each day to patrol cops; patients having to tip the cleaners and porters in public hospitals to ensure they weren't ignored or badly treated. Almost every government department had similar issues. Graham began to understand how badly this commission was needed right now – otherwise, as the territory became more prosperous, petty corruption would expand in significance, nibbling at the fabric of society, at which point it would be too late to address the problem.

Not knowing a word of Chinese made Graham's work

particularly difficult, and local customs and practices left him at a loss at first. Still, he'd been appointed for his experience, to teach the relatively untutored locals how to carry out an investigation, gather evidence and follow protocol in operations that would lead to corrupt individuals being brought to court. Before the commission was set up, the most experienced investigators in Hong Kong were of course in the Royal Hong Kong Police. Unfortunately, the force itself was rampantly corrupt, and needed to be investigated – so the commission had to look elsewhere to recruit and train its staff.

The issue of police corruption had serious implications for law and order. Ever since Hong Kong had opened up for trade, outlaws and Triads had used bribes to convince the force to shut one eye. Police sweeps of illegal gambling clubs, vice shops and drug dens weren't intended to rid the territory of crime, but to collect more under-the-table payments. In order to make it look like the officers were doing their job, criminals would arrange for some of their number to go willingly to jail, handed over as a 'gift' together with the necessary evidence. The money from drugs, gambling and so forth which they offered up was a tiny proportion of the trade, of course.

If you joined the police and you were honest, you had to keep your head down. There was a saying within the force that bribery was a car; you could 'get in the car' and take your share, or you could refuse, in which case you would be expected to 'run alongside the car' and not interfere. If you insisted on reporting each incident to your superiors, that'd be 'standing in front of the car', and you'd probably get knocked down and run over, ending up with multiple injuries. Only those with no idea what they were up against would try to stop this vehicle, and even if they weren't completely destroyed, would probably still end up neglected, frozen out of the hierarchy, all hopes of promotion gone.

There'd been an internal anti-corruption division within the police force, but as it was staffed with existing officers, it had too many connections to other departments to be effective.

The commission sought to break this stalemate; it reported directly to the Governor of Hong Kong, and so was able to operate independently.

Graham Hill had investigated several corrupt police officers in his first year on the job. At the start of the second year, he started uncovering more cases involving higher-ranking officers – the top brass were as bad as their subordinates when it came to sheltering criminals. The commission had to be very careful to separate truth from slander – many suspects were willing to denounce 'corrupt police officers' in exchange for a reduced sentence, so it was necessary to investigate each complaint carefully. Graham Hill believed outlaws were the same the world over, and even without speaking the language, he always had a good idea if they were lying, if the details of their evidence was contradictory.

At the moment, his team had just received a new case which he was slowly realizing was on a far bigger scale than anything he'd seen before.

The previous spring, April 1976, the Commerce and Industry Department's Anti-Smuggling Squad had found a cache of drugs in a building near Yau Ma Tei Wholesale Fruit Market. Several men were arrested and charged, one of them half-American, and four months later, the police swept twenty-three locations across the territory, confiscating more than twenty thousand dollars' worth of heroin and arresting a further eight suspects, including the purported mastermind of the Fruit Market smuggling ring, all of whom asked to speak to someone from the commission while they were being held, claiming they could expose organizational corruption in law enforcement. After being found guilty a month ago, they were now formally prosecution witnesses for the commission as part of their plea deal. The gang had paid handsomely for police inattention, not expecting they'd get caught a year later by Commerce and Industry, which took a more serious view of the issue. And so they chose the nuclear option, in order to teach these ineffectual police a lesson.

The drug pushers had kept detailed accounts of the bribery

in code. When they'd 'paid squeeze', they'd only had a vague idea of the rank and department of each receiving officer. Turning these hints into concrete allegations would require legwork. Investigators from the commission had to ensure that there were no conflicts of interest that would invalidate any of their evidence, which mean Graham had to scrutinize how all the people in this case were related and follow the paper trail carefully. He didn't understand the Chinese words, so his colleagues translated them, and he was able to match up the symbols to dig deeper. Eventually he began to recognize certain Chinese characters – though these were of no help in his daily life, because they were just code words. For instance, '本C' ('this C') meant 'Yau Ma Tei Criminal Investigation Department'; '老國' ('the old country') meant 'Kowloon Regional Special Duties Squad'; 'E' meant 'patrol car of the Emergency Unit' and so on. In order to familiarize himself with these pictograms, which might as well have been symbols from a ouija board, Graham began bringing documents home to study them in his spare time. Of course, these sensitive materials normally lived in his safe. Not even Stella was allowed to look at them.

Very soon he saw how much larger the case was than he'd first thought. It didn't just involve frontline officers. According to the testimonies and accounts they'd received, Regional and even Headquarters figures were involved, including some of superintendent rank and above. Graham and his colleagues realized that this was a far cry from a few dollars changing hands as 'tea money'. Once they began, they'd surely turf out several hundred serving police officers, bringing down an entire network of corruption.

It felt like the commission's three years of existence had all been preparation for the upcoming battle.

No matter how good the commission was at keeping things under wraps, nothing in this world can be entirely secret. Once the Fruit Market mastermind was brought to justice, rumours began circulating that the commission had the police in their sights. After this, there was an antagonistic relationship on both sides – the commission believed the police were a nest of vipers, while the police believed the commission had become drunk on power.

When Graham got back to Nairn House and heard what had happened from his terrified wife, apart from being shaken to the core, he was also unsure whether he ought to call the police.

The bloodstained shirt and clipped hair told him the kidnappers were serious. As an enforcement officer, he knew it was foolish to obey the criminals' instruction not to call the police, because the odds of a kidnap victim being released after a ransom was paid were fifty–fifty. Having the police on your side was the best chance of rescuing the hostage. He'd seen a case in England where kidnappers had planned to kill a captive after they'd got the cash, but fortunately the police tailed them, found their hideout and saved her.

But what if the officer who responded to his call found out he was in the ICAC and neglected the case – or, worse, took advantage of the situation to extract revenge by obstructing a rescue, causing his son's death?

As he hesitated by the phone, wrestling with the problem, Stella collapsed onto the sofa, clutching the little lock of hair and howling.

The seconds and minutes went by. Now it was half past one. Graham looked at the grimy uniform shirt, and thought of it being ripped off by these thugs. Now his son was sitting, barechested and terrified, in some dark room. That made up his mind. He picked up the receiver, knowing that even if the Royal Hong Kong Police had something against the commission he worked for, they were also the only people he could turn to at the moment. He simply had no choice.

3

'HEADMAN, YOU STEP in this time,' said Mac from the driver's seat of the small car, not looking back.

'Every minute counts in a kidnapping. With the hostage's life on the line, of course they'd want to use our Big Bon.' Before Kwan Chun-dok could answer, Sergeant Tsui had piped up from beside him. Inspectors were known in Hong Kong as 'Bon-pans', after an old term for Chinese officers who spoke English in the Qing Dynasty, so senior inspectors naturally became 'Big Bons', a coveted position in the regional departments.

Kwan Chun-dok didn't agree or disagree, but smiled noncommittally and went back to staring out the window. In his current post at Kowloon Regional CID, he'd been promoted from inspector to senior inspector at the start of the year – his high crime-solving rate over the last few years must have caught his superiors' attention. For Kwan to have such a high rank before the age of thirty had attracted admiring gazes, and of course jealous murmurs that he was the running dog of the British, that after two years in the UK he'd forgotten he was Chinese. Some also mocked him for being merely lucky, his swift ascent possible because he'd caught the eye of a white officer. But whether they were respectful or envious, no one in the force was in any doubt as to Kwan's abilities. He was the real thing, and especially after returning from training in 1972, he'd performed outstandingly in every investigation he took part in.

Inspector Kwan had three subordinates in the car with him as they headed to Nairn House. The driver Mac – Mak Kinsi – was the youngest of the group, twenty-five, and only a year into his CID stint. Despite his inexperience, he was quick-witted and nimble, and once chased a suspect ten whole blocks before apprehending him. Next to him was twenty-eight-year-old Detective Police Constable Ronald Ngai, with Old Tsui and Kwan in the back. Despite his nickname, Sergeant Tsui was only thirty-six, but he had the face of a man pushing fifty.

Kwan had decided to use these three men mainly because they all spoke English. Police reports had to be in English, and there was a language requirement to join the force, but many officers' ability still left a lot to be desired. There was a joke going round the force that a traffic cop had to write up a report about a collision, and the best he could do was, 'One car come, one car go, two car kiss.' Kwan didn't want to take any chances. The caller had been a British national who didn't understand the local language, and if any investigator present didn't have fluent English, they'd lose a lot of time on translation – which they couldn't afford in a kidnapping case.

'Hey, Ron, have you checked the call tracer? Don't want something going wrong like last time,' said Old Tsui.

'Yes,' answered Ngai curtly. During the previous operation, he hadn't noticed the fuse had blown on a surveillance device, which failed to tape the suspect's words at a crucial moment. It took a week's extra work to gather enough additional evidence to secure an arrest.

'As long as you checked it,' Old Tsui insisted, almost as if he was trying to irritate the younger man. 'If anything goes wrong, that's a life at stake. It's not like we'd get another chance.'

'I checked it three times.' Ron Ngai turned around to glare at Old Tsui.

'Uh huh.' Old Tsui pursed his lips, avoiding his gaze. Looking out the window, he added, 'Wow, it's posh around here. No wonder someone looked at that kid and saw dollar signs.'

'But the caller is some British investigator brought in by the ICAC. He can't be that rich, can he?' interrupted Mac.

'Who says?' sneered Old Tsui. 'You know Morris, in Shaw? I heard that fellow comes from quite the family – his dad and brother both have bottle caps, they're in parliament or some high official post, I don't know. Anyway, he's come to Hong Kong to get some practical experience, and after a few years he'll be back in Britain, in diplomacy or government intelligence, that sort of thing. This director who got his kid snatched, I'd wager his background's about the same as Morris's.'

'Shaw' was what they called Special Branch, on the grounds that its initials were the same as the movie studio Shaw Brothers. SB was, on the face of it, a police department, but in fact reported directly to MI5, and outsiders were only allowed to know a little about their cases some time after they'd been resolved. Morris was a high-ranking officer in Special Branch, whose father and brother were both in the British government and had been awarded OBEs – the decorations nicknamed 'bottle caps' in Hong Kong for their resemblance to a certain brand of soda-bottle top. In truth, the Morris family wasn't particularly wealthy, but to many Chinese people, if you had an important government job or an official position with power, the money would come from somewhere.

'So that guy's from the commission – but when something goes wrong, he still has to lean on us,' snorted Ngai. 'He spends all day thinking of ways to hobble us, until we're all walking on eggshells. Then the criminals come for him, and he has the nerve to ask us for help. The nerve.'

'Ron, it doesn't matter who he is, we're just going to do our jobs.' Kwan finally broke his silence.

The other three grew quiet at their leader's words. Mac focused on driving, while Ron and Old Tsui stared out their windows. None of them noticed that Kwan was speaking less than usual, as if he had something on his mind.

When the car was still one block away from Nairn House, Kwan tapped Mac on the shoulder. 'Stop here.'

'Huh? We're not there yet, Headman.' Even as Mac spoke, his hands were obediently turning the wheel so the car drifted to the side of the road.

'Old Tsui and I will walk there, and the two of you can drive to the parking lot. We don't know if the kidnappers are watching,' Kwan explained. 'Ron, you and Mac tell reception that you're here to see Liu Wah-ming from the Fire Department – he's on the fourth floor – while Old Tsui and I will say we have an appointment with Senior Superintendent Campbell on nine. They've been notified, so if the receptionist calls up, we'll be covered.'

'Headman, we're lying to reception too?'

'Anyone might be an accomplice,' said Kwan, getting out of the car. 'When we're all in, let's meet in the corridor.'

Ding dong. As soon as they were all together, Kwan pressed the doorbell. Mac was gawping at everything – he'd never been to this sort of fancy lodging. He himself lived in North Point Police Quarters. With ten rooms to each floor, it was crowded and noisy. There were only two apartments on each floor here, and everything was so quiet. He couldn't stop marvelling at the difference.

'Good afternoon, I'm Inspector Kwan Chun-dok from Kowloon CID,' said Kwan when the front door opened, producing his badge. His English was British-inflected, reminding his subordinates that he'd studied there. The accent alone would give him a certain intimacy with the white officers that they'd never have.

'Uh... I'm Graham Hill. Come in.'

In the living room, Stella had stopped crying, but still sat disconsolately on the sofa, not reacting at all to the arrival of the police, as if her soul had left her body. Kwan looked around until he found the phone, and gave a look to Ngai, who walked over with his bag of tools and began fitting the recording and tracing devices. The other three sat on the longer sofa, facing Graham.

'Mr Hill, was it you who made the report? Could you tell us what happened?' Even that final 'l' in 'Hill' sounded British in Kwan's mouth.

'Uh, yes.' Graham leaned forward. 'My wife was woken by a phone call at twelve forty-five...'

Graham recounted the sequence of events he'd heard from Stella – the threatening words, the call to the school, discovering the uniform shirt and hair. As an experienced investigator, he knew how to describe an incident in an orderly manner. Without needing to ask a single question, Kwan learned the basics of the situation.

'So he said he'd call again at two thirty.' Kwan looked at his watch – it was 1.52 p.m. 'Of course, he might phone earlier. Ron, is everything done?'

'All connected, just testing it. Seems fine.' Ngai popped in his earpiece and flashed the OK sign.

'Mac, bag the shirt, hair and cardboard box. There might be fingerprints or other clues. Call the Identification Bureau and tell them to send someone dressed as a delivery person for it – don't forget, the kidnappers might be watching.'

'Got it.'

'Mr Hill, I'd like to ask some questions about your family, to see if there are any leads there,' Kwan said solemnly. 'Had you recently encountered any suspicious individuals? Or has anything out of the ordinary happened?'

Graham shook his head. 'No. I've been very busy, often doing overtime and getting home late. I haven't met anyone at all, and I don't think Stella's mentioned anything strange.' He turned to his wife and shook her arm. 'Stella, Officer Kwan wants to know if you've seen any strange people or behaviour?'

Stella Hill looked up blankly. As her eyes swept across the policemen, she bit her lip and shook her head as if in pain. 'No... nothing at all... but this is all my fault...'

'Your fault?' Kwan asked.

'I've thought about nothing but work all these years. I've never taken good care of Alfred. His nanny did everything... Is God punishing me for being an unfit mother? I hardly said a word to him when I got back from work this morning. Oh God...'

'Stella, you're not to blame. I've neglected Alfred too.' Graham hugged his wife, letting her bury her face in his chest.

'Mr Hill, could you tell us if anyone goes in and out of your home regularly, other than the nanny?' Kwan steered them back to the point.

'There's a cleaning lady, she comes twice a week.'

'I'll need the names, ages and addresses of both women. Could you write them down?'

'Officer Kwan, do you think they're... connected to what happened?'

'In a kidnapping case, anyone who has regular contact with the victim is a suspect, especially employees who aren't part of the family.'

Graham seemed to be swallowing a protest. Working in law enforcement, he knew Kwan was absolutely right, but just couldn't believe it.

'I really don't think they'd harm Alfred. Of course, for the investigation, let me go and get the information.' Graham stepped into his study, returning with a little notebook from his desk drawer.

'The nanny's name is... Leung Lai-ping. Her English name is Liz. She's forty-two,' he said, reading from the book.

'Leung Lai-ping... how do you write "ping"?' asked Kwan, scribbling down the information.

'Like this.' Graham indicated the characters on the page.

'And that's her address and phone number?'

'Yes.'

Kwan, Old Tsui and Mac all took down this information.

'And the cleaning lady?' asked Kwan.

'She's Wang Tai-tai. Aged fifty.'

'Mac, call both their homes, see if there's anything we can find out.' Mac went over to the phone and picked up the receiver.

'Liz lives alone, and often spends the night here. She has her own room,' added Graham. 'Although we hired her as a nanny, she also helps us with cooking and manages the household.'

'How many nights a week does she spend here?'

'It varies, depending on Stella's work.' Graham turned to glance at his wife. 'When she's on the night shift at Kowloon Hospital, Liz stays here with Alfred, especially as I'm often late back too. If Stella and I get home at a reasonable hour, she'll leave – she says she doesn't want to be in the way. Oh, but we don't think of her as an outsider.'

'And the cleaner, Wang Tai-tai?'

'I don't know much about her.' Graham shook his head. 'We didn't want to overburden Liz, so I hired Tai-tai to help with the cleaning. She only understands simple English, so I've hardly spoken to her. According to Liz, she lives with some "sisters" – I don't think she plans to get married.'

'That sounds like the Sun-tak Sisterhood,' interjected Old Tsui. Graham had heard this term during his three years here, but had supposed it just meant elderly, single maidservants. He had no idea that Sun-tak was a place in Guangdong province, where these female workers who had taken a vow of spinsterhood came from.

'Headman, I made the calls,' said Mac, returning to his seat. 'No one answered at Leung Lai-ping's place. Wang Tai-tai was home. I pretended to be from the Mutual Aid Committee, asking questions about her work and home situation. She didn't suspect a thing. I doubt she has anything to do with this case.'

'Then Liz must be our suspect,' said Old Tsui. 'Mr Hill's kid goes missing, you'd expect the nanny to be the first to know. But no, she hasn't come back here, hasn't gone home. Maybe she's in cahoots with the kidnappers. As long as she was around, they wouldn't need any tricks. The kid would just go willingly and no one would pay any attention.'

'Liz wouldn't...' Old Tsui's words had touched a nerve, but Graham said no more. He had to acknowledge it was a possibility.

'Or perhaps Leung Lai-ping has been kidnapped along with the child,' said Kwan in a level voice. 'Or even worse, they've already got rid of her. The kidnappers would just want a white-skinned child. A yellow-skinned middle-aged nanny is of no value to them.'

Graham Hill gasped. He'd spent all this time worrying about his son, without sparing one thought for Liz – and what Kwan said sounded very likely. God only knew if the blood on the uniform was Alfred's or his nanny's.

'Have you noticed any recent odd behaviour on Leung Lai-ping's part?' asked Kwan.

'No...' Graham hesitated.

'Thought of something?'

'Nothing major. Two weeks ago, I got back from work and had a shower. When I came out of the bathroom, Liz was in our bedroom. She said she was looking for a shopping list. But she seldom goes into the master bedroom – at least not when I'm at home.' Graham's face displayed conflicting emotions. 'I wondered if she was stealing from us, but I counted the cash in my wallet and it was all there. Then later she said she'd found the list on the balcony, and I realized I was worried about nothing.'

'So you were suspicious of her?' said Old Tsui.

'No, no, I just thought of it because Inspector Kwan asked. Liz got on very well with Alfred. I don't believe she'd ever do anything to harm him.'

'In any case,' said Kwan, 'can we take a look at her room?'

'Please do.'

Graham led Kwan to Liz's room. Old Tsui and Mac followed, leaving Ngai alone by the telephone. The room wasn't large, and didn't contain many personal items apart from clothes and toiletries – nothing of value to the investigation.

The group returned to the living room and sat in silence, waiting for the kidnappers to call. Kwan didn't ask any more questions, but seemed sunk in thought as he sat on the sofa. Mac and Old Tsui paced around the living room from time to time, trying not to let the atmosphere get too heavy, staying away from the windows in case the kidnappers were watching.

While they waited, two men from Identification turned up to collect the shirt and other items. They were dressed as workmen with heavy gloves, pushing a trolley on which was an enormous cardboard box, so it looked like they were delivering a fridge. In fact, the box was empty. Mac loaded it up with the evidence and they wheeled it away. An onlooker would have assumed they'd got the address wrong and had to lug the fridge away again.

Now and then Mac glanced at an ICAC plaque on the shelf – an award Graham had received at the end of his second year, in recognition of the many corruption cases he'd broken. Mac thought how unbelievable this must look from the outside, the police in the same room as the man in charge of investigating them, doing battle together. As if cats and dogs could put aside their differences to fight jackals and wolves together, then resume their own quarrels when peace returned—

Brrring... The bright peals of noise broke the silence. It was exactly half past two. The kidnapper was punctual.

'Drag this out as long as you can. It'll take time for the tracing device to find out where the call's coming from.' Kwan and the others pulled on their headphones and signalled for Graham to pick up the phone. Ngai raised a thumb at Kwan, indicating that everything was in working order.

Graham answered. 'Hello,' he said cautiously.

'Are you Alfred Hill's father?'

'Yes.'

'Your wife did as we asked. Not bad. Did you get my gift?'

'If you harm one hair on Alfred's head...' Graham couldn't stop his angry outburst, provoked by the other man's mocking tone.

'What if I do? Mr Hill, let's get this clear. I'm the one who gives the orders.'

'You...' Graham was filled with despair. 'What demands do you have?'

'Before we get into that, let me ask you – did you call the police?'

'No.'

'I hate people lying to me. The deal's off.'

Click. He'd hung up. Graham clung numbly to the phone, listening to the monotonous dial tone, which sounded to him like a whetstone sharpening his executioner's blade. He glanced blankly at Kwan, allowing the receiver to drift back down.

Brring... Without waiting for Kwan's signal, Graham picked up the phone right away.

'Please don't – I'll do anything—' he gabbled.

'I'll give you another chance. Did you call the police?' It was the same man.

Graham was on the point of blurting out 'Yes, I'm sorry!' but he looked up in time to see Kwan holding up a sheet of paper on which was scrawled the word 'BLUFFING'.

'No! I wouldn't gamble with my own son's life!' Graham blustered. He was terrified the kidnapper would see through his lie, or that Kwan's guess was wrong, but in this moment he could only trust he was making the right choice.

'Good, good.' He didn't hang up, and Graham let out a shaky breath. 'You're an honest man. So we can talk business. A minute ago, you said you were willing to do anything. All I want is money. Give me cash and you get your kid back.'

'How much do you want?'

'Not much. Five hundred thousand Hong Kong dollars. Quite a bargain.'

'I... I don't have that much money...' said Graham helplessly. The sum was worth over £60,000.

Click.

'Hello! Hello!' Graham was dumbfounded – he hadn't thought speaking honestly would enrage the other party.

He set down the receiver. Inspector Kwan asked Ngai, 'Did you trace it?'

'No, not long enough.' Ngai shook his head.

'Officer Kwan, what'll we do?' asked Graham.

'The criminal—'

Before he could finish, the phone rang for a third time.

'The criminal's testing you – he wants to squeeze you dry. He's not actually going to terminate the negotiation. But you need to tread carefully,' said Kwan.

Graham nodded and picked up the phone. 'Please don't hang up! Can we just talk?'

'You said you had no money. What else am I supposed to say?'

'But I really don't have that much money.'

'Huh, that's ignorance for you…' Then silence.

'Hello? Hello?' Graham thought he'd hung up again, but there was no dial tone.

'… Liz? Are you there? Liz?'

Graham felt tears spring to his eyes. It was his son's voice.

'Alfred! Are you hurt? Don't be scared, Daddy's going to bring you home.'

'Alfred!' Hearing her husband's words, Stella lunged at the telephone.

'Mr Hill, you see that I'm serious.' The kidnapper's voice was back. 'It's too bad of you to keep saying you have no money. Your business fluctuates by millions in a single day – what's five hundred grand to you?'

'Where would I get a million-dollar business? I'm just a salaried public servant!'

'Since when do public servants live in Kowloon Tong and send their children to fancy schools?'

'Nairn House is government accommodation! My son's school fees are subsidized!'

A sudden silence.

'Hello? Hello?'

'… I'll call you later.'

'Hello!'

But the kidnapper had hung up.

In that instant, Graham realized he'd said the wrong thing. If the kidnapper really thought he was a wealthy man, and if that's why he'd kidnapped Alfred, then finding out he couldn't afford a huge ransom might make him decide to get rid of the hostage. Why hadn't he said he could borrow it from friends?

'Ins... Inspector Kwan, have I ruined everything? Graham stammered, looking at all of them.

'It's too early to say. The kidnapper might not have done sufficient research,' said Kwan calmly. 'From what he's said so far, we can guess that whoever's masterminding this is an expert in psychological manipulation. If they were mistaken, they'll want to work out a new ransom. You've been very co-operative so far, so they'll probably feel you're still of value to them, and if they give up now, they'll have nothing to show for their pains.'

Graham understood that when Kwan said 'give up', he meant 'kill Alfred', but that he was trying not to agitate Stella further.

Two minutes later, the phone rang again. To Graham, those two minutes were like two hours.

'Hello?'

'You... really are a public servant?'

'Yes.'

'Where do you work?'

'The Independent Commission Against Corruption.'

'Right, that's what your son said too. At least you're not lying.' The voice softened a little. 'That's bad luck – I made a mistake.'

'Please let Alfred go! I'll give you everything I have!'

'How much is that?'

'About seventy thousand dollars...'

'Seventy thousand? Your family lives in Kowloon Tong, and all you have saved up is a piddling seventy thousand?'

'I came to Hong Kong to work, because I had debts to pay off...' Graham didn't dare conceal anything. They could verify what he was saying by asking Alfred, who knew about the family's financial situation.

The kidnapper cursed in Cantonese, then switched back to English. 'Listen carefully. I want a hundred thousand, and you have to get it within an hour... no, within forty-five minutes. Otherwise your son is dead.'

'Where am I going to get thirty thousand dollars in forty-five minutes?'

'How would I know? If you don't have cash, make up the difference with jewellery. You're in fancy government housing, I guess you must have an important position? I don't believe your wife doesn't have some baubles for when she hangs off your arm at those la-di-dah banquets you high officials attend. If you can't get that together in forty-five minutes, then prepare to pick up your son's corpse.'

Once again, the line went dead.

'Ron, did you get a fix on that?' asked Kwan, plucking off his headphones.

'I'm sorry, sir. Not enough time.'

'He kept hanging up, seemingly because he was angry at Mr Hill, but it might also have been a precaution,' frowned Kwan. 'He might have presumed we'd be listening in, so kept each call short to prevent us tracking him down. Everyone, be on your guard.'

Kwan turned to Graham. 'Mr Hill, do you really only have seventy thousand in savings?'

'Yes.'

'It's two thirty-five now. Forty-five minutes takes us to twenty past three. That's not enough time for us to get you marked bills. I think you'd better follow the kidnapper's orders and draw all your savings out of the bank.'

'And the other thirty thousand?' interrupted Mac. 'Mr Hill, could you get an advance on your salary?'

'Not in forty-five minutes. And that'd be four months' wages.'

Kwan stroked his chin. 'Mr Hill, the police can't provide the money, but I can lend it to you privately...'

'Headman, that's against the rules!' said Old Tsui. All three subordinates were shocked – not that their leader was willing to help their sworn enemy, the ICAC investigator, but that the famously stingy Kwan Chun-dok was willing to loan thirty thousand dollars that might never get paid back.

'Sergeant Tsui is right,' said Graham, nodding to show his gratitude. 'Stella has some jewellery left to us by my parents. We weren't willing to sell it to pay our debts, but they're insignificant compared to Alfred.'

'The jewellery is worth thirty thousand?' asked Kwan.

'We had it valued at between fifteen hundred and two thousand pounds back in England, so at most twenty thousand Hong Kong dollars, but jewels fluctuate in price, don't they? Hopefully it's worth more by now.'

'See? I told you Brits were all rich,' whispered Tsui to Mac in Cantonese.

'Stella, you don't mind, do you?'

She shook her head. After being too late to hear her son's voice on the phone, she seemed sunk even further in despair.

Kwan walked up to Stella and took both her hands in his. 'Mrs Hill, we'll bring your son safely back. I guarantee it.'

Stella looked up at Kwan and nodded sadly.

'Mr Hill, is the bank far from here?'

'Five minutes by car.'

'Then you'd better get there as quickly as possible. Mac, hide in Mr Hill's back seat and be on the alert for anything unexpected. Make sure no one sees you.'

'Yes, Inspector.' Mac departed with Graham.

The other four, left in the living room, said nothing. Kwan sat on the sofa, apparently staring at a horizon far away. His subordinates and the mistress of the house had no idea he was contemplating an entirely different matter.

What Kwan Chun-dok was considering was the 'police corruption' revealed by the Yau Ma Tei Fruit Market drug-smuggling case.

4

At three o'clock, Graham Hill and Mac returned.

According to Mac, nothing out of the ordinary happened on the way. He'd peeped out the car window in all directions, and hadn't noticed anyone following them. The Hills had HK$70,000 in a fixed-term deposit that matured in a month. Graham had had to close the account to get it out, which meant losing all the interest. With the cash in an envelope, he returned to the car parked just in front of the bank. It all went very smoothly.

Now he stacked the new bills on the living-room table: seven bundles of twenty $500 notes each. Although Hong Kong had issued a new $1,000 bill three months ago, most banks still supplied the familiar 'Big Bull' $500 notes. $70,000 would be six or seven years' salary for the average clerical worker, but looking at the piles of paper on the table, Mac thought it looked much less than he'd expected.

'Mac, write down the serial numbers.' Before Kwan had even said anything, Old Tsui was giving orders. 'There's not much time.'

Mac nodded and sat at the table, ripping off the paper that held each stack together and diligently copying down the number of each note. As soon as any of these went back into the bank system, the police could start tracking down the perpetrator by following the flow of money.

'And the jewellery to make up the rest?' asked Kwan.

'I keep it in my study,' said Graham, walking in that direction.

'Not in your bedroom?'

'We had so much debt before last year. Of course we store our valuables in the safe. Imagine if we'd kept them unsecured and a burglar helped himself – that would have been the very little we had, completely gone.' Graham sighed. 'It's funny how things work out. I'm going to be handing them over anyway.'

Kwan followed Graham into the study. Old Tsui followed, as if wanting to see a bit more of this world. The study wasn't large, but very orderly, with shelves full of books on law, procedure and crime detection. The wall next to the bookcase held several paintings – nothing particularly beautiful, just childishly executed watercolours.

'These are Alfred's,' Graham explained. 'He loves painting. Extra-curricular activities don't really interest him, just painting. Give him a brush and some paper, and he'll sit and paint all afternoon. Stella sent him to some after-school drawing class, and he was completely hooked. He insisted I hang his work in my study, saying a study ought to be decorated with paintings.'

Graham's smile quickly faded, to be replaced with sheer misery. Kwan and Old Tsui understood that this pleasant memory had become a psychological torture.

Opening a wooden cabinet by the bookshelf, Graham revealed a grey-blue safe, about seventy centimetres wide and a metre tall. Kwan couldn't see how deep it was. Graham turned a key in the lock, then rotated the dial left and right. The door snapped open. He carefully removed a purple velvet box and shut the cabinet door, retrieving the key.

When Graham opened the box, Kwan and Old Tsui almost jumped. Inside was a necklace with a dozen dazzlingly bright diamonds dangling from it, coiled around a pair of diamond earrings of the same design, while three rings lay to one side, two of them the same design as the other pieces. The remaining ring wasn't a diamond but a ruby.

'This lot is only worth twenty thousand?' whistled Old Tsui.

'I'm not sure,' answered Graham. 'The jeweller said fifteen hundred pounds, but maybe he was trying to cheat me.' He shut the box and sighed, 'Stella's had this necklace and earrings so many years, but she's only worn them three or four times. Since we arrived in Hong Kong, I believe the only occasion was last November, when we went to a colleague's wedding. She's always loved them. She'll give them up for Alfred, but I'm sure she hates to.'

The three men returned to the living room, where Mac had finished copying down the numbers. Five of the seven stacks had contained only new bills in sequence, which made his job easier.

'Headman, isn't it strange that the kidnapper didn't specify old notes and small denominations?' said Mac.

Old Tsui shrugged. 'Maybe he wants to get this over with quickly, and didn't think of those details.'

'Or he's already got a plan to cover that,' said Kwan, walking over to Ngai. 'Hand me the thing.'

Ngai knew what his commander meant, and removed a small black box from his equipment bag. It was plastic, about the size of a cigarette lighter, with several vents on the underside through which could be seen a jumble of wires. On the front were four screws, and in the middle an unobtrusive button.

'Mr Hill, this is a transmitter.' Kwan placed it on the table. 'The battery inside is good for forty-eight hours. Press the button when you slip it into the bag with the money, and we'll be able to track the signal. As soon as the kidnapper picks up the ransom, we'll have a colleague follow him, and when we know where his hideout is, we'll rescue your son.'

'But what if the transmitter gets discovered?'

'You can choose not to use it – we won't force you. But please understand that once the kidnapper gets the cash, he won't necessarily keep his word and let his hostage go. Rather than seeing this as a gamble, try regarding it as an insurance policy. If you trust the Royal Hong Kong Police, then please do as I ask and put it in the bag.'

'I understand.' Graham nodded.

'The kidnapper may instruct you to transfer the money and jewellery to a different bag during the handover. You'll have to play it by ear.' Kwan tapped the transmitter a couple of times.

Mac bundled the notes up again into their original seven piles. Graham quickly counted them, then put them back into the envelope. The jewellery box was too large to carry around, so he found a small cloth bag for the necklace, earrings and rings, then pulled the drawcord and stuffed that into the envelope too. He picked up the transmitter and was about to place it with the cash and jewels, then changed his mind and put it in his trouser pocket, thinking he'd wait and see if the kidnapper gave him any particular instructions first.

While they waited, Kwan made two phone calls, to the Hong Kong Island and Kowloon Criminal Investigation Departments. As soon as the kidnapper told Graham where to go, Kwan would brief the relevant district's officers to set up surveillance and an ambush.

Ten minutes later, the phone rang. It was 3.20 – again, right on time.

Everyone put on their earpieces and Ngai once again switched on the tracing and recording machines. Kwan nodded at Graham, who picked up the phone.

'Hello.'

'Have you got the money?' The same man again.

'Yes. Seventy thousand in cash and thirty thousand in jewellery.'

'You see, where there's a will, there's a way!' jeered the man.

'I want to speak to Alfred,' said Graham, trying to drag out the conversation as Ngai indicated he needed more time.

'Don't bargain with me,' said the man coldly. 'I'm only going to say this once.'

'But I want to speak to Alfred—'

'Within twenty minutes, drive alone to Lok Heung Yuen Coffee Shop on Wellington Street in Central. Bring the ransom with you. Order a cup of milk tea. You'll receive new instructions there.'

'Wait, I want Alf—'

Before he finished, the man had hung up.

'No trace,' said Ngai, removing his earpiece. 'These calls are all too short to get a fix.'

'Ron, you stay here. I want you to examine the recordings of all the calls so far – see if you can find any clues, background noises, that sort of thing,' said Kwan, removing his earpiece too. 'Mr Hill, with a twenty-minute time limit, you'd better set out now. Do you know where Lok Heung Yuen is?'

'The D'Aguilar end of Wellington Street, right?'

'Yes, that's the one. Mac won't be able to go with you. The kidnapper emphasized you should come alone, and if he happened to find another person in your car, that might not be good for your son's safety. But Mac, Sergeant Tsui and I will wait nearby, and as soon as you get a chance, let us know his next instruction and we'll mobilize the others. I'll get in touch with CID over the car radio and tell them to put an undercover officer at Lok Heung Yuen.'

Graham nodded.

'Mac, go get the car. Meet me and Old Tsui at the street corner.'

Graham didn't set off right away. Instead, he went over to Stella, still slumped on the sofa, and knelt to hug her.

'Don't fret, I'll bring Alfred back home,' he murmured into her ear, sounding confident. Stella's eyes filled with tears again, but she nodded and clutched her husband tightly. She knew she had to be strong, so Graham wouldn't worry about her as he went off alone.

Graham picked up the envelope and went down to the parking lot. Placing the ransom on the passenger seat, he started his car, trying to work out which route to take. As he drove out the main gate of Nairn House, he saw Kwan and Old Tsui walking past the security kiosk towards the street.

Along the way, Graham kept glancing at his watch. It was about a twelve-minute drive to Central, but if traffic were bad, he might not make it within twenty. He glared anxiously at each red light he came to, and floored the pedal with each amber, zooming ahead like a Grand Prix driver with a medal in his sights.

Fortunately, rush hour was still some time away, and traffic was smooth. The only problem came in the Cross-Harbour Tunnel, where the clumsy toll-booth cashier cost him an extra ten seconds, and even after Graham snapped that he didn't need change, the blockhead still took his time raising the barrier.

Graham reached the coffee shop at 3.37. Lok Heung Yuen was known locally as the Snake Pit – Cantonese slang for shirking from work was 'Snake King', and each afternoon the place filled with white-collar workers who'd snuck out of their offices for an illicit break. This was the peak time for afternoon tea, and every single table was taken, leaving Graham at a loss.

The Snake Pit was a place for regular people – foreign bosses or high-level executives would never go there – so when Graham stepped in, he attracted some attention. People assumed he must have come to the wrong place, or that he was trying to track down an employee who'd abandoned his post at a crucial moment.

'Sorry, no seat. Do you mind... *daap toi*?' The waiter spoke broken English, ending with the Cantonese for 'share a table', gesturing to show what he meant.

Graham suddenly caught sight of some familiar faces – Kwan Chun-dok and Old Tsui in a four-person booth. He went over as casually as he could, and slipped in next to Kwan. The inspector was apparently absorbed in a newspaper, while Old Tsui had his arms folded across his chest, seemingly sound asleep. Both had typical Snake Pit behaviour down to a T, and no one would ever have suspected they were policemen. For all that Graham had hurried here, Mac drove with the reckless speed of a young man, and he'd got the officers here a few minutes ahead.

Kwan didn't make a sound, only glancing at Graham as if to say, 'What's this foreigner doing, sharing a table with us?' Graham didn't speak to them either, only followed the instructions he'd been given, ordering a cup of Hong Kong-style milk tea from the waiter.

Lok Heung Yuen's tea was famous, but Graham wasn't in the mood to appreciate it. He took a sip, then began looking around, waiting for the kidnapper to show up.

Although he'd arrived just minutes before the deadline, it still seemed to take the long hand of his watch forever to creep closer and closer towards the 8. When it was almost there, the same waiter came over with his half-baked English. 'You... Mr Ha? Telephone.' Once again, he had to mime to get his message across.

This was strange. Clutching the ransom envelope, Graham went to the public phone. The receiver was on the counter, and no one was nearby.

He gingerly picked up the phone. 'Hello?'

'You're on time, good.' Once more, the hateful man.

'Show yourself. You can have my money, I only want my son back.'

'If you do what I say, you'll see him very soon,' said the man levelly. 'Right now, I want you to find a jeweller and change the seventy thousand dollars into gold.'

'Into gold?'

'Yes, gold. The price of gold today is about nine hundred dollars per tael... I'll give you a discount. Buy me seventy-five taels of gold. You can keep the change.' Hong Kong still used the old system of weights for trading gold; a tael was equal to ten maces and a mace was about 3.75 grams.

'Change the cash into fifteen five-tael gold bars, then drive to Kennedy Town swimming pool in West Point. Order a cup of coffee at the poolside cafe and wait for my next order.'

'Kennedy Town swimming pool?'

'Don't make me repeat myself. I'll give you half an hour, get there by four fifteen.'

'Will you bring Alfred—'

Click. He'd hung up.

Banknotes could have their serial numbers copied down, but gold was untraceable. If necessary, ingots could be melted down.

Graham returned to his seat and gulped down some tea, then whispered, 'The kidnapper wants me to turn the cash into seventy-five taels of gold, then meet him at Kennedy Town swimming pool cafe.'

Kwan said nothing, his gaze remaining fixed on the paper. He only placed his right hand on the table and tapped twice gently in acknowledgement. Graham called for the bill and quickly left the cafe, still clutching the ransom.

Now he had to find a jewellery shop. Central was the heart of Hong Kong Island, and walking a little way west on Queen's Road he found himself amongst all manner of shops, including several jewellers. He picked one at random and went in past its window display of gold bracelets and rings. The staff perked up to see a white man walk in. By this point the locals had almost caught up with the foreigners in terms of wealth and status, but older Hongkongers couldn't shake off the idea that a non-Chinese face meant money.

'Welcome. How may I help, sir?' The balding, bespectacled clerk spoke fluently, although with a strong accent.

'Gold. I want gold bars,' said Graham.

'As an investment? This is a good time to buy gold. How much?' said the clerk delightedly.

'Five taels of solid gold. I want fifteen of those.'

'Sir... did you say fifteen five-tael bars?' The clerk thought he'd heard wrong.

'Yes, seventy-five taels in total.' Graham pulled the cash from his envelope. 'Do you have it here? I need it now, tell me if you don't and I'll go. I'm in a rush.'

'We do! We do!' The clerk's eyes almost popped out of his head. It wasn't that he hadn't seen such big sums before, but no foreign visitor had ever been that open-handed. It was enough to buy a triplex apartment in Wan Chai.

The clerk hurried into the back of the store and returned a

minute later with a tray bearing fifteen ornate boxes. He opened them one by one to show that each contained a slab of glittering gold, stamped with its weight and serial number, and a certificate stating the provenance of the ingot.

'We have scales here, if you want to inspect...'

'No, and I don't need the boxes, just give me the gold.'

'Gold is selling for eighty-eight dollars per mace today... so that's a total of sixty-six thousand dollars.' The clerk discreetly pointed at a sign on the counter that said, 'Fine Gold: $88 per mace. No bargaining, please.' He checked his calculations quickly on an abacus. 'Will you be paying in cash?'

Graham shoved the piles of banknotes in front of him, as if rebuking him for asking unnecessary questions.

'I'll need to examine the notes, please bear with me,' said the clerk gingerly, trying not to annoy the customer.

'Hurry up.' Graham checked his watch. It was only a ten-minute drive from Central to West Point.

The clerk inspected the cash. Because they were large denominations and many were in sequence, it didn't take him long to count out $66,000.

'Here's your change. I'll write you a receipt.'

'I don't—'

'Sir, it's better if you keep the receipt, to prevent any dispute later.' The clerk found it very odd that this foreigner was in such a hurry – perhaps these were stolen public funds, and he was preparing to abscond? Of course, it didn't matter to him what the story was – these were real notes and the transaction was legal, so even if the police showed up, he should be able to hang on to the money.

While the clerk was scribbling out the receipt, Graham shovelled the gold bars into his envelope. Each ingot was only a little larger than the average eraser, and the A4 envelope was easily able to hold all fifteen. They were heavy, though – about three kilograms, almost ripping the paper. Seeing this, the clerk handed over the receipt, then reached for a plastic bag.

'Thank you,' said Graham, British politeness automatic even at this moment.

'No, thank you for your business.' The clerk shook his hand warmly. 'Sir, if you require anything in the future, please be sure to visit our humble store again.'

Graham nodded and placed the envelope and receipt in the plastic bag, then hurried out. Only when he was leaving the store did he notice Old Tsui by the window, pretending to browse. As he brushed past, neither so much as glanced at the other. Graham guessed Superintendent Kwan must have radioed ahead to send someone to the pool, or else he and Mac would have driven there straight away to see if there were any sign of the kidnapper.

Graham sprinted to his car and set off.

Kennedy Town pool on Smithfield had opened two years previously. In addition to a viewing area and changing rooms, the pool also had a public cafe. Each morning the place was packed with breakfast customers, and after the rush of the morning swim, seniors would turn up, many of them with bird cages – a little bird-appreciation club. It was a bustling scene.

At five past four, Graham arrived at the pool. He'd never been there before, but having investigated so many corruption cases, he knew the addresses of public facilities by heart. As soon as he turned onto Smithfield, he saw his destination at once. Parking in a nearby lot, he saw roadside hawkers and a market opposite the entrance. Smithfield was at the western end of West Point, near two large public housing developments – Kwun Lung Lau and Sai Wan Estate – as well as private housing, with more than a hundred thousand residents in all. Apart from street snacks, you could also buy clothes or fruit here, or get your watch repaired, your shoes fixed, your keys cut, your blades sharpened. These last hawkers carried whetstones and other tools around, shouting, 'Knives and scissors!' as they roamed the streets, summoning housewives downstairs with their implements to be made sharp again for a dollar or less.

It was after school, and the snack stalls were busy with students clamouring for fishballs and tripe soup, or sweets like Cantonese steamed cakes, peanut candy and dragon's beard. Graham squeezed through the hordes of ravenous young people to the pool entrance and followed the signs to the cafe upstairs.

This wasn't as crowded as the Snake Pit – there were several empty tables. He spotted Kwan sitting alone, but, afraid he was being watched, slid into another booth with his back to the policeman. Although facing in opposite directions, they could still hear each other if they whispered.

'What would you like?' said a waiter in Cantonese. Graham had no idea what he'd just said, but guessed this probably wasn't a message from the kidnapper – who'd presumably know not to send someone who didn't speak English. He pointed at coffee on the menu, which fortunately was bilingual.

Sipping his coffee, Graham studied his surroundings. He had no idea if there were other undercover officers around. The two at the round table in front might be police, but equally could be the kidnappers. The twenty-something guy a little to the back was suspicious too; he kept staring at Graham as he drank his iced lemon tea. Graham followed his gaze and realized he might not necessarily be the target – right in front of him was a ravishing young woman enjoying a sandwich.

As he was looking around, the waiter came up again and pointed at the counter, where the phone was off its hook. Was the waiter in cahoots with the kidnapper? No, he could easily have said, 'Please ask the Westerner who just ordered a cup of coffee to come to the phone.' He'd probably picked this venue because not many foreigners came here. Still, Graham now realized something.

Both here and at the Snake Pit, he was being watched by the kidnapper's co-conspirators. As soon as he arrived, the observer would have left, or else found some way to notify his colleague outside, to phone the restaurant at once and give Graham his next order.

As he made his way to the counter, Graham swept his eyes

across every face in the room to see if he recognized anyone from the Snake Pit. But there was no one. He couldn't claim he never forgot a face, but he certainly would notice running into the same person twice in half an hour.

So the kidnapper had more than one assistant – different watchers in Central and West Point.

'You bought the gold?' It was the same man on the phone.

'Yes. I'll give you the gold and jewellery, just return my son to me.'

'Mr Hill, don't worry, when I get the ransom, I'll send your child home to you. But I'm not stupid enough to do the exchange face to face,' said the man coldly. 'I've left a cardboard box by the flower trough at the cafe entrance. Your name is written on it. Go look.'

He hung up. Graham didn't bother returning to his seat, but handed the waiter some money, then walked out. Sure enough, a box stood where the kidnapper had said, with 'HILL' on one side in big letters. He ripped it open to see a pair of red swimming trunks, an odd-shaped white canvas bag and a typewritten note:

'Go into the pool area, change into the trunks. Place the gold and jewellery in the bag and carry it with you. I've left a special coin in the centre of the main pool. When you've found it, you'll understand the next step.'

All of this was baffling, but Graham had no choice. He made sure he hadn't missed any items in the box – or any clues – then took the swimming trunks and bag downstairs, past the reception desk. Kwan followed him, so he palmed the folded note and left it on the railing for him to pick up – he couldn't afford to speak to Kwan, not knowing if his observer was still nearby.

After paying, Graham went down the passageway into the men's changing room. There were no lockers here, only a counter where an attendant would give you a wire basket for your possessions. The baskets were about the size of a desk drawer, and each had two metal tags attached – you were given one tag when you deposited your property, then your basket went back on the rack. The attendant had six or seven empty baskets ready on the counter for use, which he constantly replaced. These went back on the rack in order, for easy retrieval.

Graham didn't quite know how this worked, but watched the people in front of him and quickly got the idea. There were seven or eight other men in the room, getting dressed or undressed; he didn't know which of them were police or kidnappers. Taking a basket, he went into a corner and undressed, then slipped on those bright red trunks. Looking around to make sure no one was watching, he opened the envelope and transferred the gold bars to the canvas bag one by one.

The bag was long and narrow, more like a belt, with a buckle and clasp at either end and a long zip down the middle. It looked as if it had been specially commissioned by a smuggler, rather than something you could buy in a shop.

A footstep behind him arrested his movements. He turned around hurriedly to see Kwan Chun-dok, who now sat next to him, not acknowledging him in any way, pretending to change – he didn't have any swimming trunks with him.

Graham continued transferring the gold bars and then the jewellery. Just as he was about to pull the zip shut, he remembered the little black box and couldn't help crying out so sharply that even Kwan was forced to turn and look at him.

So that was the purpose of his dip – the gold and jewellery would be fine, but if he put the transmitter in the canvas bag it would probably be ruined by the water.

Should he take the risk and put the transmitter in? Or hide it somewhere by the poolside, and try to find a way to slip it in later? But what if the kidnapper found it?

His brain filled with questions.

He'd taken the black box from his pocket as he removed his trousers, and now held it in his palm, flashing it at Kwan as a question. Kwan stretched lazily, shaking his head.

True, if the transmitter stopped working, then it became a straightforward liability – its discovery could only harm Alfred.

Graham tossed it into his basket next to his watch and keys, tugged the zip on the canvas bag shut, and went to the counter to hand over his possessions. In exchange, he got a tag on a string that he could wear around his wrist.

'You can't take that belt in, sir,' said the attendant. He spoke first in Cantonese, and when he realized he wasn't being understood, repeated himself in English.

'No, I have to.'

'No personal items. Please leave it here, we'll take care of it.' His face was grumpy.

Losing his temper, Graham pulled open the zip to reveal the glittering gold bars. 'If these go missing, will you take responsibility?'

The attendant's eyes popped wide open and his chin practically hit the floor. He just about managed to mutter, 'Please... please go ahead.' Graham guessed he'd probably never seen so much gold in one place. But then, half an hour ago, neither had he.

As he left the changing room, Graham glanced at Kwan Chun-dok, who gestured briefly to indicate he should go on in. Graham understood – the longer he delayed, the more danger Alfred was in.

Clipping on the belt, Graham walked past the training pool to the deeper main pool. There were about twenty people swimming. He swam past them to the very centre, where he trod water and scrutinized the bottom of the pool.

There was nothing there.

Desperate, he looked again, even diving so his face was almost touching the bottom. It remained stubbornly empty.

Graham broke the surface and took a deep breath, then went down again. Perhaps he wasn't quite in the centre, or the coin had been shifted by the water. He searched a wider area. Still nothing.

How was this possible? Now and then he bumped into other swimmers, spitting out quick apologies as he continued his hunt.

'A special coin – could it be transparent?' he wondered.

Running his hand along the pool bottom, he felt nothing, just smooth tiles.

Could the kidnapper have mixed up the two pools? He got out at once and turned to the training pool. Kwan, now in swimming trunks, stood by the poolside, but Graham made no attempt to speak to him. He'd already wasted ten minutes and was no closer to finding that damned coin.

It was the same story in the training pool – nothing at all resembling a coin. There were more people in here. As he kept diving, some young girls thought he was up to something suspicious and quickly got out of his way.

'God, could someone else have picked it up?' The horrifying possibility occurred to him. A cardboard box by a flower trough was fairly unremarkable, but a coin at the bottom of a pool could be picked up by a curious stranger.

He returned to the main pool and asked a few swimmers, but no one had seen a coin. Some just ignored him and went on with their lengths. He tried the lifeguards too, with no more success.

Graham began to feel dizzy. The belt hung heavily around his waist, and no one appeared to snatch the ransom. He thought of appealing to Kwan for help, but looking around, he found the inspector nowhere.

Had Kwan seen someone suspicious? Was he tailing that person? Could the kidnapper not have managed to put the coin in place? Graham thought of various possibilities, but there was nothing he could do. His only option was to keep searching for a coin that might or might not exist.

He glanced at the clock by the pool. It was 4.45 – he'd been searching for half an hour. There were more people in the pool now, probably schoolchildren. Once again, he dived through the throng and made for the centre, and this time he spotted it.

A gleaming, silvery coin.

He didn't know how he could have missed it earlier. It was as if someone had cast a spell to keep him from seeing it. Picking it up, he saw it was a British 25-pence coin, issued by the Royal

Mint that February to commemorate the Queen's silver jubilee. A hole had been drilled in it, through which had been threaded a string attached to a metal tag.

When you've found it, you'll understand the next step – and sure enough, he did.

Without hesitation, Graham leaped from the pool and charged back into the changing room. There was a long line at the counter. He charged up to the front and pushed in. There was some grumbling, but no one dared to stop him. He frantically flung the coin and tag onto the counter, scaring the attendant into taking a step back. The man quickly glanced at the number and rushed to fetch the wire basket. He seemed to find its contents odd, but didn't say anything.

This basket contained only a pair of flip-flops and a piece of paper folded in four. Graham grabbed both and unfolded the note.

'Within thirty seconds, walk out of the main entrance to the road and head north. Hold the bag with the gold bars in your left hand. Don't forget, you only have thirty seconds. My associate is watching you now.'

Graham cast a panicky look around the changing room. Everyone was now staring at him. Not caring about anything else, he slipped on the flip-flops and dashed out, still drenched from the pool.

'Out of my way!' he yelled as he sprinted down the passageway, barrelling through the one-way door to the outside. He ran to the roadside, remembering that Smithfield went uphill to the south, and so turning downhill. He pulled the dripping canvas bag from around his waist and held it up with his left hand, confused as to what this would achieve.

Within seconds, he knew.

A motorcycle zoomed up. The rider, all in black with a black helmet, grabbed the bag and sped off into the distance. It took Graham a second to realize what had happened, and then he ran after the motorbike, shouting, 'Where's my son? Bring my son back!'

Everyone turned to look at him. What happened next was completely unexpected – including to the kidnapper.

Three seconds after the rider snatched the bag, something small and dark fell from the motorcycle.

Graham didn't know what that was at first, but as they kept coming, he saw.

Gold bars, glistening and bright, each weighing five taels.

That first dark object must have been the bag with the jewellery in it. The rider saw what was happening and slowed down, but a car roared past Graham and the black-clad rider sped off again, with the car in pursuit. A trail of gold bars remained behind, like a dotted line marking this strange occurrence.

Graham remembered – he'd pulled the zip open to show the attendant the gold.

He probably hadn't closed it fully afterwards.

While he was diving so many times into the water, the little ingots would have collided repeatedly, forcing the zip to open wider.

Neither he nor the criminal could have expected that the opening would be facing downwards during their exchange, nor that the force with which the bag was snatched would cause it to give way altogether.

5

IN THE CAR pursuing the motorcycle were members of Hong Kong Island CID. After being alerted to the Hill kidnapping, they'd followed orders to prepare for action at the scene and were awaiting further instructions. When a man clad only in swimming trunks, dripping wet, burst out and began acting oddly, the investigators paid attention. They didn't know what Graham Hill looked like, but it seemed likely this was the hostage's father. A moment later, a motorcyclist swooped in, grabbing an item from the man in trunks, and the CID officers understood at once they were witnessing the moment of exchange. If they could nab this rider, they'd gain valuable information, and so they dived in on their own initiative, chasing after the bike, not caring if this exposed police involvement.

But they didn't catch him.

Motorcycles are nimble – the criminal only had to turn into Belcher's Street and slip into the gaps between cars to vanish into the distance. The police car wasn't far behind, and found the abandoned vehicle on Sands Street, but the culprit was long gone, leaving behind his black jacket, his helmet and the canvas bag. The officers asked passers-by if they'd seen the suspect, but their answers were inconclusive. An off-duty policeman said he'd seen a man dashing into a taxi, but he hadn't taken note of the licence number, and anyway that might not have been the suspect. A quick check showed that the motorcycle had been reported stolen.

When Graham saw the gold bars fall and the kidnapper get away, his mind went completely blank. He didn't run forward to retrieve his property, just stood stock still, staring at the disappearing motorcycle as if it were his son vanishing into the distance.

'Quick, pick up the gold bars, get changed and go home. The kidnapper might phone again. I'll assist the officers in the pursuit,' said a soft voice.

Graham turned to see Kwan Chun-dok standing beside him, already back in his clothes. Having given his instructions, Kwan walked briskly to a car on the opposite side of the road. Graham helplessly picked up the valuables. It was only then that the surrounding crowd realized what they'd seen, which added to their astonishment.

Clutching the gold, Graham persuaded the flabbergasted counter clerk to let him back in and then retrieved his possessions from the oblivious attendant. The black box was where he'd left it, next to his watch and keys. Glaring at this useless bit of machinery, Graham flung the gold and jewellery onto a bench and punched the wall. Not caring that he was still sopping wet, he pulled on his clothes, shoved the gold back into the envelope in the plastic bag, and departed amidst bemused looks from the bystanders.

Back in his car, he listlessly started the engine and drove back to Nairn House. None of this felt real. His son being kidnapped was already something he'd never expected in this lifetime, but his misadventures in the last hour and the failure of the ransom payment made him feel he'd wandered into a dream. All the way home, he thought about Alfred – how he'd looked as a baby, his smile the first time he said 'Daddy', how he'd cried on his first day of school, holding hands crossing the road. When they'd said goodbye that morning, he hadn't realized those might be the last words they'd ever exchange.

Are you having trouble with your homework? Do you have good friends at school? What are you learning in art class? Do you want Mummy and Daddy to take you to the carnival? – how he regretted not saying these things to Alfred. He and Stella had handed over responsibility for raising their son to the nanny while they buried themselves in work, so Liz had asked all these questions for them. Alfred had probably wished to hear them from his parents, but had been afraid to ask. Before they left England, each time Alfred asked him or Stella for something, they'd only reply, 'We can't afford it right now. Mummy and Daddy have to work hard to pay our debts. Let's see after we've done that.'

But the debt had been cleared a year ago. Why hadn't he paid more attention to his son after that?

Graham was so agitated he almost drove his car into a streetlight to punish himself.

At ten past five, he rushed into the apartment. Stella leaped up from the sofa when she saw her husband, but when she saw he was alone, the hope in her eyes flickered into despair.

'Alfred...'

Graham shook his head. 'The exchange failed.'

'How? What happened?' Stella broke down, grabbing her husband's shoulders. Ronald Ngai, who'd been sitting to one side, rushed over to see if he could help.

'The kidnapper got the ransom, but it fell from his motorcycle...' Graham couldn't meet his wife's eyes.

'Oh God, what will happen to Alfred?' Stella's legs weakened under her and she tumbled to the floor. Graham and Ngai quickly lifted her up and laid her on the sofa.

The three of them waited helplessly. Ngai didn't have much time for the ICAC man, but at this moment, even he thought the couple before him were truly pitiful. Stella sobbed as if she'd watched her child die in front of her. Indeed, from Graham's account, it would seem the boy's chances weren't good.

Fifteen minutes later, the doorbell rang. Kwan, Old Tsui and Mac came in. From their stricken faces, it was immediately obvious that the investigation had run into difficulties.

'We didn't catch the motorbike rider,' said Kwan. 'CID found the bike, and the Identification Bureau have gathered what evidence they could from it. Hopefully that'll provide a lead.'

And with that, the Hills' last hope snuffed out.

'Those Island CID officers were too rash. If they'd followed unobtrusively, we might be in a better position. But let's not worry who's to blame right now. We'll deal with the situation as it stands.' Kwan's voice remained level. 'The kidnapper might know you called the police, Mr Hill, but he might only suspect it. I've notified the media to describe what happened at the pool as a snatch theft. Plain-clothes officers happened to see a motorcycle-riding thief grab a foreigner's bag, and set off in pursuit, but the criminal got away, while the victim left the scene on his own. This will be on the six o'clock TV and radio news. They'll add that police are seeking the Westerner who was robbed – hopefully that'll convince the kidnapper this was just a coincidence.'

Graham nodded. His mind had switched off.

'If that works, the kidnapper will phone again. We just have to keep waiting.'

Kwan took Graham through every detail of what had happened that afternoon, and Graham answered as best he could, though with each sentence he couldn't help wondering what on earth he could have done differently to avoid this disaster.

'The pool attendant might be able to identify the kidnapper,' said Mac. 'Surely depositing only a pair of flip-flops and a sheet of paper would attract attention?'

'Some people have too much stuff for one basket, so they grab a second one,' Old Tsui butted in. 'As long as he did that, the attendant probably wouldn't have taken any notice.'

Several hours seemed to go by as they waited for the phone call. The atmosphere was heavy, a sense of disappointment hanging in the air. When it was time for the news, Graham turned on the TV, while Ngai and Old Tsui put on the radio, and they listened intently.

The living-room clock coldly swung its arms as the minutes

and seconds slipped away. The phone didn't ring again. The envelope holding the gold bars and jewellery sat on the table. Graham wished these riches would just disappear, if that could bring his son back.

Click.

A sound from the front door seized everyone's attention. The door swung open and Stella shrieked.

A woman said, 'Oh, do we have visitors today?'

The officers recognized the woman from the photos in the living room. It was Liz, Leung Lai-ping, the nanny. But the person who made Stella scream and Graham stare was standing behind her.

'Alfred!' Stella half ran, half crawled to her son and grabbed him. Graham did the same, kneeling down to embrace both his wife and son.

'What's going on?' said Liz, looking startled.

'I'm Inspector Kwan Chun-dok,' said Kwan, flashing his ID. 'How did you find Alfred?'

'What?'

'Alfred, are you all right? Liz, did the kidnappers do anything to you?' Graham looked up from holding his son, who seemed confused.

'Kidnappers?'

'You and Alfred were kidnapped!' shouted Graham.

'I don't understand. Alfred and I have been together all day. Nothing's happened.'

Everyone stared at Liz.

'You weren't kidnapped?' Mac cut in.

'I met Alfred after school, took him for lunch, and then to his sketching class.'

'Sketching?' Graham repeated.

'Yes, didn't I tell Mrs Hill last week? The art class had a special outing.'

'What's this?' gaped Stella.

'You seemed quite tired when I told you. Maybe that's why you don't remember? But you signed the consent form – they were taking all the kids out to the countryside, so there was a letter for parents.'

'When did I sign that? I don't remember.'

'It was last week. I gave it to you with some other school documents.'

'But – but you should have known I might forget. Didn't I tell you if there were any changes to the schedule, you should leave me a note on the day?' Stella, in her confusion, was scolding Liz, when really her son was back and she no longer cared about anything else.

'I did! I know how busy you are, so I made sure to leave you a note this morning.'

As Liz spoke, she went over to the shelf where Graham's commendation plaque stood, and felt around on it, then knelt down and pulled a slip of paper from behind a potted plant.

'It fell down,' she said, handing it to Stella. Everyone leaned forward, and sure enough, it said in English, 'After school drawing class activity, afternoon I take Alfred for lunch outside, evening come back.'

'Liz, have you really been with Alfred all day?' asked Graham.

'Of course. I met him at eleven thirty, took him for some wonton noodles, and then we went to the meeting point. The other children and parents were there. We took the bus to Sai Kung. The children drew pictures, and I chatted with the parents and other nannies. It was nice to be in the countryside, breathing fresh air.'

'Really?' asked Stella, still hugging Alfred, who said nothing, taking all this in.

'You can ask Alfred, or call the art teacher, if you don't believe me,' said Liz. 'What on earth happened?'

'Someone said they'd kidnapped Alfred, and demanded a hundred thousand dollars from Mr Hill,' Kwan explained.

'Oh no!' Liz's mouth fell open, and she turned to Graham. 'Mr Hill, did you pay? No, I remember Mrs Hill saying you don't have that much in the bank...'

Mac's face changed, and he ran over to the dining table to look in the envelope. He'd suddenly thought there might have been some kind of switch, but when he tipped it out onto the table, every gold bar was present and correct, and so was the jewellery. He picked up an ingot and tapped it on the table. It seemed genuine.

'Heavens! So much gold!' exclaimed Liz. 'So you're serious?'

'Did you think we were joking?' sneered Old Tsui.

'So that was no kidnapper – just a fraud,' murmured Graham.

'But how did he guess Mrs Hill would forget about her son's drawing class?' said Old Tsui.

'Miss Leung,' said Kwan, turning to Liz, 'do you know if there are any other kids at Alfred's school who have the same colour hair as him?'

At this unexpected question the group stared dubiously at Kwan.

'I think... there might be three or four,' Liz replied.

'Old Tsui, call the school and get their names from the principal.'

'Headman, do you mean...?'

'The kidnapper might have got the wrong person.'

Graham stared, confused. He was naturally delighted to have his son back, but hearing Kwan's words, he began to worry again. If this *was* a kidnapping case, then his own child had been spared only through a string of coincidences. And at that moment, another innocent child was going through a torture meant for Alfred.

'Going by Mr Hill's many conversations with the kidnapper, if this was a case of mistaken identity, we'd need to find someone fitting this description: the child would have to have red hair like Alfred; his father may work in the same place as Mr Hill, though it's also possible that the child gave the wrong answer in his fear, or that the criminal got mixed up between ICAC and some company name like ICA or ICC; thirdly, there'd need to be someone called Liz or Elizabeth in their household.'

Kwan's words made Graham think back to the phone calls. When he'd heard the child calling for Liz, he'd immediately assumed it was Alfred. But actually, from just those few words, he couldn't be certain that had been his own son's voice.

'Mr Hill, we'll have to trouble the four of you to come down to the station to assist with our inquiries,' said Kwan. 'If all of this is true, then you're the key figures in this case, and we'll need each of you to provide a detailed statement. We'll need to know more about your circumstances, and see if you've come into contact with any suspicious individuals.'

'But if they grabbed the wrong child, we might get another phone call here?' Mac protested.

'The exchange of gold bars, using the swimming pool to destroy our transmitter, leaving the school uniform outside the building – this is a criminal who's thought of everything. He surely has an associate watching this place.' Kwan shook his head. 'With the nanny and Alfred returning home in plain sight, they'll know something's gone wrong, and won't be phoning again. We'll have the latest news at the station, and it'll be easier to dispatch people from there. Don't forget, a child's life may still be at stake.'

'Stella, let's go down there,' said Graham. 'If another child is suffering in Alfred's place, we have to do our best to rescue him.'

His wife nodded. After today, they'd both realized that debt was no big deal – money can be paid off some day, but a broken family can never be mended, and you can't embrace a missing child.

'Must I go too?' asked Liz.

'Naturally. For all we know, the criminal might have shown up around the drawing class. You might have seen him.' Kwan glanced at Liz, then turned back to Graham. 'Mr Hill, you should make sure the gold bars and jewellery are put away safely. After everything you've been through today, why don't you leave it till Monday to turn the gold back into cash and put that back in the bank?'

Graham did as he was told, scooping up the gold bars and heading to the study. Kwan followed him.

'I wouldn't have minded losing all of these, if it got Alfred back,' said Graham, turning the dial on his safe.

'We have a saying in Hong Kong – "Money is just a thing out-side your body." Hongkongers might be materialistic, but on this point, we're pretty certain what's really important.'

'You're right.' Entering the last digit of the combination, Graham inserted the key and opened the safe. He placed the gold inside, and was about to return the jewellery to the purple case, but thinking about it, chucked the cloth bag into the safe too. Money is just a thing outside the body.

Graham closed the safe and went back into the living room with Kwan. The Hills changed their clothes while Kwan stood out on the balcony – Mac guessed that as there was no longer any need to worry about being seen, his commander wanted to survey the surroundings, to see if he could spot any clues.

The Hill household, including Liz, followed Kwan out of the apartment. He'd arranged for a car to meet them. Graham and Stella would only want to hold Alfred tight at this moment, and given earlier events, it would be asking too much to have Graham drive right now.

The two cars headed for Kowloon Police Headquarters in Mong Kok. Kwan instructed his subordinates to take statements from the Hills and from Liz, going into every detail, including all their friends and acquaintances, and any strange events near Nairn House.

'Headman, where are you going?' asked Old Tsui, seeing Kwan had put his coat back on and was heading for the exit.

'I have to run some errands. You take charge for now.'

'Old Tsui, do you think Headman's a bit odd today?' asked Mac, when Kwan had left.

'Is he? Maybe he didn't get a good night's sleep.' Old Tsui shrugged.

Kwan headed for the parking lot, took out Mac's car keys – strictly speaking, they were the CID's keys – and drove away quickly. He only had a short time to make use of this opportunity. Turning off the car's radio comms, he stepped on the pedal and was soon at his destination.

Nairn House on Princess Margaret Road.

Instead of driving in, he parked near the building.

'Ah, mister, it's you again,' said the security guard.

'Superintendent Campbell has a whole lot of jobs for me today – no help for it,' said Kwan casually, once again using William Campbell on the ninth floor as his excuse.

He took the elevator up to the ninth floor, then walked down two flights of stairs.

'I'd really rather not be doing this sort of thing.' He pushed open the stairwell window and looked out, then hauled himself up to the window sill. Looking to his right, he could see the Hills' balcony, a couple of metres away.

Making sure no one below was paying attention, Kwan reached out to grab a protruding corner of the outside wall, then stepped out onto the shallow ledge just below the window. His right hand still gripped the window frame, but he was now on the outside of the building.

Should have brought a rope, he thought. Still, no time to waste. He let go of the frame and moved his right hand to the protrusion, then moved his left hand to grab the balcony railing. He had a strong grip, so even though this looked absurdly precarious, he felt quite secure.

With his left hand on the railing, he gave a sharp tug so his whole body lurched over. A second later he was tumbling onto the balcony.

After making sure no one was inside, he pressed down on the balcony door handle, which opened easily, letting him into the living room. While leaving the apartment earlier, he'd pretended to lock that door, but hadn't actually pushed the bolt all the way in. Knowing he didn't have much time, he pulled out his torch and went into the study, opening the wooden cabinet to reveal the blue-grey safe.

This was government housing, so even the furniture was provided by the state, hence this model of safe was not unfamiliar to him. It was British-made with a double lock, one opened by a combination and one by a key. The combination could be changed by the owner at any time – with the door open, you only had to depress the metal bar and enter the new code. Cautious individuals changed the combination at regular intervals.

'82 left, 35 right, 61 left...' Pulling a glove on, Kwan turned the dial. Graham had opened the safe in front of him twice, so he was certain of the combination.

With a click, the first lock opened.

As for the second one, he had to rely on luck. From his pocket he pulled a little piece of metal and a pair of pliers. The metal plate was flat and had little jags on both sides, like a key.

It was indeed a copy of Graham Hill's safe key.

While Graham had been frantically searching for a coin at the bottom of the swimming pool, Kwan Chun-dok had executed his plan.

He'd waited for the pool attendant to need the bathroom, then slipped behind the counter. Having watched Graham change, he knew which was his basket. Identifying the safe key on Graham's key ring, he pulled out from his own pocket a container the size of a matchbox that opened like a book. Inside were two pieces of green clay. Sprinkling talc from a little bottle over the clay, he brushed off the excess powder, put the key between the clay pieces, shut the box and pressed down hard. When he opened it again and removed the key, it had left behind a perfect impression. He wiped the key clean, replaced it and swiftly left.

After accompanying the Hills to the station, he'd found an excuse to return to his own office. There he'd pulled from his drawer a lighter, a metal spoon and a small quantity of alloy with a low melting point. Together with the clay, they were a kit for copying keys – he'd stumbled upon them many years ago in a shop that sold little playthings like these. Placing the alloy in the spoon over a flame, he melted it – it was probably mainly lead, he guessed – then poured it carefully into the mould.

After a short while, he opened the box again, and there was what looked like half a silver-grey key, nestling inside.

Would this work? He'd only know when he tried it – it was a crude copy. Besides, low-melting-point alloys are brittle, and it could easily snap off in the lock. It would be annoying if that happened.

Still, he had to take the risk.

It had been a while since he made the copy, so the metal should have had time to harden. He placed it between the pliers, slowly inserted it, made sure it was correctly positioned, then very slowly turned it...

Click.

The second lock opened.

Kwan let go of the pliers, then held his breath as he shone the torch into the safe. The gold bars glittered back at him, but he ignored them. They weren't his target.

He was after documents. The informants' testimonies from the Yau Ma Tei Fruit Market drug case.

The accounts that recorded payments to corrupt police officers.

These papers were the ICAC's most potent weapon against the police. If they were to fall into the hands of anyone in the force, the whole operation could break apart. Many officers were anxious about these documents, terrified that their sins would be exposed.

And at this moment, looking through these incriminating papers, was Inspector Kwan Chun-dok of Kowloon Regional CID. The accounts were in code, but Kwan was familiar with underworld slang, and with a bit of imagination, he worked out roughly which departments were on the list, and even which individuals. He paid particular attention to the officers from the Kowloon region.

'Hmm, this fellow owes me a big favour now.'

He slipped the folder into his pocket and shut the safe, turning the copied key with the pliers – making sure he didn't leave any metal fragments behind – then closed the cabinet door. His task was done, and now he just needed to get out.

Kwan left the apartment the same way he got in, with that

risky climb over the balcony. He was sure-footed enough not to feel a moment's panic. In a few seconds he was back in the stairwell, and then saying goodbye to the security guard, then in his car returning to the station. He'd been away less than an hour.

'Headman!' Mac approached as soon as he entered the office. 'I've checked with the school – no missing children at all.'

'None?' Kwan put on a surprised face.

'Not one. There are five students with red hair, and they're all safely at home. Besides, we haven't received a single appeal for help or missing person report. To be sure, I asked the principal to get each form teacher to call every child in their class. The only one they couldn't get hold of was Alfred.'

'Because he's here.'

'Yes. Which means the entire school is safe and well.'

'So our perp wasn't a kidnapper, just a fraudster.'

'Mm, but it's hard to believe a con man would go this far. He almost tricked Mr Hill out of his entire savings.'

'How are the Hills?'

'They're relieved that no other child's in danger. They've gone to grab a bite in the canteen.'

'No one's with them?'

'No.'

'Wow, you let the ICAC man sit in the police canteen, calmly eating away? Aren't you afraid our colleagues will recognize him, get carried away and beat him up?'

'Argh!' Mac cried out in alarm and dashed down the corridor to the canteen. Kwan smiled to himself – he'd only been joking. Graham Hill on his own might have attracted some trouble, but he had his wife and son with him, and at most he'd get a few dirty looks.

Kwan went over to the canteen himself to have a few words with Graham. After saying goodbye to the family, he returned to his office and locked the door. Taking out the stolen ICAC documents, he read every page carefully.

Just think how many favours I could trade this for, he thought.

6

ON MONDAY AT noon, Kwan Chun-dok made an excuse and left the station alone. He took a bus to the south of Hong Kong Island, getting off at Repulse Bay.

There weren't many people on the beach, but Kwan wasn't here for fun. He had someone to meet. There were too many eyes and ears in the city, and even though excuses could be made, he and the other party would still be in trouble if they were spotted together.

Walking along the coast road, he came to a car. Going up close, he made sure he had the right person, before heading round to the other side. Without knocking, he opened the door and settled himself into the passenger seat.

'Kwan, why'd you want to meet? And in such a godforsaken place?'

Without saying a word, Kwan pulled an envelope from his coat pocket and gave it to the other person, who opened it, blanched, and flipped through the whole stack of records – the coded list of names of every corrupt officer.

'Aren't you going to thank me? You almost got into a lot of trouble,' laughed Kwan.

'You... You... Where'd you get these?'

'Where else? From your home.'

Graham Hill returned Kwan's gaze, stunned.

'My home!' he yelled. 'When did you...'

'Last Friday, while you were all at the station giving your statements. I guess you haven't looked in the safe since then?'

Graham paused. 'That's right. Stella and I spent the whole weekend with Alfred. She was actually scheduled to do a shift, and I had some overtime to get through, but we both took the time off. Yesterday and the day before, we took him to a film and an amusement park. Today I'd only just got to the ICAC when you called and said I absolutely had to meet you out here in the middle of nowhere.'

'Anyway, you have your documents back, and Alfred is fine, so all's well.'

'I have absolutely no idea what's happening! My God, Kwan. Why on earth did you break into my home to get these papers? Don't you know how serious that is? If anyone found out, we'd both be in deep trouble.'

'You really don't know, do you?' Kwan smiled grimly. 'Let me ask you, do you think Alfred's kidnapping was the work of a conman?'

'You mean it wasn't?'

'Of course not. A grifter that good could get a million dollars if he wanted, never mind a hundred thousand. Of course, even if he was just after a hundred grand, he still wouldn't have come to you. You're pretty much a pauper.'

'I don't understand.'

'This case, this kidnapping or con or whatever you want to call it – the whole thing was a sham. All misdirection, aimed at you.'

'Misdirection? Then what was the real target?'

Kwan reached out and tapped the papers in Graham's hand. 'These documents?'

'Exactly. To the criminals, these were the most valuable objects in your home, not your pathetic savings or those damn diamonds.'

'You mean... the criminal was a police officer?' Graham yelped.

'Yes. And not just one, I'm afraid, but a whole group of them.'

'But what's the use of stealing this? It's just a copy! The one that's going to be used as evidence, the one with legal standing, that's still in my office. Taking the copy won't affect their case at all!'

'You really are a dimwit. They don't want the evidence, they're after information.'

'Information?'

'You've been at the ICAC three years now, don't you know the principles of bribery? Criminals will pay the police what they ask for, but they'll also say: the more people we bribe, the safer it is for the crooked cops. Police corruption might be rampant, but it's not centralized – there's no one person running the show. Most of the time, it's little squads keeping their ears open, hearing of where open-handed criminals can be found, and going in to get their share. Of course, criminals are willing to pay "squeeze" to more people, but they don't allow double-dipping, so the police themselves won't know which of their colleagues are getting paid off – but the drug pushers have comprehensive records.'

'So they want that list of names...'

'To find out what company they're keeping. If some corrupt officers think they're going to be arrested, they'll want to launch a pre-emptive strike: find others under suspicion, band together with them and start planning, or threaten them into co-operating. Even better if the list includes inspectors or superintendents – higher-ranking officers might be able to work together and pressure the top brass into shutting down the ICAC. Even more scarily, the records also list all the intermediaries who helped facilitate the bribes, and if the corrupt cops think any of them might turn informant like the pushers, those people will have to be dealt with.'

'You mean... killed?'

'Possibly. There are many methods – they could say the guy got aggressive during a routine traffic stop, leaving them no choice but to shoot; or that he was trying to flee and accidentally fell from the roof of a building. From time to time I wonder if there's more to certain suspects' deaths than meets the eye. But if a case is closed, I can't investigate.'

Graham took a deep breath. 'So in order to get their hands on this, they faked Alfred's kidnapping? These two things were unconnected!'

'They're connected,' said Kwan with certainty. 'But before I say how, I have a question for you – how were they able to fool you and your wife?'

'I still don't understand! How could so many coincidences have stacked up in the conman's favour, to make me believe Alfred really had been snatched? They didn't get the wrong kid at all, did they?'

'That was just some nonsense I made up – you didn't really believe it?' smiled Kwan. 'They didn't get the wrong kid, because they didn't get any kid. You mentioned "so many coincidences" – what were they?'

'Loads of them.' Graham stroked his chin, trying to remember. 'Even if the criminal knew Alfred was with Liz in the country-side, he couldn't have known Stella would forget about that outing. If Stella had remembered, that first phone call would have gone nowhere. And if Liz's note hadn't fallen on the floor, Stella and I would have seen it. Or if Alfred had mentioned to one of us that morning that he was going on a sketching trip... Yet these all happened by chance.'

'Chance my ass,' Kwan chuckled. 'The three things you mentioned all involved one person – your nanny, Leung Lai-ping. Liz. These coincidences were all manufactured by her.'

'Liz?' Graham gasped. 'She's been bought?'

'Of course.'

'But I don't believe she'd ever do a thing to hurt Alfred!'

'And indeed she didn't. Her affection for Alfred, though, doesn't necessarily mean she has affection for his parents.'

Graham stared at Kwan.

'Your first preconception was that Alfred was the victim. And because you knew Liz wouldn't hurt Alfred, you ruled her out as a suspect,' said Kwan. 'But you were wrong from the start. The real victims were you and your wife – though the harm you'd suffer was only half a day's worry and the loss of some property. For the right reason – or the right price – quite a few people would say yes to that. Or perhaps Liz felt she was making the right choice for Alfred. Look, isn't he now suddenly getting a lot more attention from his parents?'

'But how could she manufacture all those coincidences? Liz didn't *make* Stella forget about the outing.'

'Your wife didn't forget anything. She was never told about it.'

'But she signed the consent form—'

'Signatures can be faked.' Kwan waved dismissively. 'If I had constant access to someone's signature, I could probably copy it easily. Liz noticed your weak point as a couple – you were both so distracted by work that, in the shock of the moment, it would be easy for her to push the blame onto your wife, and you'd believe it.'

'And the note?'

'That only came to light when she returned home. She had it hidden in her hand and pretended to discover it under the shelf. I took note of every item in the room when I first came in. There was nothing on the floor there.'

'What if Alfred had mentioned the outing to one of us that morning?'

'Then they'd have changed the plan. Liz was there, so she'd have known if Alfred had mentioned it – but even if not, your wife would just have dismissed the first phone call as a prank, and the criminals wouldn't have lost anything. The main thing was that Liz didn't give herself away. To be honest, Liz knew Alfred probably wouldn't say anything, because you'd grown apart – she saw all that very clearly.'

Graham thought back to that Friday morning. Although Alfred hadn't mentioned the outing, there'd still been a clue – he normally disliked going to school, but he'd actually been quite cheerful, probably looking forward to being out in the country.

'Hang on.' He thought of something. 'That means – the

school shirt and the hair, and when I heard Alfred's voice on the phone...'

'It wouldn't be hard to get hold of a uniform shirt – Liz could just have bought an extra one. And the hair probably *was* Alfred's – she just had to grab a few strands when she took him to get it cut. As for the voice, any tape recorder would do. All he said was "Liz? Are you there?" She just had to wait till she was alone in the house with him, which was most of the time, set the tape running and hide till he called for her.'

Graham was speechless. As the details mounted, he saw that Liz was indeed the only person who could have made all this happen.

'All right. Now I can make clear what this fake kidnapping had to do with stealing the documents.' Kwan pulled something from his pocket and tossed it to Graham with a metallic clink. 'One of their motivations was this.'

Graham recognized it at once as a copy of his safe key.

'Where... where did you get this?'

'While you were enjoying your swim, I copied it through the crudest methods,' smiled Kwan. 'You shouldn't be concerned about this one, but about the one the criminals have.'

Graham looked between the key and Kwan, unable to understand what he was talking about.

'I said that on the face of it, the kidnapping – or the con – failed, but in fact the criminals got what they were really after. They brought about all the conditions they needed to steal the documents.'

Graham looked at Kwan, waiting for an explanation.

'Going to Lok Heung Yuen and waiting for instructions, buying the gold bars, getting to a particular place by a certain time – all of those tasks were designed to blind you to what was really going on. At the pool you were set searching for the coin, apparently to keep you from tampering with the ransom – it kept you from planting the transmitter – but in truth, it was so you'd be away from something you'd never otherwise let out of your sight.'

'My keys.'

'Right. If the kidnapper really just wanted to make sure you hadn't booby-trapped the ransom, he didn't need to make you waste half an hour in the pool. Look, every step before this had been perfectly planned and flawlessly executed. Even the phone calls were right on time. Why would something go wrong with the coin? If it really had been moved by a third party, you wouldn't have found it after half an hour. When I saw from the poolside you were having trouble, I sensed at once that the criminal had some other plan. Add that to my earlier hunch, and I knew they were after your keys.'

'Wait!' Graham interrupted. '"Earlier hunch"? You already knew the kidnapping was fake?'

'I realized when we were sitting in Lok Heung Yuen.'

'That early? What tipped you off?'

'Remember that waiter who didn't speak much English? What he said to you?'

'He... he said there was a call for me.'

'He said your name, but not your real name.'

Graham recalled. 'But so what? Plenty of my colleagues in other departments just look at the transliteration of my name and call me Mr Ha.'

'The kidnapper said at one point he'd thought you were loaded, which means he didn't know much about your background. All the documents at Alfred's school are in English, so your surname would only appear there as Hill, not Ha. So why would the kidnapper have said "Ha" to the waiter, a name he should have no knowledge of? Of course, the waiter could have misheard or changed it into Cantonese himself, but what are the odds he would land on the same unusual transliteration of your name? I reckon the kidnapper must have been speaking in Cantonese and said to call a foreigner to the phone, and when the waiter asked for a name, he said "Mr Ha" automatically. That was when I started thinking the whole thing was a sham. Actually I had my doubts from the start. Abductions normally take place after a lot of preparation. What kind of kidnapper would make a basic mistake like snatching the son of a penniless public servant? But anything is possible in this world, so I had to take the investigation seriously – after all, Alfred's life could have been at risk.'

'But that one sentence made you think the criminal was lying?'

'That was the start of it. The second piece of evidence came with that money belt, and the plan for you to find the instructions in the pool. There was just enough room in the canvas bag for the gold bars, right?'

'Yes, so?'

'Don't you remember how much the kidnapper initially asked for? Half a million dollars – that would have bought a hundred and thirteen five-tael gold bars, which you certainly couldn't have fitted into that bag. More importantly, it would have weighed more than twenty kilos. How would you have carried all that weight on you while diving for a coin? With everything so meticulously planned, this couldn't have been thrown together at the last minute. That means the criminals knew from the start you'd only have three kilos of gold on you, which means they knew exactly what your financial situation was. All the rest was play-acting.'

Graham smacked his forehead. If he'd only managed to stay a little calmer, he wouldn't have fallen into this trap.

'Although I knew this was a bluff, I couldn't tell you; if you'd shown any sign of knowing, it would have scared them off. So in order to find out their true intentions, I decided to keep playing along,' Kwan continued. 'At the pool, by the time you'd spent nearly twenty minutes searching for the coin, the thought popped into my mind that they were after your keys. In order to prove it, I went to back to the changing room and got dressed, went back to the car and got my copying kit, then snuck in through the employees' entrance to wait for my chance.'

Kwan kept a tool chest in the boot of his car that was filled with all kinds of odd items, including fingerprint powder, photographic developer fluid and luminol. Mac, guarding the car, had watched curiously as Kwan hurried over, grabbed something, then headed back to the pool.

'I slipped past while the attendant was on a bathroom break – lucky for me. Otherwise I'd have had to frighten him a bit by flashing my badge. I entered the basket storeroom and found yours. When I looked at the safe key, as I expected, there was metal dust on it. So I took an impression with my pieces of clay, and left before I was caught.'

'Metal dust?'

'Meaning, while you were busy treading water, the criminals had already got their hands on your key and copied it.'

'Oh!'

'I'm guessing at least one of the people in the changing room was an accomplice, probably one step ahead of you in line, so he could remember the number of the next empty basket on the counter – you'd take that one, and he'd know your tag number. He had one ready without a number, so when you'd finished changing, he just had to write your number on his blank tag, wait a while, then go up to the counter and say he needed to grab something. When he'd got your basket, he'd pass your keys to another accomplice, who'd head out and find a locksmith who could make a copy. Then he'd return your keys to the basket and go back to the pool. They didn't have much time, so didn't bother brushing off the metal filings from the copying. They probably reckoned you'd be too upset to notice, anyway.'

'So the coin in the pool – they only planted it when they knew they'd succeeded?'

'Yes, probably.'

'And the gold bars falling out – that was part of the plan.'

'No, I think that really was an accident,' Kwan grinned. 'They'd got this far, they might as well take the ransom too. Someone was probably watching over you, to make sure they didn't manage to take all your savings.'

'Yes, that motorcyclist was unlucky, then.' Graham couldn't help chuckling. 'And he was almost caught!'

'No, I don't think he would have been caught – they'd chosen where the exchange would take place, and thoroughly prepared every detail. My guess is the off-duty policeman who said the kidnapper got in a cab – he was the man on the motorcycle.'

'What?'

'Like I've been saying, the criminals were cops. What kind of person is least likely to be suspected, do you think? Someone from your own tribe, of course. The motorcyclist just had to throw off his helmet and jacket, then tell the officers running up to him that he'd seen the criminal heading off, and they'd believe him. The reason you had to put the gold in a money belt was so he could wear it under his clothes. No one would subject a fellow officer to a pat-down.'

Graham leaned back, both hands on the steering wheel. So he'd almost been cheated of more than a year of savings. A few years ago, what he'd thought was a stable investment had landed him deep in debt; this time, he could have lost everything he owned, but by a miracle had clung to it. He couldn't help thinking God must be fond of practical jokes.

'Well, even if the criminals copied my key, the safe still has a combination lock. The key alone won't open it.'

'I opened it.' Kwan gestured at the documents in the other man's lap.

'You... ah, dammit, you remembered the combination!' Graham laughed.

'Yes, I saw it and memorized it.' Kwan's expression turned stern. 'But, you know, I wasn't the only one.'

Graham looked worriedly at Kwan. He remembered the moment he got the jewels out of the study safe.

He thought of the person who'd been next to him.

'Old Tsui must definitely be one of the bribe-takers.' Kwan frowned. 'I've always suspected someone in my team was involved, but had no way to find out who. Now, with this case, the fox has shown its tail.'

'But... isn't it a bit of a leap to assume he's guilty, just from this?'

'Remember when I offered to personally lend you money? Old Tsui put a stop to that at once. He doesn't really care about police regulations, but he knew that if I made the loan, you wouldn't need to open the safe to get the jewels, and he'd miss an opportunity to see the combination. Also, right from the start, he brought up the possibility of Liz being an accomplice, so when we realized the kidnapping had never taken place, we ruled out the idea of Liz the kidnapper's assistant, and no one thought of the other possibility: Liz, the conman's moll.'

'That's...' Graham couldn't find the right words. He understood how unhappy Kwan must be that one of his own team had turned out to be a criminal.

'Don't worry about me, I can take care of myself.' Kwan's expression relaxed.

'How would the criminals have known about the jewellery?'

'Liz told them, of course. She must have seen your wife wearing it. The details about your household probably all came from Liz. When I told her someone had tried to extort a hundred thousand dollars, the first thing she said was that you didn't have that much money in your bank account. She's tucked away a fair bit of information.'

Graham felt ill. He'd never imagined someone so close to him and his family would be despicable enough to spy on them.

'As for Liz, she may not have thought she was doing anything wrong,' said Kwan. '"It's just information – if I don't tell them, someone else will." "It's just a little favour." "It's just a bit of money in exchange for a small job." Her part wouldn't have seemed like a big deal. That's the general attitude of society now – that's why the governor had to set up your commission.'

'How did Liz know I was bringing documents about the corruption case home?'

'She probably didn't, but from what she said, and what the criminals already knew, it can't have been hard to work out. It's no secret that you're at the ICAC, nor what cases each team is dealing with. With your temperament, you'd be very likely to bring work home to deal with, and if Liz told the criminals, "When my boss gets home, he locks himself in the study to work," they'd probably guess you had important documents at home.'

'But there's something I don't understand. If all they wanted was the key, why all that effort? With Liz on the inside, couldn't she just have stolen it?'

'She tried, but failed.'

'How do you know?'

'You told me.'

'I did?'

'You said about two weeks ago, Liz slipped into your bedroom while you were having a shower. She must have done so at the criminals' urging, to take the key. I don't know whether her instruction was to make off with it, or if she had a piece of clay to take an impression, like I did, but even if she'd succeeded, there'd still have been the combination to deal with. Speaking of which, do you still have the habit of changing that regularly?'

'Yes, twice a month.'

'Right, that'd be a headache for the criminals. So they'd have to come up with a method that killed two birds with one stone. And if they could get your savings as well, that'd be three birds.'

'Kwan, if that's the case, you ought to have told me right away.' Graham picked up the documents and waved them in front of Kwan's face. 'If you'd said someone wanted to steal these papers, I'd have moved them elsewhere, or changed the combination right away.'

'When did I say the criminals wanted to steal the documents?'

'You did! Just now!'

'They didn't want to steal the documents, just the information they contained. And what's more, they don't want you to know that they've got that info.'

Graham tilted his head to one side and stared at Kwan, looking lost.

'If you discovered the documents were missing, that'd only alarm the ICAC. The criminals would rather avoid that – far better that they operate in darkness. If they wanted to turn the tables, it was better you didn't know how many chips they had left. When you and your family went to the movies and the amusement park at the weekend, did Liz come with you?'

'Hmm, no... she said she'd let us spend some time together as a family.'

'So yesterday or the day before, she received the copied key and combination from the criminals, and opened your safe. She was probably told to take photos of the documents.'

'But when she discovered the documents were missing...'

'Have a careful look at what's in your hand.'

Once again, Graham removed the papers from his envelope and flipped through them.

'Hey, there are eight pages missing.'

'I left those eight pages in the safe,' smiled Kwan. 'If the criminals wanted intelligence, I thought I'd give it to them. I like placing my gambling chips out in the open. Except the criminals only see what's in my hands and think that's all of it, when actually the chair I'm sitting on has dozens of chips underneath.'

'You... you deliberately misled the criminals?'

'Liz will only have found eight pages in the safe. They'll assume the drug pushers didn't give up everything, only a small portion of their data in exchange for a lighter sentence. They'll let their guard down towards the commission. And they'll stop trying to dig up more about you, engineering a second or third fake kidnapping, a fake murder or the like.'

Graham finally understood why Kwan had taken the documents. He wanted to set the stage for the ICAC to nab as many corrupt cops as possible.

'Kwan, did you ever imagine they might have kidnapped Alfred for real? I mean, because I'm an ICAC investigator and they wanted to teach me a lesson, stealing the documents and kidnapping Alfred too. I guess there was no way of knowing whether Alfred was truly safe or not.'

'No, once I was sure their target was to copy your safe key,

I relaxed, because a copied key meant someone would steal the documents later. They wouldn't have wanted to alert you, which meant they had to have an insider. If Alfred had really been kidnapped, it would have been on Liz's watch, and even if he came back unharmed, you'd probably still have fired her. Why make the situation that complicated? Kidnapping Alfred for real would have been difficult and pointless.'

Once again, Graham was in awe of Kwan's intellect. He'd known Kwan Chun-dok was a smart investigator, but how he'd grown in just a few years. His deductive and strategic skills were impeccable, as was his ability to zero in on particular details. He felt embarrassed now to recall how he'd once tried to play the mentor to Kwan and teach him investigation skills. That was seven years ago, when Kwan was just twenty-three and had been assigned to Graham's team during his London training. Naturally, when Graham had phoned asking for help, they'd agreed it would be best not to acknowledge they knew each other in front of the other officers.

'Thinking about it, I've been in Hong Kong three years, and still haven't taken you out for dinner,' he now laughed.

'Ah, but you're at ICAC, and I'm in CID. If people saw us together, there'd be gossip. While the police and commission are at odds, I don't think we'll have much chance to meet.' Despite their old acquaintance, Kwan knew he'd have to maintain a certain distance from Graham Hill – that would make everyone's job easier. On Friday, when he'd received the phone call, he knew Graham wouldn't have got in touch unless he were in serious difficulties. Kwan had figured it was likely the criminals would have insiders within the CID, and if Graham had just called the general police number, a team would be assigned to the case who would likely cover up Old Tsui's part. Even if Old Tsui were exposed, the rest would still be hiding within the force. It would take Graham and his colleagues to root them all out at once.

'Kwan, it's a bit rude to ask, but why did you help me? Shouldn't the police be on the side of the police?' asked Graham thoughtfully.

'I agree officers ought to support each other against common enemies, but only if everyone shares the aim of upholding justice. Blindly supporting another person just because he wears the same uniform is foolish. Police corruption is an epidemic and we can no longer solve it ourselves – we need outside help. I've always hated that cowardly idea of "running alongside the car" – yes, standing in front of the car will get you killed, so I'd rather sabotage the car and let it fall apart.'

'Do you think we – I mean the commission – will succeed?'

'I don't know. If there are too many officers involved, the governor might be forced to face reality and issue an amnesty. But if things get that far, I'd still want the bad apples exposed and brought to trial, found guilty in the eyes of the law and sentenced. And those who've covered up guilt for the sake of personal gain – I want them to know that if they don't reform, that's the downfall awaiting them.'

Kwan Chun-dok looked out at the deep blue ocean, as if he could see the future of the police force. He was worried, but at the same time carried a thread of hope. Graham Hill, sitting next to him, was sharing these thoughts. They might notionally be on different sides, but their ideas were pointing in the same direction.

'I won't ask whether you're planning to fire Liz – that's your decision,' said Kwan, getting out of the car. 'But be sure to ask for a new safe as soon as you can.'

'Wouldn't you like a lift into town?'

'No, it's better if no one sees us together. I'll take the bus.'

'Kwan, you've been a great help to me today. I'm truly grateful – I owe you so much. If there's anything I can ever do for you, just say the word. Anything at all.'

'Heh, now you mention it, you do owe me dinner – though that'll be tricky in the next year or two.' Kwan smiled through the car window. 'I had to run around all over Kowloon to get you that stack of prospectuses. My fiancée must have thought I had a bastard child somewhere, ready to start school...'

VI

BORROWED TIME:

1967

1

I DON'T KNOW how Hong Kong ended up like this.

Four months ago, I had no idea that our city would wind up in this state.

Standing on the border of madness and reason.

And the border's growing blurry. We can no longer tell what's sane or crazy, what's just or evil, what's right or wrong.

Perhaps all we can ask for is to be safe – continued existence as the only purpose in life.

Laughable.

Perhaps I'm thinking too much about this. I'm a young guy of less than twenty, after all, and can't really get worked up about these deep theories. They're beyond my ken.

Every time I bring up the state of the world with Elder Brother, he laughs and says, 'You don't even have a job, what do you know about these big ideas?'

He has a point.

Elder Brother is three years older than me. We're not related by blood, but we've known each other many years, and now we live in the same boarding house – so we're related by difficulty, so to speak. Like Patrick Tse and Bowie Wu in *My Intimate Partner*, that film from a few years back, two poor devils struggling to earn a living. Of course, we're not quite as badly off as them, cheating and stealing to feed themselves, but while we just about have a place to stay, and stave off hunger pangs with tea and plain rice, we haven't managed to save a cent.

My parents died early and I had to find a job before even finishing high school. I've been doing odd jobs for some years now, but ever since the 'disturbance' erupted this May, it's been hard to find anything. With all the unions agitating for strikes and protests, even ordinary factory work seems impossible to come by. So for now I'm helping my landlord take care of his store, and now and then running errands for extra cash.

My landlord's name is Ho Hei. He's somewhere between fifty and sixty, and runs a store with his wife on Spring Garden Lane in Wan Chai – it's named Ho Hei Kee, after himself, with the standard business-name suffix. I can't remember what Mrs Ho is called. To be honest, I only remember Mr Ho's full name because it's right there in big letters on that sign I see every day. I just call them Mr and Mrs Ho, or sometimes 'Landlord-Father' and 'Landlady-Mother'. Ho Hei Kee is on the ground floor of a four-storey building. The Hos live on the first floor, and after their children moved out some years ago, turned the rest of that property into a rooming house, for single young people like us. It's freezing in winter and boiling in summer, full of mosquitoes and other insects, and there's a big rush for the shared bathroom and kitchen in the morning, but the rent is so cheap I can't complain. I have it a lot better than many others. Mr and Mrs Ho are good people – they've never gone after anyone for owing rent, and on holidays they'll share a meal with us. You'd never guess from the way they look, but I believe Mr Ho must have quite a bit saved up, and doesn't need to worry about money. They only seem to keep the shop open out of habit, and don't care if it makes a profit or loss.

Mr Ho often says that young people ought to be ambitious, rather than settling for a lifetime of odd jobs or shop work. I know that very well, and Elder Brother is always urging me to better myself in my spare time, flip through the dictionary to improve my English, so that when the time comes I can achieve something great. Sometimes, when sailors from the US Navy come to the shop to buy soda or beer, I try speaking to them in English, although I have no idea whether they understand what I'm saying.

I look through the newspaper ads every day, hoping to find a suitable job. There's another way out – I could always apply to the police force. Although there's that saying 'Good men don't become cops', I think it's actually a cool idea – fighting for justice, putting fear into the hearts of bad guys, a stable income, separate quarters once you get married. Some people say the police just get ordered around by their British superiors, but if I were a clerk in Central, my boss would just as likely be white. All that talk about 'the racial spirit' – that's so much hot air, in this society. The thing is, Elder Brother's always been against me joining the force. He says police lives are cheap, and the government pays for Chinese officers to serve as cannon fodder, protecting the British elite. If the colonial government ran into trouble, the Chinese would wind up as collateral damage.

I'd never have guessed how right Elder Brother was.

Thinking back, this whole affair began over a tiny incident. In April, there was a dispute at a factory in San Po Kong in Kowloon – the management had imposed some strict new conditions, no time off, that sort of thing, which the workers objected to. When they couldn't come to an agreement, the boss found some excuse to fire the union representatives, which touched off a demonstration. Some workers' associations began blocking production until the police had to be brought in. The demonstration became an uprising, with workers hurling stones and glass bottles at the police, who responded with wooden bullets. The authorities imposed a curfew on East Kowloon, and several of the larger unions joined in the fight, taking advantage of revolutionary fervour on the Mainland to make a stand against the colonial government. What started out as a labour dispute became a political struggle.

And now the situation's out of control.

Within a month, the row had escalated to a national quarrel

between China and Britain. Leftist workers, with support from Beijing, set up the Hong Kong and Kowloon Anti-Hong Kong British Persecution Struggle Committee – the Anti-British Struggle Committee for short. Crowds surrounded the governor's mansion, accusing the colonial government of being fascist oppressors. The government wouldn't give an inch, and police officers were dispatched to put down the unrest, dispersing the crowds with tear gas and forcibly arresting 'troublemakers'. More workers went on strike, shops closed, schools shut down, and quite a few citizens supported this, while the government hit back with more curfews – the most seen on Hong Kong Island since the Second World War, two decades ago.

At the start of July, a group of Mainlanders crossed the border at Chung Ying Street, entering Hong Kong territory in order to 'assist' the workers and take part in the protests. The Hong Kong border guards opened fire on them, and militiamen from China retaliated. The Hong Kong side were trapped when they ran out of ammo, and by the time the British had dispatched troops to help, five officers were dead.

'Does the Mainland want to take Hong Kong back early?' I remember Mr Ho saying that day, as we listened to the news on the store radio. God knew if Chairman Mao planned to send the People's Army in to chase away the British ahead of time. After all, 1967 is just 1997 with one digit flipped over.

In the days after the gunfight, people said the British were preparing to retreat and leave Hong Kong to its fate. If China really did go to war with the UK, they'd want to evacuate, and the police would have to make sure they were able to get away, no matter the damage to themselves. Even though Elder Brother didn't bring up my wanting to join the force, I knew he must have been thinking, 'I told you so.'

We're now two months on from those events, and there haven't been any further clashes, but from time to time, people still talk about 'the Communist Party liberating Hong Kong'. On 22 July, the colonial government declared a state of emergency, not only forbidding the possession of firearms and ammo, it became illegal even to be in the same place as a restricted item, or to travel with an armed companion. Inflammatory leaflets and anti-government posters were outlawed, and gatherings of more than three people were declared to be illegal assemblies. They couldn't stop the major newspapers, which received direct support from Beijing, but several smaller leftist papers were shut down. They talked about the 'spirit of the law' and 'freedom of the press', but that was just bull.

Still, it takes two hands to clap, and it can't be denied that the leftist workers went too far in their 'anti-British struggle'.

The leftists had already used blast-fishing bombs and acid in their attacks on the police, but since British troops sent helicopters to assist a police raid on the Struggle Committee's headquarters, they've started using more powerful explosives. In the last month or so, the streets have been full of real and fake bombs – the Honkongers call them 'pineapples' – the idea being to run the police ragged. All of them look perfectly innocuous, just a metal or cardboard box; some contain a mixture of metal shrapnel and soil, while others are actually deadly explosives. These haven't just appeared outside government offices, but also at tram stops, on buses and in non-leftist schools – every place touched by the surging wave of unrest.

Just walking down the street could get you blown to death these days. I had some sympathy for the workers to start with, but at this point I can't condone them. The leftists say this is 'to meet violence with violence' and 'a necessary evil', insisting that a little sacrifice is worth it to defeat the British.

I really can't understand what's 'worth it' about hurting the people you ought to defend.

We're people, not ants.

In an atmosphere of panic, we can only pray to be spared.

I'm particularly worried for Elder Brother, because of his work. He's a broker, introducing people who might want to do business together, earning a bit of commission. He has no basic salary and when his luck is bad, we have to rely on my pittance to feed ourselves. But when he does seal a deal, he'll take me out to a tea house – not the cheaper lower floors either, but all the way upstairs. What extravagance. He runs around Kowloon all day finding clients, so he's much more likely than I am to get caught up in some street clash or bombing. I always tell him to be careful, and he answers, 'If you're fated to die at three o'clock, then no matter what, you won't live to see five. If I was scared of death, I couldn't earn any money, and then we'd both starve. Since I'm going to die anyway, what's there to be afraid of? You have to take some risks to get rich in this world!'

I might not be like Elder Brother, criss-crossing Hong Kong Island and Kowloon, but when I leave the shop on a delivery or collection for Mr Ho, I'm always on the lookout for danger. Every minute I'm on the street, I'm aware of any suspicious people or objects around me. The leftists often paste up anti-government slogans looking like Chinese New Year couplets where they plant their bombs. 'Roast the white-skinned pigs' on one side, 'Fry the yellow-skinned dogs' on the other, and across the top: 'Comrades keep clear', but on white paper. 'White-skinned pigs' means the British, while the 'yellow-skinned dogs' are the Chinese police 'helping the tiger to devour others'. I guess they think Chinese people who willingly serve the British are no different from collaborators during the Japanese occupation – all traitors who've betrayed the sovereignty of the people.

More than once, I've seen the police treat civilians with an iron hand. The Chinese officers seem even angrier than the British ones. Their hatred for the leftists seems even more evident.

This is a time of extremes. Most people know to be careful and stay out of trouble. If questioned by the police, whatever happens, don't argue or you'll be in their sights, meaning you'll probably end up in prison. Before the May violence policemen already had privilege. For instance, if some of Mr Ho's goods occupied a tiny bit of the sidewalk, a policeman could give him a ticket, unless Mr Ho gave a little 'tea money' to the cop, in which case the issue could be settled privately. But now the police are out of control, at liberty to arrest 'suspicious elements' for 'obstructing a police officer in his duties', 'resisting arrest', 'taking part in unrest', 'unlawful assembly' – all of which rely solely on the police officer's word to establish guilt.

I never thought that kangaroo-court justice would show up in Hong Kong today.

On our street in Wan Chai, Spring Garden Lane, I often bump into a couple of beat cops – their badge numbers are 6663 and 4447, and I've secretly nicknamed them 'Cop 3' and 'Cop 7'. Cop 3 seems older. Last month, I saw someone handing out anti-government leaflets who had the bad luck to be arrested by those two. Cop 3 gave him no chance to explain – his left hand on the man's shoulder, he beat him with his police truncheon till the poor guy bled from the head. I saw it clearly; the man wasn't resisting at all. But no one present would have dared testify against the cop – if you spoke up, you'd be branded a collaborator, and then you'd be in trouble too.

Cop 7 didn't step in to stop his colleague, but I know he's more honest than Cop 3. They often stop to buy a soda at Mr Ho's shop while out on patrol, and Cop 3 never takes out his wallet – Mr Ho says not to bother over such a trifle – but Cop 7 always insists on paying. I once told him the boss said he didn't have to, and he answered, 'If I didn't pay up, the boss would earn less, and if you lost your job because of that and fell into crime, I'd have even more work to do.'

He sounded like Elder Brother.

Everyone in the neighbourhood thinks Cop 7 is a good guy, only he can be a bit too by-the-book, following orders scrupulously. When I see Cop 7, I feel that being a policeman might not be a bad job. Or so I thought, before all this unrest kicked off. The way things are right now, it would be dumb to join the force. The 'yellow-skinned dogs' have made themselves into targets. I keep expecting to see Cop 3 and Cop 7 being paraded down the street, with wooden placards around their necks listing their crimes.

After this latest round of violence, I've heard that police recruitment has fallen. Some Chinese officers have quit because they were persuaded by the leftists not to stand alongside the 'fascist' British. Others are afraid of being killed, or caught up in some incident like the Chung Ying Street gunfight. Mr Ho's lived in Wan Chai for a long time and knows some of the local officers quite well. They've told him that all leave has been cancelled for months, and they have to be on alert twenty-four hours a day – and apart from their main jobs, they also do overtime on the riot squad. The government has given each officer a three per cent raise and increased overtime pay, even providing free meals. Mr Ho said the sergeant in charge of disbursing salaries often has thick stacks of banknotes in his briefcase for these handouts.

The government is enticing policemen to stay with cash. Actually, what the leftists are doing is not much different.

When workers go on strike, they lose their income, and if they can't feed themselves, what kind of 'struggle' can they take part in? So the union leaders support them, giving them one or two hundred Hong Kong dollars per month. I don't know how they come up with the money. Some people say the Chinese government is supplying them with cash 'for the revolution'. All I know is, this conflict isn't simply about ideology. Money is very much involved as well. Perhaps that's just reality.

I heard from the horse's mouth about payments to striking workers – our neighbours in the boarding house just happen to be a pair of leftists. Mr Ho lets out three rooms – one is occupied by me and Elder Brother, one by a journalist called Toh Sze-keung, and the third one by Sum Chung, a textile worker. At the end of May, Mr Sum responded to his union's call to strike, and was swiftly fired. I asked how he was managing to keep up with his rent, and he told me 'union leaders' were paying him a wage, and there was also more money on offer if he took on special projects. He advised me to join their ranks, working together to overturn British colonialism – this was a rare opportunity, and if the revolution succeeded, comrades like us with 'pure thought' would become tomorrow's leaders. I didn't turn him down in so many words, just said I had to talk it over with Elder Brother before making a decision. I suspect if I'd said no right away, he might have labelled me an 'anti-revolutionary element' – and I didn't want to think about what the consequences of that might be.

In contrast to the ideological certainty of Mr Sum, Toh Sze-keung was driven by desperation. He used to work at a newspaper as chief financial correspondent, but the government decreed that the paper was leftist and shut it down, leaving him out of a job. The only choice left to him was to join the struggle, partly because the stipend from the union would solve his pressing money problems, partly because if the movement were successful and the newspaper reopened, he'd be employed again. He told me all this with a frown on his face, and I don't think even he believed the government would relent and allow the newspaper to publish again.

That's the paradox of my life. Every day, I worry that Elder Brother and I will be blown up by bombs, that public order is deteriorating, that the government will fall, that society is paralysed, that the city will collapse into war – and yet, day after day, I pretend nothing's wrong. I take care of my landlord's store, wish my neighbours good morning even though they represent the 'opposition', and sell soft drinks to the 'fascist' police officers. Radio broadcasters scold the leftists for bringing misfortune to our city and destroying the peace, while the newspapers sympathetic to China criticize the British and Hong Kong uniformed forces for their 'insane persecution' of patriotic organizations. Both sides proclaim they're standing up for justice, while we citizens are helpless, crushed between power and violence.

Before 17 August, I thought I would continue with this helpless life until the fighting stopped or the British left.

I didn't expect to overhear one sentence that would pull me out of the middle ground and into the turmoil, right in the crosshairs of danger.

2

'THE PINEAPPLE WON'T blow up while we're delivering it, will it?'

I heard this sentence while still half asleep. At first, I thought it might have been a dream, but as my brain cleared, I knew it was real.

The voice had come from the other side of the wall.

That morning, Mr Ho's new refrigerator had arrived at the store. We scrambled to fill it with soda and beer from the old unit, then hoisted that one onto a cart and pushed it five blocks to the second-hand shop. When I came back with the money, Mr Ho said he could take care of the shop on his own that afternoon. I'd been running about all morning in the hot sun and must be tired, so why didn't I go and have a rest? It's rare for him to be so considerate, so I decided to take him up on it, and after lunch I went up to my room for a nap.

Then I was woken by those words.

I glanced at my alarm clock. It was ten minutes past two – I'd been asleep for an hour. It must have been Sum Chung who had spoken – his high-pitched voice was easily recognized. But the cubicle next to ours was the unemployed journalist's. Why was Sum Chung in Mr Toh's room?

'Mr Sum, please don't speak so loudly. What if someone hears you?' This had to be Toh Sze-keung.

'Old Ho's wife went out earlier, Old Ho and the two guys next door are at work. No one will hear,' said Sum.

'Anyway, so what if someone overhears? We're the proud sons of China, and we carry ourselves with a lofty revolutionary spirit. We're not afraid of spilling our hot blood. Even if we fail, the imperialist oppressor will one day bow before the noble socialism of our motherland.' All of this was in a very loud voice, and it was easy to imagine the speaker's expression of righteous zeal. This must be Sum Chung's 'comrade', a youth named Chang Tin-san. Mr Sum had once introduced him to me as one of the laid-off workers from the textile factory.

'Ah Chang, don't talk like that. The colonials are crafty, and we have to be cautious around them. Don't give the enemy an opening.' A voice I'd never heard before.

'Master Chow's right, we can't afford to fail,' said Sum Chung. I didn't know who this Master Chow was, though from the way Sum addressed him, I guessed he was the leader of the group.

'So anyway, Ah Toh and Ah Sum will set off from North Point, and I'll wait here,' said Master Chow. 'When we're assembled, we'll start as planned, and afterwards disperse immediately from Jordan Road Ferry Pier.'

'But what exactly is the plan for the operation?' Sum Chung's voice.

'You and Ah Toh create a diversion, and I'll strike.'

'Master Chow, it's easy for you to say "create a diversion", but we have no idea what that means.'

'Play it by ear when the time comes. I don't know what the situation will be. But I only need thirty seconds – that shouldn't be too difficult.'

'But can it really be so simple? Number One won't be easy to deal with...'

'Ah Toh, relax, I've confirmed this several times – the target is more vulnerable than we imagined. The white-skinned pig won't be expecting this move, so when the pineapple goes off, he'll be left open-mouthed, staggered by the intelligence of the Chinese.

That'll send a shockwave through the British Empire.'

In this moment, I suddenly realized I was listening to something horrific. The four men in the next room were planning a bomb attack. I broke into a cold sweat, shivering despite the heat of the day, and didn't dare move a muscle, lest the old bed creak. I even made my breathing more shallow. If they knew I'd overheard their plans, I thought they might kill me to keep me quiet, in the name of the People.

'As for the other side of it, we'll have to look to Ah Chang,' said Sum Chung, sounding quieter now – probably he'd been standing by the wall, and had moved away.

'Chairman Mao says, "Be determined, don't fear sacrifice, overcome ten thousand difficulties, and achieve victory." I hold these words in my heart at all times. I'll carry out the mission and strike a painful blow against the enemy. I'll defend the Mao Zedong Thought and continue the struggle.'

'Ah Chang, you can relax. After the incident, the Leader won't forget you.'

'Rewards are just like drifting clouds to me. Even if the fascists try to take my life, I'll fight to the end.'

'Well said. Ah Chang is an example to us all of true patriotism.'

'But...' This was Toh Sze-keung's voice. 'Is it really right, what we're doing? A bomb? We could hurt an innocent civilian...'

'Ah Toh, you're wrong,' said Sum Chung. 'Imperialism has bullied and humiliated us. It's left us with no choice but to fight back.'

'Yes, it's improper not to "reciprocate",' said Master Chow. 'The white-skinned pigs shoot our comrades dead, frame innocent people for violent assault, and stop at nothing to destroy us. A pineapple isn't one-tenth as barbaric as what these fascists are doing. Our aim is not to injure people, but to paralyse the Hong Kong and British uniformed forces with intelligent guerrilla warfare. If we wanted to hurt civilians, why would we write "Comrades keep clear" beside each bomb?'

'"Revolution is not a dinner party", "Death is a common

occurrence" – Ah Toh, have you forgotten the primary directives of our leaders?' This was the loud-voiced Chang Tin-san. 'If we have to sacrifice a few common people to secure the fall of the British Empire, then how justified their deaths will be! Their blood and sweat will bring victory to our motherland. They'll be martyrs for their comrades and country.'

'Yeah. Think about Choi Nam, killed by the white-skinned pigs, or Tsui Tin-por, beaten to death in a police station. If we don't rise up, the next dead body could be yours or mine,' said Sum Chung.

'But...'

'No more buts. Ah Toh, you've seen for yourself how they shut your newspaper down. Those unscrupulous yellow-skinned dogs burst in, beat up your colleagues and labelled you as dissidents. Don't you have even a spark of rage about that? Don't you want to teach them a lesson?'

'You have a point.'

The three of them kept going back and forth until the weight of their words crushed Toh Sze-keung's objections.

'Remember, the first wave is the day after tomorrow,' said Master Chow. 'When the first blast sounds, it'll shake the hearts of the colonials. Then the second wave the day after that, and the third wave the next, and we'll be able to demand the British surrender. The Portuguese have already given up. Can the end of British Hong Kong be far behind?'

In December last year, there was a clash between the police and citizens in Macau. The Portuguese government had imposed martial law, and the police shot dead many Chinese residents. The Guangdong provincial government objected, and after many rounds of negotiation, Portugal had to apologize and pay compensation. This strengthened the resolve of the leftists. If the Macau Chinese could successfully oppose the Portuguese, surely the days of the British in Hong Kong must be numbered?

'Ah Sum, Ah Toh, after we leave here today, don't try to get in touch with me. I'll see you the day after tomorrow, when the operation commences,' Master Chow said. 'If there's a need, we'll use this room as our base. My apartment is already being watched by the yellow-skinned dogs – it's not safe.'

'You live nearby anyway, Master Chow, so we can look after each other easily,' laughed Sum Chung. 'As long as those yellow-skinned dogs didn't follow you here.'

'Ha! How careless do you think I am?' chuckled Chow. 'Worry about yourself – make sure *you* don't catch their eye before the operation.'

'Some day I'll send them running with their tails between their legs, and then turn them into dog-meat hotpot,' growled Chang Tin-san.

'So everyone knows what they're doing? Here's some cash – a bonus for your special duties. Eat well these next couple of days, drink some beer to build up your courage. Ah Chang, we're counting on you.'

'Aren't you coming for dinner with us, Master Chow?'

'No, I might get you into trouble if we're seen together. I'll go now. You should wait a while before leaving.'

'All right. See you in two days.' Sum Chung's voice again, then a door closing. I slipped out of bed and pressed an ear to my own door, listening to the other three saying goodbye to Master Chow. Our cubicles had ventilation panels in the walls separating them from the communal area, and there were frosted glass panels in the doors, so I had to squat low – otherwise they might have seen a figure moving about inside. They didn't return to Mr Toh's room, but stayed outside, idly chatting about which nearby tea house had the cheapest yet tastiest food. It was half an hour before they finally left, and I sighed in relief.

Cautiously I opened my door and stuck my head out, and after making sure I was the only one there, rushed to the bathroom. I'd been on the brink of relieving myself into a bottle.

Back in my room, I thought back over the conversation I'd overheard. If Mr Toh or Mr Sum were to come back now, I could easily pretend I'd only just arrived home, and they probably wouldn't be suspicious. But how should I deal with this secret?

Master Chow sounded like he was in his forties or fifties – perhaps a cadre from one of the unions. Toh, Sum and Chang were all in their twenties, passionate and hot-blooded. Their rage at the present situation had no other outlet, and it just happened that the leftists desperately needed manpower. Maybe their thinking was correct, and their starting point was purely to fight against injustice in society, but bringing bombs into it was crazy. Master Chow's words resonated, but the way I saw it, Sum Chung and the rest were exactly the same as the 'yellow-skinned dogs' they talked about, just cannon fodder.

This is how power works. The ones at the top make use of ideals, beliefs and money to entice those below them to give up their lives. People want to find some lofty reason for existence, or else to lead a quiet life. You'd need to give them a big incentive for them to willingly enslave themselves. If I'd said anything like this to Mr Sum, he'd scold me for having been contaminated by fascism , because the noble Party and motherland wouldn't treat their patriotic comrades unfairly – though I can guarantee these little people will be forgotten. This is an eternal truth – when all the rabbits are caught, the hunting dog will be eaten; when all the birds are shot, the bow is put away. If the British stay put, then all those jailed by them will be lauded as 'unyielding warriors' for a while, but in the long term, will they be looked after? I doubt it. The more of these bit-part players there are, the less important they seem. Do you think setting off one bomb means you've accomplished some great task? There are hundreds or thousands of sacrificial victims just like you, not to mention the collateral damage of innocent victims.

In reality, power and money will always be concentrated in a very few hands.

That night, when I saw Toh Sze-keung and Sum Chung, Mr Sum seemed exactly the same as always – as soon as he saw me, he started encouraging me to join his union. Mr Toh seemed much more guarded than normal, though. Mr and Mrs Ho didn't notice anything, and I didn't say anything to Elder Brother, for fear he'd let something slip to Toh or Sum. I slept badly that night – whenever I remembered their 'operation', worry flooded my mind.

The following day, I pretended everything was normal as I went to work at the store. Business was slow as the streets were still pretty empty. Mr Ho sat behind the counter reading a newspaper, while I stayed by the door, fanning myself and listening to the radio. The broadcaster was once again cursing 'leftist kids' for disrupting the order of society – he called them 'shameless, low-down bastards', adopting a sardonic tone and mocking them and their abilities. I laughed this off, but it would have been biting for the leftists.

Around eleven o'clock, a man came by. He seemed somehow familiar, then after a moment I realized he was one of the plotters I'd overheard – Mr Sum's friend Chang Tin-san.

'A bottle of Coke.' He put down forty cents.

I took the money and got his drink from the new refrigerator, then sat back down. Mr Ho had stepped out, so I was alone in the store. Picking up the newspaper he'd been reading, I kept a corner of my eye on Mr Chang, wondering if he was here looking for Sum Chung. He stood in the store for some time, left hand in his trouser pocket, leaning against the icebox as he drank his soda. He kept looking towards the street corner, trying to seem casual. *Please just finish your drink and get out of here!* I thought. I knew Cop 3 and Cop 7 would be showing up on their rounds any moment, and God knew if this guy would try to start something with them.

Even before I could finish my thought, the two policemen appeared. Just like always, they walked side by side, passing by the bakery, pharmacy and tailor before reaching the store.

'A Coke and a Super Cola, please,' said Cop 7. As usual, he put down thirty cents to pay for his share, the locally produced Super Cola being ten cents cheaper than Coke.

I got the two sodas from the fridge and handed them over.

They kept chatting as they drank, blissfully unaware that they were standing right next to a bomber, drinking the same beverage, while I shook with fear.

'This is the eleven o'clock news,' came the melodious voice on the radio. 'A bomb has been discovered at Causeway Bay Magistracy. Police have sealed off that stretch of Electric Road to both traffic and pedestrians. At ten fifteen this morning, employees discovered a suspicious object at the entrance to their office, and called police. Investigations are ongoing, and it is still unknown whether this device was real or not.'

I noticed one corner of Mr Chang's mouth curving upward – could he be the one who'd planted it?

Next item. 'The British Royal Air Force Vice Chief of Air Staff, Air Marshal Sir Peter Fletcher, arrived in Hong Kong this morning for a five-day visit. Air Marshal Fletcher is meeting the Governor of Hong Kong this afternoon, and tomorrow will visit the Royal Air Base to personally thank the British troops stationed here, as well as to attend a banquet jointly organized by the British Overseas Forces and police. Air Marshal Fletcher has said he agrees with Far East Commander-in-Chief General Michael Carver, who said on a previous visit that the Hong Kong people are the first line in the defence of peace in this territory, while the police are the second line, and British troops the third. British soldiers will only assist the government when necessary—'

'What bullcrap! Lying white-skinned pig!'

My skin prickled. I looked up at Mr Chang uncertainly, to see his face full of contempt as he sipped his half-empty cola.

'Hey, what did you say?' barked Cop 3.

'Did I say something wrong?' Chang Tin-san didn't even turn round.

'I heard you say "white-skinned pig".'

'Oh, you looked quite dark to me – don't tell me you're a white-skinned pig too?' Not only was Mr Chang not backing down, he was answering back. This meant trouble.

'Put down that bottle and stand against the wall!'

'What law have I broken? What right do you have?'

'You seem to have too much free time, and I suspect you're concealing a weapon or leftist propaganda, so I'm going to search you.'

'So you hear someone say "white-skinned pig" and you're going to make a big thing out of it. Just like a yellow-skinned dog,' sneered Mr Chang.

'You're dead meat, leftist boy. You dare to repeat that?'

'Yellow. Skinned. Dog.'

Then everything started happening at once. Cop 3 pulled out his truncheon and smashed Mr Chang in the face. The Coke bottle flew from his hand and shattered on the ground, while he tumbled to the side. Cop 3 struck a second blow as he fell, right in the middle of his chest.

'Aah—' As Mr Chang lost his balance, he pulled his left hand out of his pocket, as if trying to grab Cop 3's collar. My attention was caught by something else, though – a scrap of paper fell from his trouser pocket and landed in front of me. I instinctively picked it up and glanced at what was written on it, then, realizing I shouldn't interfere, handed it over.

It was Cop 7 who took the note – fortunately. Cop 3 would probably have insisted I must be a confederate of Mr Chang, and hauled me off to the station too.

Cop 7 looked at the paper and furrowed his brow, then whispered something to Cop 3, who was still beating up Mr Chang, and held the paper before his eyes. Cop 3's expression changed immediately.

'Where's the phone?' Cop 3 said urgently. I pointed at the one on the wall.

Cop 3 put the bleeding Chang Tin-san in handcuffs and ordered Cop 7 to keep watch over him, then dialled a number. He only spoke a few words before hanging up, and minutes later, a van pulled up with several officers in it. They slung Mr Chang into the vehicle, then climbed in and drove away.

During the whole incident, neighbouring shopkeepers and

assistants had stuck their heads out to watch. I thought this wasn't curiosity but fear – they wanted to know if they should run away. After the police van departed, peace resumed. I swept and mopped where the bottle had broken and went back to taking care of the shop.

When Mr Ho returned, I gave him a brief report, saying the police had arrested a man who said the wrong thing. Mr Ho sighed, 'At a time like this it's best to be careful of your words. Trouble only arrives when you show your strength – you'll live a long life if you just keep quiet.'

Is that really true? Keep quiet to live a long life?

Should we never say anything, and just suffer in silence?

I knew too much.

I had only glanced at Mr Chang's note, but its contents were burned in my mind. Turns out having a good memory isn't always an advantage.

The paper just had a few lines on it:

18 Aug

| X. | 10.00 a.m. | Causeway Bay Magistracy (real) |

19 Aug

1.	10.30 a.m.	Tsim Sha Tsui Police Quarters (fake)
2.	1.40 p.m.	Central Magistracy (fake)
3.	4.00 p.m.	Murray House (real)
4.	5.00 p.m.	Sha Tin Train Station (real)

The afternoon news continued to report on the incident at the Causeway Bay Magistracy. The British sent a bomb disposal expert to carry out a controlled explosion, confirming that it was a genuine 'pineapple' and could have caused serious harm.

Just as Mr Chang's note promised.

Everything matched – the date, time and place, and that it was 'real'. The X wasn't clear at first, but I thought it probably showed the task was complete and crossed off. That meant tomorrow, bombs, some real and some fake, would be planted at the police dormitory in Tsim Sha Tsui, the magistracy on Arbuthnot Road in Central, Sha Tin railway station and Murray House in Central, one of the government's main offices.

Even if the Causeway Bay bomb wasn't the work of Mr Chang, the note incriminated him. In the current state of emergency, just the words 'Causeway Bay Magistracy' would have been enough for the police to take him away for questioning. Even if Cops 3 and 7 hadn't got the reports from Causeway Bay because they were on patrol, they'd surely have heard the radio news.

Cops 3 and 7 had got all worked up over those last four lines. Knowing the targets in advance, the police would just have to spread a net and wait for the rabbits to fall into it.

But I felt something was wrong.

Those four targets all made sense – they were exactly the sorts of places the leftist groups were attacking. Police quarters were home to 'yellow-skinned dogs', Central Magistracy was shamelessly carrying out unjust interrogations, and Murray House was where the 'white-skinned pigs' worked. Sha Tin station wasn't a government building, but the leftists also believed in creating as much chaos as possible, and a bomb in a crowded station would certainly achieve that, striking at people's trust in the colonial government.

But there was one thing that niggled at me. The day before, I'd heard Master Chow and Sum Chung say, 'We'll disperse immediately from Jordan Road Ferry Pier.'

So why wasn't the pier on that list?

3

On Saturday 19 August, around ten in the morning, I was yawning and bleary-eyed as I helped Mr Ho with stock-taking. I'd had nightmares all night long, starting awake several times.

When I'd finished work the night before, I paid close attention to our two neighbours, looking for any reaction to Mr Chang's arrest. Sum Chung wasn't any different, whereas Toh Sze-keung seemed unsettled. On Saturday morning at nine, while I was busy in the store, I saw the two of them head out together, empty-handed. Mr Sum even called out a greeting to me.

I distractedly finished checking the stock, then went back inside to watch the store for Mr Ho – he was meeting a friend he hadn't seen in a while for tea, and would be back around noon.

Staring at the clock, I thought about the note.

It was still ten minutes until 10.30. Would the police be waiting at Tsim Sha Tsui? If Mr Sum or Mr Toh really did turn up to plant bombs, would they see the trap and abort in time? Or had their leaders already learned of Mr Chang's arrest and changed the plan?

Earlier that morning, Elder Brother had told me he was showing a client some land in the New Territories that afternoon, and if he closed the deal it would mean a big commission. He was spending the night at a friend's place, and told me not to wait up for him. I asked him not to take the train, saying something vague about how 'pineapples' were appearing on public transport and in stations these days.

'My client has a car, you don't need to worry,' he'd smiled.

I turned on the radio and listened intently to the news, but no bombs were mentioned. There was another report about that British Air Force guy's visit, as well as the latest development – a British journalist named Anthony Grey had been put under house arrest in Beijing. A little after eleven, Cop 7 came by, his uniform neatly pressed, and asked for a soda.

As I handed over the bottle, I made a decision.

'Are you all alone today, Officer?' I didn't know whether it was a good idea to speak to a policeman at this point, but Cop 3 seemed to be somewhere else, and Cop 7 wasn't the sort to arrest people without a good reason.

'Yes, we're short-staffed, so I'm patrolling alone.' Laconic as ever.

'Is... everything prepared at the Tsim Sha Tsui Police Quarters?' I asked carefully.

Cop 7 put down the bottle and looked at me. I felt a little worried, but then looking at his expression, I knew my words hadn't ruffled him too much.

'So you did see it,' he said. He picked up the bottle again and kept drinking, as if I hadn't said anything unusual. I'd been right about him – he was much friendlier than Cop 3, who'd probably be shouting at me by now, calling me a 'leftist kid'.

'I saw what was in the note, and I know that fellow,' I said boldly.

'Oh?'

'He's called Chang Tin-san. He used to work in a textile factory, but after going on strike, he joined these organizations instead.'

'And you too?' His tone remained the same, which startled me.

'No, not at all. I have nothing to do with them. But that Mr Chang is friends with one of my housemates, so I've seen him a few times.'

'I see. And you have something to tell me?'

'Well...' I stumbled over my words, not sure what I could say without getting myself into trouble. 'The day before, I happened to hear Chang Tin-san and his friends planning an attack.'

'The day before? Why didn't you call the police at once?'

Damn. Now he was going to blame me for the whole thing.

'I... I wasn't sure what I'd heard. I'd just woken up from an afternoon nap, and only heard bits and pieces of a conversation. If I hadn't seen that note, and heard about the Causeway Bay bomb, I still wouldn't be sure.'

'So what did you hear?'

I gave him a rough account of the discussion. Of course, I omitted all mention of 'white-skinned pigs' and 'yellow-skinned dogs'.

'So you're saying this Master Chow, the journalist Toh Sze-keung and the worker Sum Chung are connected to the case? Fine, I'll tell the investigation room.' Cop 7 wrote down the names as he spoke. 'I've run into that reporter a couple of times before, but don't think I've seen Chow or Sum...'

'Officer, you don't understand.' I shook my head. 'There's something strange about all this.'

'Strange?'

'I heard them talking about Jordan Road Ferry Pier – but that wasn't on the note.'

'What did the note say?'

'Causeway Bay Magistracy, Tsim Sha Tsui Police Quarters, Central Magistracy, Murray House and Sha Tin Train Station.'

'Good memory.' There was a hint of mockery in his voice. Did he suspect I was working with Mr Chang and trying to trick him?

'I make deliveries for Mr Ho, and have to remember four or five addresses at a time, so I've become good at it,' I explained.

'So you think it's odd that the places on the list didn't include a pier.'

'Yes.'

'If the criminals really were following the list, they'd need to use a boat at some point, so naturally a pier would come into it,' he said breezily. 'Toh Sze-keung and Sum Chung live here, and Sum mentioned that Master Chow lives nearby. If they were going to Tsim Sha Tsui to plant their fake pineapples, they'd need to take the ferry across the bay. In fact, if they were really following that itinerary, they'd need to go back and forth between Hong Kong Island and Kowloon two more times, because after the Tsim Sha Tsui bomb, they'd have to get to Central for the Magistracy and Murray House, and then drag themselves all the way out to the New Territories for Sha Tin Train Station.'

'That's not possible.'

'Not possible?'

'There were times on that list too, remember?'

'Yes, so?'

'Murray House was down for four p.m., and the train station for five p.m. How could you get all the way from Central to Sha Tin in just an hour? The ferry alone would take you thirty minutes.'

'Maybe the times meant when the bombs would go off, rather than when they'd be set,' Cop 7 retorted. 'A bomb could go off at four p.m. but have been placed there hours earlier. The previous location is Central Magistracy, just ten minutes away from Murray House.'

'No, it has to mean when they were set.'

'How can you be so sure?'

'Because the Causeway Bay bomb didn't go off at ten a.m. yesterday.'

Cop 7 lowered his head and was silent for a moment, as if turning my words over in his head. Besides, I wanted to tell him, two of the bombs were marked as fake – they'd hardly have a detonation time.

'So,' Cop 7 looked up at me. 'You believe Toh Sze-keung, Sum Chung and this Mr Chow were splitting up the tasks?'

'That wouldn't work either. There were four of them, so it

would seem logical to be in charge of one bomb each, but I heard Sum Chung and Master Chow talking about working together; they said, "When we're assembled, we'll start."'

'There might be more conspirators.'

'That's possible, but there's still something I don't understand.'

'What's that?'

'Today's Saturday, so government offices are only open in the morning.' I indicated the wall calendar. 'Why would they want to bomb them in the afternoon? They should strike on a week-day, or Saturday morning, for the greatest possible impact.'

Cop 7 looked surprised. The police were so overworked, he'd probably lost track of where he was in the week.

'What do you think, then?' He looked more serious than before, as if realizing that I had a point.

'I think that list is fake.'

'Fake?'

'Chang Tin-san was bait – his job was to mislead the police,' I explained. 'He knows you two pass by here every day at this time, so made sure to pick a fight with you, and then let you dis-cover the fake intelligence.'

'Why would he do that?'

'To conceal the real targets, of course. Today, the police and bomb disposal experts are all gathered at the locations on the list, while the comms and strategy teams will be busier than usual. Security at other places will be weaker. And unlike before, when they leave the bombs at the real targets, they won't be marked with clear warnings. They're seeking to create maximum impact, "to shake the hearts of the colonials". Master Chow said to Chang Tin-san, "We're counting on you," as if he was making some kind of sacrifice. And Sum Chung said Mr Chang would be taking care of "the other side". I think that means they're giving up one comrade in order to secure victory through misdirection.'

Cop 7's face sank. After a moment, he walked over to the phone and picked up the receiver.

'Hang on!' I yelled.

'What's up?' He turned to look at me.

'Are you phoning your superiors?'

'Of course, do you need to ask?'

'But everything we've talked about is just conjecture.'

Cop 7's hand hesitated on the dial.

'If you report this to the higher-ups and they reallocate every-one, and then real bombs do go off at Murray House and Sha Tin station, you'll be in big trouble.'

Cop 7 furrowed his brow and replaced the receiver. I guess he agreed with me.

'What do you suggest, then?'

'Um... we could find some evidence?' I pointed above us. 'They said Toh Sze-keung's room would be their base; maybe they've left some clues there. You can go in and search, and if anyone comes in, we'll say you're my guest.'

'I'm not a detective, searching for evidence isn't my job...'

'But you're a police officer! Do you want me to go and search on my own?' How stubborn he was, I thought.

Cop 7 was silent again. 'Okay. How do we get upstairs?'

'You're in full uniform – no matter what we'll do it'll look like you're on official business, which'll put them on alert!' I said urgently. 'Anyway, I have to watch the store until Mr Ho comes back at noon.'

Cop 7 looked at the clock. 'I finish my shift at twelve thirty. I'll change into civvies and come back. Meet at the corner at one, and you can bring me upstairs?'

'Fine. Wear a hat with a brim or something like that. If we bump into Mr Toh or Mr Sum, they might recognize you.'

'I'll think of something,' he nodded.

'And change your shoes.'

'What?'

'Your black leather shoes are too obviously police issue. Even if you change everything else, your shoes give you away at once.'

'All right, I'll make sure of that,' he smiled. Who'd have thought I'd be giving him orders like a commanding officer!

Soon after Cop 7 left, Mr Ho returned. I told him I had some personal matters to attend to in the afternoon, and he gave me the rest of the day off without asking any questions. At one o'clock, I stood in front of the pharmacy at the corner, but there was no sign of Cop 7, only some young guy who suddenly came up to me as if he wanted to talk.

'Ah!' I stared at the other man's face. It took a few seconds for me to recognize Cop 7. He was in a white short-sleeved shirt with a pen in his pocket, a tie and a black briefcase. You'd have thought he was a clerk in some foreign firm who'd just finished his Saturday shift. He wore glasses, and his hair was pomaded into a side parting. He looked like a different person.

'Let's go.' He seemed pleased with my shock. As we passed, Mr Ho even said, 'Oh, is this a friend of yours?' I noticed a smug little grin on Cop 7's face at that.

Carefully opening the door, I looked in to make sure Mr Sum or Mr Toh weren't about to bump right into Cop 7, which might give us away, but the communal area was empty. Although I'd seen them go out first thing in the morning, and they couldn't get back in without passing by the store, I might still somehow have missed them. Tiptoeing, I listened at both their doors, then checked the kitchen and bathroom, and only let Cop 7 in when I was sure we had the place to ourselves.

Our rooms didn't have locks, which made our task a lot easier. We usually kept valuable items locked in our drawers, though it wasn't like any of our possessions were worth much. Only a very stupid thief would bother with us.

I lightly shoved open Toh Sze-keung's door, and inside it seemed the same as always.

'I thought you'd refuse an illegal search like this,' I teased, as we looked into every corner of the room.

'During a state of emergency, the police are empowered to search any suspicious person's residence. It might not be within my duties, but I'm not going against any rules.' He was calm and serious, as if he hadn't noticed I was joking.

There wasn't much in Mr Toh's room, just a bed, a desk, two wooden chairs and a chest of drawers. The bed was against the right-hand wall, on the other side of which was the room I shared with Elder Brother. At the head of the bed was the chest of drawers, with the desk and chairs on the left side of the room. A couple of shirts hung from hooks on the wall – wretches like us made do with this, not being able to afford anywhere nice enough to have wardrobes.

The desk and chest of drawers contained quite a few books, as well as notebooks. I guessed he must have used the latter when he was a journalist. The desk also held a lamp, a penholder, a Thermos flask, a cup and some metal storage boxes. On top of the chest were a radio and an alarm clock. When I tugged at the top drawer, it turned out to be locked.

'Let me see if I can open it,' said Cop 7.

'I don't think there'll be anything important inside,' I said, taking a couple of steps back.

'Why not? It's locked.'

'Toh Sze-keung might put important items in a locked drawer, but I don't think Master Chow would.' I knelt to look under the bed. 'If I'm right, and Chang Tin-san's arrest was a tactical sacrifice, then they're preparing to attack from a different direction. People with a scheme like that wouldn't lock evidence in a drawer. That would be the first place the police would search. I bet it contains a stack of inflammatory leaflets or something like that, but definitely no clues to do with the bombings. The police would find those, and that'd be enough to charge a suspect, so they wouldn't look any further.'

Cop 7 stopped trying the drawer and nodded at me. 'That makes sense. I'll see if there's anything in the books and notebooks on the desk.'

I checked under the bed and beneath the mattress, but there was nothing suspicious. Cop 7 was flipping through each book, and when I asked if he'd found anything, he just shook his head. We opened all the unlocked drawers, but apart from some tattered underclothes and other unimportant objects, there was nothing.

'When you overheard them plotting, was there anything else that struck you?' asked Cop 7.

I tried my best to recall every detail. What was it Master Chow said? Something about Ah Toh and Ah Sum leaving from North Point, and he'd wait here...

'That's right! It's a map!' I yelled, as the answer flashed into my brain.

'A map?'

'Master Chow said he'd wait "here" for Mr Toh and Mr Sum. I thought he meant this room, but now I think about it, how could he? The landlord and landlady don't know him, so it would be strange for them to just let him in. I think when Master Chow said "here", he must have been pointing at a spot on a map.'

Cop 7 nodded in agreement. 'But where is it? I've flipped through all these books, and there's nothing there.'

I thought back to the conversation. Was there another clue?

'No, I can't think of— Ah!'

I'd been moving away from the bed, but suddenly thought of something. The room had two chairs, so with four people present, two would naturally have sat on the bed. When Sum Chung was talking about 'a diversion' and 'striking' with Master Chow, his voice had grown softer. If he was holding the map, preparing to put it away, then his voice dipping would mean he was moving away from me, which meant away from the bed.

On the other side of the room was the desk.

I walked up to it and bent down, but there was nothing on its underside. And nothing between the desk and the wall. I thought I must be wrong, but just as I was about to turn my attention somewhere else, I noticed the large base of the lamp. Lifting it, I prised away the bottom plate, which came away with a click. In the space behind it was a folded map.

'Excellent work!' Cop 7 exclaimed, eyes wide.

We opened it out and placed it on the desk. It showed the

whole of Hong Kong, with lots of pencil marks, and numbers next to some locations. At Causeway Bay Magistracy was an 'X', and next to it '18 August, 10.00 a.m.', while the other locations on the list were numbered 1 to 4, but with no dates or times. Jubilee Street and Des Voeux Road near United Pier in Central were circled, and above that was written 'Number One T – 19 August – 11.00 a.m.' Another circle ringed Jordan Road Ferry Pier in Yau Ma Tei. I remembered the plotters mentioning North Point, but that bit of the map was untouched, apart from a few pencil dots on Ching Wah Street. Between United and Jordan Road Piers was a straight line, also with an 'X' on it.

'This should be enough evidence to arrest Toh and the others,' muttered Cop 7.

'But if you give the order now, you won't stop them.' I pointed at the Central circle. 'This says 19 August at eleven in the morning, two hours ago. They've already started their operation. Toh Sze-keung said something about a "Number One" target. Could that be on Des Voeux Road? It does say "Number One" there.'

'No,' said Cop 7, 'that's Number One Tea House, at the junction of Jubilee and Des Voeux. It's been in business almost fifty years. Haven't you been there?'

I shook my head. To be honest, I haven't really been anywhere. Elder Brother and I can only afford to go to a tea house a few times a year. We've eaten at Double Happiness and Dragon Gate near here, and out of the Central tea houses, I don't know a single one apart from Ko Sing and Fragrant Lotus.

'Number One Tea House must be their meeting point.' Cop 7 studied the map. 'If Chow was there at eleven and met Toh and Sum, then they'd leave from United Pier, headed for Jordan Road. Is their real target the ferry or the dock? Or maybe it's United *and* Jordan Road Piers. If they could destroy both piers, there'd be no car ferry service between Kowloon and the Island – these are some of the busiest routes in Hong Kong. It'd take a long time to fix all of that. Or perhaps they plan to turn vehicles in the gridlock into sitting ducks for an attack.'

Were they trying to start an all-out war?

I banished this conjecture from my brain, and said to Cop 7, 'You've got your evidence, so I guess I've helped as much as I can. Whatever their target is, I hope you're able to stop them as soon as possible.'

Cop 7 looked at me expressionlessly, as if making some calculation, then refolded the map, stuffed it back into the lamp base and closed the bottom panel.

'Huh?'

'You were right earlier. Even if I called it in now, there wouldn't be enough time,' said Cop 7. 'We don't even know what their target is – and we can't be sure there won't be real bombs at Murray House and Sha Tin Station. If I report this and officers are dispatched to the wrong locations, it might lead to a greater tragedy. Better to nab Toh Sze-keung and Sum Chung when they come home. Right now, we'll just have to investigate this ourselves, uncover the real target and get the bomb squad in to deal with it.'

I hadn't expected Cop 7 would bend the rules like this. Was it Cop 3's bad influence? Or was he just cutting loose because Cop 3 wasn't here to see? I just hoped I wasn't the one who'd planted these reckless ideas in his mind.

Hang on – did he say 'we'?

'You said... but I'm just a regular citizen...' I stammered.

'But you have the brains for it. It's thanks to you that we have this map.' Cop 7 patted me on the shoulder. 'I can't do this on my own. I can follow rules and obey orders, but you're different. Your thinking might seem crude, but you notice clues I miss. Besides, you're a crucial witness because you heard Toh and the rest plotting. Only you can find the flaws in their plan and stop them.'

I'd been about to say no, but in these circumstances, I felt I was already riding a tiger. I couldn't dismount now.

'Fine, I'll come with you,' I sighed.

Cop 7 grinned happily, but didn't leave Mr Toh's room right

away. Instead, he went back to the desk and opened a particular book, pulling out a photograph.

'Is this Toh Sze-keung?' He handed over the picture, and sure enough, it was Mr Toh. I nodded.

'Easier to get information with a photo.' He put it into his pocket.

I'd been about to ask if this was theft, but no doubt he'd just have brought up the state of emergency again. It seems right now that the police are above us ordinary folk, and they can do what they like.

4

WE ALSO SEARCHED Sum Chung's room, but didn't find anything. Par for the course, I suppose. Around twenty to two, Cop 7 and I left the building. He walked along Spring Garden Lane to Gloucester Road, and I didn't like to ask why, so I just mutely followed along.

It turned out he was taking me to Wan Chai Police Station.

'Why... why are we here?' Although, as the saying goes, you don't need to be scared of hell unless you're dead, I didn't want to walk into the station for no good reason.

'I want to drive to Central,' said Cop 7. 'If you don't want to come in, just wait outside.'

In order to prevent rioters from attacking the station, the whole place had layers of protection – steel barricades, barbed wire, even sandbags around the entrance. It felt like you could really sense the coming storm in this place. I stood outside an ice-cream parlour at the corner, uncertain how the oppressive sight of these fortifications would affect the people who lived nearby.

Two minutes later, a white Volkswagen Beetle pulled up in front of me. Cop 7, still dressed like a clerk, waved at me from the driver's seat.

'You own a car!' I said, getting in. Although police officers earned a stable salary, wouldn't it still be quite difficult to afford one of these? Of course, if you skimmed 'extra income' off brothels and gambling dens, even a Jaguar would be easy enough to get – but it didn't seem like Cop 7 was the sort.

'This was second-hand... no, third-hand. I had to save up for two years before I could afford it – I'm still paying it off every month.' Cop 7 smiled grimly. 'It breaks down from time to time, and there are days when I have to kick it hard to get the engine to start.'

I don't know much about cars, and can't really tell new from old, first- from second-hand. To me, all privately owned cars are luxurious toys. The tram only costs ten cents, and takes you all the way from Wan Chai to Shau Kei Wan. If you drove that far, the petrol alone would probably cost some astronomical sum.

Once we got to Central, the traffic was bad around the Bank of China building and the Cricket Court, so we didn't get to Jubilee Street till almost half past two. I guess the police had shut the roads around the Magistracy and Murray House, creating the snarl-up as everyone tried to take a different route. Although Cop 7's face remained calm, his fingers drummed incessantly on the steering wheel, so I knew he was agitated – after all, the criminals could be leaving the tea house at that moment, planting their bombs in some secret location.

Finally, Cop 7 parked and we hurried across the road to Number One Tea House. An enormous green sign stretched across the second and third storey of its facade, topped with a giant thumbs up with the name below. It would have grabbed anyone's attention, except the Chung Yuen Electrical Company billboard next to it was even larger.

The ground floor only sold cakes and pastries to take away, so we went upstairs.

'Table for how many?' asked a middle-aged waiter, teapot in one hand.

'We're looking for someone,' answered Cop 7. Hearing this, the waiter took no more interest in us, turning to greet other customers.

Even though it was already past two thirty, the tea house was full of people – every table seemed noisily occupied. The dim sum girls carried metal trays with shoulder rests, each piled high with stacked bamboo baskets like little hills, steam rising from them. They wandered between the tables calling out their wares, and diners waved them over.

'Toh and the rest might still be here,' shouted Cop 7 in my ear, struggling to be heard over our noisy surroundings. 'If they're preparing for some big operation, with the risk of getting arrested, Chow might want to treat them to a slap-up last meal. You search this floor, I'll take the one upstairs. If you see them, come up and get me. I don't think Toh would recognize me looking like this. If they spot you, just say you're meeting a friend here.'

I nodded and started squeezing through the narrow gaps between the tables, looking for Toh Sze-keung or Sum Chung. I went all the way around the resaurant, but didn't see them. I then scrutinized every diner, looking for unaccompanied men – perhaps the other two weren't here yet, and Master Chow was waiting for them. I went from table to table listening to conversations in the hopes of hearing a familiar voice.

Most of the diners were in couples or groups. There were only four lone men. Just as I was trying to think of some way of getting them to speak so I could hear their voices, one of them called for more tea. He spoke Cantonese with a strong Teochew accent. That ruled him out.

I found some excuse to talk to the other three – 'mistaking' one for someone I knew, asking another if he'd seen something I'd lost. The third one had a wrist watch, so I simply asked for the time. All three sounded different from the man I'd heard yesterday. So I went upstairs to see if Cop 7 had done any better.

Before I even got there, I met him coming down the stairs. He shook his head.

'Haven't you found your friends yet?' The same waiter as before, his tone unfriendly. He probably thought we were local ruffians who couldn't afford to eat there, so we'd just turned up to hang out on the stairs and pretend to be better than we were.

'Police.' Cop 7 flashed his ID.

'Ah! Sir, you should have said. Sorry if I offended you. Is it for two? Let me show you to a private room...' His snobbish attitude had reversed completely – he was even starting to bow to us.

'Have you seen this man?' Cop 7 pulled out the picture of Toh Sze-keung.

'Ah... no. I could ask the other waiters...'

'No need, we'll do it ourselves. Just don't get in our way.'

'Yes, of course!'

Just like a lowly eunuch bumping into the emperor, the waiter scurried away reverentially. Being a police officer certainly opened doors. Even a regular beat cop was not someone most people dared to offend. Perhaps this unfair treatment was adding fuel to the flames, one of the reasons leftists cursed yellow-skinned dogs and opposed the government. I really don't know.

'Police. Did you see this man after eleven o'clock this morning?' Cop 7 held his ID and Toh Sze-keung's photo in the same hand, holding it up to each waiter and dim sum girl in turn. The answers were 'No', 'Not that I noticed' and 'I don't know.' We did the same thing on the upper floor, with the same result.

'Officer, we have a constant stream of customers. How could we remember any one face? Of course if it was a regular, we'd know them, but I have no memory at all of this man,' said an elderly dim sum girl – really, she was more of a dim sum auntie.

'Could we have misunderstood the words on the map?' I asked as we trudged back downstairs.

Cop 7 was about to say something when the toadying waiter came over and asked, 'Officers, have you found him?'

He'd assumed I was a policeman too.

'No,' said Cop 7.

'Have you asked our Sister Lovely in the bakery downstairs? She's right by the entrance, she might have seen the person you're looking for,' he cooed ingratiatingly.

Cop 7 thought about it. 'Could you bring us down to talk to her?'

'Of course! This way, please.'

We followed him downstairs. At the counter, an older but very fashionably dressed lady was chatting and giggling with a customer.

'Hi, Ah Lung, shouldn't you be upstairs? If the boss catches you again, you'll be fired for sure,' she said to the waiter.

'Sister Lovely, these two officers have something to ask you.' Ah Lung's face had a smile forced onto it.

'Ah, really?' Sister Lovely looked stunned, like a student who knows she's in trouble with the teacher, but not what for.

'Have you seen this man?' Cop 7 placed the photo on the counter. 'He might have been here after eleven o'clock today.'

Sister Lovely let out a breath and stared at the picture for several seconds. 'This young man... ah, yes! This morning, around half past eleven, he showed up with another guy, about the same age. They hovered around the entrance for a long time, and they were new faces, so I remembered them.'

'Hovered around?' I asked.

'They looked like they'd never been here before, sticking their heads in and peering everywhere on their way up to their table. They left around twenty to one, with an older man, maybe in his forties or fifties, a bit plump. He bought quite a few sweetheart cakes on his way out. That made me wonder if they were still hungry after their meal.'

'When the two young people arrived, were they carrying anything?' Me again.

'That's... I think so. One of them was holding a black bag. But I may be remembering wrongly,' said Sister Lovely, brow crinkled.

'When they left, did they still have the bag with them?' said Cop 7. I guessed he was trying to eliminate the tea house itself as a target. Although none had been struck so far, a bomb here would cause a lot of casualties.

'I think so... Yes, they did, I remember. The other young man had a black bag both arriving and leaving. When I sold those sweetheart cakes to that older guy, I remember wondering if he was going to put them into the bag, because it looked quite full, and I worried they might get crushed before he got home.'

A chill went through my heart, and I guess Cop 7's too. This morning, I'd seen Sum Chung and Toh Sze-keung leaving the house empty-handed, and at eleven, they'd arrived here with a heavy bag they'd picked up some time during those two hours.

'Did you see which way they went?' asked Cop 7.

'No idea. God knows where they were driving off to.'

'Driving off?' I asked.

'They got into a black car parked across the road – where that white car is now.' I looked out – by coincidence, the white car was Cop 7's Volkswagen.

'Do you remember what model of car it was? Did you get a look at the licence plate?' asked Cop 7 urgently.

'Not even the Monkey King would be able to make out the licence number from clear across the road! As for the model, I don't know anything about cars. All I can say is it was neither big nor small, it had four wheels...'

This description was useless, but at least we now knew the gang was driving, which probably meant they were taking the car ferry from United to Jordan Road Pier.

Cop 7 thanked Sister Lovely, then turned to me. 'We won't catch up with them now, but we could go to the pier and have a look around... You haven't had lunch, have you?'

I was taken aback by the question. Had I been staring at the pastries like a starving orphan? Embarrassed, I shook my head.

Ah Lung was still hanging around, so Cop 7 said to him, 'Go wrap up a few baskets of dim sum. Pork and shrimp dumplings, and some sticky rice with chicken or char siu buns.'

'Yes, Officer!' Ah Lung vanished up the stairs, and appeared less than a minute later with five or six takeout boxes.

'So many! How will two of us eat all this?' laughed Cop 7.

'Your work is so hard, it's better you eat a bit more,' smiled Ah Lung.

Cop 7 opened one box – I glimpsed at least ten little dumplings, packed tightly together. 'Three of these boxes will be plenty. How much?'

'This is just a little token from us, don't worry about paying.'

'How much? Don't make me ask you again.' Cop 7's face was stern. I thought Ah Lung had probably never encountered such a stubborn police officer.

'Uh... uh... four dollars twenty.'

Cop 7 handed over the cash and walked out with the three boxes. I hurried after him.

'I don't have enough on me to pay for my share,' I said as we got in the car.

'I forced you to come and help me, I can at least give you lunch.' He took off his glasses and loosened his tie. 'Us policemen sometimes end up starving – when you're after a suspect, there isn't always time to even take a sip of water. But there's no reason you civilians should suffer that way. I haven't had lunch either – and if it was just me, I'd skip a meal. So it's good you're here to remind me to eat.'

I'd been about to thank him – normally I spend less than a dollar per meal, so this was a banquet – but then I thought it was his case, and he'd dragged me in, so this was just payment. Besides, I was a civilian, so Cop 7 would get all the credit for catching the bombers. Four dollars seemed quite cheap, when you put it like that.

'I'll drive us to the pier, you go ahead and eat.' Cop 7 had to turn the key three times before the engine finally started.

It wasn't much more than a block from Des Voeux to the pier – I'd only stuffed down two shrimp dumplings when we arrived. They were truly delicious – the tea house was not called Number One for nothing.

There was a long line of cars waiting – perhaps because it was Saturday, when many people worked half the day and now needed to get home to Kowloon. Getting on the ferry might take thirty to forty minutes. Instead of joining the queue, Cop 7 parked by the side of the road.

'You keep eating, I'll go over to the terminal – I want to ask the staff if they've seen any suspicious people or objects. It'll be dangerous if the bombs are in there. Wait here for me.'

As Cop 7 walked towards the building, I kept popping tasty morsels into my mouth whilst studying his car. Its interior was spartan, with no ornaments whatsoever. A piece of paper was pasted to the windshield with the Hong Kong Police insignia – probably so he could drive in and out of the station without being stopped. I looked at the dashboard, then below it, until I found the controls for the radio. Turning it on, I tuned it to an English pop song.

I'd almost finished the first box of dim sum when Cop 7 reappeared. 'I didn't see anything. The staff said nothing unusual's happened so far this afternoon.'

I handed him one of the boxes and turned down the radio. 'So they probably took the ferry to Kowloon?' It was half past three, two and a half hours since the plotters left the tea house. What if they'd already finished their tasks and 'dispersed', as Master Chow said?

Cop 7 picked up a char siu bun and gulped it down in a couple of bites. With his mouth full, he mumbled, 'Very possibly. I've shown Toh's photo to the staff but they didn't remember him. All we can do is keep on their tail and gather intelligence.'

'Actually, I've been thinking...' I opened the third dim sum box and grabbed a bun. 'The docks probably aren't their targets.'

'Why do you say that?'

'Remember that X on the map?'

'You mean on Causeway Bay Magistracy?'

'That was one of them, and the other one was on the straight line between United and Jordan Road,' I said, munching. 'I think they might represent the real bombs.'

'The real bombs? You mean at Murray House and Sha Tin?'

'No, forget the list, the list was just a decoy. The map shows their real plan. The police found a real bomb at Causeway Bay yesterday, and there was an X there. So that other X on the water might be their other real bomb.'

'You think the target is the ferry?'

'Well, yes, I wasn't suggesting they'd just drop a bomb into the water.'

'But what's the point of blowing up a ferry?'

I shrugged. I wasn't sure either.

'Right, keep thinking about that. In the meantime, let's get in line.' He started the car.

In the half hour we waited, I kept thinking about the possible meaning of every marking on that map. The police quarters and the other three locations from the list that had no times attached were probably just picked out in order to waste the authorities' time.

'United Pier probably isn't the real target, because it's close to the fake targets of Murray House and Central Magistracy, and the officers who'd been sent there could rush over quickly,' I pointed out. Cop 7 nodded.

Still, we couldn't work out from there what the criminals' next move would be. I could only guess that the 'operation' they'd talked about would take place on the boat. Maybe Master Chow would use Mr Toh and Mr Sum to distract the crew. But the terminal staff had noticed nothing unusual, so we'd have to ask the sailors ourselves.

At four o'clock, after two ferries had set off in front of us, we finally got on board. The two-storey car ferry was named *Man Ting*, and I guessed each deck must hold twenty or thirty cars. I'd been on passenger ferries, but this was my first time sharing the space with vehicles. On the boat, some drivers and passengers stayed where they were, snoozing, chatting, reading newspapers or listening to the radio, but most got out and stood on deck enjoying the ocean breeze.

Cop 7 and I approached the crew.

'Police.' He showed his ID. 'I'd like to ask you all if you've seen this young man, some time after twelve forty p.m. today?'

A few of the sailors gathered round and studied the picture of Toh Sze-keung, but all shook their heads.

'Have you encountered anything odd today?' Cop 7 asked next.

'No, Officer. Today's been the same as usual, lots of cars and people, nothing odd about that,' said a bearded crew member.

'Nothing on our boat, but during the shift change just now, I heard there was a disturbance on the *Man Bong*,' said another sailor, in his forties.

'What kind of disturbance?'

'They said about an hour and a half ago, on the Central-to-Yau Ma Tei boat, two young people started shouting about something or other. The crew were afraid they'd come to blows, but after yelling at each other for a while, they seemed to become friends again. Kids today!'

'Can I reach the *Man Bong* crew to ask more?'

'Of course, but we've just left Central, which means the *Man Bong* will just have left Yau Ma Tei. They'll arrive at Jordan Road about half an hour after you.'

We were scheduled to dock at half past four, so the *Man Bong* would arrive at five.

'Could their target be the *Man Bong*?' I asked, once we were back in the car.

'Back to the ferry bomb theory?' said Cop 7.

'Sinking a ferry wouldn't achieve much, but maybe they're after a particular person on that boat.' I frowned in thought. 'That would make their conversation much easier to understand. Mr Toh and Mr Sum pretended to have an argument to distract the crew, while Master Chow placed a bomb on the boat. When Mr Toh said the target wouldn't be easy, he meant there would be too many witnesses on the ferry – but Master Chow said it was more vulnerable than he imagined, because no one there would expect a bomb. It wouldn't be too hard to kill someone in a city this busy – getting away would be the hard part. But a ferry thirty minutes into its journey is completely isolated – even the coastguard and firefighting boats would have trouble getting to it, and the lifesaving equipment on board isn't always in good working order. Most importantly, the culprits would be long gone.'

'Damn!' Cop 7 leaped from the car. I followed closely behind. Sprinting up to the bearded crew member, he gasped, 'I need to radio to the *Man Bong*.'

'Officer, I don't have the authority to do that, you'll need to talk to the captain. But if you're just going to ask about your suspects, you might as well wait till we've docked, it's not like you can send a photo over the air...'

'No, I need to send the *Man Bong* a message.' Cop 7 grabbed the sailor's arm. 'They need to search for suspicious objects – I think there's a bomb on board.'

All the crew within earshot looked stunned, and after exchanging looks with the others, the bearded man said, 'Officer, is this real?'

'I don't know, but it's a possibility. Ask the *Man Bong* crew to carry out a search, without alarming the passengers.'

'Understood. Please wait here.' The sailor nodded and went off to the wheelhouse, returning with the captain. Cop 7 explained the situation, and the captain headed back to telegraph the *Man Bong*. Cop 7 and I sat with the resting sailors, waiting for his return. Although the scenery was beautiful in the bay, and the cool breezes refreshing, we weren't in the mood to enjoy any of it.

'That's the *Man Bong*,' said one of the crew, pointing at a ferry coming towards us. Looking at that vessel, I couldn't help imagining it blowing into smithereens and sinking right before our eyes, plunging the passengers and crew into a nightmare few would survive.

But the *Man Bong* didn't explode, only passed quietly by.

About fifteen minutes later, when our ferry was almost at the Jordan Road terminal, the bearded sailor hurried back and said, 'Officer, the *Man Bong* crew say they've found nothing.'

'Nothing?'

'They searched twice, but there were no suspicious objects at all. Is your information correct, Officer? Their captain said he could take the boat out of service when they get to Central, but if it turns out to be wrong, he'll get into big trouble – he doesn't want that responsibility.'

Cop 7's face contorted, as if he was having trouble making a decision.

'No need to take it out of service – tell them to continue as normal,' I interrupted, making my voice sound authoritative. 'The *Man Bong* should reach United Pier around four thirty, and then should be at Jordan Road by five? We'll wait at Jordan Road and get on the boat ourselves to investigate. Tell the crew to stay vigilant for now – the bomb might be set to go off on the next trip.'

'Yes, Officer.' Beardy dashed off once again to the bridge.

'We'll wait in the car – let us know if there's any news,' I said to the other crew members, who nodded in acknowledgement.

Back in the car, Cop 7 turned to me with an unhappy expression. 'Why'd you let the *Man Bong* continue its journey? What if the crew have missed something, and there's a disaster at sea?'

'We don't even know that there really is a bomb on board!' I snapped. I was getting used to working with Cop 7, and was even beginning to feel like his equal. 'Anyway, I noticed something strange, and now I think we may have been wrong.'

'Strange how?'

'Didn't that crew member say earlier that the dispute on the *Man Bong* took place an hour and a half ago, on the Central–Yau Ma Tei route?'

'That's right.'

'That was the two-thirty ferry. It's less than a half-hour journey from Central to Yau Ma Tei, call it an hour there and back, including turnaround time. While we were waiting to board, I observed four car ferries in rotation on this line, leaving every fifteen minutes. Sister Lovely said Toh Sze-keung and the rest left Number One Tea House around twelve forty. If they had to wait in line, say, half an hour to board, they'd have been on the one-fifteen ferry – but they ended up on the two-thirty one. Don't you think that's suspicious?'

'Maybe they were targeting the *Man Bong* specifically,' Cop 7 shot back.

'They could just as easily have done that on the one-thirty trip.'

'Or maybe they did board the one-fifteen or one-thirty boat, and got right back on after disembarking at Jordan Road, which would bring them back to Central in time to get on the two-thirty one.'

'Not possible. They'd have to queue again each time – they couldn't just get back on. And they couldn't have stayed on board, or the crew would have mentioned it when you asked if anything odd had happened. Besides, that probably isn't allowed, with these ferries being so crowded.'

Cop 7 was silent, as if thinking it through.

'Now I think about it, there's an issue with our previous supposition,' I went on. 'They might be targeting a particular person, but there'd be no way to be sure which boat the victim would board. So I have a new idea.'

'Yes?'

'A car bomb.'

Cop 7's eyes widened.

'Think about it – everything makes sense.' I gestured at the cars surrounding us. 'The criminals' target is some British person. They wait near the dock, and when they see the victim's car approach, they follow and get on the same boat. Toh and Sum then fake a fight to distract the target long enough for Master Chow to plant a bomb in his car.'

'Why a British person?'

'Master Chow said, "The white-skinned pig won't be expecting this move."'

We went looking for the bearded sailor once more, asking him to get in touch with the *Man Bong* again.

'Officer, we're about to dock – I have a lot to do.'

'Just one question – please,' implored Cop 7. 'Ask if there were any foreigners on the Central-to-Yau Ma Tei boat – this is the last time I'll bother you.'

Beardy seemed surprised a police officer would ask so humbly, and went off reluctantly.

He was back a minute later.

'No, they said not a single one.' He looked as though he no longer trusted us.

'None?'

'It was a boatful of Chinese people,' sighed the sailor. 'Officer, why not just wait at the dock? The *Man Bong* will be along at five o'clock, and then you can question them for as long as you like.'

Cop 7 and I could only nod and move away, watching the sailors getting ready to land. At four thirty, we disembarked from the *Man Ting* at Jordan Road Terminal. Cop 7 showed his ID to the dock workers and said we needed to carry out an investigation on the *Man Bong*, which was docking at five o'clock.

'Actually, not many British people use the car ferry these days, do they?' mused Cop 7 as we waited.

'But don't the British need to go between Hong Kong Island and Kowloon?'

'High-ranking officials can take government boats. And with things the way they are, British people probably are trying to go out as seldom as possible – some have even gone back to the UK because they don't feel safe here. I know quite a few British police officers have told their families to stay at home, or to remain in their own neighbourhoods.'

This made sense, but I still felt my hypothesis was right.

We might as well have been sitting on a bed of nails for that half hour. Cop 7 turned the radio up to see if there'd been an explosion at Murray House – a real bomb there would knock over all our previous theories like dominoes.

At 5 p.m., just as the *Man Bong* was approaching the pier, the news came on.

'Royal Air Force Air Marshal Sir Peter Fletcher has visited the Royal Air Base to see British forces stationed here, praising their noble work assisting the Hong Kong government in quelling recent unrest. This evening, Air Marshal Fletcher will attend a banquet at the base. Lieutenant General John Worsley, Police Commissioner Edward Eates and Colonial Secretary Michael Gass will also be in attendance.'

'No explosion at Murray House – that would have been the first item,' said Cop 7.

'Ah!' I yelped.

'What?'

'Mm... but that doesn't seem right...'

'What are you talking about?'

'We've missed a key word.' I scratched my head. 'But then that still doesn't seem possible.'

'What key word?'

'I'd thought the bombers had a "Number One Target" and "Number Two Target", but actually "Number One" was the name of the target – the Police Commissioner's car, because its licence plates just have the number 1 on them. But how does that make sense? A high and mighty Police Commissioner is hardly going to take the car ferry. And he's always accompanied by a full police escort...'

Before I'd even finished speaking, Cop 7 had leaped from the car, and I had to scurry after him. Grabbing a dock worker, he yelled, 'Quick! Did Number One car pass by here today? The Police Commissioner's car – was it here?'

The poor man stammered, 'Yes... yes. Number One car takes the ferry several times a month – it's very normal.'

Cop 7 released the worker and rushed back to the car. I got in too. 'What's up? There can't be a bomb in the car.'

'There can!' Cop 7's face was tense. He started the car as he explained, 'The Commissioner would have to take Number One car to an official banquet. But if the banquet's in Kowloon, the car will be sent across first, while the Commissioner takes another government car to Queen's Pier, then boards a Marine Police boat, only getting into Number One at the Kowloon docks. Otherwise he'd have to get on the car ferry with a full escort, which would cause chaos! His bodyguards would follow the Commissioner, not the car. Which means Number One car might have been left unguarded on the ferry!'

I stared at Cop 7 in shock.

'It's very likely they've placed a bomb in that car.' Cop 7 stepped on the gas. 'They're planning to assassinate the Police Commissioner!'

5

'The Commissioner's chauffeur is from Shandong – that's why the *Man Bong* crew said they didn't see any foreigners,' said Cop 7. I clutched the door handle tightly as we sped down Jordan Road. 'Toh and the others must have heard ahead of time that the Commissioner was attending a banquet today, and hatched this plot. They'd have waited at United for Number One car, like you said, to plant their bomb. Master Chow bought those snacks because he didn't know how long they'd be waiting.'

'Since... since we already know the target, why not just tell the Commissioner's protection detail?' I stuttered, the swerving of the car almost causing me to bite my tongue off.

'There's no time! I've seen the briefing – the banquet starts at five thirty. Everyone's very punctual at these events – you can't have the British Commander waiting around for the Police Commissioner and the Colonial Secretary. Which means Number One car is probably already waiting at Kowloon City Pier, and the Commissioner's about to arrive by boat. It'll be faster driving straight there than trying to get to him through official channels.'

'How would the bombers know his route?'

'Government activities are all on public record, and the route could be worked out from the times and locations. Or internal papers might have been leaked.'

'Will... will we be in time?' I yelped.

'Should be! I can get us there in eight minutes.'

Surely Kowloon City Pier was more than eight minutes from Jordan Road? But I didn't dare open my mouth again, for fear of distracting Cop 7 from the road. Never mind stopping this car bomb, our own lives were in peril at that moment.

We got all the way from Jordan Road Terminal in West Kowloon to Hung Hom in the east in under five minutes. The whole way, I prayed non-stop to Buddha to keep us safe, and fortunately Cop 7's driving skills were razor-sharp. We got there in one piece, though we had a few close shaves with pedestrians.

As we turned into Dock Street, though, our luck ran out.

In front of us was a crowd, maybe twenty or thirty people. Not many, but enough to block off the road. Some were waving placards, chanting slogans. Cop 7 was forced to slow down, and as he drew closer, I could read the signs they were holding up: 'Stop illegal harassment of residents', 'Investigate the bloody murders', 'Patriotism is not a crime, unrest is justified', 'We'll surely win, the colonialists will lose' and so on.

'Damn, an illegal assembly.' Cop 7 stopped the car. Last month, the Hong Kong police had launched a surprise attack on the Kowloon Dockyard Workers' Union and Workers' Children's School in Hung Hom, resulting in a battle by the docks in which news reports said 'violent elements' from the unions had been shot dead. These looked like leftists drumming up local support.

Cop 7 looked behind us, preparing to put the car into reverse – but a couple more vehicles had pulled up, so there wasn't enough space.

'Just honk at them to move.' I reached for the horn.

'No!' But Cop 7 didn't grab my hand in time, and the *parp* sounded loud and clear.

A few seconds later, I understood why he'd tried to stop me.

The crowd turned, attracted by the noise. To start with, they just glared angrily, but then a murmur started up, and their eyes took on a murderous look. Advancing step by step towards us, they looked like a wolf pack closing in on its prey.

Ah, right. I'd forgotten.

Cop 7's car had a police badge on the windscreen.

Things started happening very fast. A few men ran up to us and began hitting the bonnet with metal sticks. One of the headlights shattered crisply.

'Tear apart the yellow-skinned dog! Revenge for our comrades!'

'Sit tight!' Cop 7 suddenly put the car into reverse and stepped on the gas. There was a red car behind us, which he crashed straight into. In the tiny Beetle, I was so badly jolted I almost threw up the shrimp dumplings from earlier.

'Don't let them get away!' roared the protesters.

The Beetle couldn't ram the red car out of the way, so Cop 7 abruptly changed gears and zoomed forward. Startled, the mob froze. As soon as they'd backed off a short distance, he reversed again.

One man wasn't giving up – he ran alongside the Beetle, and with a whack, his metal pole smashed my window. I covered my face, watching in horror as he got ready for a second blow. Cop 7 turned the wheel towards him, shoving him away.

The red car's driver probably understood what was happening, and began reversing too. We sped away from the crowd, and then just as I thought we were out of danger, something terrifying happened.

Another man, clutching a glass bottle, was sprinting towards us.

Flames licked the mouth of the bottle.

'My God! Molotov cocktail!'

No sooner had I said the words when the bottle hit the car, and suddenly our windscreen was a sheet of fire. Flames slipped in through the broken window, but in my panic I didn't feel any heat.

'Don't be scared!' yelled Cop 7. He continued to reverse, and although he couldn't go fast like this, he was still able to outpace a human being. The car's motion pulled the flames away from us. We went almost two blocks back but the fire showed no sign of abating, and I got scared, thinking we were sure to be burnt to death. Cop 7 had said his car broke down sometimes. If that happened now, my little life would surely go up in smoke.

'Get out!' Cop 7 suddenly stopped the car, and without thinking about it, I pushed open the door, jumped out of the burning Beetle and made a dash for it.

'This way! This way!' screamed Cop 7.

I'd been too busy running to notice he was by the roadside. Next to him was a stunned-looking man in a helmet, standing beside his motorcycle.

'Police! I'm requisitioning your vehicle,' Cop 7 said.

Before the man could react, Cop 7 was already on the bike, motioning for me to get on. Thinking it was our only chance for survival, I jumped on and Cop 7 started the engine, leaving the hapless owner behind. Hopefully the leftists would leave him alone – he wasn't a 'yellow-skinned dog' – but then neither was I, and I'd still almost got a metal pole right in the face.

'Are we going for help?' I yelled over the wind, arms wrapped tight around Cop 7, deathly afraid I'd fall off at the next corner.

'To the docks! Stop the Commissioner's car! Lots of police there!' he shouted.

I'd never before taken a car ferry or sat on a motorbike, I'd never had a petrol bomb thrown at me, and I'd never taken a vehicle from someone by force. Now, in just half a day, I'd had all those experiences. What other excitement lay in store, I wondered.

In a blink, we'd arrived at Kowloon City Pier. There were no police cars or Marine Police boats anywhere. I looked at the large harbour clock – 5.16 p.m.

Cop 7 looked around, jumped off the motorcycle and ran towards a uniformed officer.

'Did the Commissioner just get in his car?' he panted, showing his badge.

'Yes, he left about five minutes ago.'

'Dammit!' Cop 7 looked around again, then said, 'Go tell your superiors the Commissioner's in danger. Someone's interfered with his car. I'm going after him.'

The officer gaped in shock, as if not quite understanding what he'd just heard. But Cop 7 didn't waste any more time on him. He got back on the motorcycle and we sped off again. We probably couldn't depend on that officer to raise the alarm, and even if he did, by the time he got through on the phone, the bomb might already have gone off.

'The air base is on Kwun Tong Road,' shouted Cop 7. 'The cavalcade won't go too fast. We might still catch up!'

Our motorcycle ate up the road, but there were too many cars – probably because we were near Kai Tak Airport. Everyone coming in or out of the country would need to take this road.

'We're not going to make it,' I moaned.

'Let's take a short cut.'

Cop 7 turned the bike into an open-air marketplace.

'Out of the way! Police!' he shouted.

When they saw the motorbike bearing down on them, pedestrians and vendors jumped out of the way, scrambling for safety. We were on a narrow path between fish and vegetable stalls, bamboo baskets and wooden boards freighted with all kinds of greens and meat encroaching on our passage. Curses and screams came after us: 'Damn you!' 'What are you doing?' 'My broccoli!' We knocked over quite a few stalls, but didn't slow down. If we'd fallen off the bike here, we'd probably have been torn limb from limb by irate stallholders – a worse fate than the leftists would have dealt us.

'Look out!' I yelled. Not far ahead of us was a vegetable hawker with two huge bamboo baskets, standing paralysed in the middle of the path as if uncertain which way to jump. Even if Cop 7 avoided him, we'd surely crash into one of those baskets, but it was too late to brake.

With a screech, Cop 7 slowed down. Just as we were about to

hit the hawker, the motorbike swerved to the left. Its front wheel went up a wooden board leaning against one of the stalls, launching us into the air. When we landed, I almost tumbled off. In an instant, we were back on the main road, though I still smelled fish, and there were vegetable leaves plastered all down my thighs.

'I see him!' A line of vehicles ahead of us, the last one flashing police lights. Instead of going straight after them, Cop 7 swung down an alleyway to the right, pulling out ahead of the cavalcade.

Cop 7 stopped the motorcycle in the middle of the road and held up his police badge, facing the oncoming vehicles. I stood to one side, keeping my distance. Hopefully the police cars would stop when they saw us, but if not, I wanted to be able to get out of the way.

Fortunately, the traffic cop leading the procession waved to the others to stop. 'What the hell do you think—' he barked, but then broke off, perhaps noticing the police ID.

'Number One car might have a bomb in it!' yelled Cop 7.

Three or four officers had starting running towards us, but they froze when they heard these words, and immediately turned towards a black car with the number plate '1'. They shielded a foreign man as they ushered him out and into another police vehicle, which sped off with two police motorbikes beside it. At the same time, an impressively built white officer with thick eyebrows walked up to me and Cop 7. A Chinese officer stood beside him – his deputy, by the looks of it.

'Who are you?' he said to Cop 7. At least I think that's what he said – he was speaking in English.

'PC 4447, stationed at Wan Chai, sir!' Cop 7 saluted smartly, speaking in Cantonese. 'I've received some intelligence and suspect that criminal elements have planted a bomb in the Commissioner's car. The matter was too urgent to notify my superiors, so I could only get the information to the Commissioner in this way, sir!'

The Chinese deputy translated this into English, and the white officer said something to his entourage. A moment later, a uniformed cop hurried up and said a few words. The British officer's face changed.

'Unidentified object near the fuel tank,' Cop 7 whispered to me. 'You understand English?'

'A little. But I speak it terribly – wouldn't want to inflict it on the superintendent.'

So this white man was a superintendent. Elder Brother was right – learning English really was important.

The superintendent said a few more things to Cop 7, and the deputy translated. 'Well done, the army bomb disposal expert is on his way. Come over here and tell me what happened.'

'Sir! The bomb is going to go off any minute now!' Cop 7 remained standing at attention. 'The criminals are very organized – this was meticulously planned. The bomb is due to go off at five twenty-five, when the car would have been driving into the base.'

'Everyone away from Car Number One! Repeat, all personnel stay away from Car Number One!' the deputy bellowed, at the superintendent's instruction. Some of the officers quickly sealed off the road at both ends, preventing traffic or pedestrians from getting any closer.

'Officer, what's the time?' Cop 7 asked the deputy.

'Twenty past five.'

'May I inspect the bomb?' asked Cop 7. The deputy translated, and the British officer stared hard at Cop 7.

'Why take the risk?'

'Car Number One represents the Hong Kong Police Force. If it were to be destroyed, our morale would take a big blow. Even if the Commissioner survived, destroying such a symbolic vehicle would encourage the leftist insurrection, and make citizens think we can't keep order. This isn't about the cost of a car, but the value of the entire force. I've spent some time in the bomb squad and know the basics. If it's a simple design, I might be able to defuse it and preserve the car.'

The superintendent nodded. 'Can you do it alone? Do you need help?'

Cop 7 looked all around, and then at me.

Was he joking?

'This is a dangerous task. I couldn't ask anyone to do it – but if someone were to volunteer...' said Cop 7.

Was I meant to put up my hand? I wasn't a police officer, all I'd got out of this was half a box of dim sum.

'I'll do it, sir. I've studied some books on bomb design.'

While I was still hesitating, the officer next to me spoke up. I turned to look – it was the one who'd reported the foreign object just now.

'All right, do what you can, but don't push it. Your own safety is most important,' said the deputy.

Cop 7 grabbed a tool kit that someone handed him, and together with his volunteer, hurried over to Number One car. The rest of us stood at a safe distance. The deputy asked who I was, and I explained briefly. He passed this on to the white man, who nodded a lot but didn't otherwise respond.

Cop 7 was on the ground, half his body under the car, the other officer next to him holding a torch. I didn't dare look directly at them, so instead fixed my eye on the deputy's watch, as the minute hand crawled.

My hallucination of the ferry exploding reappeared before my eyes. Time slowed down, barely moving. At any second, there might be an enormous bang, taking away the new companion I'd only met that day.

The minute hand settled onto the 5...

Boom.

A plane passed overhead, and for an instant we were unable to hear each other. As the ear-splitting engine roared, all of us looked up at that giant metal bird.

As my gaze drifted back down, I saw an unexpected sight.

Cop 7 and the other officer were by the Commissioner's car, their faces split into wide smiles. Cop 7 was holding up his right hand, giving the thumbs up.

They'd done it.

6

At 6.20 p.m., the bomb disposal experts arrived. It probably took a whole hour because they'd been sent to Murray House and Sha Tin in readiness. They looked at the device and confirmed that Cop 7 had defused it – it could be taken away without a controlled explosion. This wasn't a particularly powerful bomb, but being next to the fuel tank, would have turned the car into a fireball.

Cop 7 and I were driven to Kowloon City Pier in a squad car, then brought back to Hong Kong Island on a Marine Police boat. In between, several high-ranking officers – I think they were high-ranking – kept coming up to us with questions, and we went over the whole sequence of events in vivid detail, including the conversation I'd overheard, Chang Tin-san's arrest, the map we found in Mr Toh's room, what happened at Number One Tea House, and how we guessed the truth on the ferry.

All the officers looked grumpy, as if they might throw a tantrum at any moment, but Cop 7 quietly told me that they were actually very happy with these results. There'd be some trouble, but once they arrested the criminals, the matter would be dealt with.

'Of course, this was a serious security breach, and the Commissioner was very nearly killed. They'll have to take some of the blame for that. Toh and his friends are in for a rough time when they're caught,' Cop 7 explained.

We arrived at Wan Chai station around half past seven, and I
walked into the imposing building I'd refused to enter just hours
before. The exterior was as forbidding as ever, the sandbags and
barricades even more terrifying by night – it looked like a street
in wartime.

Inside the station, we were taken to the centre of operations,
where we told a plain-clothes detective the whole story yet again.
Several white men in neat suits were also there – Cop 7 said they
were from the Special Branch.

'Can you identify the men in these photographs?' said a detective, placing three pictures in front of me. 'Are they Toh Tze-
keung, Sum Chung and Chow Chun-hing?'

'That's definitely Mr Toh, and that's Mr Sum. As for Master
Chow, I've only ever heard his voice – I never saw his face.'

'Chow Chun-hing lives on Ship Street. He used to run a car
repair service, but it folded in the economic crash some years
ago. Informers have indicated he's closely associated with leftist
leaders – we've had our eyes on him for some time.'

Ship Street was only two or three minutes' walk from Spring
Garden Lane. And he was a car mechanic – he'd have found it
easy to plant that bomb.

'Don't go home now. A team will be there soon to arrest Toh
and Sum,' warned Cop 7.

'Will they be armed?' I asked. 'My landlords are good people
– they're innocent.'

'I know. I'll tell the officers – they won't try anything.'

Fortunately Elder Brother was still away on business.

'I should phone Mr Ho and tell him I'm spending the night
with a friend.'

'Hey, are you trying to tip off the gang?' said a plain-clothes
officer in an unfriendly tone.

'If he was helping the bad guys, he wouldn't have put his
life at risk to expose this plot,' Cop 7 replied. The other officer
frowned, but didn't bother me any more.

I told Mr Ho that Elder Brother and I would both be away

that night. He grunted in acknowledgement, and that was that.
A few hours later, a squad of uniformed officers would barge
into the building, no doubt scaring him and his wife to death,
but there was nothing to be done about it.

They put me in a corner of the room and told me to wait. I
was to listen to Master Chow's voice, to confirm he was the plotter I'd heard. A plain-clothes officer, the one who hadn't been
particularly friendly earlier, now asked me if I was hungry, then
went down to the canteen to get me a plate of delicious spare
ribs and rice. It had been a hard day, and I'd had some real
scares, but lunch and dinner had been sumptuous – some silver
lining! Every time Elder Brother came into some money, he'd
treat me to a good meal. A shame I couldn't return the favour
now. But for all I knew, he'd think it was bad luck to eat police
food, and be unable to choke it down.

A little after ten, Cop 7 came to visit me. He'd changed into
uniform, and even had a helmet on. There also seemed to be
more weaponry hanging from his belt than usual – they were
preparing to move out. Cop 3 was there too, looking as mean as
usual. I jumped when I saw him, but he gave me an unexpected
smile and said, 'Good boy – you did well.'

After they left, I dozed off on the long bench, until a commotion woke me at half past midnight.

'You bastards! Going straight for the top, eh? How dare you
target our Commissioner!'

'Patriotism is no sin! Unrest is justified!'

The voice shouting slogans was high-pitched – Sum Chung.
I remained on the bench, hidden from view by a stack of files
on the table in front of me. I peeped through the cracks between
piles of paper. The plain-clothes officer next to me, who was
sorting through the documents, didn't try to stop me. I thought
he probably understood.

When I saw Sum Chung, I couldn't help letting out a little gasp.

His face was covered in bruises and his right eye was badly
swollen. There was no blood on his head, but his clothes were

streaked with it – terrifying. I almost couldn't recognize the man who tried every day to persuade me to join the union. Toh Sze-keung was with him, less badly bruised but still showing signs of a beating. He kept his head down and said nothing, dragging his left leg – I wondered if the police had broken it. Last of all was a plump, middle-aged man, like Sum Chung so badly beaten up he barely looked human. I couldn't have said if this was Chow Chun-hing from the picture. They were all handcuffed, and each was accompanied by two or three officers, while a few in combat uniform stood to the side, Cop 7 among them.

'Walk faster!' An officer kicked the plump man.

'Yellow-skinned dog,' he yelled back, which earned him a couple of blows with a truncheon.

And now that he'd spoken, I was sure who he was. Turning to the officer beside me, I said, 'That's his voice, that's Master Chow.'

The officer nodded and slipped away, whispering a few words to a man in a light-blue long-sleeved shirt who looked like his superior. The three plotters were locked up in separate cells – presumably their interrogation would continue. I didn't dare imagine how much more suffering they still had to endure.

Cop 7 walked over to me. 'Mr and Mrs Ho are a little shaken, but the team was very careful not to damage anything in your room,' he smiled. 'We took the map as evidence. So that's the end of the case. You've been through a lot today.'

I was about to deny it politely, but I really had been through the wringer.

'Attention!' came a voice from the door.

The white officer from before strode into the room, with the same deputy by his side. Everyone stood and saluted. The superintendent looked more relaxed than before.

'You've all done very well,' the deputy translated. Then, turning to me, 'Have you thought about joining the force? Superintendent Got was very impressed by your performance today. We need bright young men like you. Each applicant needs two people to vouch for him – but if you don't have a boss or anyone like that,

Superintendent Got will make an exception and personally give you a reference.' So that was his name, I thought – though probably it was just that his English name started with a 'guh' sound.

'Um, I'll think about it. Thanks!' I nodded.

'Leave your details with the sergeant. When you want to apply, just come and have a word with him.' The deputy gestured at a man of about forty standing behind him.

Superintendent Got praised Cop 7 again for thwarting such a major plot. Cop 7 responded respectfully, saying he was just doing his duty, and so forth. A whole lot of polite talk, in other words.

As they spoke, a plain-clothes officer came up to them.

'Sorry to interrupt, sir. I need to talk to PC 4447.'

'What is it?' said Cop 7.

'Toh Szc-kcung is willing to make a full confession, but he'll only talk to 4447.'

'Me?' Cop 7 looked alarmed.

'Don't fall into that trap,' said the man who looked like he ran this room, the one in light blue. 'He must have something up his sleeve. These scumbags deny everything, and we have our own methods of getting the truth out of them. You're a uniform – best stay out of this.'

'I... I understand, sir,' Cop 7 replied.

I almost told him he was making a mistake, but swallowed the words.

The officer went back out, and I heard faint moaning and sobbing from the next room. Meanwhile, everyone around me was congratulating each other on the end of the case. The contrast between their celebrations and the suffering next door made the whole situation seem unreal.

We were truly living in an age of paradoxes.

I spent the night at the station. Someone offered to give me a lift home, but Mr Ho would surely get suspicious if I arrived home after midnight, when there was a curfew. Cop 7 found me a folding canvas bed and I passed a reasonably comfortable night in a corner. There were fewer mosquitoes than in my room.

I walked home from the station at seven in the morning. Back home, I pretended to be shocked at the news of Mr Toh and Mr Sum's arrests. Mr Ho vividly described the whole process, a hair-raising saga. I thought if I did tell him about the previous day's events, he'd surely spice it up even more, telling the whole neighbourhood a tale more fantastical than any radio serial.

Elder Brother came home and left again in a hurry. He must have been close to striking a deal – he seemed full of energy, despite having to do business on a Sunday.

As usual, I opened and minded the shop for Mr Ho, while he went off to drink tea with his friends. The radio news contained nothing of what we'd been through – it looked like the police were keeping the secret for now. It was hard to blame them – a serious matter like this had to be completely resolved. A headline like 'Commissioner Escapes Car Bomb' with no further context would cause chaos.

Cop 7 didn't come by – another officer was on patrol. I thought he'd probably been given the day off.

Closing up the shop that evening, I began moving the candy and biscuit tins back inside. Mr Ho stayed behind the counter, fanning himself and humming an out-of-tune Cantonese opera aria.

Then, on the radio: 'Breaking news. Two young children have been killed in an explosion on Ching Wah Street in North Point. The deceased are a brother and sister, aged four and eight, surname Wong. They lived near the site where the home-made bomb exploded. The police have promised to do everything they can to solve the inhumane crime. There are no government buildings on Ching Wah Street, and government spokesman has commented that it is hard to understand why leftists would choose to place a bomb in a residential district. He labeled it a senseless act of evil by the communists...'

'Terrible,' said Mr Ho. 'These leftists are going too far. Just imagine if China takes Hong Kong back – those fellows will become ministers. Us regular folk will be in trouble then.'

I didn't answer Mr Ho, only shook my head and sighed. So that's how it was.

The next morning, I saw Cop 7 again. He was just as before, striding along with a calm expression, appearing round the corner.

'A Super Cola, please.' He put down thirty cents.

I handed him a bottle and returned to my seat. Mr Ho was off drinking tea again, and I was alone in the shop.

'Are you going to join the force?' Cop 7 said after a long pause.

'I'm thinking about it.'

'With Superintendent Got backing you, if you do join, you'll be sure to rise quickly.'

'If I have to be completely obedient to my superiors, I don't want to join.'

Cop 7 looked at me strangely. 'The police keep strict discipline. Duties of higher and lower ranks are very clear.'

I broke though Cop 7's lecture. 'You've heard the news? That brother and sister blown up in North Point?'

'Hmm? Yes, I know, poor things. We haven't found the killer yet.'

'I know who did it.'

'Huh?' Cop 7 was staring at me. 'Who?'

'The man who killed those two little kids,' I stared straight into his eyes, 'was you.'

'Me? What are you talking about?'

'You didn't place the bomb, but they died because of your ignorance and stubbornness,' I said. 'Toh Sze-keung wanted to speak to you, but that detective just said a couple of words and you didn't dare to so much as fart. Mr Toh was trying to tell you about North Point.'

'What... what do you mean?'

'I told you, I overheard Master Chow telling Mr Toh and Mr Sum to set off from North Point and meet him at the rendezvous. They were empty-handed when they set off, but by the time they got to Number One Tea House, they were carrying explosives, which means they must have picked them up in North Point.

I remember all those pencil marks around Ching Wah Street on the map. Master Chow might well have made them while showing it to Mr Toh and the others. You have to be very careful fetching bombs from their maker. I don't mean in case they explode, but because of the risk of exposure. If the bomber were someone like Master Chow, already under police surveillance, they'd just need to follow him to get to the bomb-maker – and the leftists would lose one more precious skilled worker.'

I paused and looked at Cop 7, who was dumbstruck. 'So I don't believe they'd do anything as risky as meeting in person for the handover. The simplest method would be to agree on a place where the bomb-maker would leave the device for some foot soldier to pick up. Don't you remember me saying, Master Chow said that in the following days, there'd be a second and third wave of attacks? Toh Sze-keung was trying to tell you this because once they were arrested, they had no way to stop the bomb-maker dropping off the second device as planned. With no one to pick it up, it ended up as a plaything for curious little children.'

'Toh Sze-keung was trying to tell me this? Why me? He could have spoken to any of the officers there,' cried Cop 7, his expression all wrong for his uniform.

'The incident room is notorious for beating and torture. Do you think any of those fellows would have believed him? Mr Toh knew you were an upright person, with a good reputation in the neighbourhood, so he asked for you. But a few words from a superior, and you gave him up. You knew Mr Toh wasn't like Mr Sum, he wasn't a fanatic, just unfortunate. But you ignored your instincts to protect your job, and followed that order you disagreed with.'

'I... I...' Cop 7 struggled to find an answer.

'For the sake of the "morale of the force", you were willing to risk your life defusing the bomb in Car Number One. But yesterday, two innocent children lost their precious lives. Are you here to protect police symbols or the safety of ordinary folk? Are you loyal to the colonial government, or us Hongkongers?'

My voice remained level. 'Why on earth did you want to be in the police force?'

Cop 7 said nothing. He put down the soda, even though he'd only had a couple of mouthfuls, and walked slowly away.

Watching him leave, I wondered if I'd gone too far. Who was I to speak so harshly to him? I decided that the following morning, I'd give him a soda by way of apology.

But the next morning, Cop 7 didn't appear, nor the mornings after that.

Mr Ho had some connections in the force, so I asked if he knew why Cop 7 hadn't turned up for some days now.

'4447? Who? I don't remember their numbers,' said Mr Ho.

I struggled to recall the name I'd glimpsed on Cop 7's ID. 'Something like Kwan Chun-dok, Kwan Chun-jik...'

'Ah Dok!' said Mr Ho. 'I heard he'd had some great achievement, and been transferred to Central, or maybe it was Tsim Sha Tsui.'

So he'd been promoted. Well, never mind. That saved me the cost of a soda.

I'd let rip, scolding Cop 7, but actually I was no better than him. I hadn't accused Mr Toh and the others in the interest of justice, or anything like that. I'd just been worried for myself and Elder Brother.

The way things were, nothing happened for a clear reason. It was already stressful living under the same roof as leftists, at constant risk of being tarred with the same brush. When I heard them plotting, I grew even more uneasy about what would happen if Elder Brother and I got mistaken for members of their gang.

Sometimes self-defence means striking the first blow, neutralizing Master Chow and company.

I'd started out only intending to help Cop 7 find his evidence, and not to get involved. As the saying goes, it's easy to get things done when you know someone in the imperial court. With Cop 7 testifying that I was the whistleblower, it wouldn't matter how much Mr Sum tried to blame me – Elder Brother and I would be spared. And I wasn't worried the leftists would find out I'd accused them. The police wouldn't release my name. They only wished there were more people like me.

But I was too easily swayed – a few words from Cop 7 and I obediently got in his car, running all over Kowloon and Hong Kong Island. I was an idiot who'd let them use me.

Two days later, Elder Brother arrived home in high spirits – he had something to talk over with me.

'I closed the deal I've been working on. My commission's three thousand dollars,' he crowed.

'My God, so much!' I hadn't realized his deals were so big-time.

'No, the money isn't so important, the main thing is I have a good relationship with this boss. He's thinking of expanding his business empire and starting a new company – he's recruiting right now. Me striking this deal is like a successful job interview – I'm in! It's just to be a regular clerk, but who knows whether I'll get to be a supervisor or manager in the future.'

'Congratulations, Elder Brother!' I almost said I'd passed my own 'interview', but he'd always hated the police.

'There's something in it for you too.'

'For me?'

'I told them I had a good little brother, a capable guy who I could guarantee would do a great job. So if you're agreeable, we could be working in the same office.'

Working alongside Elder Brother? Excellent, that sounded much better than that nonsense police job.

'All right! What's the company?'

'Have you heard of the Fung Hoi Plastic Goods Factory? The boss is Mr Yue. He's preparing to move into the property and real-estate markets. We'd only be probationary clerks, but the prospects for promotion aren't bad! Young Tong, your surname's Wong and mine's Yuen, but all these years I've thought of you like my own brother. I've shared all my good fortune with you, and we've faced adversity together. Now let's move ahead together. This job is just the beginning. We'll achieve great things.'

AFTERWORD

I HADN'T INITIALLY planned to write an introduction or afterword for this novel. I believe that once a work has been 'birthed' by its writer, the text takes on its own life, and readers are free to see and receive whatever they want from it, each person embarking on a unique journey. Rather than having the author go on at length about what is or isn't there, why not allow the reader to experience it in person? When I submitted the novel to my publisher, however, I included a summary and explanations of some of my creative choices, breezily scrawling a few thousand words, and my editor later said to me, 'You should turn this into an afterword! People are interested in that sort of thing.'

Let's start from the beginning.

In the autumn of 2011, I was fortunate enough to win the Soji Shimada Mystery Award, and immediately began thinking of the subject of my next book. Nothing came to mind. Then the Mystery Writers of Taiwan held a short story competition for its members with the topic 'Armchair Detectives', that is, detectives who have to base their deductions only on reported evidence, without being able to visit the scene of the crime for themselves. I decided to push the idea further, creating a situation where an armchair detective could only answer yes/no questions, and wrote 'The Truth Between Black and White'. I completely failed to keep the length under control, however, and exceeded the word limit. In the end, I decided to keep this piece as the basis for a longer work, and submitted something else to the competition – a detective story with science fiction elements.

After that, I started thinking how to expand the story of Kwan Chun-dok and Sonny Lok. My first idea was very simple: to write another two stories of about thirty thousand Chinese characters ('Black and White' was thirty-three thousand characters long), and get them published together. I'd decided from the start to use reverse chronology, though in the beginning I was considering this book purely as a detective novel, driven by its plot.

As I continued writing an outline and creating the mysteries, however, I grew more and more uneasy.

I was born in the 1970s and grew up in the 1980s. During this time, many Hong Kong children thought of policemen as akin to superheroes in American cartoons: strong, selfless, righteous, brave, honest, serving the people. Even as we grew up and began to understand that the world is a complex place, we maintained a mostly positive image of the police. In 2012, however, this view was shaken again and again by incidents and news items concerning the Hong Kong police. I began to suspect that my police detective novel was growing to resemble propaganda.

With even the author feeling this uncertain about his story, how could any reader trust in it?

And so this novel underwent a complete change in direction. I no longer wanted to simply describe criminal cases, but the story of a personality, a city and an era.

The book expanded vastly, more than I could ever have expected.

If you're familiar with detective novels (particularly Japanese ones), you probably know about the split between the classic and social genres. The former rely on mysteries and plots, placing their emphasis on solving clues and logical deduction, while the latter are more concerned with reflecting the state of society, focusing on character and situation. I'd started out planning to write a classic detective novel, but now I'd pivoted towards writing a social one. These two varieties aren't necessarily at odds with each other, but it wouldn't be easy to mix them together – the flavour of one would easily overpower the other. In order to solve (or avoid) this problem, I chose the structure of six stand-alone novellas, each one fuelled by mysteries and clues, but all six fitting together to form a complete portrait of society. The idea was to create a book in which every part felt like a classic detective story, but looking at the big picture, you'd see it was actually a social realist novel.

Each story is set during a crucial year for Hong Kong, though these historical events might play an important part in the story, or might only be mentioned in passing. The only exception is the first story, which is set at a point after I'd finished the book. I'm no Nostradamus, and had no way of knowing the future. Still, with the public's trust in the police eroding as we moved from 2012 into 2013, it seemed like a reasonable bet that this trend would continue.

I don't intend to go into the background of each story, the meaning of each character, the symbolism of each detail, or the broader intellectual context for the novel – these are best left for each reader to discover in person. There are just two things I want to talk about. Readers unfamiliar with Hong Kong might not realize that we keep revisiting the same locations throughout these stories. For instance, the playground where Sonny Lok and Kwan Chun-dok meet in Chapter 2 is close to Chapter 5's Nairn House – both are near Argyle Street. Kwun Lung Lau in Chapter 3, where the sighting of a suspicious individual wastes a great deal of police time, is next door to Kennedy Town Swimming Pool in Chapter 5. The West Kowloon reclamation project, where Candy Ton is attacked in Chapter 2, was previously Jordan Ferry Terminal, where Cop 7 and the narrator of the final chapter wait for the *Man Bong* ferry. Graham Street Market in Chapter 3, the restaurant where Kwan Chun-dok and Benedict

Lau have lunch in Chapter 4, and the 'Snake Pit', Lok Heung Yuen, in Chapter 5 are all around Wellington Street in Central (Lok Heung Yuen is no longer in business, but an establishment of a similar name is currently trading there). If some readers were inspired to visit these places after reading the novel, I'd be delighted.

The other point I wanted to mention was that Hong Kong today is in just as strange a state as in 1967.

We've come full circle, back to the beginning.

I have no idea whether Hong Kong after 2013 will be able to recover as it did after 1967, pulling itself onto the right path, step by step.

And I don't know whether we'll ever recover the image of the police as strong, selfless, righteous, brave, honest, serving the people – so the small children of Hong Kong can once more be proud of them.

CHAN HO-KEI,
30 April 2014